Posy: Book One

Mates

By Mary Ann Weir

Table of Contents

Prologue: Alone   5
1: Rescued   7
2: By Father's Command   11
3: Introductions   18
4: Meeting Lark   25
5: Saying Goodbye   31
6: A New Home   39
7: Brothers and Teammates   47
8: Seeking Sanctuary   52
9: Going Shopping   61
10: What a Mess   67
11: Quartz the Comforter   73
12: Apologies   76
13: New Life, Rough Start   84
14: Dinner with Friends   93
15: Sleepover   99
16: Waking Nightmare   106
17: Meeting the Betas   111
18: The King Arrives   120
19: Diner Disaster   124
20: Aftermath   133
21: Kinds of Strength   138
22: My Mate is Who?!   144
23: Getting Comfortable   152
24: Leaving Her Mark   160
25: Ticklish Matters   171
26: Running with Wolves   179
27: Morning Mating   186
28: Learning Curve   193
29: Slaughter All   202
30: Getting Schooled   210
31: First Kiss   215
32: Get Well Soon   223

33: Ice Pops and Party Planning   231
34: Interrogations   241
35: Plan of Attack   247

Prologue: Alone

Posy

I turned eighteen years old alone in a dark room, whimpering from the pain that racked my whole body.

I'd displeased my father again, and his punishment had been brutal.

They always were.

While Mom was still alive, it hadn't been so bad. Father and I didn't have much interaction. He kept his distance and Mom cautioned me to let him. I remembered being jealous of watching him play with my two older brothers, and always wondered why he disliked me more day by day.

Six years ago, a disease swept through shifter communities around the world. It attacked indiscriminately - young and old, alpha and omega, male and female. Almost a year passed before our doctors developed a cure. By then, thousands had died, my mother among them.

With her gone, there was no barrier between my father and me, and his dislike turned to outright hatred.

I asked myself over and over what was so wrong with me. Had I done something as a child I couldn't remember? What could have set him against me so much?

I tried to make things right. I was on my best behavior at all times and followed his rules, yet nothing was ever enough. There was something about me that infuriated him.

Same with my brothers.

I missed James and Aiden so much, it made my heart hurt. We'd had nothing but fun together growing up. Then, one day out of the blue, they turned against me, and all those happy memories became ashes. They even convinced Father that I didn't need to go to school, trapping me in this house with him.

Most of the time, I was locked in this small, dark room. It didn't even have a window or a closet. The only positive was the tiny attached bathroom, just a sink and a toilet, but enough to make do. Once a week, Father permitted me to take a shower in the guest bedroom. I wasn't allowed warm water or more than ten minutes, but it was still heavenly to wash the grime and blood away.

When he'd first ordered me into this dark hole, he'd watched as I'd moved in my clothes, shoes, and pillow, then said that was all I needed. Over time, I snuck in a few comforts. Mr. Nibbles, my stuffed bunny, who I managed to keep hidden from him by some miracle. A blanket. A yoga mat to sleep on. Once, I tried to smuggle in a small

5

lamp, but he caught me. That punishment took two full weeks for my wolf to heal.

Each day, Father let me out for a few hours to clean, cook, and do the laundry. Despite the chores, I savored that time away from my room. At least it gave me the chance to look out the windows. No matter what the weather was doing, I found the view perfect. It was the only joy in my life.

I couldn't remember the last time I went outside. The last time I breathed fresh air or ran through the forest and smelled the goodness of dirt and growing things. Felt the breeze on my face. Laid in the grass. Enjoyed the sun's warmth.

Simple things all denied to me for a reason I couldn't guess. Simple things I yearned for with all my heart.

Especially whenever my wolf slept.

I hadn't felt Lark stir in weeks, not since the last dose of wolfsbane Father had administered. The aconite put a shifter's inner wolf to sleep, although too much could be lethal. I'd built up a tolerance to it, and Father had to constantly adjust how much to give Lark to keep her docile, but still able to heal me.

The last dose, though, had been part of a punishment after we'd tried to escape. He hadn't killed my wolf, but he'd come close. *Very* close. I'd tried to find some nightshade or foxglove to counter the wolfsbane, but hadn't been that lucky. Weeks later, she was still in a coma.

Poor Lark. I pitied her for being stuck with me. She was so strong and had hung in there long after most wolves would have gone insane or faded back to the Goddess. She kept herself going with two hopes: being free of Father and finding our mate.

I didn't crush her optimism, even though I knew neither would ever happen. Father would never let us out from under his thumb and even if we *did* meet our mate, he would reject me in a heartbeat. Father had guaranteed that.

I had scars on scars and bruises on bruises. My hands shook all the time and my vision was narrow and dark around the edges. Having been denied food for weeks at a stretch, I was skeletal and weak, and the world spun with every step I took.

The plain truth was that I doubted I'd make it to see another birthday, let alone gain my freedom or find my mate.

But what did it matter? Who would care? I had no pack. No family. No mate. Not even my wolf at the moment.

I was alone in the dark, and death was the only escape I could hope for.

1: Rescued

Posy

The click of the lock opening woke me. Instantly, my eyes darted to the widening sliver of light that came from the door swinging in.

Is it Father? His beta? Or one of my brothers?

"Get up, Posy."

Beta Roy.

Father only ever called me runt, and I hadn't seen the boys in months. After they'd moved out three years ago, they rarely came around, and certainly never to see *me*.

Beta Roy wasn't as bad as Father, but was unpredictable. Kind one moment and cruel the next.

I scrambled to my feet, careful to keep my head down and my bruised, swollen face hidden in the curtains of my grimy hair.

"Guests are coming. Alpha wants brunch ready in an hour. Five visitors, myself, Gamma Alex, and alpha, but make enough for ten in case your brothers come. I'll set the table. You just worry about the food."

His offer was a godsend. Even if it was only for the moment, I'd take it. I needed all the help I could get after my midnight beating.

The ribs on my right side were badly bruised, and I suspected at least one was broken. Something was wrong with my head, too. It ached terribly, and the sunlight streaming in from the windows stabbed my eyes like toothpicks. On top of that, my shirt stuck to the raw wounds on my back. I hoped that none of them opened too much as I worked. There was nothing worse than a blood-soaked waistband to gall your skin.

I followed Beta Roy into the kitchen, washed my hands, and got right to work. Since it was brunch, I knew Father would want both sweet and savory items. I decided to start with fruit and cheese plates. I could get everything cut up and plated, then into the fridge while I worked on the rest.

As I sliced a block of cheddar, I tried to think of what else to make, but my brain wasn't up to the task. I could barely focus on the cutting board and knife in front of me.

Get these made first, I told myself. *If you don't cut off any fingers, we'll go from there.*

It wasn't easy, but I did it. Covering the plates in plastic wrap, I stuck them in the fridge.

A glance at the clock showed me I was down to thirty minutes. Did it really take that long to cut up fruit and cheese?

Frantic now, I rummaged in the fridge and found three packs of bacon. I could bake it in the ovens, which would free me up to make other dishes. Running over, I flipped two ovens on, then laid parchment paper out on four big pans. It took a few minutes to open the packages and arrange all those strips, but the ovens were still preheating when I finished.

Thinking as quickly as I could, I organized some jellies, jams, and butters into little dishes and popped some ready-made rolls and scones into bread baskets, then covered them with a cloth. By then, the ovens were ready for the bacon.

"Table's set." Beta Roy came into the kitchen. "Are these ready to go out?"

He gestured to the bread baskets and things, and I nodded. He started carrying them into the dining room, which made me feel both guilty and grateful. It wasn't his job, and Father wouldn't like to know he'd helped me. I would do something nice for him the next time I had a chance.

Behind Father's back, of course.

I started the coffee pot and looked at the clock again. Fifteen minutes left. What else could I make? I stuck my head back in the fridge.

Eggs! Perfect!

Getting out the biggest skillet, I melted butter, then added a dozen eggs. I was super careful not to break the yolks since Father liked sunny side up. Soon they were sizzling away.

Phew. Good.

The timer went off on the ovens, and I ran over to pull out the bacon. Patting off the grease and getting it plated took a few minutes, and by then the eggs were cooked, too.

"Hurry, Posy!" Beta Roy hissed. "Alpha's almost here! Let me take those, then I need to meet him outside."

Nodding, I handed him the platters of eggs and bacon and whirled to the fridge one last time to grab the fruit and cheese trays. I hustled them out to the dining room before I ran back to the kitchen to finish up the coffee tray and fix some pitchers of orange and apple juice.

I'd just finished filling the sugar bowl when several delightful scents filtered into the room. They worked in harmony, yet each one was a distinct note in the bouquet: campfire, pine, maple syrup, roses, and vanilla. All my favorites.

The smells were addictive and I inhaled as much as my lungs could hold, ignoring my ribs as they screamed in protest.

Where is that coming from?

8

Then my father stalked into the kitchen, and all my attention diverted to him. Glancing at his face to gauge his mood, my heart sank. He was fuming.

Twisting his hand in my hair, he yanked my head back hard, hurting my neck. With a whimper, I dropped to my knees to try and relieve the pressure.

"Where are the waffles?" he shouted. "Can't you do *anything* right, runt?"

I didn't answer. I'd be punished if I spoke and I'd be punished if I didn't. Either way, I was done for.

Beta Roy didn't say anything about waffles. Did he set me up to fail? But why? Especially with guests here?

With one hand still tangled in my hair, Father punched me full-force in the face, and a loud *crack!* echoed through the room. Blood and saliva splattered on the floor as I screamed in agony, knowing my jaw was broken.

Suddenly, tell-tale electricity raised the hair on my arms as someone shifted into their wolf, frightening me to death. Had Father finally lost his mind enough to sic Basalt on me?

"What do you think you're doing?!" roared a stranger's voice.

"How dare you harm our mate?!" bellowed another.

"Mate?" my father sneered. "This pathetic runt? She's a worthless whore. A useless slut. Take my advice, boys. Reject her quick and take a chosen mate."

Everything rattled as two thunderous growls shook the room. Alpha power flared in rich waves, stronger than I'd ever felt from anyone, and Father released his hold on my hair. I slumped to the floor and curled into a protective ball, my hands covering my head.

Fierce snarls soon erupted all around me. Beta Roy scooped me up and carried me to the far corner of the kitchen. He set me on the floor, then crouched in front of me in a defensive pose.

"Don't watch, Posy," he muttered.

I couldn't have even if I'd wanted to. I was too hurt to keep my eyes open any longer. The vicious sounds of wolves fighting kept me conscious, though, and questions whirled through my mind. Were the guests attacking my father? Was I next? And why was Beta Roy guarding me instead of aiding my father?

It wasn't a long fight, and it ended with the loud *snap!* of a neck breaking. I couldn't bring myself to care who won. If my father had, nothing would change; if someone else had, everything would. Either way, I would have to deal with the aftermath.

But not right now, I thought weakly. *Right now I am going to lie here and melt into the pain, and the world will have to spin on without me for a while.*

9

Loud, upset voices surrounded me, startling me from my daze.

"Are you okay?"

"She's obviously not, idiot!"

"Why isn't her wolf healing her?"

"I can't even *feel* her wolf. Can any of you?"

"What do we do?"

"Let's get her off the floor to start with. Beta, get the pack doctor."

Hands slid under me and scooped me against a hard chest. The smell of pine engulfed me, and I felt myself being lifted up just as a door slammed open.

"What's going on here?"

I recognized that voice. It was my oldest brother, James.

"*Posy!*" And that was my other brother, Aiden.

"Posy? Is that her name?" asked the one holding me.

"What's it matter to you?" James barked. "Give her here! How dare you touch her!"

"I dare because she's ours! Our mate!"

"Mate!" James yelped.

Mate?

The word bloomed in my heart like a flower.

"To whom? Not ... not all *five* of you?" Aiden faltered.

I forced my eyelids up half way and stared blearily at the faces surrounding me. Only two were familiar.

I have ... mates?

That's when I gave up and faded into the darkness.

2: By Father's Command

Posy

I woke up in a bed. A real one, not a yoga mat with a thin blanket.

Sunlight streamed through the curtains, and I turned my face toward it, loving the feel of it on my skin.

I didn't know where I was or how I'd gotten here, but I was going to enjoy the sun for as long as I was allowed to.

I wish I could bottle it, I thought wistfully, *and take it with me when I'm forced back into the dark room.*

"Posy? You awake, little girl?"

Beta Roy? What was he doing here, wherever here was?

I nodded, despite my confusion, and turned my head to see him getting up from the chair in the corner.

"Thank the Goddess," he muttered. "I linked your brothers that you're up. They're so worried about you. We've been walking on eggshells around here. Dealing with so many agitated alphas hasn't been fun."

I nodded again. I wondered who he meant by *alphas*, plural, but couldn't ask since he didn't give me permission to speak.

And, truthfully, I was in too much pain to care. My aching jaw had a deep thrumming solo in the symphony of aches, and my ribs hit all the high notes anytime I moved. If only Lark would wake up, she could help. Without her, I healed as slow as a human.

Lost in my thoughts, I nearly jumped out of my skin when the door burst open and people poured into the room. I scrambled to sit up against the headboard and bared my neck in submission, being very careful to keep my eyes down.

I recognized two of the scents as my brothers. The other five were the same scents as the delectable ones I'd smelled earlier in the kitchen.

Mates? my heart whispered. *We have mates?*

As with the sunshine, I knew it wouldn't last. All I could do was savor the gift for as long as possible.

My brother James came over and sat on the edge of the bed. I drew my knees up to my chest and wrapped my arms around them, trying to be as small as possible.

"How are you feeling, Posy? You've been asleep a long time. Are you in pain?"

Scared of him and all his questions, I curled up in a tighter ball to hide how I was shaking.

I know this trick. Father does it all the time. If I say no, he'll punish me for lying. If I say yes, he'll punish me for being weak.

Staying silent was always my best option. Sometimes, Father would still punish me for being insolent, but other times he saw it as submission and let me go with only a few slaps or kicks.

"Hey, it's okay. We won't hurt you. You can talk to us," James sounded like he was pleading. "You don't need to follow Father's stupid rules anymore. He's gone."

My head flew up and my eyes went right to James' dark blue ones.

"He's dead, Posy," James said and waved a hand at the five men standing behind him. "These alphas put him down this morning."

Five alphas? And I'm their mate? Oh, Moon Goddess, what were you thinking?

The strangers stayed silent, and James didn't tell me their names. I knew I wasn't worth an introduction, and they probably didn't see the point. After all, it wasn't like they were going to keep me.

Until they reject me, I guess I'll identify them by their scents.

"We're finally free," James went on. "This morning, I stepped up as alpha and named Aiden my beta. The whole pack has been in party mode since."

Aiden came over and slowly sat on the other side of the bed. He had my stuffed rabbit in his hands, and my eyes widened with panic.

Oh, no. Not Mr. Nibbles!

"Here's your bunny." He held it out to me. "I washed him up for you. He's nice and fluffy again."

Despite how badly I wanted Mr. Nibbles, I didn't move. This was another trick. Father used it a lot, too. If I reached for whatever he held out, he'd punish me for being greedy. If I didn't reach for it, he'd punish me for being ungrateful. Then he'd destroy whatever the item was. Flowers. Food. Pictures of my mom. Clothes. Shoes.

Before I could stop it, a tear rolled down my cheek. I didn't want to lose Mr. Nibbles. He was the only good thing I had left in my life. And I couldn't take another beating.

Let this be the last one, I begged the Moon Goddess. *Let me die at my brothers' hands. I don't want to do this anymore.*

Two of the strangers whimpered. Why were they in pain? Did they get hurt during the fight in the kitchen?

Then I heard one of them shift their feet. As the air stirred, maple syrup wafted to my nose.

My mates had intervened with Father. Would they intervene with my brothers, or let them hurt me?

Why would they help a worthless runt? No one else ever has.

12

Aiden stretched his arm closer to me.

"Please take it, baby sister," he murmured.

Baby sister? When was the last time I'd heard that? How many years?

My confusion and heartache must have shown on my face because James sighed and scrubbed his hand over his face.

"Posy, we never *wanted* to hurt you. Father made us. Aiden and I fought as hard as we could, but no one could defy him when he gave a command in his alpha voice."

I was too stunned to answer.

"That's why we moved out." Aiden set Mr. Nibbles next to my hip. "Ignoring you was miserable, but hurting you was worse. Every time I had to hurt you, I died a little inside. I'm sorry, baby sister. I'm so, so sorry!"

"It made our wolves crazy and harder to control," James went on when Aiden choked up. "Slate and Agate tried to protect you as much as they could, but his alpha command bound them, too."

"You didn't know *any* of this? You thought we hurt you by choice?" Aiden looked devastated, his blue eyes welling up with sorrow and hurt.

I stayed silent as my tired brain worked to process everything. *They ... don't hate me?*

After six years of isolation and abuse, it was hard to believe. Deciding to take a risk, I asked the question that had plagued me for so long.

"Why?" I whispered.

It was the first time I'd spoken to someone other than Father in years.

"Why what, baby sister?" James asked. "Why did he treat you that way?"

I nodded.

"I'd like to know that, too," said Campfire.

"I think we all would," Roses added.

My brothers looked at each other, then at my mates.

"When we were pups, our mother was kidnapped by rogues," James began. "They had her for three months before Father found and rescued her. Seven months later, little Posy was born."

"She was *Mama's* baby, not Father's," Aiden said. "He never forgot or let her forget, either."

James must have seen the confusion on my face.

"Father wasn't your father," he explained. "One of the rogues was your father."

That was even more confusing. Why would Mama want a baby with a rogue?

13

James realized he hadn't made anything clearer and tried again.

"She didn't have a choice. He, uh, forced her." He rubbed the back of his neck, then muttered, "Your mates can explain it to you later."

"Thanks, dude," Vanilla said. "Way to pass the buck."

Aiden said something back to him, but I was too busy in my thoughts to pay attention. I gathered the courage to ask another question since my brothers were being so nice to me.

"The pack?"

"Do you remember when you first shifted into your wolf?" James asked. "It was your twelfth birthday."

I nodded.

How could I forget? That beating had nearly killed me. It had taken four months for Lark to heal all my injuries.

"Mom had just died, and your wolf is a mirror image of hers, right down to the white on the tips of your toes. As soon as he saw it, Father flew into a rage and gave the pack orders on how to treat you."

I blinked up at James. Father hated Lark because she looked like Mom's wolf?

"We pulled you out of school then, remember? I know we did it in a harsh way, but if he thought we were doing it to protect you, he wouldn't have agreed."

I remembered that day. They'd told me I wasn't worth an education.

"Why bother sending her to school, Father, when she can cook and clean here?" Aiden had asked.

"It's a waste of time and money to pay a housekeeper when Posy won't amount to anything even with a diploma," James had said.

That argument had sealed the deal. Everyone knew of Alpha Kendall Briggs' miserly ways.

"We still wanted you to get as much of an education as you could, so we snuck books and stuff to you whenever possible," Aiden said.

My eyes widened with wonder and shock.

I was always finding books of all kinds tucked here and there. The laundry basket, under my blanket, in my bathroom cupboard. Sometimes, a sheaf of paper would slide under my door early in the morning, or I'd find pens stuck in my apron pocket. One glorious afternoon, I'd returned to my room after lunch to find a box of art supplies: watercolors, brushes, assorted paper, colored and drawing pencils, and even some air-dry clay.

Those mysterious gifts had given me hope, as did knowing at least one member of the pack was kind enough to provide the runt with such treasures.

"I know taking you out of school isolated you even more, but it saved you, Posy. If no one saw you, they wouldn't be forced to hurt you." James took a deep breath. "That's why we all kept our distance and avoided you. None of us wanted to hurt you. It sickened the whole pack."

"Why didn't you take over as alpha when you turned eighteen?" asked Maple Syrup.

"The old man wouldn't step down and even together we weren't strong enough to take it from him."

I stared at James.

"You don't know how many times we challenged him, Posy," he said, "but his wolf was too strong."

"After our last try failed, we decided to bide our time until Posy turned eighteen," Aiden explained. "We had hoped Lark would be strong enough to help us fight him, but we didn't know she was MIA until we tried to talk to her."

"What did he do to her, Posy?" James asked. "How long has it been since you last sensed her?"

I didn't want to tell them about the wolfsbane, and I'd lost count of the weeks. I hid my face in my thighs. I didn't want to look at any of them anymore.

"Is that why we can't sense her wolf?" Roses asked. "Alpha Kendall Briggs did something to her?"

"Most likely," James answered. "We'll probably never know everything, but she's lived in hell these past few years."

"When we realized something was wrong with Lark, that our plan wasn't going to work, we contacted the king for assistance," Aiden explained. "It was clear that Father was never going to give up the alphaship. We *might* have been able to reason with Basalt, his wolf, but Father was a whole different story. He was insane."

"Yeah, that's what King Julian said before he asked us to come here," Maple Syrup replied.

Wow. My mates are powerful enough that they help the king with other packs?

Someone touched my arm, and I flinched before drawing myself into a tighter ball.

"Someday, I hope you can forgive us, baby sister." Aiden's voice was full of pain. "We can never make up for failing you so badly, but please know that we love you very, very much."

"We always have, Posy," James added, "and we always will."

15

I peeked up at them. Their faces were so sad, it broke my heart. If what they said was true, they hadn't failed me. They were victims as much as I was. And I had never stopped loving them. I didn't have the courage to say any of that, but I wanted to make a peace gesture.

Maybe if I ask for their help, they'll understand.

"Thirsty," I croaked.

They fell over themselves in their hurry to reach the bottle of water on the nightstand. James got there first, twisted the cap off, and held it out to me. My shaking hand reached for it, and I guessed he knew I wouldn't be able to take it without spilling it everywhere because he didn't release his hold on it. He let me place my hand on his and guide it to my mouth, but he controlled the bottle otherwise.

"Dr. Swedes left some pain meds for you," Aiden said. "How about you take them now?"

I nodded, and he shook two white pills out of the little container and handed them to me. James helped me with the water bottle again, then I dropped back against the headboard.

"More water?" he asked.

I shook my head.

"I'll leave it here if you want it later." He set the bottle back on the nightstand. "You can ask any of us for help."

He swept his hand out to include my mates, but I wasn't brave enough to look at their faces.

Campfire stepped closer to the bed.

"Can we have a word with her in private?" he asked my brothers.

"Only for a few minutes." James shot him a warning look. "She needs to rest, especially since Lark isn't there to help her heal."

"Of course."

After my brothers left the room, my mates moved a little closer, and I took a glance at each of their serious, unsmiling faces before dropping my eyes back to my knees.

Despite Lark's silence, I sent her my sincerest apology and hoped she heard it. She didn't deserve to die like this. After being tortured and suppressed for so many years, she finally found a mate - mates - and now they would kill her.

Oh, not on purpose, but female shifters rarely survived being rejected by one mate, and I had *five*. I was as good as dead.

At least I'll join my mother in Heaven now, and leave the torment of this world behind.

"Please say something to us, little mate," Roses said. "We want to hear your sweet voice again."

Since he'd given me permission to speak, I took it and asked for the only thing my heart desired.

"Can I have one more minute, please, before you do it?"

"Do what?" Vanilla sounded confused.

Closing my eyes, I twisted my fingers together and inhaled their scents one last time.

"All right. I'm ready." I nodded.

"Ready for what, honey?" Pine asked.

"For you to reject me."

"Why would we do that?" Vanilla made it sound like a ridiculous idea. "We would never reject you or leave you."

"We love you already, princess," Maple Syrup said.

My eyes flew open and zipped from one face to the next.

I didn't dare to believe it. I couldn't. This was all a cruel trick. It had to be.

Is Father even dead? Did he set this up as a new kind of torture to make me pay for sins I never committed? Was every word out of my brothers' mouths a lie?

"What?" I whispered.

"You're stuck with us, sweetness, until we draw our last breath." Roses grinned down at me.

"You are the perfect mate for us." Pine sat on the bed next to me, but didn't try to touch me.

I stared into his pale green eyes and allowed myself to hope.

"Your future is going to be a happy and bright one with us," he murmured. "For now, though, you need to rest. Close your eyes. We'll be here when you wake up."

Is this true? Could it be possible? Maybe.

Feeling like I was in a dream, I curled into my nest of blankets and pillows. My broken jaw ached like mad, and I raised one hand to it.

"No, sweetness. Don't touch."

A hand grabbed mine and pulled it away. Sparks danced up and down my skin where Roses' fingers touched it. I didn't know how I felt about that, but I was too weak and tired to react.

"The pain meds will kick in soon."

Then he surprised me by tucking Mr. Nibbles into my arms. I squeezed my bunny against my chest and hid my face in his soft fur.

The rest of my injuries combined with the exhaustion to rob me of what little strength I had. My eyelids fell down and I couldn't lift them again.

"Go to sleep," he whispered.

So I did.

3: Introductions

Posy

When I opened my eyes again, I knew right away something was different.

I here! yipped a sweet voice in the back of my mind.

Lark! You're back! Tears flooded my eyes and spilled down my cheeks. *I missed you so much!*

I miss you, too! But I here now. Here and strong and healthy!

I'm so glad. Oh, Lark! Guess what happened while you slept? Our mates found us. They killed Father and said they weren't going to reject us!

Lark howled with joy and excitement.

"Posy?"

Five boys suddenly crowded around my bed and stared down at me with wide eyes.

"Are you all right?" Pine asked. "Why are you crying? Do you need more pain meds?"

I shook my head.

"Did your wolf wake up?" Maple Syrup asked. "Sid says he can hear her now."

I nodded with a little smile.

"Can she heal you?" Campfire asked.

I nodded again.

Lark? These are our mates. I don't know their names yet, but show them what you can do, girl!

Wiggling with happiness, she repaired my broken body at lightning speed. Soon the only thing left was my back.

Posy, someone need to clean this. Dry blood making shirt stick to boo-boos.

No. I don't want them to see.

Sorry, but has to. I tell one of mates' wolves if you no tell them, she threatened.

"What's wrong, little mate?" Vanilla sat down on my left side. "Your injuries seem to be better, but is there something your wolf can't fix or needs help with?"

I closed my eyes and bit my bottom lip.

A thumb gently pried my lip away from my teeth, and sparks ran over my skin, startling me. My eyes flew open to see Vanilla had moved a lot closer. His light blue eyes glittered with silver strands, and I wanted to stare into them forever.

"You can tell us anything," he promised in a soft voice.

"My back," I whispered.

"Okay. Let's have a look."

He reached for me, and I scrambled away, my eyes huge and my heart racing.

"I won't hurt you." He let his hands drop to the bed. "None of us will ever hurt you. It may take you a while to believe that, but we'll prove it to you every day. Now, can you roll over so we can help you?"

I really, *really* didn't want to, but I did. Once I was flat on my stomach, someone's hands moved my lank, greasy hair out of the way, then fingers rolled up the hem of my shirt. They didn't get far before the fabric stuck, and I hissed as my wounds pulled.

"Warm water," Maple Syrup said. "I'll be right back."

"Posy, did your father do this?" Pine asked.

I nodded, hiding my face in the pillow.

"Was it his belt?"

I shook my head.

"A whip?"

I shook my head again. They would understand once they saw it.

Maple Syrup returned. Dabbing gently, he worked his way up my back, and Vanilla began to ease the damp fabric away from my wounds. In no time, my shirt was pulled up to my neck, exposing the deep, bloody cuts.

"A knife?" Campfire rumbled. "He used a *knife*?"

I nodded.

The aroma of vanilla dipped closer, and something soft brushed my left shoulder. The sparks returned and tickled me, making me squirm a bit.

"This is good to heal now, little wolf," Vanilla murmured.

Lark went to work, and each wound closed with a pinch that made me wince a little.

"Let's get you a fresh shirt," Roses said. "Take that one off of her."

"No!"

I didn't want to disobey them, but I didn't have a bra on. With the state my back had been in, that would have only added to the torture.

"Shh." Pine laid down next to me and stared into my eyes. "We won't look. You have nothing to be embarrassed or worried about. We only want to take care of you, okay?"

I couldn't look away from his light green eyes. I got so lost in them that I barely noticed when Vanilla eased my arms out of my sleeves.

"I'm going to move your hair again, honey," Pine whispered, "so we can pull this shirt off."

19

I nodded, not caring what they were doing so long as I could keep drowning in his eyes.

His big hands did just what he said, and I was embarrassed for him to feel my greasy hair a second time. He didn't seem to mind, though. Our eye contact was broken for a brief second as Vanilla pulled the shirt over my head, but there he was again, waiting for me when the fabric disappeared.

Suddenly, fingertips skimmed down the knobs of my spine, and I jumped. Not only was I unused to being touched so tenderly, but it also stirred up those delicate sparks again, which tickled.

"Sorry," Vanilla muttered.

Then another bunch of fabric blocked my vision as a different t-shirt slipped over my head. I sank my nose into it and hummed as the lovely fragrance of roses engulfed me. Before I knew it, the boys had my arms through the sleeves and were tugging the back down as far as it would go while it bunched up at my collar bones in the front.

"Lift up for a second, baby," Vanilla said in my ear.

Again not wanting to, I obeyed so I didn't get punished, and he whipped the shirt down my front without letting his fingers stray to my skin.

"Why did he hurt you like that, Posy?" Campfire's tone was even, but I could hear the underlying anger.

"I was bad." I was ashamed to admit it, but I wouldn't lie to my mates. "I had to be punished."

"How were you 'bad'?" Roses asked.

I closed my eyes and trembled. They would leave now, once they knew how terrible and unlovable I was.

"I disrespected him," I whispered.

"Can you tell me how? What did disrespect look like to Kendall Briggs?" Pine spat the name.

Tell them, Posy, Lark demanded. *Father was bad one, not you.*

"I told him no, then accidentally called him Father instead of alpha."

"He made you call him alpha?" Maple Syrup asked.

I nodded. That rule made more sense to me now that I knew he wasn't my real father.

"What did he want you to do that you refused?" Pine asked.

Shaking hard at the memory, I buried my face in the pillow and didn't answer. It was too shameful and would only disgust them.

"Posy, what did he want you to do?" Pine demanded again.

I shook my head.

Two hands rolled me onto my back. Panicking a little, I brought my arms up as a shield over my face, but Pine grabbed my wrists and pinned them above my head. Feeling trapped as he hovered over me, my heartbeat sped up and my lungs went into overdrive.

"What did he want you to do, Posy?" he bit off each word.

"Please don't make me tell, alpha," I whimpered, tears trickling down my cheeks.

"Calm down, Cole! You're scaring her."

Campfire grabbed Pine in a headlock, pulled him away, and dragged him over to the far corner of the room.

Cole? Is that Pine's name?

Still shaking, I squeezed Mr. Nibbles tightly and kept my eyes on the bedspread.

"Shh. You're okay, sweetness." Roses sat down next to me. "You don't have to tell us anything, okay? And don't call us alpha. We're your mates."

I nodded, but didn't look at him.

"Cole's just upset. He wouldn't hurt you. None of us would. He's worried about you. We all are."

"Oh, my Goddess!" yelped Vanilla, making me flinch. "Granite says you don't know our names!"

"We forgot to tell you our *names*?" Sounding horrified, Roses slapped his palm over his face. "Jeez. We're lousy mates already. Sorry, love. I'm Jayden. Jayden Carson. I'm nineteen. My wolf's name is Quartz. I'm an avid reader. I try to read at least a book a week. I also like to play the guitar. Acoustic, *not* electric."

I didn't know the difference, but learning anything about him was interesting.

I studied his striking face and blond-streaked brown hair, then met his eyes and couldn't stop staring. If Pine's pale green eyes were beautiful, Jayden's were exquisite. The irises glittered golden around the pupil, then transitioned to sage and were encircled by dark blue rings.

Dragon eyes, Lark said.

A kind dragon.

Very kind, she agreed. *Very sweet. Very nice. Very gentle. And Quartz none of that.*

I paused for a second, then asked her what she meant.

Quartz going to be difficult, she murmured as if to herself.

Oh?

He violent. Not feral, just ... brutal. So far, he no speak to me. Jayden tired from controlling him sometimes. Lark's voice became determined. *Between us, we help them. We help them both.*

Definitely, I assured her.

Vanilla moved to stand behind Jayden.

"Hello, cutie. I'm Wyatt Black and my wolf is Granite. I'm eighteen. All of us are into sports and video games, but I also like working on cars."

Granite say Wyatt full of mischief, Lark informed me with a snicker. *Oh, Posy, you going to have fun with this one!*

Ignoring her, I studied Wyatt. His white t-shirt stretched across his broad shoulders and drew my eye to his defined biceps. His short blond hair gleamed in the sunlight and his blue eyes glittered with silver threads. He was so gorgeous, it made my breath catch.

Knowing I had other mates to meet, I turned my attention to the next boy. He bounced on his toes and excitement lit his dark brown eyes, which made a smile bloom on my face.

"Your dimples are so precious!" Maple Syrup covered his mouth with both hands for a second, then launched into his introduction. "I'm Ash Mitchell, and my wolf is Obsidian, but everyone calls him Sid. I'm also eighteen. I don't really have hobbies other than what Wyatt already said. I'm going to call you princess, and also cupcake when you're being cute!"

I held back a giggle as I took in his mess of brown curls and easy grin. Lark thought he was adorable, and I agreed. The more I watched him, the more I saw he never really stopped moving. He had a lean, athletic build and was the tallest of my mates, almost freakishly so. He stood almost a full head above Wyatt, who was the shortest of the five, although even *he* was at least six foot.

I'm going to look like a dwarf next to him, I thought anxiously.

He no care. Lark was having a great time sharing her wolves' insights with me. *Obsidian say Ash want to tuck you in pocket and carry you around.*

As if he knew what Lark was saying, Ash winked at me, and I blushed.

"What's your bunny's name?" he asked.

"Mr. Nibbles," I mumbled.

"Aw. That's such a great name for a bun. And he's *almost* as cute as you are, cupcake."

Of course that made my face burn red again.

"Stop teasing her," said Campfire as he came over and stood next to Ash. "I'm Mason Price, little flower. My wolf is Garnet. I'm twenty-one. I enjoy all the things already mentioned."

Short and to the point. Okay.

Mason was easily the most dominant of all five boys. He had dark brown hair, gray eyes, and a blank expression on his handsome face. Several tattoos ran up and down his muscular arms, and there was one behind his ear. I couldn't see it clearly, but thought it was a luna

22

moth. They made him look dangerous, which Lark liked, but it intimidated me. He radiated power and intensity, which didn't help.

I liked the way his gray eyes crinkled up at the corners when he smiled at us, though.

Lark? I questioned when she stayed silent.

Garnet say Mason grieving, she said at last. *His heart hurt. His thoughts sometimes go to dark place.*

My eyes burned and my chest seized up to know that one of my mates was in pain.

Is this how they felt when they saw my father hit me?

Wolves say yes, Lark answered, although I'd been talking to myself. *Only a thousand times worse.*

I didn't know the root of his grief, but I decided then and there that I would do everything I could to help Mason.

Even if he does kind of scare me.

I looked over at my last mate. He hadn't moved from where Mason had put him.

"My name is Cole Barlow, honey." His voice was calm and quiet again. "Topaz is my wolf. I'm twenty. I like playing chess and cards and shooting pool."

The top of Cole's straight, midnight-black hair was pulled back into a man bun. His pretty eyes glowed in sharp contrast to his tan skin. Like most shifter males, all my mates were muscular, but Cole looked as if he could snap my spine without any real effort if he wanted to. He'd already shown me that he had a temper, and I shrunk into myself and hunched my shoulders.

His eyes dimmed when he saw that, and a spike of pain stabbed my heart. I wished I could find enough courage to speak to him.

Trust him, Lark encouraged me. *Yes, he has temper, but Topaz say he never, ever hurt you.*

Taking a deep breath, I decided I could take one small risk. I raised my hand and held it out to him. His eyes widening, he slowly walked over and laid his hand in mine. Gentle sparks danced over my skin where our palms connected.

I looked up at him.

"What is that?" I wondered.

"The sparks? It's the mate bond. Feels nice, doesn't it? Like sitting by a warm fire on a freezing night."

He was right. It did.

"I'm sorry for scaring you," he murmured.

I squeezed his hand and smiled at him, hoping he knew that meant I forgave him. Smiling back, he rubbed his thumb over the back of my hand.

23

"Posy, would you like to rest now?" Mason asked. "We have some matters to settle with your brothers, then we can pack your things and take you home with us."

I nodded.

"Do you want one of us to stay with you?" Ash asked.

I shrugged and lowered my eyes. I did, but I knew they had to take care of business.

"I know the pack comes before all else," I whispered.

No. For the first time, one of my mates' wolves spoke directly to me. *You come before all others. Always. Forever.*

Deep in my mind, Lark stirred. I couldn't tell which wolf had spoken to me, but it had shocked her.

Suddenly, Jayden plunked down on the edge of my bed as if his legs couldn't hold him up anymore. His amazing eyes widened and glistened as he stared at me.

"Quartz spoke to you." A single tear rolled down his cheek. "I'm so happy."

As my other mates quietly left the room, Jayden leaned forward and buried his face in my blanket-covered lap. My mouth fell open, but I had no words, so I did what I thought a mate would do. Laying my cheek on his head, I wrapped my arms around his trembling shoulders and held him.

4: Meeting Lark

Lark

"Should we wake her? I want to get her home."

"She needs her rest. The poor little thing is exhausted."

"And starved. That sick excuse for a father not only beat her, but also worked her down to skin and bones. Did you see how every bone in her spine stuck out?"

"Yes, Wyatt, we all saw. At least we got a cup of broth in her earlier. And after she's back on her feet, we can feed her until she's nice and plump."

I giggled at that, and heard five sharp inhales.

"Posy? Are you awake?" asked one of my mates.

My eyes popped open to find five boys stationed around my bed.

"Posy sleeping," I told them. "I no want to be plump!"

They all chuckled, which made me smile. For the first time in years, I felt alert and well and happy.

"Hello, Lark." Jayden gave me a toothy grin. "Your silver eyes are so pretty."

I dropped my head, feeling shy.

"Hello, Lark. It's nice to meet you," Cole said. "Our wolves were worried at first because they couldn't reach you. What happened?"

I frowned. I'd never talked through Posy's mouth before, and I had to concentrate hard. It didn't help that I could hear their wolves. They were yipping with excitement because I was awake again, but I had five humans wanting answers at the same time.

"Posy no want to tell, but I had get wolfsbane out," I explained. "It took long time."

"*Wolfsbane?!*" they all shouted.

"Why did you have wolfsbane in your system, little wolf?" Wyatt asked.

"Alpha gave it when I protect Posy." Tears gathered in my eyes. "Posy hurt all the time. I no can do anything."

Their wolves suddenly stopped their happy barking and howled. It made my head hurt. I whimpered, and they stopped right away. Their howling woke Posy up, though. She listened in the back of my mind, but didn't ask to take control.

"She's gone through so much." Mason was talking quietly to my other mates, but I could hear him. "We're going to have to be very careful with her."

25

I closed my eyes to hide my grief. Their wolves sensed it, of course, and begged me to tell them what was wrong.

"We understand. We know we too broken to be luna," I whispered. "Why you no reject us when she ask? It hurt more now you make us believe you keep us."

They all went silent, both men and wolves. Then I felt feather-light touches skimming my arms, my legs, and my face, leaving trails of sparks. My eyes flew open to see my mates hovering over me with pain and worry etched on their faces.

"Oh, we're keeping you, little wolf." Wyatt leaned down and pressed a kiss to my forehead. "If you can't believe anything else, believe that."

"And you're not broken, precious. You're a survivor." Mason frowned, his brows drawing together.

"We said we'd never reject you and we meant it." Cole picked up my left hand and stroked his thumb over the back of it.

"We'll make you believe it." Ash grabbed my other hand and brought it to his lips to kiss my knuckles. "We love you and want you in our lives."

"That's right," Jayden said. "We're going to take very good care of you."

I looked at each one of them, studying their faces and meeting their eyes. Posy and I talked for a moment, then agreed we'd believe them until they gave us a reason not to.

I hope they knows how much courage it take to trust them, I told her nervously, not realizing the mate bond would carry my thoughts and words to my wolves.

We do, sweetheart. You're so brave, and we're so proud of you.

It was one of my wolf mates, but I'd forgotten which wolf went with which human.

"Can you say names again, please? I no want to offend you or wolves by making mistake."

I was as polite as possible. Alphas were touchy, and I was still too weak to defend us if I angered them. They didn't look angry, though.

Maybe they won't hurt us, Posy said with hope in her voice.

Neither as man nor wolf will we hurt you, vowed the same wolf. *And if anyone else ever does, we will kill them.*

I sent him a smile of gratitude, then turned my attention to Wyatt as he spoke.

"Sorry. The mate bond is new to us as well. And don't worry about offending anyone. There is nothing you could do to offend us, okay?"

26

Then they went around and made sure I knew which wolf was whose: Cole with Topaz, Jayden with Quartz, Ash with Obsidian, Wyatt with Granite, and Mason with Garnet, the one who'd just talked to me.

"Now tell us about you," Ash said.

"Oh. Well, we just turn eighteen." I paused. Human tongues and mouths were annoying! "I like run in woods, but I no allowed outside for really long time."

All of the wolves growled, and I felt their fury. I didn't think it was directed at me, but a shiver of fear went down my spine.

No, dearest. We're angry at the one who abused you, Topaz explained.

And the rest of my wolves sent me a rush of comfort, which made me shiver for a whole different reason. I couldn't wait to meet these wolves in the fur!

"What about Posy? What are some of her interests?" Wyatt asked.

"She no allowed to have interests. She learn to be silent. She learn to be still. She learn to survive." I dropped my head and embarrassed both of us by frantically blurting out, "We feel like we no enough. You all handsome and nice clothes, but Posy no allowed shower or food for days and day—"

Fierce snarls ripped out of all of them, and my head shot up. All of my mates' faces were twisted with rage.

They're going to wolf out on us! Posy warned.

I scrambled off the bed and pressed my back against the wall, then edged over to the corner, never taking my eyes off of them. A whimper slipped out, and their heads snapped to me.

All those wolf-eyed stares frightened me even more. Shaking hard, I slid to the floor and curled up to protect my head. I was too weak to fight and too slow to flee. All I could do was freeze.

The next thing I knew, a pair of hands picked me up and settled me in a lap. From the rich smell of maple syrup, it was Ash. He ignored my flinches and held me tight to his chest.

"Shh. We're sorry," he crooned in my ear and rocked me back and forth. "We didn't mean to scare you. Shh. You're okay. You're safe. We will never hurt you. Never, ever."

After a few minutes, I was calm enough to relax from my protective ball and look at him. His long, black eyelashes were wet and spiky around his dark chocolate eyes.

"I sorry." I took a risk and touched my fingertips to his cheek.

"No, *you* don't apologize. You did nothing. We weren't prepared for how furious it would make us to hear how you've been mistreated."

27

I nodded, not really knowing what else to do.

"We're so happy to meet you." Jayden crouched next to us, laid his hand on my head, and stroked my hair. "We'll get you a shower and food and anything else you want as soon as you feel up to moving."

"You could be covered in mud and you'd still be beautiful. Some blood-stained clothes and messy hair can't hide that." Wyatt's smile was as bright as the sun as he stood over us.

Posy pushed me to make one last attempt to show them how unsuitable we were to be the mate of such handsome, powerful alphas.

"We have nothing to give you. No fortune. No power or skill or talent. Not even beauty."

"Your sweet self is all we want," Mason said. "You are the greatest treasure we could ever hope to have."

"And you are the most beautiful girl we've ever known," Cole added. "Inside and out. We may rule a pack, but you rule our hearts."

My heart was going to explode from so many compliments. I ate them up, but Posy was flustered. She wasn't used to being treated so nicely and didn't feel worthy of any kind of admiration.

We already admire you more than you know, Garnet said. *You are worth the world to us.*

We will shower you with lovey words every day! Obsidian added.

Thank you, Garnet. Thank you, Obsidian, I murmured shyly.

Call me Sid, my darling, Obsidian bubbled. *Everyone does.*

Ash interrupted my pleasant conversation with my wolf mates.

"Lark, as much as we like talking with you, can we have Posy back, please?"

"She shy." I smiled at him. "Just a minute."

Posy, your mates want to know you, and I want to talk to my wolves. Too hard for me to talk to so many at same time. Please come out for your mates.

I felt her hesitancy, but she agreed.

"Here she is," I told the boys.

Then I sank to the back of her consciousness, excited to get acquainted with my wolves.

#

Posy

I blinked. That was the longest I'd ever let Lark control my body.

I guess that's what she feels like when I control her wolf body.

I smiled at the thought, then remembered I wasn't alone.

"Welcome back, Posy," Ash said from above my head. "We love getting to know your wolf as much as we love getting to know you."

My face burned, which made him chuckle. He was still holding me and didn't seem disgusted by it, so I took the chance and hid my face in his chest. That made the rest of them chuckle, too.

"I'm sorry for Lark's rambling," I mumbled into his shirt.

"There's nothing to apologize for." Jayden continued to stroke my hair.

"It's dirty," I told him. "My hair. You should stop."

He only smiled and kept doing what he was doing.

"How about a shower, honey? We'll get you some food after that, then we'll pack your things and head out. We're excited to show you your new home."

Cole said it as if it were a request, but I could tell that they wouldn't allow me to say no.

I'll let them fuss over me a little, I guess. I'll enjoy them being nice for as long as it lasts.

"A shower sounds wonderful."

They helped me stand, and their hands on me sent a million sparks through my whole body. It startled me, and that made them chuckle again.

"You'll get more comfortable with it soon," Wyatt assured me.

I nodded shyly, and he led me to the bathroom.

"We'll leave fresh clothes for you on the bed and wait outside your room. We'll guard your door from the hallway so you can feel safe."

"You don't have to—"

"We want to, and we're going to," was his simple response.

He made sure I had everything I needed, then turned to go. Without thinking, I reached out and caught his sleeve. He stopped walking and turned back.

I bit my lip, almost too scared to ask, but my dread of a cold shower overcame my nerves.

"What is it, cutie?" Wyatt tilted his head in a very wolf-like gesture. "Is something wrong?"

"Um, am I allowed to use warm water?"

His whole body stiffened as his eyes went wolfy. I stepped back, moving away until my calves hit the toilet.

Crap! Why do I always have to ruin everything? Now my mate will punish me for being greedy and inconsiderate.

"I'm sorry, alpha. Cold is fine. I'll hurry. Fast as I can." Now I was rambling in my panic.

The best thing I could do was shut up, so I did.

29

"Posy." Wyatt's power-filled voice froze me in place. "Look at me."

My head whipped up to meet his glowing eyes. When he spoke again, it was with a clenched jaw and gritted teeth.

"*Don't* call me alpha. Just Wyatt, or whatever nickname you want."

His voice grew gentler and his eyes turned back to silvery blue as he got Granite under control.

"You take a shower at any temperature you want to, whenever you want to, for as long as you want to. If you had any restrictions on using shampoo or soap or anything at all in the bathroom, they're gone now. Do whatever you want in here with whatever products you want to, okay?"

I nodded with wide eyes.

"Say okay, cutie."

"Okay, cutie."

When I realized what I did, I slapped a hand over my mouth and waited to be punished. Instead of yelling or hitting me, though, Wyatt surprised me with a roar of laughter. He left the bathroom, shaking his head and grinning, and I stood there in shock for several long minutes before I headed to the shower. A small smile tugged up my lips.

For the first time in years, I felt hopeful for the future.

5: Saying Goodbye

Posy

Packing my things didn't go so well. When my mates followed me into the dark room, they all froze in shock. Then the rage took over. I could *feel* it radiating off them. In the end, only Jayden stayed while the others slammed out without a word.

I bit my lip and hunched my shoulders and dug my fingers into Mr. Nibbles' soft fur.

"They're mad at your father, not you," Jayden assured me. "Mason and Ash are usually better at keeping their temper, but it challenges all of us to see what our mate was forced to live with for so long."

I glanced at him with a question in my eyes.

"Yeah, I'm angry, too, but—" He sighed. "I didn't want you to know this so soon. My wolf is really violent and aggressive. When I let him out, usually people die."

I nodded. Lark had already told me that, so I wasn't surprised.

"So, from the time I was a pup, I had to learn to keep my temper locked down tight. It's hard, and some days are draining, but look how it's working out now." He gave me a big grin. "I get alone time with our lovely mate while my brothers are out busting knuckles on hard surfaces."

I giggled, then realized what I'd done. Looking down quickly, I covered my mouth with my hand.

"Sweetness, your smile is so pretty. Please don't hide it."

He slowly reached over and wrapped his long fingers around my wrist, then pulled my hand away. I raised my eyes to his dragon ones and saw only kindness and care. Maybe even love.

"I'm allowed to be happy?" I whispered.

His eyes glowed a faint gold, his wolf stirring, but he blinked and swallowed hard and the glow disappeared.

"You are allowed to be whatever you want to be. Happy. Sad. Upset. Angry. Joyful. The only thing I *don't* want you to be is scared, but I know that will take a long time."

"I don't know how not to be scared," I admitted, still staring into his beautiful eyes.

"We'll help you learn. If anyone scares you, tell one of us. If one of us scares you, tell another one. We can make a safe space for you at the house, too. A room that's all yours, but it definitely won't look anything like this one."

I thought about it for a few minutes, then nodded.

"I'd like that. Maybe— Maybe it could have a window?" I asked, nervous hope fluttering in my chest. "Just a small one? I'd like to see the sun."

He didn't respond, didn't blink or even seem to be breathing, and I scolded myself for overstepping.

"Sorry. I'm being greedy."

"Sweetness, may I give you a hug?"

I wasn't sure about that, but he wouldn't like it if I said no. Biting my lip, I looked at the floor and nodded.

Moving slowly, he wrapped his arms around my shoulders and drew me closer until Mr. Nibbles was squished between our fronts. I stood as stiff as a board, trying not to hyperventilate while debating if I should hug him back.

"We will make sure your room gets lots of sun, baby girl."

Something soft pressed against my forehead, then he laid his cheek on top of my hair. Since he was being so gentle and nice, I dared to put my hands on his waist. Not a hug exactly, but better than no response at all.

"Thank you," I told him.

"We all want you to be happy and comfortable." His hands moved to frame my face. "Posy, could you do something for us?"

I nodded.

"It's going to take a lot of courage," he warned me.

I had a short supply of courage, but I'd try. For him.

I nodded.

"Tell us no when you don't like something or don't want to do what we ask, and don't apologize for it. For example, I don't think you really wanted me to hug you, but were too afraid to say no."

I bit my lip and looked down at Mr. Nibbles.

"Now I feel like I forced you to hug me," he sighed, "and it hurts me to know that."

"You didn't *force* me," I murmured.

"Maybe not physically, but you weren't really willing, either, were you?"

He raised an eyebrow, and my cheeks heated up.

"Look, here's the deal," he sighed. "Except for Mason, my brothers are pretty oblivious. They'll take your yes at face value. They mean no harm, and it's not that they don't care. They just won't realize that you're too afraid of getting in trouble to disagree with them. If they figure it out later, though, it will hurt them."

I understood. Raising my face, I met his eyes and nodded.

"I'll try," I promised.

"Good enough. Now, what would you like to pack? And where's your suitcase?"

32

"Um, I don't have one. We can get a box from the kitchen. And not much. I don't have many clothes and only one pair of sneakers. Could I take some of my books, though?"

"Posy, take anything you want. Take everything. Take nothing. We'll go shopping for whatever you want." Frowning, he plowed a hand through his sun-streaked brown hair. "I'll go find a suitcase or duffel bag we can use. I'll be right back."

I nodded and turned to my task as he went to do his.

#

I stood inside the front door and anxiously peered outside. My brothers waited on the porch, my mates stood behind me, and I couldn't bring myself to cross the threshold.

I craved the sun on my face, but it looked so open and scary out there.

"What's she doing?" Wyatt whispered.

"When were you last outside, Posy?" James asked.

"Almost six years ago." I squeezed Mr. Nibbles tightly.

"You— You haven't left this house in *six years*?" Cole growled, making me jump.

I heard shuffling behind me, then Jayden stood at my elbow. I looked up at him, and he gave me a gentle smile.

"We're right here at your side, sweetness, and your brothers are, too. You can do this."

I took a deep breath, held it, and let it out slowly. Squaring my shoulders, I took one step, then another and another until I was through the door and down the front porch steps.

Closing my eyes, I lifted my face. The summer sun burned my pale skin a bit, but I didn't care. I could *bathe* in the golden light and still not get enough.

"Posy?"

I opened my eyes, looked at the seven concerned faces around me, and smiled.

"I forgot how good the sun felt," I whispered.

Cole, Wyatt, and Aiden's faces all darkened, and I took a step closer to Jayden. I was fairly sure they weren't angry at me, but the lessons of the past made it hard to trust anyone, especially if they were in a temper.

James took my hand that wasn't clutching Mr. Nibbles.

"I feel like we just got you back and now we're losing you." He smiled. "Please come visit us soon. You are welcome here anytime, baby sister."

I glanced at my mates. Could I ask them to allow my brothers to visit? Did I have that right?

"Everything we have is yours, Posy," Ash said. "Our pack is yours. Our house is yours. You can have your brothers over any time you want."

A wide smile spread across my face and I did something without thinking: I launched myself at my mate and hugged him around his waist. I froze, my entire body tense as I waited to see if I was going to be punished for touching him without permission.

A soft sound huffed out of him, then his long arms wrapped around my shoulders and squeezed me. I listened with wonder to the strong thump-thump of his heart far above my ear.

He doesn't mind it! I think he might even like it!

"Hey, hey, cutie! Can we get some affection, too?" Wyatt teased. "May I hug you?"

When I nodded, he carefully pried me away from Ash, then lifted me off my feet in a big bear hug complete with a playful growl that made me hide my smile in his neck.

The boys passed me around, each one hugging me. Cole even dropped a kiss on my cheek, which made my face burn bright red. I was slowly getting more comfortable with the idea of mates, but physical contact and affection still made me nervous.

I ended up back in my brothers' arms.

"We have something for you."

James picked up a slim package that had been sitting on the porch rail and held it out to me with a smile.

I looked at it, then pointed to myself.

"Yeah, baby sister. For you. Open it."

Tucking Mr. Nibbles under one arm, I reached for it hesitantly, afraid he'd pull it back when my fingers touched it, but he didn't. I unwrapped it to find a framed photo of the three of us when we were pups.

Little five-year-old me sat in the middle of a field with a brother on either side, our cheeks smooshed together and huge grins on our faces. In my lap was a big bunch of daisies, chicory, and Queen Anne's lace. Mr. Nibbles, who went everywhere with me back then, sat on the ground in front of us.

"Do you remember that day?" Aiden asked.

I nodded.

Mom had taken us to pick berries. Afterwards, I'd convinced the boys to help me gather flowers from the field. At five years old, I had thought my older brothers were the coolest people on the planet.

A hot tear slipped from my eye. James wiped it away with his thumb, then squeezed me in a super-tight hug.

"I love you forever, Posy."

Then Aiden came over and wrapped his arms around both of us.

"Me, too. I love you forever, baby sister."

I sniffled and hugged them back.

They let me go after each gave me a kiss on the forehead.

"Be happy, Posy," Aiden said.

"And if these mates of yours don't make you happy, you tell us, baby sister." James gave them a dark scowl which frightened me a bit, then he turned back to me with a grin. "I know they will, though."

With that, James severed my link to the pack, freeing me to leave his territory and join my mates' pack.

"We'll see you at your luna ceremony," Aiden promised.

I smiled and waved goodbye as my mates led me to their big, black SUV, Wyatt walking next to me and holding my hand.

"I'm driving!" Jayden shouted and headed for the front seat.

"Do you want to ride up front?" Cole asked with a soft smile.

I shook my head rapidly. To tell the truth, I was a little afraid. I hadn't been in a vehicle in years.

"I call shotgun!" Ash ran around to the passenger side.

"Can I have your photo, cutie?" Wyatt asked. "I'll put it in a safe place for the trip."

With a nod, I gave it to him, and he went around to the back of the vehicle.

"How about right behind Jay?" Cole opened the back door for me. "After you, honey."

I looked at the height of the seat and prayed I wouldn't embarrass myself. I tossed Mr. Nibbles in first, then grabbed the door frame, swung one leg up, and tried to pull myself into the vehicle. Unfortunately, I was still very weak. I lost momentum and balance and started to fall backward.

Cole caught me around the waist and sat me down in my seat.

"Sorry," I whispered, lowering my head.

"Not a problem, Posy."

He closed my door, went around to the other side, and climbed into the back row. Mason followed him without a word. I'd already figured out that he was the quietest of them all.

Wyatt swung into the seat next to me.

"Ready?" he asked as Jayden started the engine.

I nodded, although my shoulders came up and my fingers fiddled with Mr. Nibbles' ears.

"We have a long drive, so let's get to know each other better, okay?" Wyatt reached over and took one of my hands in his. "Ask us anything!"

"Yeah. What would you like to know, honey?" Cole asked. "I'm sure you're as eager to learn about us as we are about you."

Until a couple of days ago, drawing attention to myself in any way meant a beating. Not really believing they wanted me to speak, I snuck a peek at Cole over my shoulder to see if he was telling the truth. He grinned and winked at me, which made my face burn red. I swiveled further to see Mason.

"I know it's hard, little flower," he murmured, "but try to trust us. We won't hurt you. Not ever, and certainly not for asking questions."

Encouraged, I nodded and decided to go for it.

"Why do you each have a special smell? Is that part of the mate bond?"

"Yes," they chorused.

"What—"

I paused. I wanted to know, but what if they got impatient with me? Taking a deep breath, I did what Mason asked and trusted them.

"What do I smell like to you?"

"Cookies."

"Chocolate chip."

"Fresh out of the oven."

"Makes me want to go down on you and eat you all up." Wyatt leaned closer with a wolfy grin and mischief sparkled in his eyes.

"Go *down* on me?" My eyebrows scrunched up in confusion.

"Wyatt!" Cole snapped. "Quit being crude!"

"You smell very appealing, Posy." Jayden flicked his amazing eyes to mine in the rearview mirror. "Don't worry about Wyatt's nonsense."

"Why do I smell the same to all of you," I asked, "when each of you smells differently to me?"

"Because you're *our* mate. What's my scent?" Wyatt squeezed my hand gently.

"Vanilla."

"What about me?" Ash turned around to meet my eyes.

"Maple syrup."

"Must be because I'm so sweet, just like you, cupcake." He grinned in a way that made my heart stutter.

"With a line like that, you should smell like cheese," Wyatt snickered.

Ash scowled at him while the others, even Mason, chuckled.

"What about me?" Cole asked.

"Pine." So he wouldn't have to ask, I added, "And Mason smells like a campfire."

"And me?" Jayden glanced back at me again.

"Roses."

"Aw, Jay's a flower!" Wyatt teased. "Must be your feminine side coming out."

"Um," I tried to intervene before a fight started.

"You have a lot of lip for a candle fragrance, jerk-off," Jayden shot back.

"That's—"

Wyatt cut me off.

"Candles have fire, moron. What do roses have? Limp petals that wilt?"

I was ruining things already. Should I have lied and told him he smelled like something else? But I couldn't lie to my mates.

"I'm sor—" I tried again, feeling tears prick my eyes.

"Roses have thorns, idiot. You know what candles do? They melt into a soft lump."

As they went back and forth, I started to shake. The fingers of my free hand dug into Mr. Nibbles, and I bit my lips so hard, I tasted blood.

"Shut up, both of you!" Mason barked. "You're upsetting Posy!"

"Oh, cutie, I'm sorry. We're just joking around." Wyatt brought our joined hands up to his mouth and kissed my knuckles.

"Sorry, Posy," Jayden said. "Didn't mean to scare you. We'll try to tone it down around you, but we *are* dudes, young, and alphas, which means it's our nature to compete."

"It's never any serious fighting," Wyatt explained as he rested our hands in my lap. "We got that out of our systems when we were pups."

"You grew up together?"

"Yep. We've all known each other our whole lives. Been there through the worst times and the best."

"That must have been lovely." I admired how close they were. Except for Mason, they all laughed.

Worried they were laughing *at* me, I lowered my head and played with the rings on Wyatt's hand. He wore a rose-gold band on his pinkie, a signet ring with a square ruby on his middle finger, and a pair of wings on his forefinger. That one looked like silver, but I knew it couldn't be because shifters were allergic to silver.

It plat-in-um, Lark said the unfamiliar word slowly. *Granite tell me. He say they richy rich.*

Great. Yet another reason to feel inadequate. My shoulders slumped, and I spun Wyatt's pinkie ring as I blinked back tears.

"You're not inadequate," Cole growled, making me jump. "Stop thinking things like that."

37

"How did you—"

"Lark talks to our wolves, and they talk to us."

Lark, shut up! I hissed at her. *They don't need to know every thought I have!*

Yes, they do. Especially when you being down on yourself.

"You mean the world to us, Posy, and we're going to prove it." Ash reached back and laid his hand on my knee. "It upsets us and our wolves that you doubt us."

"It's me I doubt, not you."

"Try to believe it, okay? Believe in us and in yourself." Cole stretched forward and squeezed my shoulder.

"I'll try."

"Good. That's all we can ask."

The motion of the car was making me sleepy, and a yawn surprised me.

"Go to sleep if you're tired, cutie. You need to rest to get your strength back."

I nodded as my eyelids grew heavier. I could hear my mates talking, but their voices grew fainter and fainter.

I'll close my eyes for a couple of minutes, I promised myself. *I don't want them to think I'm ignoring them. Just a short nap.*

Next thing I knew, someone was unbuckling my seatbelt and scooping me up in muscular arms. I jerked awake, frightened, until my nose filled with the glorious scent of roses.

That calmed me right down.

"Shh, little mate," Jayden whispered into my hair. "You're okay. We're home. I'm carrying you inside."

"Mr. Nibbles," I mumbled, noticing I didn't have him in my arms anymore.

"We'll find him and bring him to you. Go back to sleep."

Taking a deep inhale, I snuggled against him and closed my eyes, knowing I was safe.

6: A New Home

Posy

I woke up on a soft bed with a heavy arm draped across my collar bones, a face smooshed into the back of my neck, and my nose filled with the delicious smell of vanilla.

Strangely enough, I didn't panic.

It the mate bond, Lark explained. *Growing stronger and stronger. Makes you feel safe with them.*

The sparks tickled me everywhere our skin touched, reinforcing the truth of what she said.

"Wyatt?" I whispered.

He only huffed quietly and dug his face deeper into my hair.

"Sorry, cupcake," Ash chuckled. "He's not a morning person."

I looked up and saw him standing at the end of the bed with Jayden, both wearing big grins.

"Might as well get used to his cuddles, too," Jayden told me. "His and Cole's. They're both snugglers at night. Sometimes we put them together to give the rest of us a break."

"Or sic them on me." Ash gave him a sour look.

"Dude. You sleep like the dead. You don't even know they're there."

"Why are you talking so much?" Wyatt muttered. "Go away."

"Nope. Sorry. It's get-up o'clock." Cole came into my line of view with Mason looming behind him. "Untangle yourself from our girl. Breakfast is almost ready."

"Bacon?" Wyatt sat up and rubbed his eyes with his knuckles.

"Of course, you carnivorous pup," Cole said.

"Hey, I'm not the pup anymore," Wyatt yawned. "Posy's two whole months younger than me."

He leaned down and kissed my forehead, then half-fell, half-rolled out of bed and landed on the floor with a thump.

"Whatever you say, *pup,*" Cole smirked.

Jayden and Ash snickered, and Wyatt flipped them off as he got to his feet, then headed for the bathroom.

"It takes him a while to wake up and become his usual, charming self," Cole explained.

"Well, the two of you hogged our mate all night. It's someone else's turn tonight," Ash griped.

"Why do you care? Once you're out, you wouldn't wake up if a bomb went off," Cole retorted.

"So? I can still fall asleep and wake up snuggled next to her."

39

"Posy, how about you sleep on top of Ash tonight? That way, Mase and I can cuddle up on either side of you." Jayden looked very pleased with his solution.

"Um, I guess I can try." I sat up. "You all share one bed?"

"*We* all share one bed, including you now, cupcake." Ash waggled his eyebrows at me, which triggered my blush. "We may not be brothers by blood, but we are in every other way. We share everything important."

"You don't have to share a bathroom with us, though." Cole pointed to a door next to the one Wyatt had gone through. "You have your own separate one. We didn't decorate it or anything, not knowing what our mate's taste would be, but it has the essentials. We can pick up anything you want."

My dimples flashed as I smiled at him. I could have shared their bathroom, but they'd made one just for me. I couldn't believe how thoughtful they were.

As if he read my mind, Ash said, "When we built this place, we tried to imagine what our mate would like. As Cole said, you're free to decorate any way you want, and we can change anything as far as the structure of the house goes, too."

"We're still planning to set up that room for you like we talked about," Jayden told me. "A place for you to go when you want to feel safe or need privacy."

"Or you can't stand Wyatt anymore," Cole muttered.

Of course, Wyatt walked back into the bedroom right as he said that.

"Me! What about *you*?"

He launched himself forward and tackled Cole.

As they hit the floor and wrestled around, Mason sighed and went to pull them apart. Jayden took my hand and pulled me out of bed, and Ash joined us.

"Question, Posy," Ash said. "How would you like to go on individual dates with us?"

"But you're *all* my mates." My forehead puckered up as confusion clouded my thoughts. "Why would I want to be separated from any of you?"

"Aww. That's so sweet!" He grinned.

"It is, but we want to give you time to bond with each of us," Jayden said slowly. "We're concerned that one of us might be overshadowed by the others and get left out. While twins and triplet are common enough, not many lunas have had to adapt to *five* mates."

"We want you to love us all equally." Ash wore a lost little boy face.

Oh, my heart.

40

"I already do," I assured them both with a big smile. "I've never been on a date before, but I've always wanted to. It sounds like fun."

"Well, we're taking you on some dates then." Ash gathered me up and squished me in a hug. "You're going to have lots and lots of fun with us, Posy. I promise."

#

Breakfast was waffles, bacon, and fruits.

I looked at the enormous amount of food on my plate and panicked. I couldn't eat half of this.

They're going to be mad at me for wasting food.

My eyes filled with tears. I didn't want my mates to punish me.

They no be mad, Lark tried to tell me.

"Hey, Posy, it's okay." From where he sat next to me, Wyatt laid his hand on the table with his palm up. "Just eat as much as you can."

My eyes flashed to his face, saw his gentle smile, and darted back to his hand.

Take chance, Lark whispered. *No one going to beat you or lock you in dark room for holding mate's hand.*

With a steadying breath, I touched my fingers to his palm, and he closed his hand around them. His smile spread into a wide grin.

"It'll get better," he promised.

I nodded and picked up my fork with my free hand. I managed to eat a quarter of my waffle, a strip of bacon, four blueberries, and one giant strawberry.

I felt like I disappointed them, but they all assured me that it would take a while for my body to get used to regular meals and proper nutrition.

"Don't worry. I got you, Posy." Ash reached across the table, snagged my plate, and wolfed down the rest of my breakfast.

"I think you're a were pig, not wolf," Cole snorted.

Ash ignored him and happily munched away.

"So, Posy, we each have something we need to take care of this morning," Jayden told me, "but we'll meet back here for lunch."

"After that, we're going shopping!" Ash wiggled like a pup with excitement. "We're going to get you new clothes and shoes and hair stuff and everything!"

My stomach dropped to my feet. I dreaded what I had to admit.

"I don't have any money," I whispered and dropped my eyes.

41

"Oh, baby, don't worry about that." Wyatt raised our joined hands and kissed the back of my knuckles. "We have more money than we know what to do with."

"Honey, anything you want, anything you need, it is our duty and privilege to provide it." Cole smiled at me.

"Sorry, Posy." Mason scooted his chair back and stood. "I've got to get going. Cole, you should, too. Wyatt, Ash, you're on dish duty today. Get it done."

"I'm not some pup for you to boss around, Mase," Wyatt muttered.

Mason sent him a look that made me hunch my shoulders, and it wasn't even directed at me.

"But you *are* the one who consistently skips out on it and drops it in Ash's lap."

Mason's voice picked up a rumbly growl, and I shrank in on myself even more.

"Anyway, Posy, would you like to stay here or go with one of us?" Jayden asked, and I was thankful for the distraction.

"I'll stay here."

"It's your first day with us. I'll reschedule my meeting so I can stay with you," Ash offered.

"No. You've been dodging that meeting for a week." Cole looked from him to me. "Honey, you're welcome to go with Ash, Wyatt or Jay, if you want."

"No, not Jay," Mason growled.

My face must have shown my question.

"Could be dangerous," he muttered.

"I doubt it." Jayden rolled his eyes.

"We don't know him and he isn't pack, which means our girl doesn't go. End of." Mason's tone said 'end of' more than the words.

"I'll stay here," I repeated quietly.

"Won't you be bored and lonely?" Wyatt frowned. "You should go with one of us."

"Um, I want to, uh—" I stopped and pinched my lips together.

"Anything, Posy. You can do anything you want to do," Cole said.

"Could I please get a shower?" I whispered. "I know I already had one this week, but I'd like to wash my hair again."

They were all silent, and I made myself be brave and look at them. Except for Jayden, all their eyes glowed as their wolves fought to ascend.

Oh, no. I made them mad. I'm going to get punished! Why do I always ruin everything by being so greedy?

"I'm sorry! I don't need—" I started to backpedal in a panic.

Mason walked over and laid his index finger on my lips. The sparks made my whole face tingle and helped me calm down. I stared up into his clear gray eyes and, for the first time, my heart thumped hard for a reason other than fear.

"Of course you can. As many as you want, at any time you want, for long as you want."

"And remember what I told you." Wyatt squeezed the hand he was still holding. "Use any temperature and products. You have absolutely zero rules here."

I nodded and thanked them.

Mason kissed the top of my head, sending shivers down my spine.

"See you soon, baby," he whispered and walked out of the kitchen.

The others followed his lead, giving me a kiss on the forehead or cheek and trudging away to their separate tasks.

I flew back up to 'our' bedroom and dug around for some fresh clothing. I was embarrassed by what I had to work with, which were basically rags compared to theirs. The desire for a nice, long shower was stronger than those thoughts, however, and I hustled into the bathroom with a happy skip.

As I waited for the water to heat up, I stripped down, then worked the twist-ties out of my ponytails. I hated them because they always tangled up and the wires jabbed my scalp, but they were all I had to use if I wanted to put my hair up.

Maybe I can convince the boys to buy me a couple of real hair ties while we're shopping today.

I tell you, they dirty rich, Posy! Lark snorted. *They can buy more than hair ties. They love you so much, they buys you a whole beauty store!*

I don't want to be greedy or make them think I only want their money, I scolded her. *And it's filthy rich, not dirty rich.*

Lark just rolled her eyes at me and went back to sleep.

After my shower, I decided to let my hair air dry while I enjoyed the sunshine. Grabbing someone's brush from the boys' bathroom, I headed for the front porch and took a seat on the top step.

Lost in the rhythm of brush strokes, I almost missed hearing the heavy footsteps coming up behind me, but fingers sinking into my hair got my attention real quick.

I froze. Fear dried my mouth and turned my heart into a galloping horse as the smell of maple syrup surrounded me.

What did I do to displease Ash?

"Please, alpha," I begged. "Punish me however you want, but *please* don't pull my hair out."

43

Shaking hard, I didn't dare look at him as his hands fell away. I knew I was taking a huge risk. Father would have done exactly what I'd begged him not to. My mates had been kind so far, however, and I had high hopes that they'd show mercy.

"I'm sorry, princess." Ash's voice sounded raw and hurt. "I'm sorry I scared you. I didn't mean to, and I'll be more careful from now on. I promise."

He sat down on the same step as me, but on the other end and didn't try to touch me. I took a few slow, deep breaths until my heart calmed down, then glanced over at him.

He sat with his elbows on his thighs and his hands clasped between his spread knees. The boy's legs were so long, his feet were on the bottom stair. He watched me with worried eyes.

"I'm sorry," I whispered.

"You don't have anything to apologize for."

"I over-reacted."

"It's understandable. Your father pulled your hair out as a punishment, didn't he?" He raised his eyebrows, and I nodded. "I will never punish you, and I will never pull your hair. I only want to play with it. Jay's mom taught me how to when I was younger, and I used to practice on Jay all the time. He had really long hair until he got it cut last summer."

"Why?"

"Why did he get it cut?" He laughed. "He said it was too hot, but I think he just wanted me to leave him alone."

I shook my head with a frown.

"Oh, you mean, why did I learn? I wanted to know how to do it for our mate when we found her."

His smile melted my heart.

"Okay," I said. "You can play with it."

"I can? Like, *right now*?"

I nodded, and he jumped to his feet. His sudden movement made me flinch a little, but he either ignored it or didn't notice.

"Oh, we are going to have so much fun! Where are your scrunchies and hair products?"

Dropping my eyes to the ground, I held up the two twist-ties I'd grabbed from the kitchen's junk drawer before coming out here.

"You don't have *anything*?" he faltered, but recovered quickly. "That's okay. While we're shopping this afternoon, we'll take care of it. I'll get some stuff for now. Sit tight."

He was back in minutes with a tray of supplies and one of the kitchen bar stools. With one long arm, he picked me up and sat me on it like I weighed nothing. For the next half hour, he played with my hair,

44

trying out different styles and rambling on, and I let him. Surprisingly, I enjoyed it as much as he seemed to.

"Has it always been one length? Have you thought about bangs? We'll need to add a curling iron to our list. That way, whenever you wear it down, we can curl the ends to make it sexy."

My cheeks flared red at that comment.

Finally, he coiled my hair into two big knots on either side and pulled out a few baby hairs to frame my face.

"There! Beautiful! Next time, I want to try Dutch braids, if that's okay with you."

I didn't know what Dutch braids were, but, if he wanted to wear his arms out wrangling my mass of hair, I wasn't going to say no.

"Sure."

"Posy?"

"Hmm?"

"Can I ask you a hard question?"

I hesitated for a moment. Who knew what he meant by *hard*? However, there were only a couple things he could ask that I didn't want to answer.

In the end, I decided it wouldn't hurt to hear the question, so I nodded.

"Why did your father give you enough wolfsbane to put Lark into a coma?"

"Tried to escape." I swallowed hard, my throat suddenly dry as dust. "He caught me right as we were about to sneak out the back door."

"When was that?"

After I told him the date, we figured out that it was three months ago.

"You lived without your wolf for three *months*?"

I couldn't tell if he was shocked, amazed, or devastated. Maybe all three.

"I thought he killed her at first, but, after I recovered enough, I could feel her presence deep, deep in my mind."

"Recovered," he said flatly. "You mean he dosed you with enough wolfsbane to nearly kill your wolf *and* he beat you?"

I nodded.

Ash's breathing grew heavy.

"And you had no wolf to help you heal. I assume that wasn't the only time he hurt you during the weeks Lark slept, either. How did you survive, baby?"

I shrugged. Survive was about all I'd done. I certainly hadn't been living.

He held my face between his palms, leaned down, and kissed my forehead.

45

"Our beautiful, amazing, strong mate," he breathed against my skin.

"*Me?*" I shook my head. "I am none of those things, and definitely not strong."

"Yes, you are. Do you think *everyone* would have come out of that situation alive? Most would have given up years ago. You may have thought about ending it all, but you didn't. You endured. Every time he knocked you down, you got up and kept going."

He pressed his lips to my forehead for longer this time. When he pulled back, his dark eyes swam with tears.

"*That* is what makes you strong, baby. The getting up. In the end, you're the victor. You lived, and your abuser didn't. You got out, and he's in the ground."

My bottom lip trembled. Before I could think about it too much, I jumped off the bar stool and hugged his lean torso, squeezing him as hard as I could. I knew I wouldn't hurt him; the boy's body was as hard as stone. He seemed shocked for a second, then curled his upper half down to cocoon himself around me.

We stood there like that for a while. He dropped soft kisses on my hair and forehead while I stuffed my nose in his abs and inhaled his sweet scent.

"I need to get you a box to stand on," he said finally. "This is killing my back."

I giggled, then realized what I'd done and scolded myself for laughing at his discomfort.

"I'm sor—"

"I'm teasing, Posy," he assured me. "But I *do* need to find or make you a kissing box."

That made me blush all over.

He chuckled and straightened up, and his hands cupped the back of my head and neck. His face turned serious, and I knew he was about to say or ask something I wouldn't like.

"Can you tell us about why he hurt you so badly on your birthday? We need to know so we can avoid triggering you."

"I don't know what triggering means when you use it like that," I admitted.

"Remind you of bad things that could cause nightmares or panic attacks. It would kill us to hurt you like that, even if it's unintentionally."

I thought about that as I watched Wyatt's car speed up the driveway and zoom into his parking spot.

"I'll tell you," I said at last, "but not right now."

"Fair enough."

7: Brothers and Teammates

Posy

"I'm back!" Wyatt hollered as he climbed out of his car.

"We can see that!" Ash yelled.

"I'm not talking to you. Posy, you look so cute! I love your space buns!"

"Is that what they're called?" I raised my eyebrows and looked at Ash.

"Yep." Ash grinned down at me.

I turned back to Wyatt only to find him running toward me. My eyes widened.

Wow! He sure is fast!

"Thank you," I called out.

He was almost to the porch and still pelting along, and I clenched my fingers together.

"Don't tackle her, idiot!"

Ash's shout made me jump, and I squeaked as his arm looped around my waist and pulled me behind his long, broad back.

"I just want a hug." Wyatt skipped up the stairs. "I missed you!"

"Well, I didn't miss you," Ash retorted.

"Not you, idiot." Wyatt shoved him aside and grinned down at me. "*You.* May I please have a hug?"

I blinked. I knew they were all holding themselves back from attacking me with hugs and kisses all the time. Shifters were a very physical species, and personal space was almost nonexistent between mates.

Something to look forward to, Lark teased me.

I blushed bright red.

"Cutie?" Wyatt's face scrunched up in confusion. "You all right?"

I nodded.

"Only if you want to," he reassured me. "You don't have to. I'm not ordering you to let me hug you. If I ever *do* order you to do anything, unless it's to get to the safe room during an attack, you can punch me right in the mouth."

"I don't even know *how* to punch someone," I giggled.

I would never do that to anyone, anyway, least of all one of my mates.

"I'd pay to see you punch Wyatt," Ash said with a chuckle.

"I'm going to teach you to throw a punch." Wyatt ignored him and beamed at me. "Everyone needs to know how to defend themselves."

"She won't ever *need* to defend herself," Ash argued. "She has her wolf, and we'll always be there to protect her."

"Nah, dude. The best way for us to protect her is to make sure she can protect herself."

While they were bickering, I thought about Wyatt's request for a hug. Jayden had told me to not be afraid to say no, but I kind of wanted a hug.

What if I weigh whatever I want against whatever is stopping me from having it? In this case, is my fear greater than my desire for a hug? What's the worst that could happen in either situation?

Sucking in a deep breath, I took a baby step closer to Wyatt. He and Ash stopped arguing and looked down at me.

"You can hug me, Wyatt," I said.

"Thank you, baby."

Very slowly, he slid his arms around me and clasped his hands together right above my bum. It was a loose hold, one I could slip out of easily if I wanted to, and he didn't try to pull me against him. It was as if he knew a tight, close hug would make me feel trapped.

Tilting my head back, I met his silvery blue eyes, and any remaining anxiety evaporated. I moved a little closer and laid my palms on his chest, and his huge grin nearly split his face.

"Me, too, princess," Ash bounced on his toes. "I want a hug, too!"

"No. Get away," Wyatt grumbled. "While I was dealing with pups skipping patrol duty, you were skipping *your* duty just so you could spend time with our girl!"

"I didn't skip anything." Ash crossed his arms over his chest and looked down his nose at Wyatt. "I can't help that *I'm* so good, I finished early."

"Only because you took the easiest job."

"That's funny because the last time *you* had to hear the earnings report, you said it was ridiculously boring."

To distract them from needling each other, I laid my cheek against Wyatt's sternum. His hands went to my back and rubbed up and down. Granite purred under my ear, and I smiled.

"Where are the others?" I asked.

"Jay is interviewing a warrior who asked to join the pack. Cole's checking in with a patrol that scented rogues on the western border of our territory. Mase went to deal with a feral wolf."

I nodded because it all sounded like normal alpha duties, until he said that about Mason. Raising my head, I tensed in his arms.

"A feral wolf?"

"His mate died about a month ago." Ash ran his knuckles down the side of my face. "The wolf lost his mind, and the man's not far behind."

"Is he— Will Mason have to put him down?"

"Most likely," Ash sighed.

"And Mason went *alone*?"

"He can handle it, cutie," Wyatt told me. "He and Cole are two of the most powerful wolves in the country. In fact, they're among the top ten in the whole world."

"I'm not worried about him being in danger." I stepped back from him with a worried frown.

"Then what?"

"It will hurt him, and he's all alone."

"Oh," they said in sync, then looked at each other for a second.

"He wouldn't want anyone else there, Posy," Ash said slowly. "He doesn't like an audience for that kind of thing."

"Not an audience, but for support," I argued.

"You think he'd cry on one of our shoulders? Princess, Mase is solid ice. Even when he *does* feel upset about something, he never shows it to any of us."

"Could you check on him, please? I'm really worried." My eyes stinging, I sniffed and blinked rapidly.

"Sure. I'll link him right now."

As Ash's eyes clouded, I looked back to Wyatt. He frowned at what he saw in my face.

"Mase isn't going to crack from grief because he has to put down a wolf who needs mercy."

"I know that." I couldn't hold the tears in any longer.

"Then what's upsetting you?"

"He's alone. He's all alone to dwell on it for the whole ride home. No one to distract him or let him talk about it. And when he gets here, we'll all be busy with lunch and shopping, and he'll still have it bottled up with no chance to talk to anyone."

"He usually doesn't *want* to talk to anyone," Wyatt said, but his face showed uncertainty.

"Doesn't want to, or isn't given the chance to?"

A sob slipped out, and I put my hand over my mouth as tears poured down my cheeks.

My poor mate. How much has he had to internalize over the years? Is that why he's so aloof, even with his brothers?

"Aw, Posy." Wyatt cupped my face and kissed my forehead. "You're right. We haven't been a good support team for Mase. He's always been ours, and I guess we never really thought he needed us in that way. He does, though, doesn't he? We've been blind."

"He's almost home," Ash said, his eyes clearing up. "Should be here in a minute, the way he's driving. And Wyatt's right. We have been blind, or maybe selfish is the better word. He's the oldest and always seemed invincible."

"Ash!" Wyatt growled, and now *his* eyes were fogged over.

"What is it?" I jumped in fright. "Did something happen?"

"Mase is pissed because Ash told him you were crying." Wyatt punched Ash's arm. "You moron! Hurry up and explain that *he's* making her cry, not *us*!"

"Oh! Um, yeah. Right."

As Ash went back to linking Mason, Wyatt took my hands in his. His face was drawn with worry and something else I couldn't name.

"We took Mase for granted and, because of that, he learned to lock everything away and hide from us. We're horrible brothers, aren't we?"

"Oh, no, not at all!" I pulled my hands from his and threw my arms around his waist. "James is the same way with Aiden, so maybe it's a common big brother-little brother issue. It seems to be an instinct for the oldest to protect the younger ones."

Wyatt wrapped his arms around my head and shoulders. I felt his breath catch in his chest for a second and scolded myself.

Who am I to lecture an alpha? And about a relationship I've only recently become a part of?

"Yeah, but we're more than brothers. We're co-alphas of a huge pack. We need to make sure we have each other's backs even more than brothers." Ash frowned. "Here he comes, by the way. He wouldn't link with me again, so he doesn't know why you were crying. I really don't know how he's going to react."

I looked down the driveway and saw a rooster tail of dust approaching at an alarming speed.

"How do we even start to fix this with him?" Wyatt rested his chin on the top of my head. "I can't just run up and ask if he wants a hug. He'd either think I'd lost my mind and put me through a psych eval or else punch me and tell me to stop goofing around."

"It'll take time, but we *are* going to fix this," Ash promised. "Posy, for now, you better be the designated hugger."

Mason's big red truck came into view, and Wyatt released me and took a step back.

"Yeah, cutie, take one for the team. He won't hit *you*."

I knew Wyatt was teasing, but I hoped he was right. Mason could be scary.

50

He no hurt you. Not ever. Lark preened at the thought of hugging another one of her mates. *Garnet say he devoted to you. He adore you.*

Mason slewed his big truck into his parking space, leapt out of it, and ran towards us in a blur.

And I thought Wyatt was fast! Lightning hangs fire compared to Mason.

As he cleared the porch steps in one leap, his eyes ran up and down my body, as if checking for injuries. He stopped a foot away, took my shoulders in his huge palms, and bent down so we were eye to eye.

"Why were you crying?" His face gave nothing away, but his eyes glittered. "Do I need to beat some sense into these two?"

"Whoa, Mase!" Wyatt held up both hands. "Give us some credit, man. She was worried about *you*. It wasn't anything *we* did."

He straightened up and turned to them. His expression remained as blank as always, but I could sense his irritation.

"You told her what I was doing?"

"I won't lie to our mate," Wyatt said with narrowed eyes.

Seeing that this was headed for a confrontation, I reached up on my tippy toes, touched my fingertips to Mason's jaw, and turned his head back to face me.

"Are you okay?" I asked.

His face scrunched up in a frown, as if he couldn't even understand why I was asking him that.

"Of course."

I stared into his gray eyes without blinking for several long moments. At last, the corners of his lips twitched up a bit.

"He was a good man and a great warrior. Ending his misery was the least I could do for him. Thank you for worrying about me, little flower, but I'm fine."

Seeing the truth in his face, I moved my hands to his shoulders and tugged.

"What are you trying to do?" he asked.

"Come down here, please."

He leaned down again, but I still had to jump a little to loop my arms around his neck. He stood there for a second, still and uncertain, then very gently folded his arms around my shoulders and hugged me back.

"Posy," he muttered.

His nose nuzzled into my neck, making shivers race through me and goosebumps pop up on my skin.

"Okay, okay!" Wyatt interrupted our moment. "Now that our cutie's convinced you're not heartbroken, let's go make some lunch!"

8: Seeking Sanctuary

Jayden

We didn't get transfer requests very often. It usually only happened if a wolf found his or her mate in another pack or if a rogue or lone wolf wanted to come in out of the cold, which was hardly ever. So I was curious as to why Luke MacGregor, a twenty-four-year-old warrior, had asked for a meeting to discuss moving to our pack with his younger sister.

He showed up right on time, which was a point to the good. I introduced myself, then led him back to my office.

"Make yourself comfortable," I said as I sat behind my desk. "There's coffee, tea, and water at the table behind you."

"Thank you, Alpha Carson, but I'm fine."

I observed him as he settled on the leather loveseat and took up most of it. He was easily one of the bigger wolves I'd met. Not only did he share Cole's bear-like build, but he also stood as tall as Mase, who was six foot six. He moved with easy, athletic grace, and I had no doubt he was a competent warrior.

Can't wait to try him in fighter practice. Quartz all but salivated at the hope of a worthy opponent.

Only Cole and Mase gave him a run for his money, and only Cole could be pushed to go all out. Mase's icy control rarely slipped, but Cole's temper often got the better of him. That always made for a brutal fight.

No, a good *fight,* disagreed my psychotic wolf as he grinned disturbingly.

"So, Mr. MacGregor, you want to join our pack with your younger sister, correct?"

"Yes, alpha."

"What are your reasons for leaving Tall Pines? And why do you want to relocate to Five Fangs?"

"My primary reason for leaving is to protect my little sister. The alpha dislikes her and has ordered the rest of the pack to treat her harshly. He told them to use her appearance as an excuse to bully her."

I wondered what he meant by her appearance, but figured I'd find out eventually. I made myself pay attention as he continued.

"Not only have pack members physically hurt her, but they also robbed her of all self-confidence. They have hurt and humiliated her so often, she cringes and cowers at every sound and fast movement, and I can do nothing. It's breaking me as much as it is her."

Silver flickered in his eyes before they returned to their normal light brown.

"Our mate had a similar experience with her alpha," I murmured. "We only found and rescued her a few days ago, so we're dealing with the same thing. We've hardly been able to hug her, never mind finish the mating process."

Maybe his sister and our girl could comfort each other, Quartz suggested, which surprised me. He generally didn't care about others. Then I realized that all his concern was for Posy, not the abused girl.

"I cannot go against Alpha Halder's commands," Luke said, "but I work around him whenever I can. It's a good pack, and I hate to see it being driven into the ground. He spends the pack's money like it's his own personal wealth. Everyone lives in fear. He kills for the slightest offense, often without a hearing. If anyone stands up to him, he banishes them."

That's a troubled pack, all right. I wonder how this all stayed under the king's radar.

"I've been gathering supporters to challenge him for the alphaship, but ran out of time yesterday morning. I was coming home from night patrol when I heard Lilah screaming. I ran inside and he— He had her down on the living room floor, ripping her pajamas off and hitting her."

Again, his eyes glittered with his wolf, but only for a second. *His control is very good,* I noted. *That's a plus. We don't need any more hotheads around here.*

"My wolf, Rain, took over," he continued, "and was holding his own until Alpha Halder started to draw power from the pack."

"Which he could do since it was an impromptu fight and not a formal challenge," I said with a nod.

"Yes. Knowing he wouldn't be able to take him down like that, Rain threw Alpha Halder through a wall. While he was dazed, Rain got Lilah to her feet and out to my truck, and she drove us out of there. After a half hour or so, Rain calmed down enough for me to shift back. Lilah was shaking like a leaf, I was exhausted from coming off night patrol, and we were both covered in bruises and cuts. We drove about a hundred miles past Tall Pines' border and found a hotel. It's a good thing I keep a duffel bag of essentials in my truck, or the clerk would have gotten an eyeful."

He chuckled darkly, and I smirked.

"Anyway, while Lilah was in the shower, I called your pack. One of the betas - his name may have been Matthew? - set up this meeting and that's where we are now."

"Does Lilah need medical attention?"

"Her wolf took care of the worst injuries, but Kestrel is exhausted from day after day of healing her." Luke scrubbed one hand over his face. "I don't think a pack doctor could do much for the remaining bruises, and Lilah would be too scared to go to your clinic, anyway."

"How old is she?"

"Only nineteen. She's just a kid. She's so traumatized, she hasn't said a word since it happened. She just sits and stares and shakes."

Poor kid.

"May I ask why Alpha Halder dislikes her so much?" I asked next. "His behavior is not acceptable in any way, shape, or form, but is she disobedient or disrespectful or rebellious? Has she caused trouble for the pack?"

"No. None of that. She is sweet and innocent and shy." Luke blew a heavy breath out of his nose. "The truth is, he wanted her for his chosen mate, and she said no. She wants her Goddess-given mate, as we all do. I also believe he found out I was going to challenge him and abused her to punish me for it."

I narrowed my eyes as I studied his face. He was no mere warrior. A pack warrior wouldn't have the balls to challenge his alpha.

"I can smell your beta blood," I said. "Is that your rank in the pack?"

"It is."

Then he took a deep breath, and I could tell he was debating whether or not to share something with me. He stared at his hands for a long moment before resolve formed on his face.

"But I can no longer stand with such a cruel alpha," he said slowly, "nor will I serve one who plots treason against his king."

Instantly alert, Quartz pushed for control, and pushed *hard.* For whatever reason, he considered King Julian and his wolf, Onyx, to be his brothers. In his mind, a threat against them was a statement of war.

"Explain," I demanded, a burr of Quartz's aggression slipping into my voice despite the restraint I put on him.

Settle down, wolf, I grumbled. *It does no good to grow angry before we know all the details.*

Anger clouds the mind, he repeated dutifully and calmed a bit.

It was a mantra we'd been working on since I first shifted seven years ago. Sometimes, it helped. Other times, nothing helped.

That's when people died.

"Alpha Halder plans to lead a coup against the crown," Luke said. "He's been spreading lies about King Julian throughout the pack, which is large enough to be threatening if the majority of wolves are swayed to his side. Alpha Halder's lies might not do that, but the promise of his retribution - and his alpha command - could."

We sat in silence for a moment, each lost in our thoughts. "We'll need to call the king in on this," I said at last. "It's almost time for his annual stay, anyway."

Alpha Julian Hemming, king of the North American werewolves, visited us frequently and came for a two-week vacation every summer. We did a little pack business, of course, but mostly we relaxed and stayed up late talking around the bonfire. During the day, Onyx ran free through the woods and swam in the lake and tussled with Quartz.

I had to admit that I was a little concerned about how he'd react to Posy being here this year. He hadn't found his mate yet and, at twenty-four, was worried he never would. One of the reasons he liked vacationing with us was because we didn't have our mate, either. Now, that dynamic had changed, and I hoped he wouldn't feel like we were rubbing salt in his wounds. After all, five very young alphas had found their mate before our king had.

"That's the reason why I chose Five Fangs over any other pack," Luke told me. "Your close ties with the king are well known. And five alphas against one are odds I'll take in any gamble."

"Where is your sister now? I'm sure you didn't leave her back in the hotel room unguarded."

"She's in my truck, which is parked right outside."

I didn't think the pack house would be a good place for the girl. If it were Posy, I'd want her to be in a safer, quieter space, so I decided on the smaller guest house. The larger one was strictly reserved for King Julian's visits.

"Introduce me to her, then I'll take you to where you can stay until everything's sorted and you can find your own place. The guest house is clean and stocked with everything but food. I'll contact my beta to set up a grocery run for you."

"Thank you, Alpha Carson, for your generosity and hospitality. I can pay for the—"

"Don't even finish that sentence. Once you officially join the pack, we'll find a job for you. Your sister, too, if she wants one. Until then, we'll take care of everything."

"Again, thank you, alpha."

"You will both come to dinner at our place tonight," I continued. "I need to introduce you to my brother alphas, and our mate would love to meet Lilah, I'm sure. Do you have a phone?"

He pulled one out of his pocket and held it up, then handed it to me when I motioned for it. After adding my number into his contacts, I gave it back.

"It takes about ten minutes to drive from your place to ours. Give me a call when you're ready to leave, and I'll give you directions.

Dinner starts at six sharp. It's Mase's day to cook, so it should be good. At least you won't have to suffer through one of Ash's inedible experiments or Wyatt's frozen pizzas that he manages to burn every single time."

Luke snorted.

"As long as there's food and plenty of it, I'll be content," he said. "Uh, Lilah probably won't eat much. She isn't being rude—"

I held up one hand.

"Posy is the same way. We understand, and we don't comment no matter how much or little she eats." I sighed. "They'll get better. Just as their hearts and minds need time to feel safe again, their bodies need time to remember food and how to process it."

"Well said, alpha."

"Has Alpha Halder tried linking you?" I asked.

"Yes. Between our strength and hatred for him, Rain and I are able to resist him, and the distance is helping, too. I *am* worried about how Lilah will hold out once Kestrel wakes up again. A wolf must follow their alpha's commands, and both Lilah and Kestrel are too weak to put up much of a fight right now."

"Well, I can't induct you into Five Fangs without my brothers, but we can do it at dinner tonight. If Kestrel wakes up before then, I trust you can handle her?"

"It won't be fun, but yes."

I nodded and stood, and he followed me out of my office. As we walked outside, I spotted his truck and the girl huddled in the front seat. Even from here, I could see carroty red hair that glimmered in the morning sun. She shot timid glances at me, so I made sure to stop five feet away as Luke went up to her door and opened it.

"Hey, ladybug. Everything's okay, I promise. This is Alpha Jayden Carson. He's going to show us a place where we can stay. Can you say hello?"

Luke moved to the side and a pair of mismatched eyes - one brown and one blue - stared at me in stark terror. Under her heavy freckles, her skin turned milk white, making all her bruises stand out. She had two black eyes and a thick band of bruising around her neck like a grotesque necklace. She seemed to be wearing her brother's shirt, which covered most of her, but I could see dark fingerprints on her forearms and also on her legs where her pajama shorts ended.

It made me angry to see that, and I had to work to hide it. She was shaking hard enough without me adding to her distress.

Just like our Posy, Quartz growled. *Another innocent broken by her alpha.*

Sounds like King Julian needs to send undercover inspectors out to the packs more often, I thought to myself.

"Hello, Lilah." I smiled, but stayed where I was. "You don't have to speak if you're not comfortable. I know a man's word probably means nothing to you right now. Still, I give you mine that no one will harm you here. I swear by the moon that you are safe on our territory."

She bobbed her head in a quick, bird-like movement and dropped her eyes to the ground as her fingers twisted into the hem of her shirt. There was little I could do to reassure or comfort her, though, so I took another step back and pointed to my SUV.

"Follow me, Luke. It's a short drive."

"Sure, alpha."

#

On the way over to the guest house, I linked my brothers and caught them up on everything. They, too, were furious over the revelations of what had been happening in the Tall Pines pack. We had an alliance with Alpha Halder.

Not any more, Cole growled. *It's dissolved as of right now.*

We all agreed, and Wyatt volunteered to have the severance paperwork drawn up and delivered by the end of the week.

I'll contact King Julian as soon as I get out of this effing meeting, Ash offered.

Mase didn't say much, which was normal. He only promised he'd do his best for dinner since we had company coming.

As I pulled up to the guest house, I told my brothers I'd see them at lunch and closed my side of the link.

Jumping out of my SUV, I ran up the porch steps and unlocked the door, then ushered the MacGregors inside. It was almost as hot in here as it was outside, and I frowned.

I should have had someone come over and adjust the air conditioning.

Going over to the thermostat, I cranked it from 85 to 72 and heard the unit kick on.

"It should cool down fairly quickly," I told Luke as I handed him the house keys. "You can set it to whatever you want. Treat this place like it's your own home."

He nodded and thanked me again, and I had to admit that I liked his manners.

Through the whole tour of the place, Lilah hid behind him with her fists balled up in the back of his shirt. He didn't complain or appear irritated by it, either. He talked to her gently and gave her first pick of the two bedrooms.

More and more, I liked this guy for our pack.

And if he can fight, I will like him, too, Quartz said solemnly.

We ended up back in the kitchen, where I was proven right about there being no food in the house. I linked my beta, Crew Myers, and told him what I needed. A thought hit me and I paused my conversation with him.

"Luke, does Lilah have a phone?"

"Not anymore. Alpha Halder destroyed it."

I nodded curtly, and linked Crew to pick that up for her, too.

Luke and I were discussing what other necessities they needed when Lilah fell to her knees and squeezed her head between her palms. I glanced at Luke, and saw he understood what was wrong, too.

Alpha Halder was linking her.

"Can you tell if Kestrel's awake?" I asked him.

If she was, that would make it even more difficult for Lilah to resist her alpha.

Shaking his head, he dropped next to his sister and gathered her against his chest. His expression mirrored my own feeling of helplessness.

"Lilah," his voice was low and rough, "fight him! You can do it, ladybug. You are strong. Fight!"

Tears streaked from the big man's eyes when she began to shake as if she were having a seizure. A line of blood trickled from the corner of her mouth.

I think she bit her tongue, Quartz observed with his usual detachment, and I growled at him. *What? She is not family. She is not pack.*

She will be soon enough, I retorted and rolled my eyes at him.

Lilah tried to get to her feet, her face blank and her eyes clouded by the link, and Luke held her tighter. She struggled against him, but he was far too strong for her to break free.

"I'm afraid I'm going to hurt her," he muttered.

It was hard for a werewolf to gauge his strength, and I could only imagine myself with Posy in this situation. I - well, all of us - handled our mate like blown glass, and Lilah looked as physically frail and fragile after her ordeal.

Just make her pack already, Quartz grumped.

You know I can't make her a member of Five Fangs without—

There is another pack that is completely yours to control, he reminded me with an eye roll of his own.

"Luke, I have an idea." I ignored Quartz's complaint that it was *his* idea. "I can induct you both into the Moonset Pack. That will sever your link with Alpha Halder and Tall Pines."

"Okay, I don't know that pack, but if it helps her, please do it quickly." He grunted as one of her tiny elbows hit his throat.

"It's *my* pack," I explained as I ran over to the utensil drawer and hunted for a sharp knife. "All our old packs still exist in the eyes of the Goddess. I am the alpha, and Crew Myers is my beta. We're the only two in the pack, so your wolf might be a little lonely, but at least you'll be free of that monster."

I found a paring knife that would work well enough and hurried back to crouch next to them.

"Lilah, if you can hear me, I'm going to cut your finger."

I grabbed one of her flailing hands and nicked the pad of her thumb, then did the same with my own. Pressing the two together, I pushed out my power and felt the moon magic stir as our blood mingled. After a second, she went still and her unusual eyes met mine for a heartbeat before she lowered them.

"It's— It's so quiet," she whispered and touched her left temple. "It's so quiet in my head."

She slumped against Luke, looking exhausted and numb.

"Here, alpha."

Luke stuck out one of his hands while he held her with the other, and I repeated the process with our thumbs.

Can you hear me? I sent through our newly established link.

They turned their heads in sync and blinked at me like owls, then a wide smile broke out on Luke's face.

"We talk to each other again, ladybug," he murmured and squished her in a big hug.

Sobbing now, she dug her face into his chest and clung to him.

"Alpha Halder forbid you to use the link with each other?" I guessed.

"She wasn't allowed to use it with *anyone.*"

He'd isolated Lilah just as thoroughly as Alpha Briggs had done with Posy, which was one of the cruelest things someone could do to a shifter. Wolves needed packs. Only lone wolves could survive in seclusion. The longer a shifter went without pack contact, the more his or her mental and emotional health deteriorated.

We will kill him, Quartz promised.

"Do you want to meet Crew?" I asked. "It's only the four of us on this link."

"Sure." Luke grinned at me. "I've never heard of a four-person pack before."

"It is odd," I agreed with a smile. "He'll be dropping the groceries and other supplies off later. He'll link you when he's on his way."

"All right and thank you, alpha." He nudged the top of Lilah's head with his chin. "Ladybug, do you want to say something to Alpha Carson?"

She turned her face so I could see one red, tear-stained cheek and her brown eye.

"Thank you, alpha," she hiccuped.

59

"It's my pleasure. I can't wait for you to meet my mate. You're going to love each other. I just know it."

Her lips curled up in a hesitant smile, and I knew I was right.

"Try to get some rest," I instructed as I stood. "I'll see you both at dinner."

"See you," Luke said.

With a wave, I let myself out of the house and headed for home, anxious to see our girl.

9: Going Shopping

Posy

I felt better about shopping after Cole told me that his little sister, Peri, was going to come along. She was turning eighteen next week and was the only girl in the family, so the boys thought we would be a perfect fit.

As Mason served up meatball subs, I leaned over and tugged on Cole's shirt sleeve. When he bent down, I whispered in his ear.

"Is Peri nice? Will she like me?"

His head whipped around and his eyes met mine. My cheeks burned from how close our faces suddenly were, but I held his gaze.

"Very, and you'll like each other a lot. She's calm and sweet and, unlike me, doesn't have any kind of temper."

I hope she knows more about clothes and shoes than I do. Maybe she can help me figure out how to buy bras that actually fit.

I'd been wearing Mom's old ones that I'd scrounged years ago, and they were uncomfortable.

"Here you go, little flower."

Mason set a plate in front of me, and I looked at it with despair. After so much food at breakfast, my belly felt like it was going to erupt if I sent anything else into it.

The boys scarfed down three sandwiches each; I managed to choke down about a quarter of one. This time, Wyatt beat Ash to my leftovers, making Ash pout. I sensed a competition in the making and wondered if I should nip it in the bud or not.

Aw, let 'em go, Lark laughed. *It fun to watch!*

I offered to help clean up, but they wouldn't let me. As Wyatt and Ash did dish duty and Cole left to pick up Peri, Mason and Jayden took me to the living room.

"We have something for you." Jayden grinned.

Mason handed me a box wrapped in navy blue paper, and I held it in both hands.

"For me?" I blinked up at them.

"Yep," Jayden said.

"But I have nothing for you."

"Sweetness, we're going to spoil you, so get used to it." Jayden pointed to the box. "Now open it."

Feeling uncomfortable, I unwrapped it and discovered a brand-new phone.

"Ours and your brothers' numbers are already saved in your contacts," he said. "We'll put in our betas and the rest of the family after you meet them."

"Thank you," I whispered.

I wondered if I should tell them I had no clue how to use a phone, but Mason seemed to read my mind.

"Have you had one before?" he asked.

I shook my head.

"Then we'll show you how to use it."

"Hey, you guys," Wyatt poked his head around the corner. "Cole's going to meet us there because Peri's running late. Ash and I are ready to leave. Are you?"

"Yes."

When Jayden's knuckles knocked against the back of my hand, I laced my fingers in his without thinking about it and let him lead me out of the house.

We piled into their big, black SUV with Mason in the driver's seat and Jayden riding shotgun. Wyatt and Ash pulled me to the back row. Their reason was that they wanted to show me how to use my phone, but I think that they really just wanted to squish me between them.

#

Cole was right: Peri was super nice and a lot of fun. I hoped we'd become good friends.

Without making me feel like an idiot, she helped me pick out clothes and shoes and, praise the Goddess, knew how to buy bras. She wanted me to get some fancy ones "for the boys," but that made me squirm with embarrassment. I ended up running away from her when she held up some sheer black lingerie, which made her burst out into giggles.

Soon, I had a good number of outfits and told the boys they didn't need to spend any more money on me. They laughed and told me to stop looking at price tags and keep getting anything I wanted. I twisted my fingers, but Peri encouraged me to spend their money.

"They're loaded," she laughed. "How many guitars and game consoles and cars do they need, anyway?"

I still wasn't comfortable with it, but went through the next three stores and let Peri and the boys talk me into even more clothes, shoes, and accessories.

By then, we'd accumulated a lot of bags, and Mason and Jayden offered to take them to the car while Ash led us into a beauty supply store.

Wyatt and Cole hung out with us for a few minutes, then wandered off on their own. Ash and Peri dragged me to the hair section, but it was soon clear I didn't have a clue about the products they were discussing. They didn't ask my opinion, which was okay since I didn't have one, but I felt a little left out.

I was following them down the aisle like a lost pup when a card of barrettes caught my eye. I stopped and took a closer look. They were simple gold bobby pins, but each one had a realistic flower on the end. There was a pink rose, a red rose, a daisy, a dahlia, a sunflower, and a pansy, my favorite.

Oh, they're precious. So delicate and adorable.

"Hey, Ash, I really like these. What do you think, Peri?"

I looked up to show them, but neither turned around. My shoulders slumping, I replaced the card on the hanger.

They not hear you, Lark suggested, but I just shrugged.

I don't need them, and they've spent too much on me as it is.

Feeling a bit unsettled, I decided to find the others. I didn't smell Jayden or Mason and figured they hadn't returned from the parking lot yet, but my nose picked out vanilla and pine from the hundreds of fragrances cluttering the air in this store.

Glancing at Ash and Peri one more time, I saw they were chirping like birds at dawn, so I left them to it.

When I found Cole and Wyatt, though, I wished I'd stayed and remained ignored. It would have been better than the sickening sight before me now.

Girls surrounded them in a tight circle.

What those females doing with our *mates?* Lark snarled.

She was on the verge of taking over, and I was tempted to let her.

The smaller two girls were wolves, twins from the look of it, and most likely from the boys' pack. They lingered in the back of the group with red faces and fidgeted nervously. The other three were human with perfect hair and makeup and outfits. They were tall and shapely, too, making me even more self-conscious of my short, too-thin body, ratty jeans and t-shirt, and little-girl space buns.

Wyatt say they cute, Lark reminded me, but she didn't sound as certain as she usually did.

She was waiting for the boys to move away from the girls, or at least remember we existed.

Then one of the human girls smiled, put her hands on Cole's chest, and ran her fingers all over him.

When he only stood there and didn't push her away, I handed Lark the reins and sank to the back of my mind in utter anguish.

I knew it. I knew I wasn't enough for them.

\#

Lark

63

From my throat ripped a subvocal growl, one only a shifter could hear. I was *not* playing, and now every wolf in the vicinity was aware of it.

Wyatt and Cole whined, and I heard Ash whimper from across the store. The two she-wolves had the brains to bare their necks as I flew over there and tore the girl's hands off my mate.

"Mine!" I snapped.

"Oh, really?" The girl lifted one eyebrow and her gaze traveled from the top of my head down to my shoes, then she looked at Cole. "Babe, you may be sexy as sin, but your standards are lower than low if *she's* your girl."

Posy might not know how to throw a punch, but *I* did. The idiot girl was on the floor holding her nose in half a second, twin streams of blood trickling from her nostrils.

"Say what you want about me," I said through clenched teeth, "but *no one* insults mate!"

"Who do you think you are?!" screeched the girl.

She scrambled to her feet, but one of her human friends pulled her back before she could get in my face.

"Callie, Keeley, what kind of lunatics do you hang out with?" demanded the third human girl. "Who is this psycho?"

The she-wolves, Callie and Keeley, shot me an apologetic look and ran off.

"Hey! Where are you going?" shrieked Ms. Bloody Nose. "You can't leave us! You're our ride!"

The three human girls took off after the she-wolves, who I almost felt bad for. Why had they chosen such mean girls as friends?

Spinning around, I looked at my mates and saw their eyes aglow, Wyatt's gold and Cole's silver, as their wolves took over.

"It not what you think, my love." Granite approached me slowly with his hands up. "The she-wolves members of pack. They have question for boys."

"Then their human friends came over," Topaz went on, "and the boys didn't realize what was happening until one touched Cole."

"Why he no do something?" I snarled.

"He was too shocked at first, and was about to push her away when you intervened."

I narrowed my eyes, unsure if I believed this story. I wanted to because I loved these wolves so much already, but there was someone other than myself to consider.

"Whether that true or not, Posy *hurt*. She worried you punish her because of what I do, so I tell you right now: If your dumb boys lay one finger on her in anger, I never forgive you. *Never*."

Granite and Topaz whined, and pain rippled across their faces.

Ash ran up to us then, Peri on his heels.

"What did you two do to upset our girl?"

"And *you*!" I rounded on him. "How you not even see the *only* thing in here my girl like? She try to show you, but you too busy deciding everything for her. You no *listen* to her!"

"What? No! I..." His voice died out as his eyes turned neon green.

"My darling, I sorry," Sid whispered. "Ashy get excited sometimes and lost in his head. He not mean to ignore—"

"How none of your boys know they hurting Posy?" I spat.

Wow. I was really piling up the offenses now. This was not going to end well.

Posy?

She didn't answer me, and I knew she'd gone back to her old stand-by of stay still, stay silent, and stay alive.

"What's happening here?"

Mason's voice was so calm and quiet, it was like a balm on my frazzled mind.

Turning my head to the right, I saw him standing there with Jayden, and I wondered at what point they'd joined us.

"Lark, may I speak with Posy, please?"

Jayden also used a mild tone, as if he knew I was a shotgun on a hair trigger and needed only the lightest touch to explode.

"She no want to come out." I shook my head hard and fast. "She hurt and so scared."

Sid, Granite, and Topaz whimpered, but Garnet let out a long, low growl.

Oh, no. We really *going to get punished now.*

I'd made everything worse. Not only was I talking back to and defying the alphas, I was making my mates angry.

My lungs started to suck in air as if I'd run for miles, which I hadn't been allowed to do in ages.

"I sorry, alphas," I gulped and bowed my head. "We know you making the best of bad situation, getting stuck with worthless, damaged mate like us. I have no right to get angry if you find other females who make you happy. Punish me as you want. Give me wolfsbane and I go to sleep again. Just please no punish Posy because of me."

I covered my face with shaking hands and curled my shoulders in. The pain in my chest was worse than when Father broke both my femurs.

Just once, I wish we have someone there when we not okay. Someone who would hold us together when we falling apart. Just once.

"Lark."

65

My breaking heart stilled to hear *that* wolf's voice, and I dropped my hands to stare into Quartz's golden eyes.

"Please," I whimpered, not sure what I was even begging for.

"Come. Here. Now."

There was no arguing with an alpha's command, but Posy's frail body was giving out on us. Lungs straining, heart racing, I blinked as the world faded around the edges. My eyes rolled back in my head and I crashed to the floor.

Before my head could bounce off the hard tile, a pair of hands caught me and lifted me up into a cloud of rose perfume.

10: *What a Mess*

Mason

If they weren't my brothers, I would have killed them for upsetting my mate so badly. But they were, and she was their mate as much as mine.

I was still plenty pissed.

"My office," I barked. "All three of you. Thirty minutes." Turning to Jay, I saw Quartz was still in control and bit back a curse.

Great. A chaos cherry on top of a disaster sundae.

At least holding Posy was keeping him from becoming homicidal. He had her balled up tight against his chest with his nose buried deep in her neck, right where our mate mark would eventually go.

"Quartz, how about we drop Peri off, then take our girl home?"

Talking to him was a delicate game. If it was anything other than a suggestion stated as a question, he saw it as an order - and *nobody* ordered Quartz around.

He grunted. I waited a minute to see if he had more of a response, but knew that was probably the best I was going to get.

I took Peri's elbow, led her out to the SUV, and hoped Quartz would follow. Fortunately, he did. After I unlocked the doors, he crawled into the backseat with his precious bundle, so I offered shotgun to Peri.

"Everything was going so great, Mase." She sniffed as tears ran down her face. "I thought we were becoming friends. Do you think she hates me now?"

"Of course not," I scowled. "She doesn't know how to hate anyone."

"She's going to be okay, right?"

"Yeah. Don't worry. I'll fix it."

Like we fix everything else, Garnet muttered.

#

I clasped my hands on top of my desk and stared at my three brothers. My face was blank, my eyes, too, and I didn't move a muscle. Not even my eyelids flickered.

Over the years, I'd discovered that being quiet and still was an excellent intimidation tactic. It unnerved people, especially when those people knew just how very pissed off you were.

"I'm curious, brothers."

I flexed my two index fingers in a quick movement, and Wyatt and Cole twitched.

Garnet smirked, and I wanted to. I usually didn't enjoy scaring my brothers straight, but today was an exception.

I was finding out that *anything* involving Posy was quickly becoming an exception to all my rules.

"How did you three screw up so badly that our mate now believes we don't care about her, we'll cheat on her, and we want to put her wolf back in a coma?"

When Wyatt opened his mouth, I unclasped my hands and held up one index finger.

"Oh, and let me not forget that you upset Peri *and* got Quartz to come out and play. All in less than twenty minutes."

I shook my head and faked a smile, which made Ash flinch.

"Dang, brothers. I think that might be a new record for you."

"Shut up, Mase," Cole muttered. "I don't know what happened with Ash, but what happened with Wyatt and me was a big misunderstanding all around."

"With me, too," Ash chimed in. "I didn't realize she thought I was ignoring her."

You were *ignoring her,* we all heard Sid snarl. *I try to get you attention when she want to show you those hair flowers, but you brush me off!*

Ash gasped as he doubled over in pain.

Today, we learned something new about having a mate: If we did something to cause Posy pain or grief, our wolves became unhappy with us.

Very unhappy.

And right now, Ash, Cole, and Wyatt were suffering from their wolves' full displeasure.

"Peri already told me about that part." I looked away from Ash to glare at the other two. "Tell me what happened."

"We were looking at the jewelry counter when Callie and Keeley came up to ask us if the rumor was true that we'd found our luna." Cole scooted forward to sit on the edge of his chair. "We were about to tell them it was when three of their friends came over."

"Since they were human," Wyatt picked up, "we said that, yes, we had a girlfriend, knowing that the twins would understand what we meant."

"The three human girls giggled and came closer, and one of them put their hands on me." The disgust on Cole's face was plain as day. "Unfortunately, that's right when Posy walked over."

"You didn't realize they were flirting?" I asked.

How oblivious can they get? Garnet asked me.

68

"Not until that moment," Wyatt admitted.

I covered my eyes with one hand and shook my head.

"Did you do anything, Cole?"

I hoped against hope that he at least pushed the girl away.

"Uh, no. I was too surprised. I never thought a stranger would do that. Humans are weird. But I really didn't get a chance to do anything before Lark pulled the girl off of me and punched her in the nose because the human insulted me."

"Lark *punched* her?" I blinked.

With a nod, Cole sent me the memory through the link. On one hand, I was proud of our girl's wolf. On the other hand, I was furious. She shouldn't have had to do that.

"Okay, here's what you're going to do." I stared at each one of them for several solid seconds. "From now on, you treat any unmated females as if they are flirting with you, since you can't tell if they are or not."

"Once we're fully mated, it won't even be an issue," Cole scoffed.

"Yeah, but only with other shifters," Ash pointed out. "Humans were your problem today."

"Rings." Wyatt's eyes widened. "We'll wear wedding rings. We can get a gorgeous one for our girl, too."

I thought about it, then nodded. A good watch was all I really needed as far as jewelry went, but I was game if it helped our girl. While the boys talked about having Posy design them each a ring, I pondered the problem of how to get our mate to understand we loved her and were never going to let her go or replace her.

Mark her, Garnet encouraged, *and soon. It will strengthen the bond and reassure her.*

I agreed, but she wasn't ready for us to do that yet.

Marking works both ways, Mase.

Ah. I hadn't thought of that.

"What if we asked her to mark us?" I narrowed my eyes as I worked it out in my mind. "What Lark said today proves that neither of them really believes we want to keep and love them and only them forever. If she marks us, maybe she'll feel more secure in her role in our lives."

I could tell I caught them off guard. Females rarely marked their mates. Why bother when a male's mark was all that was needed to complete the process? Males who bore their females' mark, however, often saw it as a symbol of respect and admiration from their ladies.

After they thought about it for a few seconds, the boys all nodded.

"We'll have to talk to Jay, but I doubt he'll say no," Ash said. "She should mark us before we mark her, too."

"Why?" Wyatt asked. "I'm not against it. I want to be bound to her in every way possible. But why should she go first?"

"It'll build her confidence in us and our commitment to her. She'll see how serious we are about keeping her. And it will make her feel powerful. Maybe even give her a sense of control."

"Yeah, she probably feels like she hasn't had much of that in her life, and certainly not recently." Cole blew a heavy breath out of his nose. "It's not like she chose to have five mates or move packs or leave her brothers right after being freed from years of abuse."

"Oh." Wyatt frowned. "I was so excited to find our mate, I didn't even think about any of that. Do you—"

His voice broke, and he swallowed hard.

"Do you think she resents us?"

"Goddess, I hope not," Ash whispered.

"No. I don't believe that." I shook my head. "I believe she's very, very scared. We're all excited to find our mate, but, like I said before, we need to be careful with her. More careful than we've been so far. We need to step up our game."

"Jay will have some idea about that, once we can talk with him," Ash said confidently. "He's the best of us at those soft skills."

"Is Quartz still in charge?" Wyatt's eyebrows flew up. "Did he take over or did Jay let him loose?"

We all shrugged.

"I think Jay let him out," Ash said. "Quartz hasn't been able to forcibly take control for years now, although our mate's distress could have made Jay's control slip."

I appreciated that; however, if he gave Quartz the reins voluntarily in a human-filled store off of pack territory, we were going to have words.

"So, how do we make this right with Posy?" Wyatt scratched his head.

"After Jay gets her to calm down, we'll apologize and explain and let her know it won't happen again," Cole said.

"We should do something nice for her, too," Ash suggested, "but I don't know what."

In unison, they swiveled their heads and looked at me with raised eyebrows.

"Like I know!" I snarled.

There were two people who might have some ideas, but, man, I did *not* want to involve them!

For Posy, Garnet murmured, and that was all I had to hear.

Picking up my phone, I scrolled through my contacts, hit the one I wanted, and waited for him to answer.

"Hello, Alpha Price."

"Alpha Briggs," I returned the greeting and put my phone on speaker.

"Is Posy happy and well?"

Of course, he'd ask that first.

"I need to ask a favor." I scrubbed my hand through my hair. "What are some things she likes? We want to do something nice for her to make up for a misunderstanding."

The line was silent for a whole thirty seconds. That doesn't sound like a lot of time, but when your heart's on the line, it's an eternity.

"What. Did. You. Do. To. My. Baby. Sister?"

"Me? Nothing."

"Then why do you need a make-up gift when she hasn't even been with you for twenty-four hours yet?"

"Look, James, it's a misunderstanding, but Posy is too upset to hear anything. She's so afraid that we don't really want her."

"And you blame her for that?" His voice rose. "You only know a small fraction of what she lived through. How can you expect her to be anything other than scared? I warned you all about this before you left."

The boys squirmed in their seats.

"I know," I assured James, "and we don't blame her for anything. We're trying to show her that she can trust us. Unfortunately, this ... incident occurred and now we're back to square one."

Huh. If there was a negative square, that's where we'd be, Garnet brooded, and I had to agree.

"Why should I help you get back in her good graces?" James demanded. "You shouldn't have messed up in the first place!"

"You don't want your sister to be happy with her mates? For real, James, I love Posy so much that I'm willing to beg here."

He didn't reply, and I scowled. Plowing my hand through my hair, I glared at my brothers, and they dropped their eyes to their shoes.

"Give her flowers," James muttered after a long silence. "She loves them. Always has. Especially if you can find pansies. She used to pretend the fairies painted them."

Ah. That explains the purple pansy tattooed on his forearm and the simpler one inside Aiden's wrist.

The boys had perked up at his words, and their eyes brightened.

"Thank you," I told him.

71

"You're welcome." There was a long pause, then, "Did she have a nightmare last night?"

"No. She fell asleep on the way home and didn't move until morning."

A gusty sigh came from the phone.

"Well, when she does have one, give her Mr. Nibbles. She won't want to be touched at first, but don't leave her alone. She wants someone with her. Just keep telling her she's safe."

Red rage filled my vision. I would give anything to be able to resurrect Alpha Kendall Briggs just so I could kill him again.

We'd take years doing it, too, Garnet snarled. *Snapping his neck was too merciful.*

But, "Thanks, James," was all I said.

"One more thing, Mason."

"Yeah?"

"Whether it's you or one of your brothers, *don't* screw up again. I failed in my duty as her brother once. I never will again. She deserves to know nothing but happiness for the rest of her days. If you can't or won't deliver on that, I will do what I need to do. I don't care who you are."

"I understand and agree one hundred percent."

After I hung up, Wyatt jumped to his feet.

"Dudes, I have a great idea!" he yelled. "Come on! We have a lot of work to do!"

As they hustled out of the room, I hollered, "You also better get your butts back to that shop and buy those flower things she wanted!"

"Already done." Ash gave me a thumbs up.

At least they did that much right, Garnet grumbled.

Small favors, I grumbled back.

11: Quartz the Comforter

Posy

I woke up in Jayden's arms and realized I was back in our bed. Blinking slowly, I raised my head and found him staring down at me with golden eyes.

Quartz, then. Not Jayden.

"Feel better?" he asked.

I swallowed hard and shrugged.

"No one is angry with you," he assured me. "No one wants to get rid of you. We all love you. Topaz and Granite were telling the truth about what happened. I talked to them myself, and they would not dare lie to me."

My lips trembled, so I pressed them tightly together.

"Posy, I am only a wolf, and a violent one at that. I have no idea how to comfort my upset mate, and Lark will not speak to any of us. Please talk to me."

"She's scared that you all will hate her for defying you and talking back to you," I said at last. "She's also embarrassed she punched that girl."

Quartz chuckled, and my eyes widened.

Quartz chuckled?

Quartz?!

"I was proud of you, Lark," he said before I could get over my shock. "Not only did you stand up for your mate, you showed those girls how strong you are. Reminded your other mates, too. They made the mistake of thinking you are too gentle to defend yourself or protect others."

Thank you, my love, Lark told him. *Will my other wolves—*

"They are also proud of you. Talk to them. They need to hear your voice."

I felt Lark slip away and knew she was following his advice.

Quartz reached up and carefully undid my space buns, then ran his hands over my hair in slow, even strokes. I found myself drifting into a peaceful trance as he did so.

"Shall I tell you about the wolf I met this morning?" he murmured.

"The one who wants to join our pack? Yes, please."

"His name is Luke MacGregor. He was the beta of the Tall Pines Pack, but had an issue with the alpha. The boys are going to have to call the king about it. He has a little sister. Their pack bullied her

73

badly, which was another reason he wanted to leave. Yesterday morning, their alpha, Leo Halder, attacked her."

"Is she okay?" I tensed and sat up.

"She will be."

"You didn't put her in the pack house, did you? That might be too chaotic—"

"Jayden set them up in the small guest house not far from here."

"Good." I relaxed and laid back on his chest. "Will Alpha Halder let them move here without making a fuss?"

"Ha! Let him make a fuss. I would relish that fight. Besides, Jayden already made them part of *our* pack, the Moonset Pack, to cut the connection to Tall Pines. Halder was tormenting them through the link."

"The boys call him Jay, but you call him Jayden. What should I call him?"

"Whatever you want." He kissed my forehead. "He is Jayden, but Jay is faster to say. You can call him anything you like and he will answer."

"Tell me more about Luke's sister," I said after a moment.

"Her name's Lilah. She is nineteen."

"Why did they bully her?"

"Halder wanted her for his chosen mate. She refused because she is waiting for her Goddess-given mate. Her true mate. For spite, Halder used her unique appearance to have the pack humiliate and hurt her."

"What do you mean, unique?" I asked. "Does she have one of those port wine birthmarks on her face or something?"

"I don't know what that is. Wait. Jayden does, and he is showing— No. Not that. She has one blue and one brown eye and many freckles. What? Oh. Jayden says to tell you she has red hair, but I do not understand why that is a bad thing."

"People are cruel over the stupidest things. Can I meet her?"

"Yes. She and her brother are coming to dinner this evening." Quartz stopped petting my hair. "Little mate, Jayden wants control back very badly, and I doubt I will be able to resist much longer."

"All right, Quartz. Thank you for staying with me. For being there for me."

"I will always be there for you." He took a deep breath before continuing. "I have done terrible things, Posy, and someday you may see a side of me that you cannot love. I'll understand that, but never doubt that my heart beats only for you and Lark. The same for Jayden and all our brothers. If we can't have the two of you, we don't want anyone."

My eyes stung, and I sniffed.

"Don't cry anymore, sweetness. It breaks my heart."

Sitting up quickly, I looked into his face and saw Jayden's beautiful dragon eyes.

"You're back." I smiled.

"You know we never really leave you when our wolves are in control." He reached up and tucked a chunk of my hair behind my ear. "But yes, I'm back, precious girl."

"Thank you for letting Quartz be with me for so long."

"Not that I had much choice," he grumped, "but you're welcome. It was good for him. Keeps him calm and forces him to be gentle, which he has little experience with."

"Both of you have warned me that he's violent, but he was so tender and sweet that it's hard for me to believe."

"He's only that way with you, baby." One side of his mouth kicked up. "Trust me."

I looked down at my tangled fingers.

"Jayden, I'm sorry for ruining the shopping trip and making everyone feel bad."

"You did nothing wrong, sweetness, so no more apologies." He sat up beside me. "The others have a surprise for you before dinner. Are you ready to see them?"

I hesitated. I'd made a fool of myself, and after they'd spent so much money on me, too. I was turning out to be a terrible, ungrateful mate.

"They're very sorry, Posy. If it helps, their wolves are punishing them."

"Oh! No, I don't want that." Tears pricked my eyes. No one should be hurt because of me. "Please ask them to stop."

"You're too soft-hearted. Their egos need a little deflating from time to time. Try to remember that," he grumbled. "And you are not a terrible, ungrateful mate, nor were you acting foolish. Stop thinking things like that."

"Lark!" I hissed. "I hardly need the mindlink with her spilling all my secrets!"

He chuckled, then leaned down and kissed my forehead.

"Come on, Posy. You have some mates to make grovel."

12: Apologies

Posy

Jayden led me to a door at the end of the hallway. It was off-white and had small words painted right in the center of it. I moved closer and read, "Posy's Room" in raised, gold letters.

Whirling around, I clasped my hands under my chin and stared up at him.

"This is my room? The one with a window?" I bounced on my toes.

"Oh, it has more than a window." His smile was full of secrets. "Ready?"

"Ready!" I grinned.

He reached around me and opened the door, then waved me inside. I could smell fresh paint and polishing wax and my mates. Giddy with excitement, I walked in - and all the breath left my lungs.

It was beautiful. Off-white walls, mellow hardwood floor, beige Roman shades on the windows, *plural*, and a set of French doors leading out to what looked to be a balcony. There was a nightstand with a lamp and a bed that looked as soft as a cloud. I beamed when I saw Mr. Nibbles sitting on the pillows as if he were waiting for me.

"I know it's plain now," Wyatt said from behind me, "but I want you to decorate it in your style. Anything you want, I'll get for you, okay?"

I swiveled to see him holding a light blue pitcher full of huge pastel peonies. He held it out to me with a nervous smile, and my heart tripped.

"For me?" I whispered.

"Of course." He came closer and handed me the pitcher. "Anything for you, cutie."

Leaning down, I buried my face in the lush blooms and inhaled their sweet fragrance. It was lovely, but nothing compared to Wyatt's warm vanilla scent. I looked up at him through my lashes and smiled.

"Thank you."

"You're welcome." He reached up very slowly, like he was worried he'd scare me, and laid his palm on my cheek. "Posy, I apologize for what happened today. I have no excuse except I was too dumb to know that those girls were flirting. What can I do to earn your forgiveness?"

I went over to the nightstand and moved the lamp a bit to set the bouquet down, then ran back to him and flung my arms around his torso. He froze, and I second-guessed myself.

"Is it okay to hug you?"

"Of course it is. Feel free to throw yourself at me anytime." His husky voice was rich with laughter, which made me smile.

"You don't have to earn anything," I said into his chest. "I'm sorry I spoiled the day for everyone and made your wolf mad and hurt you."

"Oh, my darling girl." He wrapped his arms around my head and shoulders and held me tight against him. "You did none of that. *We* spoiled *your* day. The boys and I came up with a plan, though, so something like that doesn't happen again, okay?"

"Okay."

I felt something soft land on my hair again and again and knew he was kissing my head. I snuggled my face further into his chest and listened to his heartbeat.

After a moment, he loosened his hold, put his hands on my shoulders, and moved me back so he could see my face.

"Would you like to see the rest of your room?"

I grinned up at him and nodded.

He showed me the small closet that he thought I could turn into a storage area or work space for whatever hobbies I had, since I had a giant walk-in closet all to myself in our bedroom. Then he took me over to another door that led into a half bath with an adorable pedestal sink.

"Again, you can decorate it however you want. I'm a little ashamed that everything looks so plain, but this is entirely your space. I can paint the walls and ceiling any color you want. They're still a little damp, by the way, so don't touch them."

I laid my hand on his bicep to stop his anxious rambling.

"Wyatt, I love it. It's perfect. Plain works for me."

"Let's go out on the balcony. Ash and Cole want to show you their surprise."

I followed him to the French doors before I realized something. I grabbed the hem of his t-shirt, and he stopped and looked at me over his shoulder.

"You— *You* set this room up? For *me?*"

"Yeah. I wasn't sure about some things, but I went with what I thought you might like. I'm still on the fence about the hardwood floor, but it's what was here. I polished it, but it seems too dark. I wanted you to feel surrounded by sunlight."

"Wyatt."

My voice wobbled and I blinked to hold the tears back. I'd cried enough today.

"Dang it! I knew I should have gone with that plush eggshell carpeting, but the installers couldn't get here today. I'm handy with a lot of things, but laying carpet ain't one of them."

"I don't want to change the floor," I told him. "I'm happy, not upset. It makes my heart feel so full that you put time and effort into doing this."

"Well, *of course*, Posy. I'm always going to put time and effort into taking care of you."

I tugged on his shoulders.

"Come down here," I whispered when he didn't understand what I wanted.

"Oh."

He brought his face down to my level, and I kissed his cheek. A huge smile broke across his lips.

"I love you," he said and kissed *my* cheek.

My face heated up, and he chuckled softly.

"Come on, baby. My brothers are anxious to see you."

He took my hand in his and led me through the French doors to a garden utopia. On the left side of the balcony was a white chair with lavender cushions, a small table with a pink cloth, hanging wicker baskets, a lilac-colored glass lantern, a wicker plant stand, and a shimmery sheer curtain blocking off one end of the balcony. A large periwinkle basket held a few gardening tools and everywhere there were flowers: petunias, roses, tall grasses, ranunculus, and pansies.

On the right side was a comfy-looking white wicker chair with a floral cushion and a small white bench with a concrete angel sleeping on it. Pots and wicker planters were filled with more flowers, including lavender, thyme, and impatiens. A purple clematis climbed up a white wooden trellis in one corner, and a gorgeous pink rose topiary stood guard in the other corner. There was even a cute metal watering can embossed with a dragonfly and a sweet little basket filled with gardening magazines.

I covered my nose and mouth with my hands and stood there, shocked beyond words. I was barely aware of Ash and Cole joining me.

"I did the left side and Ash did the right." Cole cracked his knuckles one at a time.

"What do you think?" Ash scrubbed his hand through his dark curls. "We can change anything you don't like."

I shook my head, my throat too tight to speak.

"It was Wyatt's idea, but we picked everything out and put it together while he was painting your room," Cole said. "We know you love pansies, and we tried to guess what other flowers you might like."

"The curtain has fairy lights in it, and I strung a bunch from the ceiling, too. They're all on a timer to come on when it gets dark," Ash added.

"Oh, I can't wait to see that tonight!" I squealed, finally lowering my hands.

"So, it's okay, then? You like it?" Cole bit his bottom lip.

"Like it? I *love* it!" I opened my arms, then hesitated. "Is it okay to hug you?"

His fern-green eyes softened and seemed sad, and I worried about what he was thinking.

"Honey, you don't even need to ask. Hug me anytime, anywhere."

I snuggled into him and twined my hands around his back. My head reached slightly above his stomach, reinforcing how small I was compared to these giant mates of mine.

"Why did you look sad when I asked to hug you?" I murmured.

"You shouldn't feel like you need to ask. You're our mate. I hate what your father made you believe."

"Oh."

I didn't know what to say. I hated it, too, but there was nothing anyone could do to change the past.

With a soft sigh, Cole threaded his fingers into my hair as his other hand went around my back to hold my opposite hip. His shoulders curved down so his body enveloped me like a warm blanket.

"I am so sorry about what happened earlier." His warm breath tickled my ear. "I never meant to hurt you or make you feel unwanted. You are the only girl I will *ever* love. Can you forgive me?"

"I already have. I overreacted, too. I need to learn to trust you all more."

"With your past, it's understandable why you don't. Plus, we've only known each other for a few days. And you didn't overreact. Don't you dare feel like you're at fault in any way here. Like Wyatt said, we have a plan to prevent this from happening again. We'll tell you more about it after dinner, okay, honey?"

I nodded and raised my head to give him a happy smile.

"Look at those dimples! You're so cute, cupcake!" Ash hopped up and down next to us, making me giggle and my dimples deepen. "All right, Cole, it's my turn!"

Rolling his eyes, Cole handed me over to Ash, who swung me up in a bear hug and twirled me around.

"Ash!" I squeaked in surprise and clung to his neck. The ground was a *long* way down.

He laughed.

"Hey! What happened to your space buns?" He stopped spinning me, but still held me off the floor.

"Quartz took them down. He wanted to pet me, I think."

"Oh, no! Did he pull any chunks out?" Setting me down, Ash started to look over my head and lift sections of hair. "Did he hurt you?"

"Of course not." I batted his hands away. "He was very careful."

Ash studied my face with a frown, then shrugged.

"Anyway, I have another surprise for you, princess."

He reached over to grab a flat, white box from the little table. When he held it out to me, I shook my head.

"I don't need anything else. This," I whirled in a circle to indicate my balcony garden, "is more than I ever dreamed of having. I can't believe you did this for me."

"Well, *this*," he shook the box, "is to bribe you into forgiving me for being such a neglectful jerk today."

Cole's hand whacked the back of Ash's head.

"Owie!"

"Hurts, doesn't it?" Wyatt taunted.

"Yeah, but I don't deserve it like you do."

"You admitted that you're bribing your mate because you screwed up!" Wyatt squawked. "How is that not worthy of a slap upside the head?"

To prevent one of them from tackling the other, I took the box with both hands, which brought their attention back to me.

"Thank you," I said. "You don't have to keep buying me things. I don't want you to think I'm after your money or anything like that."

They both cracked up at that, and I frowned in confusion.

"We know you're not a golddigger. It was painful to watch you check every price tag and browse the clearance racks this afternoon." Cole ran his hand down my hair. "We want to get you little gifts, honey. We've been dreaming about spoiling our mate for years, so please let us."

"Okay, but don't spoil me too much. I don't want to become conceited or anything."

Cole snorted, and Wyatt laughed harder.

"Oh, baby, you will *never* become conceited," Ash grinned. "Now open your gift. You can think of it as a belated birthday present."

Opening the box, I found the beautiful flower hair barrettes I'd admired at the store. I touched the petals of the pansy lightly, swallowing hard as gratitude and love tightened my chest. When I was sure I could speak without choking, I raised my head and smiled brightly.

"How did you know?"

"Sid told me. Posy, I'm so sorry I ignored you today. I *will* do better in the future. I promise. Will you accept my apology?"

"Of course. And I'll do better at making myself heard and not give up so easily." I frowned when his eyes flickered green for a second. "What?"

"Nothing." He shook his head.

"It was *something* if it made Sid ascend."

"At the store, Lark said we were making do with a pathetic, damaged mate." Ash held my shoulders. "We're not *making do*; we love you, Posy. You may feel damaged, but you are *not* pathetic. Do you remember what I told you this morning?"

I nodded.

"*And?* Why are you strong?"

"Because I got up and kept going."

"Because you *get* up and *keep* going, present tense," Mason interrupted.

I looked over to see him and Jayden standing by the French doors. I hadn't realized they'd followed us out here.

"Your courage is as much a part of you as your lovely brown hair and pretty blue eyes," he continued.

I blushed at his compliments and ducked my head.

"It's true, Posy," Ash agreed, then bent down to whisper in my ear. "He'll never admit it or ask you, but Mase would really love a hug, too. He was furious that we upset you."

I glanced up at Ash, then back to Mason. His face held its usual blank expression, but I was starting to understand that his eyes were what I needed to watch. Like little chinks in his armor, they revealed glimpses of what he was feeling and thinking.

And right now, all I could see in those gray depths was something like longing.

I patted Ash's hands, and he released me with a smirk, which made me roll my eyes. I walked over to Mason.

"May I give you a hug?" I asked.

He shrugged, but I knew what to look for now. That shrug was a shout of "Yes, please!"

With a secret smile, I snuggled up next to him, wrapped my arms around his torso, and squeezed. After a few seconds, his tattoo-covered arms came up and wrapped around my shoulders ever so gently.

"You won't hurt me with a hug," I teased him.

81

"You're too delicate for us. Five rough guys and one sweet, innocent flower. You're going to have to be patient with us because we're going to screw up. We're going to screw up *a lot*." Then he lowered his lips to my ear, and his voice grew so quiet that I wouldn't have heard it without my shifter-enhanced hearing. "Please don't leave us, Posy. Promise you won't, okay? We love you so, so much. If we lost you, we wouldn't want to live anymore."

It was the most he'd ever said to me at once, and I cherished both that fact and his words. Raising my head, I met his eyes and smiled.

"I promise. I only hope—" I sighed and admitted my fear. "I only hope you won't be disappointed with me."

"That is not possible." He touched his forehead to mine. "We will treasure you forever, little flower."

"Mase, don't forget dinner," Wyatt interrupted our moment. "We have a lot of guests coming."

Mason released me with a sigh.

"Who else is coming? Jayden only mentioned Lilah and Luke." I played with my fingers as tension tightened my chest.

"And Peri," Cole said, "so she doesn't have to eat alone. Plus, she's lousy at cooking."

"I thought she lived with your parents?"

"Mom and Dad and Mama and Papa took the heathens to Disney for two weeks," Wyatt explained. "That's the only reason the horde didn't descend at dawn to meet you."

"Heathens? Horde?" I blinked up at him in confusion.

"We have a lot of little brothers between us," Cole said with a smirk. "Poor Peri is the only girl."

"For now at least. I have a feeling Mom and Dad aren't finished having pups yet." Jayden slung an arm around my waist.

"Which one of your parents are you calling Mom and Dad?" I asked.

"We have two sets of parents between us," Mason said. "Mine, whom we call Papa and Mama, and then there's Wyatt's mother, who we call Mom, and Cole's father, who we call Dad."

He didn't mention Jayden's or Ash's parents, and I decided I'd ask someone later, maybe Peri, so that I didn't accidentally say something that would hurt them.

"After my mother and Wyatt's father died in the sickness, Mom and Dad decided to become chosen mates," Cole explained. "They thought it would be the best thing to do for us kids as well as help solidify the new pack."

I couldn't imagine being with someone without the mate bond, but it sounded like they were making it work. Jayden seemed to guess what I was thinking.

"They fell in love with each other and have made two adorable pups together so far. William is five and Winston, or Winnie, is three."

"I don't know if she needs to meet those two. They'll steal her from us!" Ash laughed.

Wyatt pulled out his phone and showed me the boys' photos.

"Oh, they are so cute!" I squealed. "Look at their chubby cheeks! I want to squish and kiss them!"

"See?" Ash laughed again. "I told you."

"They're cute," Cole agreed, "but don't be fooled by their super sweet appearance. Those two are pure mischief."

I giggled.

"Okay, I really do need to get in the kitchen now," Mason said.

"I'll help," I offered.

"No. I don't need your help."

He made a move to leave, and his abruptness caught me off guard for a split second. Why was he suddenly shutting me out? Had I done or said something to upset him?

No, he just being Mason, Lark rolled her eyes. *I tell Garnet— I can handle it myself.*

I cleared my throat, a little nervous, but slowly gaining confidence with these mates of mine.

"I'll help," I repeated.

Confusion flashed in his eyes for a second, then realization. He came back over to me, laid one giant paw against the side of my face, and rubbed his thumb against my cheek.

"I wasn't shutting you out," he murmured. "It's my responsibility to cook today, and I don't want you to work on your first full day at home with us."

"Well, I want to." I made my eyes go big and soft.

"Oh, no," he groaned. "Not puppy dog eyes already!"

The others laughed.

"What are we making, anyway?" I asked as he took my hand in his and tugged me along.

"I have *no* idea."

13: New Life, Rough Start

Lilah MacGregor

Loud, rapid knocking woke me, and I shot up in bed.
My heart pounded as I gasped for breath, confused about where I was for a second. The thick curtains blocked all light from the window, and I couldn't tell what time of day it was.

Someone pounded violently on the front door again.

Something's wrong, I thought and slid out of bed.

I hurried out of my room and down the hall only to freeze when I reached the living room.

The scent on the other side of the front door was one I knew and hated.

Oh no. Not him! Please, not him! Why won't he leave me alone?

But there was no one to answer. Kestrel, my wolf, was in a deep sleep, exhausted from healing me after my latest punishment for daring to believe the Goddess had a mate for me.

"Open this door, Lilah!" roared Alpha Leo Halder.

Like a robot, I went over and flipped the lock, my whole body vibrating with fear. The door flew open and revealed my nightmare.

Alpha Halder's hands slammed into my shoulders, knocking me onto the floor. I screamed in shock and pain and scrambled back on the heels of my hands.

Then he started to kick me, destroying my already broken ribs. Weak as I was, I still fought, slashing at him with my fingernails, but that only made him hurt me more.

Kestrel! I begged with no real hope of her answering.

Unfortunately, without her, I was as feeble as a human. Not that she would have stood a chance against a full-grown, alpha wolf, but any help was better than none.

He dropped down on me and punched me in the face, breaking my nose, and more screams ripped out of me.

"Shut up!" he growled. "You ugly freak! You don't deserve to live a second longer!"

Wrapping his hands around my neck, he squeezed until I couldn't get any air in. Panicked, I thrashed against him.

I'm going to die.

The words ran through my mind over and over as my vision faded into black spots....

And I woke up screaming.

"Lilah. You're safe." Worry filled my brother's deep voice. "He can't get you here. Come on, ladybug. Wake up for me. You're safe now, and I'm going to keep you that way."

With one arm holding me tightly, Luke pressed my head against his chest and rocked us back and forth.

"Luke?"

My throat ached, and I knew I must have been screaming for a while.

"Shh. You're okay now. It was just a dream. Just your mind reliving it. It will never happen again. He'll never touch you again."

"I'm sorry," I gasped. "I'm sorry I disturbed you."

"You have nothing to apologize for." He kissed my forehead. "Everything is going to get better now, I promise."

My lungs and heart slowly calmed down. At last, I put my hand on his chest, a signal for him to stop rocking me like a baby.

"You know what? Rain has a good feeling about this place," he told me. "He says wonderful things are going to happen to us here."

Rain is just a wolf, I wanted to say, but couldn't bring myself to crush his optimism.

"I'd like something wonderful to happen," I said instead.

"And it will, ladybug. I'll make sure of it."

I reached up and scratched the scruff he called a beard. "What would I do without you?"

"Good thing you'll never have to find out," he laughed.

"Oh, someday you'll find your mate."

Then I'll be all alone.

"You'll find your mate too, ladybug. Any wolf would be proud to have you for his own."

Ha! I pity the wolf who gets stuck with me.

I didn't think he existed, but if he did, he was going to be very disappointed when he discovered I was his mate. Not only was I physically unattractive, but all the grit had been beaten out of me. I was a shadow of the girl I used to be, a shell of a person that only knew how to keep her head down and survive.

I didn't say any of that to Luke, though. I didn't want to bring him down with my negative thoughts.

He read my mind, though.

"I'm serious, Lilah. You are a beautiful, amazing girl. Someday, the right man will come along and help you see that. He'll treasure you, too, because, if he doesn't, I'll take care of him."

Luke held up one massive fist, and I smiled, knowing that's what he wanted.

"Now, come on. We need to get freshened up before dinner."

"What do you think his luna will be like?" I fidgeted with my fingers.

"*Their* luna, you mean. There are five alphas of the Five Fangs pack, and they share one mate, who they met only a few days ago."

Five mates!

"I was talking to Crew, Alpha Jayden's beta, when he dropped off the supplies earlier," Luke told me. "Her father abused her terribly. Crew said she's so traumatized that the alphas haven't allowed anyone to meet her yet."

"What— What did he do to her?" I whispered.

"Crew said the alphas are pretty hush-hush about her, but they informed all the betas and gammas that she was beaten regularly and locked in her house for nearly six years. The alphas only told them this so that, in Alpha Cole's words, when they do meet her, no one does anything dumb to upset her, which would get them killed."

Her experience sounded so similar to my own that it made me shudder. I only had to endure Alpha Halder's harassment since last spring; the poor luna had endured it for years.

"How strong she must be," I murmured.

"Just like you, ladybug."

It isn't true, but let him think what he wants.

If I had *any* strength, it came from him, and I both dreaded and anticipated the day he found his mate. Dreaded it because I would lose him, but anticipated it because he so deserved to have someone love and care for him. He was a good man; I hoped the Moon Goddess was kind with her choice for him.

Again Luke seemed to be on my wavelength, because he said, "We'll find our mates soon, ladybug. Rain says he can sense ours, and she's tied to yours. When Kestrel wakes up, I bet she'll agree."

I dropped my eyes, shaking my head in denial.

"Don't give up on yourself, sister," he murmured. "It's not over—"

"—until you're underground," I finished.

It was his favorite saying and life motto. He even had it tattooed inside his left wrist.

With a grin, he rolled off the bed and pulled me up and onto my feet.

"We're leaving in twenty minutes, so get going." He gave me a little push. "Crew brought some bags of clothes, too. I put it all in your closet."

"Did he bring any make-up? At least some concealer?"

"No, but no one will say anything about your bruises," he assured me. "Pick something pretty to wear."

I nodded, but my stomach twisted.

86

You can coat pot metal in gold, but it's still garbage underneath.

Then I chided myself, ashamed of my despondency. Luke had sacrificed so much to get us this far. I owed it to him to try harder, to take this chance to start over. I'd be foolish not to.

#

Posy

"Do you like to grill?" I asked Mason.

"Yep."

I had my head in the fridge, assessing what we had to work with. There was a ton of beef, a standard in most wolves' diet, but I also spotted some lovely red and yellow peppers in the produce drawer.

"Do you have any red onions and cherry tomatoes?"

"Yep."

"What about marinades?"

"Ah, that's probably going to be a no, but let me look."

I grabbed two packs of stew beef and put it on the counter, then went back for the peppers. Bending over, I scooped up several of each color, straightened up, and turned around only to see Mason's eyes flick up from where my bum had been a moment ago.

"Were you looking at my bum?"

"Am I in trouble if I say yes?"

I blushed and spun away, laying the peppers next to the beef.

Next thing I knew, a hand gripped the counter on either side of me and a hard body crowded against my shoulders. Warm breath tickled my skin as Mason brushed my neck with his nose, and I shivered.

"Am I, little flower?" he murmured.

Shyly, I shook my head. From the corner of my eye, I saw his ear was level with my mouth and a little imp of mischief stirred inside me.

Oh, please, Posy, Lark begged. *Please do it!*

He won't like it.

Yes, he will. Trust me, she argued. *Garnet say so, too.*

Praying I didn't get punished for it, I angled my face and blew gently in his ear.

I did not expect the rumbly noise that vibrated out of his chest or the kiss he left on my throat that sent sparks shivering all through me.

"Um, we should—" I squeaked, stopped, swallowed, and tried again. "We should get to work."

"Mmm. In a second, baby."

His lips brushed against my skin with every word, stirring up more sparks, and a soft sound escaped me. He settled his hands on my waist and gave me kisses from my throat down to my collar bone.

I felt a tingle between my legs and something twisted in my belly.

"Mason?" Confusion and a little fear tinted my voice. "What's happening to me?"

"It's okay, Posy. Your body is reacting to mine. It's the same for me. It's natural and normal for mates. You've never felt anything like this before?"

I shook my head.

"Are you scared?"

"A little," I shrugged, "because it's different and I don't understand it."

"But not scared of *me*, right?"

"No, not scared of you."

"Good. That's good, baby."

"Are you scared of *me*?" I whispered.

A husky laugh sent a gust of warm air across my throat.

"Terrified," he murmured.

"Hey!" Wyatt shouted, making me jump a mile. "You're supposed to be making food, not love!"

Mason let out a deep, heavy sigh and released me, then stepped back.

"You are a pain in the butt, Wyatt," he growled, "and you startled our girl with your yelling."

"Oh. Sorry, cutie. Anyway, Cole's leaving to get Peri and Jay's linking the MacGregors with directions. Ash is setting the table, so I guess I can help you."

"No, thanks." Mason's voice was very final.

As they bickered about Wyatt's cooking ability, or lack of it, I gathered up what I needed for a quick marinade, mixed it up, and got the beef chunks soaking in it. I was searching for a knife and cutting board when Mason interrupted me.

"What do you want us to do, Posy? Dice up the peppers?"

"Well, someone can get the grill going," I suggested, "and I need the onions and tomatoes. Do you have kabob sticks or grill baskets?"

Mason told Wyatt to handle the grill, saying it was the only thing he trusted him to do, then got out a knife and cutting board and cut up the peppers and onions.

It was interesting to watch him. He took his time and was precise in how he cut it. Everything ended up in perfect squares. By the time he was done, Wyatt was back and kindly got the kabob sticks down from the top shelf for me. He and I began to assemble the kabobs while Mason cleaned up.

"Um, Wyatt, you're supposed to alternate peppers, onions, and tomatoes with the meat." I bit my lip, not sure how he'd take criticism.

"But I only want meat on mine."

"You will eat whatever Posy prepares." Mason came over to see our progress. "For the love of the moon, Wyatt, just go back to the grill. We'll do it and bring them out to you."

"Fine!" He stalked away and slammed the kitchen door.

I flinched and curved my shoulders in. I tried to put together another kabob, but my hands shook too hard now.

I made him mad! Oh, no! I made him mad!

I couldn't breathe, and my heart sped up.

"Posy, calm down. He gets mad at me all the time," Mason said.

I shook my head and left him to finish the kabobs so he wouldn't see how I was quaking like a coward. I washed and dried my hands, intent on escaping the kitchen in case Wyatt came back. I wasn't fast enough, though.

The kitchen door banged open, and he stormed in.

"Posy?"

Fear paralyzed me and bile flooded my mouth.

When I didn't answer, he came toward me with his hands raised, and I panicked. Whimpering, I hunched down and threw my arms up to protect my head.

"Please, alpha! I'm sorry! I'll be quiet, I promise. I won't say anything again. I swear I won't!"

Alphas did not like to be told what to do and certainly not by a runt, a worthless girl who should only be seen and not heard. How many times had my father beaten that lesson into me?

And now one of my mates was going to.

Why do I always have to ruin things?

"Posy. Look at me."

I shook my head as fat tears rolled down my cheeks. I didn't want to see the hate in his eyes. That would hurt worse than any beating.

But now I was really going to get it. I'd disobeyed him, and alphas did not tolerate that, either. I'd be lucky to survive this.

I'm so sorry, Lark. I think I just got us killed.

Posy, he no hurt you. For one, Mason here and, two, Granite say—

I didn't hear what Granite said because Wyatt scooped me up in his arms and all my focus shifted to surviving. I closed my eyes tight

89

and waited for the pain to start. Was he going to throw me into the wall? Father had done that a few times...

I could hear a voice crooning to me, but it took several minutes before I could understand the words.

"Please, Posy. You need to breathe. You're safe. Baby, breathe. Can you do that? Can you breathe for me? Here. Feel me breathing. Can you copy that?"

A large hand took mine and held it against a hard chest that went up and down in a steady, slow rhythm. I did what the voice said and copied it until I came back to my senses.

Blinking, I found myself sitting in Wyatt's lap on the kitchen floor.

"Wyatt?" I whispered.

"I'm sorry. I'm so sorry for scaring you," he whispered in my ear. "I was going to hug you, not hit you. I would never hit you. Never, ever."

"But you were mad at me."

"No, no. I wasn't mad at you, sweetheart. I don't think I *can* be mad at you. Mase ticked me off, that's all."

I looked around the room, but we were alone.

"He took the kabobs to grill." Wyatt framed my face with his palms. "Can I carry you to the bathroom so I can wash your face?"

I nodded as shame washed over me. I'd made a fool out of myself by having a panic attack over nothing.

Wyatt stood and cradled me in his arms, and I tucked my face in his throat.

"Cole pokes at me all the time, and Ash and Jay tease, but Mase knows exactly what to say and do to make me lose my temper," he said as he walked. "I don't think he means to do it, but he does it very well."

"Why do you think that is?"

I didn't know if he was talking like this to distract me or because he needed someone to vent to, but I was happy with either reason.

"He thinks I'm just a kid, but I'm 18 now. I've graduated school and I'm an alpha not just of Five Fangs, but also River Rapids, my dad's pack. I do my share and volunteer for more because I know I'm the youngest and had more time than the others to goof off before assuming the alphaship."

We reached our bedroom and he carried me into my bathroom. Sitting me on the counter, he went to the closet and found a washcloth. As he turned on the hot water, he continued to talk.

90

"I want him to acknowledge that I have good qualities, but he only sees everything I do wrong. I don't remember my own dad being as hard on me as Mase is. He's harder on me than his dad is with him!"

"Mason's dad is hard on him?"

"Yeah. Dad, Mom, and Mama have all warned Papa to lighten up, but he doesn't listen. I don't get why he treats Mase that way, either. The dude never lose his temper, and I can count on one hand the number of times I've heard him raise his voice in anger since he became an alpha."

He paused to put the washcloth under the steaming water, then very gently began to wipe my face with it.

"I mean, I'll be the first to admit that I screw up and get off course sometimes and, yeah, my dad and, later, Cole's dad probably should have been harder on me, but Mase doesn't need someone standing on him all the time. He does that too much to himself. Sometimes, I think he feels he can't even breathe too deeply for fear his father will tell him he's doing it wrong."

Oh, my poor mate.

"Still," I said, "he shouldn't treat you like that. He wants the best for you, I'm sure, but that doesn't make it okay to constantly criticize you."

"I know I egg him on sometimes." He lowered the washcloth and turned the cold water on. "I can't help myself. It's like there's a devil inside me telling me to live down to his expectations."

"Well, that's not okay, either," I told him, "but at least you're able to see what you're doing to sabotage yourself. A lot of people can't do that."

He soaked the washcloth with cold water and wrung it out.

"Tilt your head back, cutie."

I did, and he laid it across my eyes. I sighed at the blissful sensation. Hopefully, that would help the redness go away before dinner. No one else needed to know about my little breakdown.

"Anyway, this isn't your problem, Posy. I'm sorry you got caught up in it."

"It *is* my problem," I argued. "I want my mates to be happy with each other, too, and I'm going to make that happen. You just watch and see, Wyatt Black."

"Okay, little bossy pants." He took off the washcloth and picked up one of my hands. "I believe you."

"Am I being bossy?" Worried I'd stepped too far, I fidgeted with his rings.

"Of course, you are, baby. That's what a luna does. She holds the alpha together so he can hold the pack together." With a chuckle, he

91

raised our joined hands to his lips and kissed my knuckles. "Sucks to have five of us, but I know you're going to excel at it, cutie."

I stared into his silvery blue eyes and saw he meant everything he said. A small smile curled my lips, and I decided to do one brave thing.

"I love you, Wyatt."

It was the first time I'd said it out loud to any of my mates. Seeing his shell-shocked expression, I knew I'd chosen the right one to start with.

"Posy," he breathed, "I love you, too."

Then the doorbell sounded, announcing that the guests had arrived.

"Oh, my gosh, I need to comb my hair and get dressed!" I fussed.

Pushing on his back with both hands, I tried to hurry him out of the room. It was like trying to move a mountain.

"All right, all right, I'm going," he laughed. "Put on something pretty and wear one of your new hair flower things."

"Now who's being a bossy pants?" I mumbled.

He laughed again, but left the room, and I reached for the brush to do something with my hair.

14: Dinner with Friends

Posy

Thanks to my conversation with Quartz, I was better prepared than the others for Lilah MacGregor's 'unique' appearance. What none of us was prepared for, however, were the dark bruises ringing her neck and dotting her arms and legs.

Her wolf must be too exhausted or injured to heal her.

I decided I'd get her alone later and ask if she needed anything. In the meantime, I slipped past my gawking mates to welcome her and her brother.

"Hello." I smiled and held out my hand. "I'm Posy Briggs."

Lilah shook my hand, and I felt the fine tremors racing through her. The poor thing was terrified, probably because of the five giants looming behind me.

"I'm Luke MacGregor," said the giant looming behind *her.* "It's nice to meet you, luna. This is my sister, Lilah."

He nodded, but didn't hold out his hand, for which I was grateful. I was wary of touching any male other than my mates, but I didn't want to appear rude, either.

I turned to the boys. Mason's expression gave nothing away, as usual, and Jayden had already seen Lilah's condition. The others' faces, however, were twisted with anger and their wolves flickered in their eyes.

Calm them down, Lark advised.

"Guys, would you please take Luke into the living room and introduce yourselves?" I asked. "Lilah and I are going to finish up with Peri in the kitchen."

"Oh, please get Peri out of the kitchen!" Jayden pretended to beg. "We want dinner to be edible."

And the simple comment broke the tension, allowing my mates to compose themselves.

"Mason, Wyatt and I made it, so it will be," I assured him. "We're just setting up drinks and stuff. We'll call you when it's ready."

As the guys shuffled off, I blew out a breath.

"Whew! It's overpowering with all of them, isn't it?" I smiled up at Lilah. She was a tall girl, almost as tall as Wyatt. "I'll introduce you to them one by one over dinner."

"Thank you." She nodded her head a little awkwardly.

"Come on. You can meet my new sister-in-law."

As she walked beside me, I watched her out of the corner of my eye. I recognized that gait. I'd moved that way myself quite a few times in the past. It was how you walked when every fiber of your being hurt, but you were trying not to show it.

"Lilah, I don't know what you may have heard about me," I said in a soft voice, "but my life wasn't so great before I came to live here. My father kept me a prisoner in our house for six years. He also routinely knocked my wolf out with wolfsbane so she couldn't help me while he beat me. Is that what's wrong with your wolf? If so, I'm sure we can get you some nightshade or foxglove."

She shook her head.

"Kestrel is exhausted. I've had a lot of beatings lately, and she was just barely keeping me going. When Alpha Halder attacked me two days ago, she couldn't even wake up enough to know what was going on."

"I've been in the same situation." I nodded. "Only rest helps. If you need anything, though, tell us and we'll get it for you. I mean it. *Anything.*"

"Thank you, luna."

"No, no. Call me Posy. Please."

By then we were in the kitchen and found Peri's bum sticking out of the fridge. Lilah and I traded grins and I giggled. Peri shot up and whirled around with wide eyes.

"Oh, it's just you." She pressed a hand over her heart. "I should have known. If it was one of my brothers, they would have smacked my butt or tried to close my head in the fridge. Stupid boys."

"Peri, this is Lilah MacGregor. Lilah, this is Peri Barlow."

"It's nice to meet you!" Peri came over and shook hands with her.

She didn't seem fazed by Lilah's appearance, and I was dead certain Cole had linked her about it.

I can't wait to get the mindlink with my mates! It'll make communication so much easier.

We organized the drinks fairly quickly and carried them into the dining room, then called the guys. I made sure to sit Lilah between Peri and me with her brother across from her. It was as comfortable as I could make her. There was a brief flurry of movement to see who would get the seat next to me, and Ash hooted in victory when he got there first. The rest of my disgruntled mates arranged themselves around the table, and I introduced them to Lilah one at a time. Then everyone dug into the kabobs.

"Posy, I *knew* that dress would look so cute on you!" Peri leaned around Lilah to tell me. "Aren't you glad you got it?"

"Yes. It's comfortable and lightweight for summer. Your dress is very pretty, too."

"Thank you! I just finished it yesterday."

"You *made* it?"

"I make a lot of my own clothes."

She shrugged as if it wasn't a big deal, while I was still picking my jaw up off the floor.

"I'm sorry I didn't dress up more," Lilah murmured. "We didn't have time to pack any of our things. In fact, if it weren't for Alpha Jayden's generosity, I'd still be wearing my brother's t-shirt with my pajama shorts."

"Well, we'll fix that!" Peri smiled brightly. "Your outfit is very cute, though."

"I just realized I forgot to have Crew pick up shoes for you," Jayden said, "and the clothes most likely came from his mom."

"You can raid my closet later," I offered. "My mates bought me a ton of stuff today. You can pick out enough to last you until you can go shopping."

"We'll go tomorrow!" Peri crowed, then looked at me. "Posy, Callie and Keeley Breckenridge are friends of mine. They'd like to meet you in better circumstances than what happened today. If you like them, maybe they can come with us. They have an awesome sense of fashion."

"Sure." I smiled at her.

"Um, hold up on those plans." Ash held up his index finger. "The king's coming tomorrow."

"*The king?*" Lilah and I gasped in unison.

"*Tomorrow?*" Peri frowned. "I thought he wasn't due until next week after the parents got back with the horde. He's getting in the way of our shopping trip!"

"You go ahead and tell King Julian that." Cole smirked at her. "I'm sure he'll change his plans."

"It's because of me, isn't it?" Lilah whispered.

I reached over and picked up one of her hands and squeezed it.

"If Alpha Halder is planning an insurrection, the king needs to investigate as soon as possible," Jayden explained with a glance at Luke.

"*And* I told him about you, too, Lilah," Ash admitted. "This is the second time in less than a week that we've had to inform him about an alpha abusing pack members. To say he's furious is understating it."

"What time is he getting here?" Peri's eyes flashed with determination.

"He's the freaking werewolf king, Periwinkle." Wyatt rolled his eyes. "He'll get here when he gets here."

"We can still go shopping. We'll leave first thing in the morning." She looked over at us. "Do either of you drive? I can't."

95

"Yeah, note she said she *can't*." Cole grinned. "Not won't, not doesn't. *Can't*. She is not capable of operating a vehicle. Well, at least not if you want said vehicle to arrive home in one piece with all of its occupants uninjured."

"Ha ha ha, brother," she sneered back.

"I have no idea how to drive," I interrupted before they got into a spat.

"I'll teach you!" Wyatt volunteered.

"Aw. I was going to say that," Ash pouted.

I wasn't really that interested in learning to drive, but, if it made them happy, I could suffer through it.

"You can take turns," I offered with a soft smile. "I'm sure I'll need lots and lots of practice and instructions."

"If nothing else, we can have the twins pick us up in Gretchen," Peri's face screwed up as she thought, "but it would be a little crowded."

"Who's Gretchen?" Lilah leaned over to whisper in my ear. I shrugged.

"Lilah knows how to drive." Luke smiled at his sister. "She's very good, too."

When everyone looked at her, her cheeks turned red.

"You can take my SUV," Cole offered. "You'll have plenty of room for everyone and whatever you buy."

"Thank you, Cole." I smiled at him, flashing my dimples.

"Of course, honey," he smiled back.

"That's settled then." Peri's eyes sparkled. "Right after breakfast, we'll take off!"

"You're not going alone."

We swiveled our heads to stare at Mason. It was the first he'd spoken since we sat down at the table.

"Why not?" Peri challenged.

He didn't reply, but his body went completely still and his gray eyes stared at her without blinking.

My shoulders came up and I nodded rapidly, more than willing to agree when he looked like *that*, but Peri wasn't so compliant.

"Oh, come on, Mase! What could possibly happen?"

"You're not going alone. End of."

"Hey, I know! Why doesn't Posy take the betas?" Wyatt asked. "They're her guard, after all, and she should get to know them."

"It *would* give my new beta a chance to interact with the others in a low-threat situation." Ash tapped his chin with his index finger.

"You have a new beta?" Luke sounded disappointed.

"Yeah. Eighteen next month and very green," Cole said, "but he was the only one in the pack with beta blood who was old enough to step up."

"He's going to be fine," Jayden said. "Just needs some seasoning, but he has all the instincts and the drive."

"Too bad you didn't get here a few weeks ago, Luke." Ash gave him a sympathetic pat on the shoulder.

"What happened to your old beta?" I asked at the same time as Luke said, "I heard the king has a new one, too."

"Everett Breckenridge was killed a couple of months ago," Ash answered me first.

Jayden's eyes suddenly burned gold and didn't subside, and all my boys grew more and more tense the longer Quartz fought to ascend. Then Jayden began to tremble.

"Jay? Not here, man. Not now," Cole said in a firm, quiet voice.

Jayden's knuckles turned white as he gripped the edge of the table, and he shook harder.

Luke half-rose from his seat, inching toward Lilah, and Wyatt held up one hand to stop him.

"Very slowly now, sit back down," he murmured. "We don't want Quartz to see you as a challenge or threat."

"That's right," Ash also spoke softly. "Everyone, sit still and quiet until Jay gets his wolf under control."

We all sat in frozen silence for several long moments, then a low rumble shook the floor under our feet and made the dishes on the table jump with a clatter. I put my hands over my nose and mouth, worried for my mate.

Jayden not going to win this one, Lark fretted.

Standing up, Mason pushed out a wave of alpha power so strong that we all bared our throats.

"Quartz. Down. *NOW!*"

I trembled under the weight of his power-filled tone and absolute authority, and it wasn't even directed at me. Watching Jayden, I breathed a sigh of relief when his eyes lost the wolf glow and returned to their normal beauty. He slumped forward with a heavy sigh.

"I'm so sorry," I whispered. "I shouldn't have asked—"

"Hush, sweetness." Jayden smiled gently. "Was my fault. Caught me off guard. Didn't realize he was still holding on to that."

I pressed my trembling lips together, wanting so badly to go over and hug him.

Do it, Lark said.

Is Quartz talking to you? I asked her in surprise.

97

Not talking, no. Grieving. He grieving, Posy. Whatever happened was bad. Real bad.

I jumped up and raced around the table. Wrapping my arms around Jayden's head, I drew his face into my neck and clutched his tense body to me. His breath brushed my skin, sending both sparks and goosebumps through me, and his arms went around my waist. He took a deep inhale of my scent, and I dropped kisses into his soft hair. When his body finally relaxed, I tuned back in to the others' soft talking.

"We may need to do some reshuffling with the guest houses," Ash was saying. "Usually, his beta stays with him, but since this one is a female, the king might not be comfortable with that arrangement."

"Then we'll move out and she can use the guest house we're in," Luke offered.

"Let's wait and see, but thank you." Cole looked over at Peri. "You know Lilah could stay with you and Luke could bunk in the pack house or with Tristan."

"He's another one of our unmated betas," Ash explained.

I was scrubbing my fingers through Jayden's hair in a gentle massage when I had a brainstorm.

"Peri, Lilah, why don't you just stay here tonight?" I asked. "That way we don't have to worry about coordinating things in the morning. Luke, I don't know if we have enough guest rooms, but you're welcome to stay, too."

"Sleep over!" Peri danced in her seat. "Yay! Which bedroom are we using? Or we could make a pillow fort in the living room."

"That reminds me!" I was excited now, too. "Lilah, Peri, you have to see the special room that my mates made for me and my balcony garden! Tonight, I'm going to see it with lights for the first time. I'm so excited!"

"Yeah, and they'll be coming on soon," Wyatt pointed out. "Before they do, how about we guys clean up while you girls check out Posy's closet for some clothes for Lilah?"

"Sure. Let's go!" Peri popped out of her seat and Lilah followed her lead.

Dropping a kiss on Jayden's forehead, I took a step back and studied his face. His hands settled on my hips and his eyes held an emotion I couldn't name.

"Thank you, sweetness," he murmured. "I love you."

Smiling widely, I dropped my forehead against his.

"I love you, too, Jayden."

15: Sleepover

Posy

"Oh, my Goddess. That is the biggest bed I've ever seen in my life."

Peri stopped dead inside our bedroom doorway.

"I know," I mumbled, my face burning. "I'm intimidated just to be in the same room with it, and that's when my mates aren't even here."

"So, Posy," she slunk up next to me, "I see they haven't marked you yet. Does that mean you haven't mated yet, either?"

"No. I just got here last night and was exhausted." I twiddled my fingers nervously. "They haven't pushed me into anything and I hope they don't, either. I don't think I am ready for that."

"They won't push you into anything," she guaranteed. "They will wait a lifetime for you if they have to. I know my brothers."

"So they *are* all brothers?" Lilah's eyes were wide.

"Not by blood. None of them are related except for Ash and Jay, who are cousins," Peri said, then went on to explain their blended family. "Ash's parents were killed, so Jay's parents adopted him. Then, after Jay's parents died in the sickness, Mase's parents took both boys in. When my mom and Wyatt's dad passed, my dad and Wyatt's mom became chosen mates to hold the families and packs together."

"And they fell in love and have two pups together so far," I added, happy that I could contribute *some* information about my mates.

"That's right," Peri confirmed with a smile. "So now I have Cole and Archer, who are my blood brothers, and Wyatt, Wayne, Wade, and Wesley, who are my step-brothers, and William and Winnie, who are my half-brothers."

"That's a lot of brothers!" Lilah grinned. "I've only ever had Luke."

"Sometimes I wish I only ever had Cole," Peri grumbled, but we could both see the teasing light in her eyes. "Anyway, Posy, once you do finally mark and mate with them, you're going to have to give Lilah and me the details. When we find our mates, we don't want to be in the dark about the whole process."

I groaned and hid my red face behind my hands.

"I'm not sure I'll find a mate." Lilah's voice trembled and she sniffed. "Even if I do, he— He won't want me."

"Don't say that!" I hurried over and hugged her. "I thought the same thing. I was convinced they would take one look at me and reject me, yet they didn't. They walked in on my father beating me, helped clean my wounds, and witnessed me having a panic attack, and they

99

still want me. If that can happen for me, it can happen for you, and I know it will."

"Even if he could look beyond my past, I'm not pretty like you two." She dropped her head and tangled her fingers together. "I'm a freak. I mean, look at my eyes and all these freckles and this carrot hair. What man would be attracted to *that*?"

"You're not a freak!" Peri joined our little hug fest. "You're beautiful! Your eyes are fascinating, your hair is so healthy and straight, and I like your freckles. It looks like fairies sprinkled you with fire."

"I like your hair color," I added. "It's so warm and pretty."

Lilah's pale skin reddened as she looked at us, and I saw hope at war with pessimism in her eyes. I sighed. I understood better than anyone how hard it is to believe in yourself.

"The Moon Goddess has someone extra special for you. Just wait and see," I told her. "And, Peri, after your birthday next week, you'll find your mate, and he'll be amazing, too."

"Oh, my," Lilah said with a sweet smile. "Wouldn't it be odd if Luke ended up being your mate?"

"I'm fine with that!" Peri wiggled her eyebrows. "He's super hot!"

"Ew! Not what I want to hear about my big brother!"

Lilah made a face, and we all broke out in giggles.

#

After Lilah picked out an outfit and shoes for tomorrow, I gave her a new bra and an unopened pack of panties. Then we joined the guys in the living room.

They were sprawled all over the armchairs and couches, and we three girls budged up together on the remaining love seat with Peri in the middle.

"So, Posy, we wanted to talk to you about our plan to prevent any more misunderstandings like what happened today at the store."

Cole leaned back in his chair and steepled his fingers together in front of his chest.

"Should we leave, alpha?" Luke raised an eyebrow.

"No, it would be good to hear other opinions."

After Ash gave him and Lilah a short summary of our shopping trip, I asked my mates to tell me the plan.

"Well," Wyatt said with excitement in his eyes, "we are thinking of rings like humans do for weddings. We'd get one for you too. We want you to design a band for each of us."

"Oh, I like that!" Peri clapped her hands.

"I think that's a great idea," Luke spoke up, and Lilah nodded.

"Another part of the plan is more serious." Mason crossed his ink-covered arms over his chest. "We want you to mark us."

100

I blinked in surprise.

"Mark you?" I wanted to be sure I'd heard right. "You want *me* to mark *you*?"

"Yep!" Ash jogged his leg up and down. "We all do, princess. We want to wear your mark so everyone knows who we belong to."

I bit my lip and looked first at Peri, then Lilah. I'd never heard of a female marking her mate, and to judge by their wide eyes, they hadn't either.

"Does it strengthen the mate bond or something?" Lilah turned to her brother.

"No, but it *is* a very special gift." Luke's face showed something that looked like envy.

"What? Why?" Peri also looked at Luke.

"When a male marks his mate, she is linked to him for life. It works the same way in reverse," he explained. "Once Posy marks her mates, they are hers forever. Even if she decides not to be theirs, they would still be linked to her and only her until her last breath."

"Aw! That's so sweet!" Peri squealed.

"And how do other males feel about this?" Lilah asked her brother.

"I only know how *I* feel," he shrugged, "and I would be honored if my future mate marked me."

They proving their loyalty, Lark said. *You mark mates, you has all power over them and they has none over you. My respect for mates growing and growing.*

Oh, my heart. If that was true, then *they* were the ones giving *me* a special gift.

"If this is what you want, I'll do it," I said quietly.

"No, Posy." Jayden shook his head. "Remember what we talked about? No more doing things that you don't want to do just to please or placate us or out of fear of a punishment."

"And you don't have to answer right away," Cole said. "You can take time and think about it. We're not pressuring you to do or not do anything."

After agreeing that I would think it over, we left the conversation there and went back to talking about ring designs. Wyatt was determined to get me a huge diamond set in platinum, but I flat-out refused.

"Something simple," I begged him. "Something small."

"I want you to have something elegant," he insisted.

"Simple can be elegant," Peri told him, "and a big, gaudy ring doesn't suit Posy anyway."

"You know, I have an idea for your mates' rings." Lilah tilted her head to the side and her eyes were far away and thoughtful.

101

"Shh! Don't tell the guys!" Peri hissed. "It should be a surprise!"

"But they should have a say in what I—"

"No, little flower," Mason interrupted me. "Whatever you create, we will wear with pride."

"Even if it is awful," Wyatt added with a straight face.

Cole chucked a throw pillow at him. He caught it and winged it right back.

"Posy, it's time for the lights to come on!" Ash shouted and jumped to his feet.

Lilah and I both flinched hard. Each of us instinctively grabbed one of Peri's arms, and the excitement in his eyes faded a bit.

"Sorry," he muttered and rubbed the back of his neck.

"It's—" I took a shaky breath. "It's okay. I've been looking forward to this so much!"

He came closer and held out his hands. He waited patiently until my panic subsided and I was able to let him pull me to my feet. He hung on to one of my hands as he led us all to my room.

"It's very plain right now," Wyatt told Peri, Lilah and Luke. "Just the basics until Posy decides how she wants to decorate it. The balcony garden is the showpiece currently."

I didn't understand why he saw the simplicity of the room as a negative.

He want to shower you with everything you miss out on last few years, Lark whispered. *He want to spoil you rotten.*

I dropped Ash's hand and went to Wyatt. Wrapping my arms around his waist, I snuggled my face into his chest. His hands linked behind my back and he smiled, which made me smile.

"Wyatt, I love my room. Thank you so much for my own special space."

"Anything for you, Posy," he murmured into my hair.

"Okay, okay, you can cuddle each other later."

Peri tugged on my sleeve, and I giggled.

"Get lost, Periwinkle," Wyatt growled.

"It's only fair, Wyatt," Ash told him. "You interrupted me hugging Posy once and Mase twice today. So suck it up, buttercup, and come on!"

Ash threw open the bedroom door, then trotted over to the French doors.

"Oh, this is the perfect set up for shabby chic or cottage style!" Peri bounced on her toes as she looked around.

"You could also do a beach theme." Lilah eyed the room with interest.

"That's true!"

As my two new friends debated the pros and cons of different decors, the guys herded us out onto the balcony, which was still dark.

"Oh!" My bottom lip pooched out. "Are the lights not working?"

Cole came up behind me and looped his arms around my waist.

"They'll come on in a second, honey," he murmured.

I shivered to feel his warm breath in my ear.

"Are you cold?"

I shivered again, and shook my head fiercely. He chuckled a little.

"Maybe you're shivering for a different reason?"

Turning my head, I caught the little smirk on his lips and a glint in his fern-green eyes.

He's teasing me!

Before I thought about it too much, I stretched up and kissed his chin. It was as high as I could reach even on my tiptoes.

His body stiffened against mine for a second, then a broad grin spread across his face and his arms tightened around me. Bending down, he pressed his lips to my cheek.

"Your skin is so soft," he whispered and brushed his nose along my jawline.

"Your beard is so prickly." Giggling, I scratched his light scruff.

"Is it okay to hold you closer?" he asked.

When I nodded, he drew my back tight against him, and I rested my head on his chest and closed my eyes. His size, which I had feared when I first met him, seemed comforting now as his bearish body engulfed me.

"Look, baby," he whispered after a moment.

My eyes popped open to see white lights twinkling everywhere.

"Oh!" I breathed, tears stinging my eyes.

I stepped away from Cole and spun in a slow circle to take it all in.

"Look at all these pretty flowers!" Peri clasped her hands in front of her chest. "And my brothers did this? Well, I'm impressed. Good job, guys!"

Giving each of my mates a hug, I thanked them with tears streaming down my cheeks. I ended up in Jayden's arms, and a wave of fatigue swept over me. I burrowed my face into his chest with a yawn and squeezed him tightly around his waist.

"Tired, sweetness?"

I nodded.

"You've had a long day. Why don't you get ready for your sleepover?"

I tugged on his shoulders, and he knew right away what I wanted. Bending down, he lowered his ear to my lips.

"I'm a little worried," I whispered. "I don't know what happens at a sleepover."

"I don't, either," he whispered back. "At least, not for girls. When we were younger, my brothers and I used to take over the living room, eat snacks, and watch TV or movies until we passed out."

"Okay, I can do that! It sounds fun, but I haven't watched a movie in years. I wouldn't know what to pick."

"We can give you some suggestions."

"Come on, Posy, Lilah!" Peri called. "We need to make a pillow nest in the living room!"

It didn't take long to set up, and everyone joined us, even Luke. That surprised me. Since he was the oldest of us at twenty-four, I didn't think he'd be interested in something like a sleepover, but he borrowed a pair of joggers from Cole and bunked on one of the couches like the rest of the guys.

Lilah looked as nervous as I felt. What if I had a nightmare in front of everyone?

"What movie do you want, princess?" Ash distracted me as he turned on the enormous TV.

"I'm open to suggestions." I thought that was better than saying I had no idea.

He and Peri wanted to watch a comedy, Jayden recommended an adventure, and Cole argued for a recently released superhero movie. Wyatt said he didn't care, and Mason, of course, remained silent.

"What about you, Lilah? Any favorites?" Peri asked as we three girls piled up on the pillows and blankets on the floor.

She shook her head, and I figured she was in the same boat I was with not knowing anything current.

"*A Bug's Life*," Luke called out, "or *Finding Nemo*."

"Those are kids' movies," Wyatt complained.

"Perfect for you, then, pup," Cole teased him.

I traded a look with the girls and we giggled.

"I'm not the pup here. Peri's the youngest," Wyatt sneered back.

"Well, as the resident pup, I like both of them, so either is fine with me!" Peri rolled herself up like a burrito in a fuzzy blanket.

"Have you watched either of those, Posy?" Ash asked, and I shook my head. "How about *A Bug's Life* first, then *Finding Nemo* if we want a second one?"

I smiled up at him, and he took that as his cue to find and start the movie.

The story was colorful and interesting, and I really enjoyed it until close to the ending when the big grasshopper picked up the littlest ant by her head. My heart started to race and my breathing became shallow.

"Posy?" came a familiar voice, but I couldn't respond.

When the main character ant confronted the grasshopper, a high-pitched buzz filled my ears and drowned out everything else. The crazy grasshopper started to beat up the ant, kicking him and tossing his body around, and I had to press my shaking hands against my mouth to muffle my whimpers.

"Posy, look at me."

Then the big grasshopper knocked the ant over and went to stomp on his head - and I was back in my father's house.

•

16: Waking Nightmare

Posy

I woke up on my eighteenth birthday with my father standing over me. Backlit by the open door, he seemed even larger and more menacing than ever. Seeing him, I woke up quickly and wondered why I was going to be punished so early in the day.

"Since you are now eighteen and haven't found your mate," he said as I scrambled to my feet, "I will make you my chosen mate. No wolf will ever want you, anyway. Your mate would reject you in a second. I might as well get some use out of your disgusting body."

My sleepy brain scrambled to understand, and when it did, panic and horror made me lose my temper for the first time ever.

"You're my *father*!" I screamed. "Fathers don't mate their daughters! And how could I even *find* a mate when you keep me imprisoned here?"

"You pathetic runt! How dare you raise your voice to me!" he roared.

He backhanded me, and I fell to the floor.

"How many times do I have to tell you? Never call me Father!"

Digging his fingers into my arms, he dragged me up and flung me into the wall so hard, my teeth rattled. Gasping, I slid to the floor in a boneless sprawl, too weak to even curl up to protect myself. He reached down, grabbed a hunk of my hair, and wrapped it around his fist twice. Tears of pain sprang to my eyes. He knew my scalp was sensitive and always took full advantage of that to control me.

Yanking my head back, he glared at me with rage-filled eyes, spit flying from his mouth and hitting my cheek. My lip curled up in disgust.

"You *will* be my chosen mate and take your mother's place in my bed."

"No," I gasped. "I'll kill myself first."

With a growl, he began to kick me viciously, and my screams drowned out the sickening sound of bones breaking.

The last thing I saw was his giant boot heading for my face…

#

"Posy. You're safe. Look at me. You're safe."

Someone was screaming, and it took a few seconds for me to realize it was me. I snapped my mouth shut and my vision cleared enough for me to see Mason kneeling in front of me. Not even caring if I got punished for it, I launched myself at him and wrapped my arms around his neck.

106

"Don't let him hurt me! I'll be good, I promise! I'll do anything you want! Just please don't let him hurt me anymore!"

I sobbed so hysterically, he probably couldn't understand a word of it.

"Shh, baby. Shh. You're safe. You're with your mates. He'll never touch you again."

One of Mason's hands ran up and down my back while the other cradled my head against his chest. The smell of a campfire comforted me and helped me calm down.

"I'm going to pick you up, Posy."

Getting to his feet, he moved one arm under my bum to support my weight, and I wrapped my legs around his torso, wishing I could crawl into his skin. Swaying gently, he massaged my neck and kissed my head until my breathing evened out and I stopped quaking.

The scents of my other mates surrounded me, but, mortified, I couldn't lift my face from his neck.

"I'm sorry," I hiccuped.

"No one's mad at you, honey," Cole said from my left. "No one's upset with you. We all understand."

"Remember when we were talking about triggers?" Ash murmured from my other side. "This is what I meant."

"Lilah's having trouble, too." Wyatt ran his hand up and down my back. "I forgot about the fight scene at the end. I'm sorry."

"It's not your fault," I whispered and shook my head.

"Please look at me, sweetness." Jayden kept his voice soft, but I heard Quartz's rough rasp in his voice.

Peeking out from my hiding spot, I found his beautiful eyes right in front of me. He studied my face for a second, then leaned around Mason's shoulder to kiss my cheek.

"I'm okay. I'm sorry I ruined the sleepover."

"You didn't ruin anything," he assured me. "Lilah got scared, too. Luke and Peri took her to the kitchen to make hot chocolate."

Went to give us privacy, more like, I thought.

"When they get back, we can fast forward to the end," Ash said. "It's happy. You'll like it."

"Okay," I sniffed and patted Mason's back.

Instead of putting me on my feet like I expected, he sank to his knees and settled us on the pillow nest. I laid on his chest with Jayden and Wyatt on one side and Ash and Cole on the other.

Tell them, Lark whispered. *They so worried.*

I didn't want to. They'd be disgusted and kick me out.

Lark didn't like that and began to show me memories from the past few days.

We would never reject you or leave you.

107

You're stuck with us, sweetness, until we draw our last breath.

Your sweet self is all we want. You are the greatest treasure we could ever hope to have.

We may rule a pack, but you rule our hearts.

You mean the world to us, Posy.

I took a minute to prepare myself for their possible reactions, then told them what had happened on my birthday.

When I was done, Ash leapt to his feet and raced out of the room, and the sound of vomiting soon echoed down the hall. Wyatt angrily swiped at the tears running down his face, and Jayden had his head buried in his hands. Mason wore his usual blank mask, but his icy eyes were murderous. As for Cole...

Pieces of clothing filled the air as he shifted into his wolf with a bone-rattling roar. I lay stone-still on top of Mason. I hadn't seen any of their wolves before and wasn't sure what to do.

"Shh. You're okay. Topaz won't hurt you." Mason stroked my hair.

"He took control because Cole was losing his temper," Jayden explained. "Trust me, Topaz is better than Cole in a rage."

I nodded, but kept my attention on the silver-eyed wolf as he came closer. I wasn't scared, not with Mason's arms around me and Wyatt and Jayden there, but I wasn't happy, either. It hurt me to know I was upsetting my mates so much.

When he was close enough, Topaz stuck his nose in my neck and snuffed, which surprised me. It tickled and made me giggle and squirm around.

Suddenly, Mason groaned and shifted me off of him and onto the pile of pillows. That confused me, especially when Wyatt and Jayden snickered.

"Was it getting *hard* to hold her?" Wyatt asked him.

Mason told him to shut up.

Their bickering faded into the background as Topaz flopped down next to me. He gave me a wolfish grin with his tongue hanging out of one side of his mouth. Wrapping my arms around him, I snuggled into his soft fur with a happy smile.

"Aw!" Ash came back into the room. "Topaz, what a great teddy bear you are for our girl to cuddle!"

Topaz raised his head and stared at Ash, then snorted and laid his chin back on his paws.

"Are you okay now, Posy?" Ash flopped back in his spot next to Topaz.

I nodded.

"Thank you for telling us." Jayden reached over Wyatt and Mason to run his hand down my arm. "I know it wasn't easy."

I nodded again.

"You're squishing me," Wyatt complained and shoved Jayden off. "Posy, do you need anything?"

I shook my head.

They worried. You stopped talking, Lark informed me.

I'm a burden to them. They shouldn't have to deal with my brokenness.

Topaz whined and nudged my cheek with his nose. I rubbed his fuzzy ears with a little smile.

"Ears are my favorite part of a wolf," I told him as his silver eyes stared back at me. "Does it feel good to have them petted?"

He huffed in approval, and I grinned.

"You're not *broken.*" Mason's chest suddenly vibrated against my back. "You're a *survivor.* If you were broken, you wouldn't keep getting up and going on."

"We love you, Posy," Ash said, and Wyatt and Jayden echoed him.

"We do," Mason said. "More than you know. More than you can understand."

"We've talked about finding you ever since we were boys," Jayden told me. "We've known for years that we'd share our true mate, our Goddess-given mate. Now that we finally have you, we are so happy."

"And the fact that our mate is beautiful and sweet and kind and so, so strong, well, it surpasses everything we dreamed of," Ash said.

Although they'd said it before, I knew I wasn't beautiful or strong.

Someday, you see yourself through mates' eyes, Lark said with a smug smile. *Then you know the truth and not the trash Alpha Briggs put in your head.*

"All right, everyone!" Peri rejoined us with a tray of mugs. "Hot chocolate has arrived."

With Luke and Lilah trailing her, she set the tray on the coffee table, which we had moved over to one side of the room. Except for Topaz of course, we each snagged a mug and sipped in silence for a moment.

"We're going to fast-forward to the end." Ash picked up the remote and looked over at Lilah, who was curled up in Luke's big arms on a couch. "It's happy, I promise, and no more violence. Is that okay?"

When she nodded, he skipped to the last scene, and he was right: it was a happy ending. I enjoyed the "bloopers" immensely, and Lilah did, too, judging by her quiet giggles.

"I think we've all had a long day," Mason said. "Time for lights out."

No one grumbled because he was right. Ash turned off the TV, Peri turned off the lights, and my mates cuddled as close as they could get to me.

Peri huffed a little.

"Seeing how my brothers took my spot, I guess I'll take a couch," she muttered.

"You can come down here with us, Periwinkle," Wyatt offered and held out one arm. "If you want to."

"Is your name *really* Periwinkle?" Lilah asked.

"No. It's just Peri. Doofus here likes to tease, that's all."

"Doofus?" Wyatt scorned. "And here I was being nice to you. Sleep on a couch alone then."

Of course, she jumped on him with a giggle, which made me giggle, too.

Mason stuffed his face in my neck and kissed my throat, which made me shiver. He chuckled and his thick arm tightened around my waist.

"Good night, little flower," he whispered.

"Good night."

And so I fell asleep with a fluffy wolf on one side and Mason's bulk at my back, surrounded by my mates and friends, feeling safer than I had in years.

17: Meeting the Betas

Posy

After breakfast and showers the next morning, we girls decided to wear floaty, dressier tops with shorts and sandals. My mates had bought me clothing in several different sizes, so I knew we'd find something Peri and Lilah could wear, but I was still worried because Peri was six inches taller than me and Lilah ten! Once we discovered that my capris fit them like shorts, though, I was relieved and happy to loan them whatever they wanted.

My mates met me at the bottom of the stairs and showered me with compliments.

"You look amazing, honey."

"Gorgeous, sweetness. Just gorgeous."

"My beautiful little flower."

"My cutie is extra cute today!"

I buried my burning face in my hands, which made all my mates chuckle and the girls giggle.

"You *are* precious, cupcake, but I need to do your hair!" Ash grabbed my hand and towed me along. "Dutch braids, remember?"

He led me to a kitchen bar stool and helped me onto it, which meant he picked me up like a toddler and sat me on it.

"He does your hair?" Peri asked, eyes agog.

"He's better at it than I am." I shrugged.

Her jaw dropped, and Lilah tittered.

After he finished, I looked in the hall mirror and gaped at myself.

"It looks lovely, Ash! Thank you!"

Spinning around, I crashed into his torso and squeezed him tight.

"It's you who are lovely," he murmured and kissed the top of my head.

"Good job, bro," Wyatt told Ash and fist bumped him. "I really like it. You have to do this style again sometime."

"Thanks," Ash said with a smile. "Jay should get kudos, too. Without him letting me practice on him for the past six or seven years, I would have forgotten everything his mom taught me."

"It was a sacrifice, believe me, but utterly worth it to see the results now." Jayden smirked and also gave Ash a fist bump.

"Betas are here," Mason interrupted the bromance going on in front of my eyes.

We went to the front porch right as three vehicles came up the driveway. I turned to my mates and knew they could see the panic in my eyes.

Jayden came over and tucked me under his arm.

"We have five betas and five gammas, one of each from what remains of our original packs," he explained. "It makes things complicated in some ways, but simpler in others."

"After the luna is found, a beta's primary duty is to keep her safe," Wyatt added. "They're your guards now, although they'll have other jobs when not on protection detail."

I looked over at Peri to see her chatting with Cole, so I checked on Lilah. She seemed as nervous as I was to go shopping with the betas. She probably wanted her big brother to come along, but knew as well as I did that one of them had to be here when the king arrived.

Same with my mates. It would have been very bad manners if they weren't here to welcome the king to their territory, even if he was their best friend.

Another thing to stress over. I bit my bottom lip. *I have to meet the king. The king! Moon Goddess, have mercy.*

Wyatt reached over and pried my lip out of my teeth with his thumb.

"Baby, each one of these guys would lay down his life for you, so don't be afraid of them, okay?"

I stared into his silvery-blue eyes and nodded.

"Peri, Callie, and Keeley know them all, too." Mason came over and laid his palm against my cheek. "Except for Tyler, who's brand new."

"They're nice guys. At least, they've always been nice to me." Peri then pulled me aside. "Speaking of Callie and Keeley, don't bring up the beta who died. Everett was their older brother, their only living relative, and they're still grieving."

"Oh!" I covered my mouth with my hand.

"I don't know the whole story," she admitted. "Only the boys do, but don't ask Jay. You saw Quartz's reaction last night."

I nodded. I wanted to know what had happened simply because it affected at least one of my mates so deeply, but knew I'd have to give it time.

Before I was ready, the yard was filled with beta wolves - and I had to meet them. Wanting to be brave for my mates, or at least not embarrass them by being a scaredy cat, I swallowed hard and took Ash's hand when he held it out. He led me down the porch stairs and over to a lean guy who stood a little apart from the others. He had dark blue eyes and dirty blond hair with long bangs and wore a gray t-shirt, dark blue cargo shorts, and gray running shoes.

"Posy, meet Tyler James. His wolf is named River," Ash said. "Ty, meet our mate and your luna, Posy Briggs. Her wolf is named Lark."

"It's a pleasure to meet you, luna." Tyler's cheeks and the tops of his ears turned pink, but he met my eyes and held out his hand.

"It's nice to meet you, too, Beta Tyler." I shook his hand.

"Just Tyler or Ty is fine, luna. I'm honored to be your guard." His face grew determined. "I'll work really hard. I won't let you down."

Oh, my heart.

"Thank you, Tyler. I can tell you're going to be a great beta, and I know we're going to become good friends."

When I smiled at him, his blush deepened.

Then one of the other betas laughed in a rude way and muttered, "What a baby!"

Of course, I heard him, as did Tyler, who shoved his hands in his pockets and stared hard at the ground.

Are they picking on him because he's so young, or because he's new to the group?

Whatever the reason, I didn't like it. Not at all. They should be welcoming him to the team, not hazing him. Besides, he, like most of us, had been prematurely thrown into a role he wasn't quite ready for.

I looked over my shoulder at the guy who'd laughed. He wore a short-sleeved white polo, khaki shorts, gray canvas shoes, and a smirk aimed at Tyler.

I glared at him. I wanted to have a talk with whichever of my mates he was beta for. I was also going to get Tyler alone today and find out how bad the bullying was.

"Matthew."

Mason's voice was the sharp crack of a whip, and the dark-haired beta instantly bared his neck. His bright blue eyes fogged up for a second and he winced. Then he walked over to us and held out his hand to Tyler.

"Sorry," he muttered, but I saw no regret in his face.

Yep. Definitely having a talk with Mason about this guy.

Tyler reluctantly took his hand out of his pocket and shook Matthew's hand, but didn't reply.

"Your apology means nothing since Mason made you do it," I told Matthew. "Be a better teammate so you don't have to make apologies, forced or genuine."

A moment of shock rippled through the group. When I realized what I'd said and done, I clasped my hands tightly and twisted my fingers. If I scolded their betas, even if they deserved it, my mates might get mad at me.

That thought was why I flinched so hard when Ash's long arm wrapped around my waist and pulled me against his side. I knew everyone saw it, too.

"You're okay, princess. No one will hurt you for correcting the behavior of someone who should know better."

Ash's voice was a rumbly growl, and I had the feeling that if I wasn't standing there, he would have cuffed Matthew on the back of his head.

"This is Matthew Rose, Mase's beta," Ash went on to introduce us. "His wolf is Arroyo."

"Hello, luna," Matthew said in a quiet voice.

"Beta Matthew."

He didn't try to shake my hand, for which I was grateful. I gave him a curt nod and received one in return. I did not like Matthew Rose very much.

Then a dark-skinned guy joined us. His black hair was braided in thin rows tight against his scalp, and he was the dressiest wolf I'd met in a while with his white button-up shirt, light blue dress shorts, and brown leather loafers. Most shifters favored clothes that were easy to get on and off in case they needed to wolf out in a hurry.

"I'm Tristan Harrington, Alpha Wyatt's beta."

His dark brown eyes were kind and warm as he held out his hand and waited to see if I'd take it. I looked up at Ash to see him smiling down at me, so I turned back at Tristan and laid my fingertips in his palm in a not-quite handshake. Very gently, he laid his other hand over top of mine.

"Hello, Beta Tristan," I murmured.

"You can call me Tristan or Tris or whatever you'd like. My wolf's name is Creek. Yours is Lark, yeah?"

I nodded and gave him a tiny smile.

"Where are we going shopping today?" he asked as he released my hand.

"I don't really know. Peri's in charge of the whole thing."

"Oh, no! We're in trouble before we leave the driveway." He grinned when I giggled. "I'm looking forward to getting to know you better, luna."

"Thank you. Me, too."

The next beta to come over had shaggy, sun-streaked brown hair and calm gray eyes that were a bit bluer than Mason's. He gave off a very zen vibe and looked to be in his early twenties. His outfit consisted of a white t-shirt, long black shorts, and checkerboard skate sneakers.

"Hey, luna. I'm Crew Myers. My wolf is named Bay. I'm Alpha Jayden's beta."

"It's nice to meet you, Beta Crew."

This time, I gathered my courage and held my hand out first. With a lopsided grin, he shook it gently.

"I'm happy you're with us, luna. Your presence has brightened everything up already."

I didn't know what he was talking about, so I nodded and ducked my head shyly.

"So, luna, you can call me just Crew, okay?"

I nodded again and gave him a small smile.

Someone suddenly spoke from right beside me, and I jumped a little. Ash's hand tightened on my waist, and I felt him drop a comforting kiss on my head.

"I'm Emerson Jones, luna," said the last beta. "My wolf is Cove."

He was the biggest of the betas, almost as tall as Mason and nearly as wide as Cole. His stance and demeanor screamed danger, and he didn't smile. A little scared and intimidated, I instinctively drew my shoulders in to look smaller and huddled closer to Ash.

A flash of something - maybe shock - zipped through his dark eyes, then he bent down with his hands on his knees to be at my eye level.

"I'm sorry I startled you, little luna," he murmured. "I didn't mean to. None of us will ever hurt you, and we'll never let anyone else hurt you, either. If one of us scares you, tell another one of us and we'll sort him out, all right?"

I studied him. He had dark brown eyes and short black hair that was slicked back. He wore a black t-shirt, camo cargo shorts, and black cross trainers.

He smiled at me, flashing white teeth and dimples, and I wondered how I'd associated him with danger.

I smiled back, showing him my own dimples, and his eyes lit up.

"Hello, Beta Emerson."

"Little bunny, you can call me Emerson or Em or whatever you want."

"Little bunny?" Ash interjected himself into our conversation.

"You got to admit, alpha, she's awful small, just like a bunny." Emerson quirked an eyebrow up at him.

"Only in stature," Ash said. "Her heart and courage would turn you and me into dwarves if they were visible."

I blushed at his words and buried my face into his side, and both of them chuckled.

"And call her by her title," Ash grumbled. "She's your luna."

"Little luna bunny," Emerson agreed.

I snickered and pulled on Ash's shirt so he'd look down at me. I gave him a happy smile, and he gave in with a roll of his eyes.

"All right, but only because Posy likes it."

I did, too, because bunnies made me think of Mr. Nibbles, and Mr. Nibbles made me feel safe.

With a deep laugh, Emerson straightened up and towered over me again, and his face returned to a blank expression that could rival Mason's.

Oh. Yeah. That's why I associated him with danger.

And now we know there a teddy bear inside, Lark laughed.

While Ash and Emerson talked, I peeked around to see that Mason had taken Matthew off to one side and was chewing him out. You wouldn't have known it from Mason's face, but Matthew's neck was bared in submission, his eyes were wide, and his body trembled.

Good.

Looking around to check on everyone else, I saw Luke and Lilah had remained on the porch with Jayden. Across the yard, Crew, Tristan, Peri, and Cole were talking with Tyler, who blushed every time he made eye contact with Peri.

Oh. OH! I need to find out when he turns eighteen!

Lark laughed at me, and I knew she'd sent my thoughts to Topaz when Cole turned his head and winked at me. I wiggled my eyebrows at him, and he snorted.

But where's Wyatt?

Stepping away from Ash, I ducked out of his loose hold and spun in a circle, looking for my errant mate.

"Are you looking for Wyatt?" Ash reached out one hand to lace his fingers through mine. "He just went to get more coffee."

Sure enough, a second later, Wyatt came out of the house with a steaming mug in his hand.

"Still needs that third cup to wake up, huh?" Emerson shook his head.

"Some things never change." Ash snorted, then brought our joined hands up to kiss my knuckles. "The twins are almost here, princess."

With Emerson in tow, we walked over to Peri's group, and Jayden and the MacGregor siblings joined us. I looked around for Mason and saw him still chewing Matthew out, and I almost felt bad for the beta.

Peri, Lilah and I formed our own circle as Jayden introduced Luke to the betas and explained a little of the situation at Tall Pines.

"So much testosterone," Peri complained. "We need to go roll around in pink glitter or something to shield us from it."

Lilah and I giggled, then I got down to business.

"I saw you talking with *someone*," I teased her with a knowing smile.

Her cheeks flushed a pretty pink, and Lilah hid a smile behind her hand. As if reading each other's minds, we put our heads together.

"He's awfully sweet, isn't he?" Peri said in a nearly silent voice. "So shy!"

"And he's adorable," Lilah agreed in a whisper. "I hope he's your mate. Seeing you two together, the chemistry is obvious, unlike with my brother."

"Luke's hot, but he doesn't *need* a mate. Not like Tyler does." Showing what a good person she was, Peri added, "Even if it isn't me, I hope his mate is worthy of his precious heart."

"Aww!" Lilah and I squealed together.

"What are you three gossiping about that has you cooing?"

I whipped my head up at Wyatt's voice. The guys were all watching us, including Tyler, whose eyes were fixed on Peri's flushed face. Luke stared at Lilah with a grin, obviously happy to see his traumatized sister giggling.

"Mind your own business, Alpha Wyatt." Peri gave him a sour look.

His eyes narrowing, he opened his mouth to retort, and I decided to intervene. Rushing over to him, I threw my arms around his waist and shoved my face into his chest.

"I'm going to miss you," I mumbled into his shirt.

His arms came to wrap around my shoulders and neck, and he took a deep inhale of my scent.

"I miss you already." He bent to whisper in my ear. "This is the first time we'll be apart since we found you. Have fun, but don't be gone too long, okay?"

I nodded and squeezed him harder.

By the time I let him go, a pink VW Bug had swerved into one of the two remaining parking spaces. The twins from the store yesterday tumbled out of the car and ran up to us.

"Alphas, is Gretchen okay parked there?" they asked in unison.

They assured them it was, and the girls came over to Peri, Lilah, and me with bright smiles.

"This is going to be so much fun!" squealed one of the twins, jumping up and down on her toes.

"Yeah, it's not every day you get invited to spend time with the new luna!" the other squeaked.

"Or spend the alphas' money," her sister quipped.

Peri laughed, and Lilah and I both smiled.

As Peri made the introductions, I realized right away I was going to have trouble telling the girls apart. Not only were their faces identical, but also their clothing, shoes, and hair styles.

Keeley have white earrings, Lark helped me out, *and Callie pink.*

Thank you, my wolfie.

Jayden ambled over as we started to say our goodbyes.

"Don't forget to buy a phone, Lilah," he reminded her.

He went to hand her a black credit card, but hesitated with a frown. Shaking his head, he turned to me with it, but hesitated again.

"Never mind. You'd be no better than she would." He finally handed the card to Peri. "Buy whatever Lilah wants or needs, and don't let her look at any price tags. Same for Posy. Anything she sees that she likes, get it for her."

"And no arguing, Posy." Mason crossed his arms over his chest and stared down at me with serious gray eyes.

I nodded and shrunk in on myself a bit. When he saw that, he immediately dropped his arms and pulled me against his torso, cradling the back of my head with one huge palm.

"Sorry, baby. I go into alpha mode when other wolves are around." He laid his chin on top of my head. "I want you to enjoy yourself today and don't worry about the money, okay?"

"Okay."

"Stay with the betas. Use your phone and text or call us if something happens, or even if you don't feel comfortable and want to come home. One of us will drop everything to come get you, even if the king is here."

He kissed my forehead, then sighed as he handed me over to an impatiently waiting Wyatt, who already had more hugs than any of the others this morning.

As Wyatt held me tight against his chest, he explained that two of the betas would drive a lead vehicle that we would follow. The rest would follow in another vehicle behind us.

"Please be safe." He smiled at me.

I nodded, and he leaned down and kissed my cheek.

As soon as Wyatt let go, Ash gently swooped me up into his arms for a big bear hug. I giggled as he growled into my neck, then squeaked when he left a kiss at the base of my throat. Laughing, he carefully set me back on my feet.

"If you find cute hair things, get them for us, cupcake."

"I will," I promised with a grin.

Then Jayden cupped my face with his palms and leaned in to kiss my forehead, then each eyelid, and finally both cheeks. My blush spread all over my face and down my neck. His husky chuckle slid over my skin like a caress, and I quivered.

"Enjoy your morning, sweetness," he murmured. "I'll see you when you get back."

I stretched up on my tiptoes and kissed the edge of his jaw, and his eyes widened before he grinned.

Then Cole came over. Holding me close against his side, he walked us to his big, black SUV and handed Lilah the keys. Peri claimed shotgun when I didn't want it, so he helped me into the seat behind Lilah's.

"Do not try to ditch the betas," he warned us with a stern scowl.

My eyes wide, I nodded frantically. No way was I going to disobey Cole when he looked like *that*.

Or ever, really.

"I'm mostly saying that for Peri and the twins, honey." Cole smirked, which relieved his dark expression. "I know my smart girl wouldn't do something stupid like that."

I smiled, showing him my dimples, and he kissed my cheek.

"Okay, okay, Cole!" Peri fussed. "Bye already!"

He winked at me, then stepped back and closed my door.

"Talk about a worry wart!" Peri snorted.

"Aw, he just loves his mate," Keeley giggled. "All the alphas all do. It's so easy to see. You're a lucky girl, luna!"

"No, no. Call me Posy," I insisted.

"Thank you!"

"All right, betas Crew and Matthew are getting into their truck. Are we ready?" Lilah asked.

"Yes!" we all chorused.

And away we went.

18: The King Arrives

King Julian Hemming

As we crossed into Five Fangs territory, Onyx surprised me by lifting his ears and going on alert.

What's up, Nyx? I asked him.

He didn't respond, which was normal. He was a primitive wolf and not the most talkative to begin with, and every year that we went without our mate, he withdrew even further. To be honest, I worried that he'd go feral if we didn't find our special girl soon.

He perked up last week when I reminded him that our vacation was coming up. He loved the Five Fangs territory and hanging out with his best buddy, Quartz. When I had to move our trip to today, I thought that he would be ecstatic, but he was too furious about Alpha Halder. Ever since Ash's call, he'd been in a filthy temper.

A frustrated sound came from the back seat, and I looked over my shoulder at my new beta.

"All good, Gisela?"

"I don't know, sire." She shook her head as her brow furrowed. "Hawk's agitated about something."

"Coal, too," said Ranger, who was driving.

"What are they doing?" I asked, curious as to what was going on.

"Coal's bouncing around like a pup."

"Same with Hawk. What about Onyx?"

"Silent as usual, but alert. Almost like he's scented prey, but not really. Hard to explain."

Ranger cut his eyes over at me.

"What do you think? It doesn't feel like danger, but should we contact the alphas?"

I thought about it for a moment. These borders were always heavily protected, and I was sure they were even more so now that the guys had found their luna. I never brought warriors from the royal pack when I visited since the Five Fangs fighters were just as qualified.

In fact, I usually never brought *anyone* with me on vacation. Official pack business, sure, but not on my much-awaited vacation. This time, I'd invited Gisela along so the five alphas could meet her. I interacted with them enough that she'd need to be on good terms with them.

"*Well?*" Ranger pushed in an aggravated tone.

I'd also brought along my yammering kid brother. I was planning to install him as the new alpha of Tall Pines. After I destroyed Leo Halder, of course.

And if Ranger didn't goad me into fratricide.

"There isn't much short of a full pack attack that the three of us can't handle," I said. "We're almost there, anyway."

A few minutes later, we sailed up the driveway and parked in front of the alphas' house. I got out of the vehicle and took a deep inhale of the fresh air, and Onyx smiled.

Onyx, who was cantankerous at best, smiled.

My eyebrows shot up. Sure, I wanted my wolf to be happier, but it was creepy seeing him go from snarling to smiling so quickly.

What's going on? I demanded.

I'd never liked surprises.

Jul will see.

I growled at him, making the SUV shimmy, and Gisela and Ranger jumped in alarm.

"What?" they asked at the same time.

"Onyx knows something, but won't tell me," I grouched.

"Jeez, Julian, give us a heart attack because you're pouting."

I snarled at Ranger, but he was already walking toward the front porch.

Jul! Onyx thundered suddenly. *What is that smell?*

I sucked in a deep breath, but didn't pick up on anything unusual. I told him there was nothing, but he wasn't having it.

Jul is dumb! Smell harder!

Chill, Nyx, I ordered him.

He didn't like it, but there was nothing he could do when I shoved him back with a burst of power.

"King Julian!" Wyatt called from the front door, then sprinted down the stairs.

"Hey, Wyatt. Good to see you." We gave each other bro-hugs.

"You, too. And Ranger! We didn't know you were coming. Awesome! How's life been?"

"Dull." Ranger smirked. "Got to clean out a nest of chupacabras in New Mexico last month, though."

"Nasty little biters," Wyatt grinned.

"Yeah. Some idiot imported 'em illegally and they got loose. Anyway, what about you? Heard you all found your luna."

Wyatt's face softened and his eyes brightened.

"Our Posy. I didn't think it was possible to love someone that much, and I've only known her a few days."

My chest burned. I was happy for my friends, of course, but, Goddess, was I jealous! I was older than all of them. Why couldn't I find my mate?

"Hi. You must be the king's new beta." Wyatt moved around us to greet Gisela. "I'm Wyatt Black."

"Gisela Bauer." She held out her hand, and Wyatt shook it.

"Come on in," he invited us. "The boys are waiting. You're just in time for lunch."

We tramped up the porch stairs and walked into the living room - and Gisela and I froze.

The luscious smell of almonds filled my nose, and goosebumps rose on my skin.

Mate! Onyx shouted.

"What is it, your majesty?" Mase asked.

"I smell my mate. Who's new in the pack that was here recently?"

"Only the MacGregors," Ash said. "They're the ones I called you about with the Tall Pines trouble. They stayed over last night. Oh, and the Breckenridge twins just turned eighteen, but they were only here for a few minutes and didn't come into the house."

My beta stepped further into the room with her nose up and quivering.

"Mate!" shouted a deep voice from the kitchen at the same time Gisela whispered, "Mate?"

She took off at a dead run, and the five alphas looked at each other with a knowing grin.

"Who is in the kitchen?" Ranger asked.

"Luke MacGregor," Cole smirked. "He's helping Jay make lunch."

"The former beta at Tall Pines?"

"Yep."

Want mate! Onyx howled. *Jul find mate NOW.*

"Where is the sister? And what's her name?" I demanded.

"Lilah. She and our mate, Posy, went shopping with Peri, the twins, and our betas," Wyatt told me. "Do you think she's your mate?"

"Who else could it be?" I scowled. "Peri's not eighteen yet, and the twins were already eighteen when I saw them at Ev's funeral."

Is this possible? Can it be true? Can I be moments away from meeting my mate?

"I'll link my beta and tell him to—"

Mase's eyes clouded over right as the voice from the kitchen bellowed, "LILAH!"

Quartz's familiar, furious roar quickly followed.

"What's going on?" Ranger and I asked at the same time.

"Posy and the girls are in danger." Cole stripped off his shirt and ditched his shoes. "Tall Pines wolves have them surrounded at Roger's Diner."

Rage burned all other emotions away, and I pelted out of the house. I was aware that the others ran with me, four of them as wolves.

I recognized Hawk, Topaz and Quartz; the other had to be Luke MacGregor's wolf.

"It'll be faster on wheels than paws!" Mase called out.

Onyx could reach fifty miles an hour when he went all out, but I couldn't remember where Roger's Diner was exactly, only that it was somewhere off pack territory.

"Ranger!" I yelled and raced to my vehicle. "We're following the alphas!"

Hawk and Luke's wolf piled in with us while the rest jumped into Ash's SUV. In seconds, we were tearing down the driveway, and I was glad Ranger was driving. I had all I could handle keeping Onyx under control and keeping my own fury and panic at bay.

I would have loved to turn him loose on the Tall Pines wolves, but I had to think of my mate. Onyx wouldn't hurt her, but he'd scare her. Plus, once he was in a killing frenzy, he'd be blind to everything but tearing out throats. Someone could harm or take our mate without him noticing.

"Hawk, Luke's wolf, get your queen and the alphas' luna to safety," I commanded in my royal alpha tone. "Ranger, capture at least one of the Tall Pines wolves to interrogate."

Ranger nodded.

Yes, sire, Hawk said through our pack link. *Rain says yes, too.*

"Good."

19: Diner Disaster

Posy

As soon as we reached the shopping center, the betas went into protection mode and fanned out around us. It was easy to ignore them for the most part, and we girls cruised through store after store, laughing and teasing each other. Soon, all of our arms were loaded down with bags.

"We're spending too much!" Lilah complained.

"The boys have plenty of money," Peri assured her as the twins giggled. "It won't even make a dent, trust me."

"Wait! This is their *personal* money?" Bright red stained her cheeks and traveled down her neck. "I thought it was pack funds! I can't accept—"

"You can and you will," Callie said. "Like Peri said, the alphas are loaded."

I felt a little guilty for spending money, too, but Ash had said to get some cute hair things, so I did. Then Peri insisted on buying a few items I'd stared at a little too long.

"We just went shopping yesterday, Peri!" I protested.

"Yeah, and it was cut short because my brothers were idiots. We didn't get to half the places I wanted to. Now you just hush and let the boys spoil you a little."

I frowned, but finally decided that, if my mates got angry, they could yell at her.

Right before noon, we began the most important debate: where to go for lunch.

"What about Roger's Diner?" Keeley suggested. "They have the best chicken tenders."

"Oh, and their onion rings are so flaky and delicious!" Callie agreed.

"Plus they have excellent milkshakes," Peri added, which made the decision for us all.

Waving Emerson over, I told him our plan.

"Sounds good, little luna bunny. We'll escort you to the vehicles, then you follow the lead car again, okay?"

I nodded and smiled, and, within ten minutes, we pulled into a gravel parking lot. The diner was a rectangular building painted bright red with a block-letter sign in dark blue. It was an isolated location, surrounded by open fields that were backed by the woods. When I got out of the SUV, I lifted my nose and smelled water nearby.

I wonder if there's a stream running along the treeline.

"Let's get inside, please, luna," Tyler said.

His eyes roved the whole area as he stood next to me, and his shoulders were tense.

"Do you smell something?" I asked him with a frown.

He shook his head.

"A feeling, that's all."

"Do the other betas also have this 'feeling'?"

"Crew's uneasy, and Tris and Em are on alert. I have no idea about Matthew."

As we walked into the diner, I laid my hand on his bicep. He looked down at me with raised eyebrows.

"How bad does he bully you? And has he always done so, or only since you became a beta?"

"Don't worry about it, luna."

"Well, I *am* worried about it. So tell me."

"He and my predecessor were best friends. I don't think it's me so much as whoever was going to take Everett Breckenridge's place."

"Hmm."

"Posy, Posy! Let's grab the big booth in the back!" Keeley came over, linked her arm with mine, and towed me along.

Once we were seated, the waitress came over and took our drinks order. We read over the menu and decided what we wanted, so we were ready when she returned. Taking a long sip of my soda, I looked around the place. It was decorated in a sports-theme, which didn't do anything for me, but it was clean and tidy.

The betas stood around the room, looking like presidential security without the suits. Their eyes never stopped scanning inside and out. I felt bad that they weren't eating lunch, but Peri said they wouldn't join us even if we asked them to.

"They are guarding you, Posy, and that is a great honor to them. Since it's the first time, they're going to be especially careful not to make mistakes."

Our food arrived, and we dug in while still chatting.

"So why were you with the three brides of hell yesterday?" Peri asked the twins.

They looked at each other, then at me with embarrassment painting their faces pink.

"We chose the wrong humans to try to befriend."

"I don't know why you even tried with that trio." Peri made a disgusted sound. "They've been mean since middle school and don't seem likely to change."

"We thought if we did something nice for them, they'd return the favor." Callie shook her head. "They made last year rough for us at school, and we wanted to avoid a repeat for our senior year."

"You go to school with humans?" I asked, tilting my head. "Why don't we have our own school?"

"An excellent question! One you should bring up with your mates!" Keeley chirped. "There are nursery and elementary schools, but no middle or high school on pack territory. If there were, so much drama would evaporate."

"Hmm. I'll bring it up and see what they say," I promised.

"Alphas Wyatt and Ash graduated in June," Callie said, "so they can tell you what it's like for shifters at a human school."

"Actually, I don't think their perspective would be a good one," Peri pointed out. "Our male counterparts in general have it far easier than we do at school. They're buff and athletic naturally, so they fit in and are automatically popular. As for my brothers, they have that alpha aura that even the humans pick up on. I don't think they've ever had to deal with the issues we have."

"What issues exactly?" I asked.

"The girls, like those ones from yesterday, pick at us and we can't really do anything about it," Callie explained. "Since we're so much stronger than they are, we could do some major damage if we get into a physical fight. And if we lose control and wolf out, well, that would be a disaster, wouldn't it?"

"So we have to act submissive or avoid the mean girls," Keeley said, "so they won't make our lives miserable. They can get vicious."

"What are some things they've done?" Lilah wanted to know.

"Steal or destroy your gym clothes, or your regular ones so you're stuck wearing your gym gear all day. Or take your towel while you're showering after gym." Keeley picked at her nails and didn't look up.

"Once, they tore my shirt off because it was exactly like one they were wearing and I didn't have permission to 'copy' them." Callie rolled her eyes and shook her head. "I had a lot of trouble controlling my wolf after they did that and had to leave school early. Of course, they thought that meant they'd won and, according to gossip the next day, I'd left crying hysterically."

I was horrified.

Maybe my brothers pulling me out of school wasn't such a bad thing, after all.

I looked over at Lilah and saw her jaw had dropped.

"Did you have humans at your high school?" I asked her.

"No, and nothing like any of this ever occurred."

I was determined now to bring this up with the guys. Even if it was for a small population, I didn't see a reason why Five Fangs couldn't have its own secondary schools.

126

Surely there are enough educated wolves in the second-largest pack in the United States to act as teachers. Other than a building, that's all a shifter school would need.

Lost in thought about what to name the new middle and high schools, I almost missed it when Lilah suddenly sat ramrod straight in her chair.

"What is it?" I asked.

"Tall Pines," she whimpered and closed her eyes. "I smell Tall Pines wolves."

The betas weren't reacting to anything, although Crew's eyes were fogged over as he linked with someone, so I swiveled to peer out the big windows.

I didn't see anything. No cars other than ours in the parking lot. No strangers. No wolves.

Maybe she's wrong—

Two black mini buses bounced into the parking lot, and I could see they were both packed with bodies.

I spun back to Lilah and saw her face had turned white as milk.

"They're coming for me," she whispered. "I don't want to go back. I'd rather die than go back to him."

Emerson was beside me in a heartbeat.

"Luna, go to the bathroom and lock yourself in," he commanded. "The rest of you are her last-ditch guards. Keep her alive as best you can."

"Yes, beta," the twins chorused.

We scurried off with Peri in the lead and piled into the ladies' room. Trembling, I drew my shoulders up toward my ears and curled forward with my arms around my stomach.

I want my mates! I screamed inside my head.

No panic, Lark soothed me. *They on the way. Be strong, Posy.*

How could I be when I was once more helpless and scared and locked in a room?

\#

Lilah

After we shut the bathroom door, we looked at each other. Posy was not doing well *at all*. Her breath came fast and shallow, bright red spots dotted each of her cheeks, and her eyes grew increasingly wild.

I fought back my own terror so I could think clearly.

The Tall Pines wolves were here to drag me back to *him*, and I made the decision that the only way I would go back was as a corpse.

They'll need to take my last breath to take me.

127

"Okay, we know help is on the way, but the betas are outnumbered four or five to one right now." Peri gathered us into a tight huddle. "We need a plan in case they can't hold the line until the others get here. We can't let anything happen to the luna."

"Behind the diner is an open field that leads to the woods," Callie said. "As soon as we hit the trees, we're on pack territory. I say we go through the kitchen, out the back door, and book it for the border."

"What if there are wolves in the back, too?" I asked, wanting the plan to be solid before we made our move.

"Twinny and I will cause a distraction," Keeley said. "We'll shift and run them in circles."

"I don't want anyone to get hurt because of me!"

Tears rolled down Posy's face, and her breathing had devolved into sharp pants.

"You're the important one here, luna." Callie gripped her shoulders. "The alphas wouldn't survive losing you, and the pack wouldn't survive losing them. Getting you to safety is everyone's top priority."

"We'll be fine," Keeley added. "If we have to shift, Sparrow and Finch are fast. Really, *really* fast."

"Lilah, are you faster on two legs or four?" Peri looked at me.

"Even with Kestrel asleep, I'm faster in wolf form."

"The only problem is, you can't link with anyone since you're not pack yet."

"Alpha Jayden inducted me into the Moonset pack," I explained. "I can link with enough people to be okay."

In fact, I'd linked the alpha, Beta Crew, and Luke as soon as I'd confirmed the nauseatingly familiar smell of Tall Pines wolves. The beta had alerted his team, which launched them into motion and ended up with us locked in this restroom.

Unfortunately, Luke had shifted into Rain and Alpha Jayden into Quartz, and *neither* of those wolves was at home to reason.

I decided linking with Beta Crew was my best bet for a while.

"Good," Peri said, "because Posy can't directly link with anyone yet."

All our eyes went to the tiny luna. She was shaking so hard now, I didn't know how she was still standing.

Half of me wanted to fall apart, too, but the other half wouldn't hear of it.

You will keep it together, I ordered myself. *These girls are all younger than you and far more valuable. Keep it together so you can help them. Remember, it's not over until you're underground.*

"Luna's not going to be able to run, Per," Callie stated what we all knew.

"My wolf is a large one. I'll carry her." I took a deep breath to calm myself as panic tried to flare again. "The three of you run guard around us. If we're attacked, buy as much time as you can for me to get her back on pack lands."

That border patrol better be close by then, or we'll both be in trouble.

The twins nodded. Peri looked conflicted for a moment, then nodded, too.

So I went into a stall, left the door open to accommodate Kestrel's size, and started to strip down. As I did, I linked with Beta Crew and let him know our plan. He didn't like it, but I don't think he would have liked *any* plan we came up with.

Peri's keeping everyone in the loop, so just focus on staying alive, he told me. *You don't know everything that happened this morning.*

What happened, beta?

You'll find out. You need to stay alive for all our sakes.

What do you mean? I asked with a frown.

I have to concentrate now. Don't die, no matter what, or all of us will.

He closed the link before I could ask anything more, and I didn't want to distract him while he was most likely fighting, so I saved the mystery for later.

I shifted into Kestrel's buff and white form, then walked out of the stall. The girls gaped at me, and I shrugged.

I'd never understood it, either. Most she-wolves were smaller than the males by about a third, and roughly half compared to alphas. Since a wolf's size was in correlation to power, it didn't make sense for me to be so large. I wasn't any more powerful than other she-wolves.

I went to Posy and nudged her cheek with my nose to get her attention. She jumped a little, then swallowed hard before she reached out a quaking hand to pet my ears.

"Up you go, luna."

After Callie and Keeley boosted her onto my back, she laid down like Luke did on his sport bike and fisted her small hands into my ruff. I could feel the tremors ripping through her whole body. The poor little thing was scared to death, and I wondered how miserable her life had been - and for how long - before the five alphas rescued her.

I'm scared, too, I thought to myself, *but I have to get her to safety. I have to ignore the fear so I can fight. Fight till I can't anymore.*

"We all know what to do, right?" Peri asked.

"Right!" the twins chorused.

I felt Posy nod her head, and I dipped mine, too.

Peri cracked the door open and peeked out, then glanced at us over her shoulder.

"Let's go."

#

I thought we were going to make it.

I really did.

The trees were so close, and I could taste the water from the stream that separated the woods from the field.

Then a dark brown wolf hit me in the side like a bullet, right in my already broken ribs. Posy flew off my back with a scream, and I rolled three or four times before coming to a stop.

The wolf who tackled me slunk closer. I snarled at him as I stood, wobbling on my paws. Twice, he lunged and retreated quickly, and it was only when I felt fangs sink into my leg that I realized he was the distraction.

A gray and white wolf clamped his jaws fast on my right front forearm. I tried to tear out of his hold, but he twisted my leg, spraining my wrist, and I yowled in pain as the world spun.

Tucking my hurt limb under me, I snapped and snarled at them as they came at me again and again, all of us pulling out tufts of hair and patches of skin. I was getting the worst of it since I was going against two of them, but I fought on until my broken, exhausted body finally gave out and crashed to the ground.

Once I was down, they sank their fangs into my ruff and dragged me along. The unbearable torture of my broken ribs bumping the ground threatened to knock me out, but I forced myself to stay conscious and watch for an opportunity.

It's not over until you're underground, I repeated.

We were halfway back to the diner when snarls and growls filled the air. More wolves raced into the field from both sides. The two Tall Pines wolves released me as a roiling mass of hairy bodies flowed over and around us and carried my attackers away with them.

I was left alone in the tall grass to pant and bleed and try to stay awake.

Kestrel? Could really use a helping hand right about now.

Still no answer, and I understood. The day we left Tall Pines, Alpha Halder had beaten me to the brink of death. Kestrel had healed the life-threatening injuries and dozens of broken bones, then passed out and had remained asleep since.

Moon Goddess, a little mercy? I begged.

While I was praying, I asked her to spare my new friends. Especially Posy because Callie was right. Those boys would destroy half the world if it saved her, and the other half in their grief if it didn't.

My pain-addled brain stopped working so hard as weariness consumed me.

I'll close my eyes for a minute. Just a minute. That won't hurt anything, will it? Either I'll live or I'll die, and the others are either safe or they're not. I know it's not over until you're underground, but maybe it can pause while you're laying on *the ground.*

My rambling thoughts froze as an amazing smell wafted past my nostrils and jolted me into wakefulness.

Freshly ground coffee. The good kind, too. Dark roast with chocolate notes. Rich, deep, complex, and almost a sin to drink.

Mate? My nose quivered. *I have a mate? And he's here?*

A mighty roar flattened the grass.

"WHERE IS SHE?"

Wolves knelt and bared their necks until only a tall, broad-shouldered man stood silhouetted against the noon sun. Even with the distance between us, I felt the power of the moon radiating off of him and realized he had to be part of the royal pack.

Oh, Moon Goddess, what are you thinking?

Although his long strides ate up the ground quickly, I still had time to study his face, and he was beautiful. Brown hair with blond streaks pulled back into a messy bun. Well-groomed beard that was neither too long nor too short. High cheekbones, straight nose, dark arching brows, and soft pink lips.

Then I met his eyes, pure sky blue ringed with darker blue, and the whole world faded to white noise.

When he reached me, he dropped to his knees and held out one fist. I sniffed it cautiously, then licked his knuckles. A smile lit up his face and eyes.

"My beautiful wolf," he murmured. "You *are* Lilah, right?"

I nodded, wondering how he knew that.

"I was at the five alphas' house when I smelled the same lovely almond perfume I smell now," he explained.

I moved a little, trying to find a better position, and let out an involuntary whimper when fire tore through my ribs.

"You're injured?"

His voice rose, and he looked at me, really *looked* at me, and saw the blood and broken bones. His eyes glinting with wolf-light, fury scored his face before he composed himself and stroked my head.

"Lilah, my darling mate, I'm so sorry I didn't get here quicker. May I carry you to a safer place where we can get you some help?"

What's the worst that could happen? I asked myself. *He drops me?*

I was already prepared for him to reject me as soon as I shifted back. Whoever my mate was, he was powerful enough to make all the wolves in the field, including Posy's alphas, submit to him. He had to be very high-ranking in the royal pack; I would have said beta if Luke hadn't told me the new one was a female.

Gamma, maybe?

Regardless, such a dominant wolf would never want a misfit like me for his mate. As hard as it was to accept, I was realistic about it. If he had been a simple, normal wolf, I might have held out some hope, but this gorgeous man would only be embarrassed every time we went out in public together.

And what would the king think to see one of the wolves in his service with a girl like me?

The Moon Goddess likes a laugh, I guess, I thought with unusual acid.

Tears stung my eyes. To have my mate so close and acting so kind was torture when I knew what was coming.

"Lilah?"

Remembering his question, I nodded, and he slid his arms under me. Unfortunately, he jostled too many broken bones, and I couldn't hold out against the agony any longer.

With a nearly soundless whine, I flopped bonelessly into darkness.

20: Aftermath

Cole

Sliding into the parking lot sideways, Ash slammed the SUV into park, jostling Quartz and Topaz around in the cargo area. As soon as Mase and Wyatt threw open the doors, we leapt out and found our five betas holding the line against twenty or so wolves who were trying to get into the diner.

Gisela and Luke's wolves streaked past us, and Ranger ran with them, nearly as fast on two legs as they were on four. The trio zipped around the side of the building, and I wondered what they knew that we didn't.

Meanwhile, Quartz dove into the fray with a thunderous growl that caused three of the Tall Pines wolves to instantly submit and drop to their bellies. He tore out their throats without a second's hesitation.

The king will want prisoners, Topaz tried to remind him, but there was no reasoning with him now.

We went out through the kitchen, Peri called through the link. *Heading for the treeline!*

What? No, no, no! Go back inside! I screamed. *We're here now.*

Too late, big bro. We're halfway across the f—

Her thoughts cut off, and I hardly needed to hear the king's shout to know what had happened.

"More enemies coming in from the west!"

"The girls are in the field out back!" Crew yelled as he fought off two wolves.

"Topaz, with me," King Julian ordered and took off.

I followed him without question, knowing Quartz alone could finish the wolves attacking the betas.

As we rounded the corner of the building, I saw Ranger had a group of about six wolves on their bellies in submission. Three dozen other wolves - our border patrol and the Tall Pines wolves - were locked in combat. The battle centered around a bloody, light-colored wolf who lay on her side and panted. I would have guessed she was an alpha based on her size alone. Luke's wolf, whose name I still didn't know, killed wolf after wolf in a widening circle around her.

The king was following his nose and headed in the direction of his mate, and I looked around for mine. About thirty feet away, Gisela's wolf stood over a lump half-hidden in the tall grass.

Posy!

Topaz shot off like a low-flying bullet and we were by her side in seconds. Gisela's wolf moved back a step, and Topaz dipped his head in thanks. After he sniffed our girl all over, he found a thin trickle of blood from a goose egg on her forehead, which told the story of what happened clearly enough.

Lark is asleep, too, he told me.

Ash, Wyatt, Mase! I linked my brothers. *Any of you still have hands, or did you all shift?*

We didn't shift, Ash replied. *Mase is trying to rein Quartz back in before he kills them all.*

Leave him and come here now! Posy's unconscious and needs to be carried.

Unconscious?! he screeched. *What happened?*

She's hurt? How bad is it? Wyatt demanded.

Wyatt, Ash, go. I've got this.

Mase's even tone didn't waver. He could have been discussing the weather. I knew better, though. The calmer, quieter he got, the more emotional he was. The younger two were only now starting to pick up on the fact that he wasn't the iceman that he showed the world.

Posy knows, Topaz murmured as he licked the blood from her forehead. *She made sure Ash and Wyatt understand now, too.*

Good.

He carefully lowered himself down on our mate, covering her tiny body completely from view. Gisela's wolf stood guard beside us, her ears pricked up and her eyes constantly scanning.

My brothers barreled over, and Topaz stood up when they reached us. He watched closely as they dropped to their knees and checked her with gentle hands.

"Looks like she hit her head," Ash muttered. "Let's get her back to the house."

Wyatt had her up in his arms before Ash could finish speaking.

"Hey! I wanted to carry her!" Ash pouted.

Topaz met Gisela's wolf's gaze, and they both rolled their eyes.

Suddenly, royal alpha power blasted across the field, sending us all to our knees. Wyatt managed to hold onto Posy as he dropped, thank the Goddess.

"WHERE IS SHE?" King Julian thundered.

After a few seconds, we were all freed to move again, and I figured he'd found Lilah. With a nod, Gisela's wolf took off in the king's direction, and I joined Ash and Wyatt. We hustled around to the vehicles, where Mase and the betas struggled to corral a snarling Quartz.

"Get her home!" Mase shouted.

We piled into the SUV, and Ash asked Wyatt how Posy was as he pulled out of the parking lot.

"Physically? Lark's already healing her. Mentally? She's shivering in her sleep, dude, and I know it's not from her injury."

"She's strong." Ash sounded like he was reminding himself of that.

True, Topaz nodded, *but even the strongest can falter.*

"Then we'll be her strength until she can be strong again," Ash told him.

Yes, I agreed. *Whatever she needs, that is what we will provide.*

#

Two hours later, I laid on the couch with Posy on my chest. Every twenty minutes or so, she whimpered in her sleep. I stroked her back and murmured sweet words until she quieted again.

I really had to pee by now and was considering linking Ash to come home just to hold her while I went to the bathroom. Before I got that desperate, though, she woke with a sharp gasp and a little jump.

"You're okay, baby," I said in a soft voice. "You're safe. I've got you."

She gripped my shirt in tight fists and sighed.

"Want some water?"

She shook her head.

"Do you hurt anywhere?"

She shook her head again, and worry bit at me. Her silence was a warning sign that Mase and Jay had picked up on and pointed out to the rest of us oblivious cavemen.

"Do you feel better now?" I tried again. "Did the nap help?"

She nodded.

"Talk to me, honey," I begged the only person I would *ever* beg.

"What happened?" she whispered. "I remember I was with Lilah and she was running and then … nothing."

I fought against the rage rising inside my chest as I thought of how close we'd come to losing her.

"A Tall Pines wolf tackled Lilah and you flew off her back. We're pretty sure you hit your head on a rock or something." I picked up her hand and touched her fingers to the fading remains of the bruise. "Is it still tender?"

"Only a tiny bit," she admitted. "What happened to everyone else? Peri and Lilah? The twins? The betas? Are they okay?"

"They are. I'll tell you everything, but give me a second, okay? I'll be right back, I promise."

"Oh. Sure."

135

She started to sit up, and I scooped her into my arms, stood, then deposited her back on the couch. Dropping a quick kiss on her cheek, I straightened up, then ran for the bathroom.

When I came back a few minutes later, I found her right where I left her, an adorable pout of confusion on her face.

"Sorry, baby. I had to pee." I chuckled when her face burned red. "Everyone is fine or going to be."

I lifted her up and got us back in the same position, wiggling a bit until I was comfortably sprawled out with our mate on top of me again.

"The betas are on watch outside along the house perimeter," I explained as she nuzzled her face in my throat. "Peri's pissed that her plan didn't work, but she and the twins weren't injured."

"Did they all go home?"

"Our gammas took Peri and the twins to our parents' place. They're going to stay with them for a while." I kissed the top of our girl's head. "Things are going to get a little crazy here once Lilah wakes up and the king returns."

"How is Lilah? She was in so much pain before the fight," Posy sounded like she was on the brink of tears.

"She has some broken bones and gashes." I couldn't lie to her. "She's asleep upstairs in a guest room with her brother and the king's beta standing guard over her."

"What? Why?" Her perfect brows scrunched up. "I mean, our betas are all around the house and you are here, too. Do you think Tall Pines will be back?"

"No, honey. She's the king's mate. He's going to use his best guards to watch over her when he can't be with her himself."

Posy lifted her head and stared at me with shock all over her face. I grinned.

"She was in wolf form when he found her. Still is, as a matter of fact. Plus, Luke's fairly certain that she has no idea who her mate is. It's going to be interesting when they meet face to face, so to speak."

"He won't reject her, will he?" Her little hands fisted up in my shirt.

"Are you kidding?" I smirked. "He adores her already. That little she-wolf has no idea how cherished she's about to be."

"You're sure? She's my friend, and she's been hurt enough."

"I'm sure, baby."

She laid her head back down, and I rubbed circles between her shoulder blades.

"Where are the rest of the guys?" she asked.

"Mase is helping the king and Ranger interrogate the Tall Pines prisoners."

"Who's Ranger?" she interrupted.

"The king's younger brother. You'll meet him and King Julian later. Anyway, Wyatt is out with a patrol unit to make sure we didn't miss any intruders and Ash is supervising the cleanup at the diner." I shook my head. "Thank the Goddess that wolves own it. As soon as you told the betas you wanted to eat there, they linked Roger and had him clear the place out for you. At least we don't have to worry about a cover up for the humans."

When I didn't say anything else, she asked what I knew she would.

"And Jayden?"

"He let Quartz out when we learned you were in danger. After the fight, Quartz, um, well, he went a little crazy. He's in an isolation cell until he calms down a bit."

Tears welled up in her big blue eyes, stabbing me straight in the heart.

"Shh. He'll be fine, honey. It happens. When he goes on a rampage, it takes a while for Jay to regain control. Don't worry too much. He isn't hurt, and he's somewhere safe."

She nodded, but I knew she wouldn't be happy until she saw him. Words of reassurance were all I could offer her, however. Jay would never forgive me if I took her to him right now. Although he realized that it was bound to happen at some point, he wanted to delay her seeing him at his worst for as long as he could.

And I don't blame him for that.

"Can I see Lilah now?" Posy asked.

"Of course. You can meet Luke's mate, too. Her name is Gisela, and she's the king's new beta."

"Wow. I was hoping it would be Peri, although Lilah thinks Peri's mate will be Tyler."

"Oh, Goddess," I groaned. "Don't talk about that stuff around me! I don't want to think about my little sister being *anyone's* mate! Eww!"

The last of my worry melted away as her giggles rang out like silver bells.

She's awake, I linked my brothers, *and she's going to be fine.*

How do you know? Wyatt demanded.

How can you be sure? Ash asked.

What's happening? Mase wanted to know.

I showed them what I was seeing and felt them relax all at once.

Thank the Goddess for that, Jay sighed.

I leaned down and kissed her sweet dimples before carrying her upstairs to see her friend.

21: Kinds of Strength

Posy

At the top of the stairs, I saw Luke standing on one side of the door to the guest bedroom and a pretty brunette with watchful dark eyes on the other.

"Posy," Luke stepped forward, "I'd like you to meet my mate and the king's beta, Gisela Bauer. Ela, this is Luna Posy Briggs."

"It's a pleasure to meet you, Beta."

I studied her as I held out my hand. She was tall, lean, and muscular without being bulky. Her clothing was simple and loose, the kind that most warriors favored for easy shifting. She wore no makeup or jewelry, but her fingernails were manicured and painted black.

She built for war, Lark murmured. *Same with her wolf, Hawk.*

Good thing she's the king's beta, then. She'll be a great guard for Lilah.

"Luna." She shook my hand with a curt nod. "It's an honor."

"I look forward to getting to know you better," I said. "For now, I'd like to check on Lilah."

"I think she's still asleep," Luke said, "but, yeah, let's check on her."

I opened the door and saw that Lilah had shifted back to human. She was curled up in a ball on top of the covers, shivering and naked except for the rainbow of bruises everywhere.

I stopped Luke when he tried to follow me in.

"What?" He looked down at me.

"She shifted. Beta Gisela, could you please help me dress her?"

"Of course, luna. And just Gisela is fine."

"Thank you. And call me Posy." I smiled as she came into the room and closed the door after her. "There is no need for titles among friends."

"Thank you." She smiled back.

I looked around and saw someone had grabbed Lilah's clothing and shoes from the bathroom at the diner. The outfit wouldn't be very comfortable with her injuries, though. After a minute's thought, I stuck my head out the door and found Cole chatting with Luke.

"What do you need, honey?" Cole asked.

"Do you know where the bags are from our shopping trip today? We bought Lilah some pajamas that will be better for her right now," I explained.

"They should all be in there. Try the closet. I think that's where Peri said she and the twins put them. If not, let me know and I'll link her."

I looked over my shoulder at Gisela. She nodded and opened the closet door, then gave me a thumbs up.

"Found them," I turned back to Cole and smiled up at him. "Why don't you and Luke take a break? Get a snack and check in with the others or something? Gisela and I got this."

Luke looked conflicted for a second, but Cole grabbed his shoulder and pulled him along.

"We're only going downstairs, buddy. And the *king's* beta is with her. You couldn't ask for a better guard."

"All right," Luke agreed, clearly reluctant to leave.

Cole looked at me and rolled his eyes, and I smiled back.

Closing the door, I turned back to find Gisela had pulled out a t-shirt nightie and pair of undies.

"We don't need to torture her with a bra, right?" she asked.

"Goddess, no."

As we approached the bed, my stomach turned to see the extent of her injuries. From the bruises and broken bones at her alpha's hands to the tears in her skin from his wolves' attack today, her body was a wreck.

"Why isn't her wolf healing her?" Gisela frowned.

"She's asleep. Exhausted. Healing daily beatings takes it out of a wolf." *I should know.* "At least the bleeding has stopped. Do you think we should try to clean some of these wounds? And I don't even know what to do about her ribs. They were broken *before* that wolf tackled us in the field."

"I think sleep is the best thing for her right now. When she wakes up, we can help her treat her injuries."

I nodded in agreement, and we gently wrestled Lilah into the soft clothing. She grimaced a few times, but never woke up.

"I hope the king is quick to punish Alpha Halder," I muttered at one point.

"The king is going to *kill* Alpha Halder." Gisela assured me. "Most likely over a long period of time and in the most painful way possible. That is, if my mate doesn't beat him to it."

Can't wait to see Lilah face when she find out she the king's mate, Lark huffed with amusement. *Luke probably loving this. Lilah for sure going to be safe and happy forever now, and he never have to be apart from her.*

I hadn't thought of that.

I also hadn't thought much about Luke's situation in general.

"I should have bought him some clothes and undies and shoes, too, today," I chided myself aloud. "He probably wanted to look good for you."

"Luke? Nah, he's a simple guy. Your mates gave him some things, and Alpha Cole wears the same size shoes, so he's good to go. I'm sure he'd appreciate the thought and your kindness, but he doesn't need much to be happy."

Her lips twitched into a confident smirk as we settled Lilah against the pillows and drew the sheet over her.

"Besides," she continued, "that sexy beast could walk around in *anything* and still make me hot and bothered, and he knows it. I can't wait to be alone with him. If he doesn't mark and mate me soon, I think I might jump out of my skin."

I wonder if I'll ever feel so confident about myself with my mates, I thought wistfully. *And how is she ready to mate after just meeting him? I mean, I know shifters move pretty fast, but they literally met hours ago.*

I knew there was a process to being fully mated. It wasn't only meeting and living with each other, although the boys hadn't pressured me to do more than that, and Peri said they wouldn't. There was marking involved, which we'd already talked about, but as far as the mating part, I was clueless and nervous and a little scared.

A little? Lark teased.

All right, I admitted with a scowl. *A lot scared.*

"You only met him a few hours ago. How do you know him so well already?" I asked, when what I *really* wanted to say was, "How do you trust him so much already?"

"Did you not know your mates the moment you met?" Gisela tilted her head to the side and wore a puzzled frown. "Maybe not their favorite colors and brand of boxers, but their essence? Who they are at their core?"

"Well, my father was beating me half to death when they found me, and my wolf was in a coma from a dose of wolfsbane. That was on Monday and— Wow. It seems like a lifetime ago."

I stopped rambling to reflect on that. Today was Friday. So much had happened over the past few days, it was hard to process.

The more I considered her question, though, the more I realized I knew them better than I'd thought.

Wyatt, for example, was a great tease. His favorite thing to do was irritate someone, but never me. He only tried to get me to smile or laugh, although he embarrassed me sometimes by saying wildly inappropriate things. He was the most talkative of the group, which I liked and could listen to him ramble all day. He got along well with everyone, although he clashed with Mason on occasion. I'd learned that this was because he looked up to Mason and desperately wanted his approval.

Mason was as quiet as Wyatt was chatty. As the oldest, he was responsible and serious and kept the others in line. He was methodical and calm and took the time to think before he gave an answer. He never lost his temper, at least not around me, and I rarely heard him raise his voice, yet everyone stepped carefully around him. He was so closed off most of the time that it worried me, but I knew now that it was because of his father and was determined to change that.

Cole had the worst temper of all my mates, but it was counterbalanced by his grumpy bear way of joking. He liked to hassle Wyatt, who ate that up and poked right back. Something I especially liked about Cole was that, when I talked to him, he gave me his complete attention. It was as if there was nothing more important in the world than whatever I was saying.

Ash was cheerful and had boundless and intense energy. He seemed to never stop moving during the day, but needed a solid eight hours of sleep every night. I wondered if that was because his body had to recover from sixteen hours of constant motion. He was sweet and appreciated small things. His enthusiasm was always genuine, too, not fake.

And then there was Jayden. Just being near him made me feel like I was wrapped in a fluffy, warm blanket. Quartz might be the most violent of their wolves, but Jayden was only ever gentle and kind to me. He was sensitive and perceptive and seemed to know what I was thinking before I did. He was everyone's peacemaker and seemed to enjoy the role. Ash and Wyatt were used to going to him for advice and guidance, even though Jayden was only a year older.

So, yes, I guess I do know them, I mused. *And I love each of them more than I've ever loved anyone or anything in my life.*

They feel same way, Posy, Lark murmured. *Your name, your face, in their minds a thousand times a day.*

While I was doing all that thinking, Gisela fetched a brush and carefully combed Lilah's long hair, then put it in a braid. She laid the brush on the nightstand when she was finished and looked at me.

"Luke told me your father was abusive. I'm sorry that happened to you. Are you scared of your mates?"

"Not of them so much as loud noises, yelling, angry voices, their hands moving too fast toward my face." I hung my head. "I'm pathetic."

"No, you're not." She stood up from the bed and hugged me. "You're a trauma survivor. That doesn't go away overnight just because you found your mates."

141

"They keep saying I'm strong, but I'm not. Today, for example, I froze. I couldn't think, couldn't move, couldn't breathe. I was helpless and useless. How could they love a coward like me when they're all so strong?"

Tears spurted from my eyes before I knew I was going to cry.

"Hey, hey." Gisela's arms squeezed me in a tighter hug. "You're *not* a coward. You reacted with a response that was conditioned into you by your father. You can work on changing it if you want to, but no one thinks less of you because of it."

She released me to frame my face in her palms.

"But not everyone is a warrior, either, Posy. That doesn't mean those who aren't are weak. There are other kinds of strength, which is probably what your mates mean."

"What kinds?" I quavered in a watery voice.

"Don't you know how much courage it takes to be kind and gentle? Your father hurt you and isolated you and ruined your teen years. You should be cold and unsociable and mistrustful of everyone, yet here you are," she waved a hand toward Lilah's sleeping form, "worrying and fussing over a girl you've known what? A day or two?"

"I met her last night," I mumbled.

Gisela laughed.

"See what I mean? Now, listen. Your mates love you very much. Anyone can see that. They know you're not perfect. Neither are they. All they want is for you to be happy and feel safe with them. Are you? Do you?"

"Yes and yes. When I feel the sparks from the mate bond, I shiver from how happy and safe I am."

"Is that the *only* reason you shiver?" She raised one eyebrow and smirked again.

Fire infused my cheeks and spread down my neck, and she laughed.

"Is it normal? What my body does around them?" I asked without meeting her eyes.

"What does your body do?"

"I get wet and achy *down there*," I whispered, "and something in my belly pulls taut. I can't breathe right and my breasts feel ... tingly, I guess?"

"Yes, that's all supposed to happen," she said. "Do you all kiss?"

"They've kissed my cheeks and forehead and my neck a couple times. I've kissed their cheeks or chins, depending on how high I can reach." My face was going to be permanently red after this conversation. "They haven't kissed me on the lips yet."

"Hmm. I think they're being very careful and waiting on you to give them a sign that it's okay to move forward with the physical stuff."

"How do I give them a sign?"

"Kiss one of them first," she suggested with a wicked grin.

I don't know if I can do that. My eyes widened. *And how would I pick one of them?*

No pick Wyatt, Lark chuckled. *He rub it in their faces the rest of his life.*

I giggled.

"Don't overthink it." Gisela patted my cheek. "Trust your instincts and go at your own pace. You'll know when it's the right time."

I nodded.

"Thank you for talking about this with me and not making it awkward and embarrassing," I said. "And thanks for helping with Lilah."

"We're going to be great friends, Posy, and it's an honor to serve my queen."

"About the whole queen thing." I twisted my fingers together. "Um, the king won't reject her, right? Lilah tried to save my life, even though she was scared and in a lot of pain. She's brave and kind and deserves to be happy and loved."

"*Reject* her?" Gisela laughed quietly. "He'll have her marked and mated by the end of the day, if he has his way."

I was still hesitant. I didn't want Lilah to be hurt anymore.

"He's a good and honorable man, Posy. You can trust him."

And mates are best friends with him, Lark reminded me. *They not have a friend who is bad or mean.*

That was true. Alpha Julian Hemming may have been a rich and powerful king, but none of those three attributes would have earned my mates' respect and friendship.

"I'm going to go downstairs and see about dinner plans." I smiled at Gisela. "Want me to send your mate back up?"

"That delicious wolf who's all mine?" She wiggled her eyebrows. "Yes, please!"

Giggling, I left the room and headed for the kitchen.

143

22: My Mate is Who?!

Lilah

I woke up with my stomach clenched in hunger.

Opening my eyes, I looked around, but didn't recognize the bedroom I was in. I inhaled and smelled Posy, my brother, an unfamiliar she-wolf, and, faintly, Alpha Cole.

I think I'm back at Posy's house.

Making an effort, I rolled out of bed and opened one of the three white doors to find a bathroom.

Ah. Good.

After taking care of business, which took a while because every movement hurt, I opened the door beside the bathroom and found a closet stuffed with the bags from our shopping trip today.

Two for two.

I pulled out a short-sleeved t-shirt and sweat shorts, panties, a bra, and fuzzy socks with kittens on them. As I was headed for the bathroom, I heard a soft knock on the door and froze until I smelled Posy.

Whew. Not my mate. He's the last *person I want to see me in this condition.*

I went to the door and opened it. She looked up, concern written all over her sweet face.

"Do you need help cleaning your wounds?"

"I don't want to be a bother," I murmured. "I'm sure I can do it."

"It's not a bother," she said with a sunny smile. "And you don't need to be embarrassed. I saw your injuries when I helped change you into that nightie."

I bit my lip and looked away as shame reddened my cheeks.

"Don't do that. I myself have looked just as bad or worse." She grabbed my hand and squeezed it. "I'll tell you about Luke's mate while I help you, okay? I just sent her downstairs because dinner's ready. She's been standing guard at your door since we got back here."

My eyebrows flew up.

"Luke found his mate?"

"Yep!" Posy giggled and pulled me into the bathroom. "She's the king's beta!"

Oh, wow. What are the odds of both of us mating with members of the royal pack?

"What's she like?" I asked as Posy helped me out of my nightie.

"Strong. Confident. In great shape. Looks like she could kick the butt of most warriors in any pack. An Amazon queen."

I grinned. She sounded just right for my brother.

The grin soon turned into a grimace as Posy started to dab alcohol on my open wounds.

"Sorry. I know how bad it hurts, but we need to keep them from becoming infected until your wolf can heal you."

I nodded and clenched my teeth against the pain.

"How are the others? Did Peri and the twins get hurt?"

"They're fine," she assured me. "No injuries. I hit my head and was out for a while. You were hurt the worst."

When she was finally done, I stood braced against the counter and tried to remember how to breathe. She wiped my tears away with a warm, wet washcloth and waited until I'd stopped wheezing to help me put on my clothes.

"Lilah, I want to thank you for your care and protection this afternoon." She looked down. "I panicked and froze, and you took action even though you were the target. You knew what they'd do to you if they caught you, yet you sacrificed your own escape to get me out of there."

She lifted her face and met my eyes with her tear-filled ones.

"I can never repay you for that. I will always count you as a friend and hope you will do the same."

"Of course, little luna." I patted her head, needing some humor to light things up. *And she's so tiny, it's impossible to resist.* "Except for my cousin Junie, I haven't had a girl friend since I was a little kid. I'm honored to be yours."

"Even when your mate takes you back to the royal pack, please stay in touch."

"You know I will." I swallowed, then whispered, "Is he still here?"

"He is." She giggled. "You're going to be so happy. He's very nice and can't wait to meet you!"

"When he sees me..." My voice died.

"He'll only fall harder for you. Be brave, Lilah. He's worth it, I swear."

I knotted my fingers together, and she gave me an understanding look.

"Come down when you're ready."

She patted my shoulder and left, and I took a deep breath. After holding it for several long seconds, I let it out slowly and opened the bedroom door. I walked down the hallway toward the sound of light chatter coming from the living room. As I went down the stairs, I clung to the banister, watching my feet carefully. My socks were comfy, but didn't have grips on the bottoms, and a fall was the last thing I needed.

I reached the bottom step, and the rich scent of coffee surrounded me. Lifting my head, I saw my mate on the other side of the living room. He was talking with my brother, but swiveled suddenly and speared me with his gorgeous blue eyes.

They grew glossy with tears, and defeat filled me.

Am I that much of a disappointment?

"By the moon," he whispered, and his next words gave me hope again. "I could not have imagined a more beautiful mate."

Then his gaze dropped to my throat and arms, and a rage like I'd never seen before darkened his face.

"*WHO?*" His roar shook the whole house. "*Who hurt you?!*"

I bit my lip. I knew I looked bad, but I hadn't expected such an extreme reaction. Shaking in fear, I took a step back - and tiny Posy Briggs darted in front of me.

"You're scaring my friend."

Her voice quavered and her body shook as hard as mine did, but she stood her ground.

Her courage made my heart hurt, and I laid my hand on her shoulder, ready to tell her it was okay, but my mate decided he was through waiting for an answer. He came toward me with fury-filled eyes.

And since Posy still stood in front of me, her alphas had a predictable reaction to an angry, male wolf striding toward their vulnerable mate.

Shreds of clothing flew everywhere as Alpha Jayden shifted into his wolf and crouched in front of Posy, which meant in front of me.

"And we *literally* just got him out of isolation," grumbled Alpha Ash as he, Alpha Wyatt, and Alpha Cole hustled between Quartz and my mate.

"Quartz, I would never harm your mate, but I need to know who harmed *mine*!" My mate's eyes glimmered green with wolf light. "Move out of my way before Onyx sees you as a threat!"

Thank the Goddess that Alpha Mason had the brains to loop an arm around Posy's waist and carry her several long strides away from me.

"Call Quartz over here, baby," I heard him tell her.

"Quartz?" she whispered. "I need you."

In a flash, several hundred pounds of malevolent werewolf bolted over and crouched at her feet.

My mate ignored them all and strode toward me. Gulping, I had to tilt my head back to maintain eye contact. At five foot ten, I wasn't short for a woman, but I was compared to him. He towered over me by six or seven inches.

I didn't have time to process much more than that. He slipped one arm around my shoulders and pulled me against his chest. With his other hand, he tucked my face into his throat. His hold was gentle, but I stayed very still in his embrace since I was unsure of what he'd do while he was so angry.

I struggled not to react as delicate sparks flared up everywhere his skin touched mine. It was the most amazing sensation, and I wanted to feel them *all* over me.

"My love," he said through clenched teeth, "I know those bruises did not come from today. Who hurt you? And why can't your wolf heal you?"

His body was as taut as a piano wire, and his heart beat furiously under my ear. His wolf yowled for Kestrel, making my head throb.

"Could you ask your wolf to calm down, please?" I pleaded softly. "I swear, Kestrel will be so happy to meet him. She's dreamed of this forever, but right now she's exhausted from healing previous injuries."

Before I even finished the words, his wolf settled into silence.

"I'm sorry," I whispered into his shirt.

"No need to be. We are the ones who are sorry. Onyx wants to meet her very much, and he's as concerned for her health as I am for yours."

"I'll be fine. I've had worse."

He growled at that, and I lifted my head to stare into his irate blue eyes.

"I will tell you everything, but can I know your name first? Mine is Lilah MacGregor."

"You don't know who I am?" His eyes widened as a tiny smile pulled up his lips.

"Should— *Should* I know you?" I faltered.

"I'm Julian Hemming."

The name rang a bell. Several bells. Several warning bells.

"Not *Alpha* Julian Hemming?" I gasped. "Not the werewolf king?"

"Only the king of North America."

My mouth dropped open.

Only. Only, he says.

"Should I bow or curtsy, alpha?" I whispered. "Oh! Am I supposed to call you your majesty?"

"Just Julian for you, darling." He grinned down at me. "There will never be formalities between us. You are my queen. My equal. My partner in all things. You are my lovely and precious mate."

"But you're the *king*," I insisted.

"You know something more important than being king?" He continued when I shook my head. "Finally finding my queen. Six years of traveling the world, visiting every tiny village and world capital, and here you are, in the home of my best friends and closest advisors."

With a smile, he moved his arms to my waist and hugged me, and I fought to hold back a scream as my broken ribs protested. I put my hands on his arms and pushed them away with a whimper.

"What is it? Lilah, what's wrong?"

"Ribs," I gasped. "Broken ribs."

"If you will allow me to mark you, Onyx can heal you through the mate bond."

"But that will tie you to me permanently," I felt compelled to point out.

"Uh, I already am?" He said it slowly, like a question, and his eyebrows scrunched up. "Do you have a concussion, too?"

I chuckled, then winced at the pain it caused.

"Probably, but I just want you to be sure that this *mess*," I drew an air circle around my face, "is what you want to wake up with for the rest of your life."

His nostrils flared as a magnificent scowl twisted his face.

"How dare you insult my mate by calling her perfect face a mess!"

I rolled my eyes.

Yep. Rolled my eyes at the *king*. If Kestrel were awake, she would have died of shame.

"*I* am your mate," I told him. "I can insult myself and call my own face a mess if I want to."

"No, you cannot. I forbid it." He put a little alpha bass in his voice, and I shivered as heat pooled in my belly. "Your little nose is perfect. Your pink lips are perfect. This gorgeous red hair is perfect. Your unique eyes are perfect. Every freckle is perfect. In fact, I'm going to kiss each one of them someday very soon."

Well, if that didn't make my heart speed up.

"And now I'm going to mark you. I don't want you to be in pain any longer."

I blinked rapidly.

"What? Right here? In front of everyone?" I squeaked.

"Everyone?" He chuckled. "They all left."

I looked and saw he was right. We were alone in the living room, and I could hear talking from the dining room.

My stomach rumbled on cue, reminding me of why I'd woken up in the first place.

"You're hungry? Okay, I'll make this fast."

"Make what—"

His hands were on my hips and his face was in my throat before I could finish. His lips explored my neck until they found the little spot of sensitivity just above my collar bone. Then his canines sank in with a sharp sting that made me grimace before pleasure exploded through my veins.

"*Julian.*"

"Moan my name like that again when we're alone, darling." His voice was husky and full of promise.

Then his tongue rasped against my new mark, and my brain shut down all unnecessary functions. I knew he was only cleaning up the blood, but each lick was a bolt of lightning shocking my whole body.

"There. Didn't even get a drop on your shirt." He raised his head and smirked. "Nyx, can you feel the bond?"

Yes. His wolf's voice was like the darkness at the bottom of a deep well. *Mate is pretty. So pretty. Pretty, pretty mate.*

"Can you heal her now and flirt later?" Julian grumbled.

Quiet, Jul! **Nyx** *talk to mate now. Where is mate's wolf?*

"Kestrel's asleep," I told him.

"If you heal her, Kestrel might wake up sooner," Julian told him.

In a heartbeat, power - so much power! - crashed into me like an ocean wave, and I staggered. Thankfully, my mate still held my hips and kept me steady.

"Gently, Nyx," Julian scolded him.

The intense power dimmed to soft pinches all over my body. Some injuries hurt more than others, and I whined a little.

"Almost over, darling," Julian whispered in my ear. "You're doing so well."

Only my ribs were left. I gripped his biceps and nodded, and my torso *burned* as Onyx mended the bones. Clenching my teeth, I closed my eyes and knotted my fingers in Julian's sleeves.

"I know, baby. I know. Onyx says seven were broken. You must have been in agony."

Julian dropped a feather-soft kiss on my cheek.

Finally it was over, and I blew out a heavy breath. Straightening, I opened my eyes and smiled up at him.

"Thank you, and you, too, Onyx. This is the first time in months I haven't been in crippling pain."

Onyx snarled as Julian's face darkened.

"Ash said Alpha Leo Halder was hurting you," Julian growled. "Did he do *all* this damage?"

"Well, the bites were from the attack this afternoon."

"But the rest?"

Biting my lip, I nodded.

"And did he ever touch you in an inappropriate way?"

I didn't want to tell him, but I couldn't lie to my mate. I was so ashamed that I hadn't been strong enough to fight him. That I'd been maneuvered into such a position.

I dropped my hands and twisted my fingers together.

"*Did he?*"

I nodded.

He let his hands fall and took a step back, his blue eyes hard and cold.

Oh, no. My lips trembled and tears burned my eyes. *Now he's disgusted!*

"How far did he go, Lilah?"

I shook my head, and a couple of tears slipped out.

"*How far?*"

"Luke stopped him before he got my clothes off," I sobbed. "I'm sorry! I'm so sorry! Please don't hate me!"

"Baby, what do you have to be sorry about? You are the victim here. None of this is your fault. And I could never hate you. I love you already. Yes, I'm angry, but not at you."

His volume rose and his tone deepened. Things began to rattle around us.

"How dare he? How dare he hurt my mate? How dare he touch what's mine?!"

Nyx will kill him, Onyx promised. *Nyx will kill him good and slow.*

I realized I needed to calm them both down before something regrettable happened. Julian's eyes showed how close he was to wolfing out, and I knew - I *knew* - Onyx would take off for Tall Pines as soon as he had full control.

I moved closer and took one of his big fists in both of my hands.

"Julian, I understand what you're feeling, but Alpha Halder will be there tomorrow. And the next day. And the day after that. Right now, I'd like to get to know my mate. And," I smiled up at him, "I'm starving. Can we eat now and plan to kill him later?"

Julian's green-glinted eyes stared at me, although I could tell he wasn't seeing me. I was just about to call his beta, Luke, or Posy's mates for help when my empty stomach came to the rescue again and growled loudly.

Jul! Feed mate!

Onyx's power-laden bellow knocked a clock off the wall and bounced several throw pillows around on the furniture. I fought back a grin, and Julian closed his eyes as he shook his head. When his eyes opened again, they were back to their normal beautiful blue and a tiny smile flirted with his lips.

"I'm sorry, darling," he murmured and covered our joined hands with his free one. "I don't usually lose control like that, yet I've done so twice since I met you. I'm not making a very good impression on my new mate, am I?"

"I wouldn't say that." I trailed my eyes down his body and back up. "I see a lot to be impressed with."

A wide grin spread across his face, and he opened his mouth only for Onyx to cut him off.

Feed mate NOW, Jul.

The werewolf king rolled his eyes at his own wolf, and I giggled.

"Come on, gorgeous. Let's feed you so Nyx can stop his fretting."

23: Getting Comfortable

Posy

As the king shouted at Quartz with wolf-lit eyes, Mason wrapped an arm around my waist, lifted me up, and carried me to the other side of the living room.

"Call Quartz over here, baby," he murmured in my ear and set me on my feet.

I didn't hesitate.

"Quartz? I need you."

He was in front of me in a flash, although he still snarled and had his lips pulled back from his long, sharp teeth.

Ash and Cole must have thought he was going to hurt me because they grabbed his ruff to pull him back. Quartz didn't like that and shook them off, then whirled and tore a long gash in Ash's arm. Horrified, I covered my mouth with my hands as Ash dripped blood everywhere until Sid could heal him.

Quartz snapped and snarled at Cole, trying to drive him and Ash back, and Mason swore under his breath.

"Can you command him like you did at dinner yesterday?" I asked as I kept my eyes on Quartz.

"Not once he's in full control. All we can do now is wrestle him back into his cell and hope no one loses a limb in the process."

"Let me try." I pulled his arm away from my waist.

"What? No! He'll hurt you without meaning to, sweetheart, and Jay will never be able to live with himself."

"He won't hurt me."

I shook my head and went to kneel, but Wyatt stopped me by grabbing my elbow.

"You don't know him. Not this version of Quartz. He's deadly, Posy, and he's not too particular about who he's killing."

"He came when I called him," I disagreed. "He recognizes me as his mate, and he is not the kind of wolf that would ever hurt his mate."

"I'm not risking your life on a romantic sentiment!"

Frowning at him, I tugged my elbow out of his grip, then I went ahead and did what I wanted.

"Quartz?" I murmured and went to my knees. "Will you come to me, please?"

Before I knew it, my face was full of snow-white fur as he laid on top of me. My other mates all leapt forward, ready to save me, but Quartz only rested his head on my shoulder. His chest rumbled with growls, but I ignored that and threaded my fingers through his silky fur.

152

"Shh. It's okay now."

As I petted him, I hummed a song that I remembered my mother humming for me at bedtime. It was one of those old, wordless tunes that was both comforting and relaxing.

The growls quieted, and I nuzzled my face in his throat.

"Everything's okay," I told him. "I know you want to protect me, and I am so grateful that you care about me, but please don't hurt your brothers. It hurts me to see them hurt."

I didn't mean to, he muttered.

"I know." Lifting my head, I rubbed his ears and smiled at him. "I'm not mad at you, I promise. Are you comfortable with returning control to Jayden now?"

Few more minutes. Rub inside my ears.

I laughed a little and complied with his request, then giggled again when he made the canine equivalent of a cat's purr as I massaged his ears.

I'll go upstairs and shift now, my love.

"All right. Then we can eat dinner." I wrapped my arms around his neck and hugged him. "I love you, Quartz."

I love you more.

Right then, Luke, Gisela, and Ranger came in the back door. Ranger looked at Quartz, who was scampering off, then turned toward the living room, where we could hear the king and Onyx getting upset about something.

"What did we miss?" Luke wanted to know as Mason helped me stand up. "Is Lilah okay?"

"She's meeting her mate." I smiled wide enough to show my dimples. "We're giving them some alone time. Where did you guys go?"

"I sent them to supervise the betas handing over the watch to a patrol of our warriors," Mason explained.

"Why is Julian pitching a fit?" Ranger sat down at the table. "I could hear Onyx all the way outside."

"He saw her bruises."

By the time Cole finished summarizing what happened, Lilah and King Julian were walking into the dining room. They held hands and couldn't take their eyes off of each other, and I squealed inside.

My friend was going to be fine.

"Can we eat now?" Ash looked at me with wide, hopeful eyes.

"As soon as Jayden—"

"I'm here." Jayden trotted into the room. "Do you need help bringing it out from the kitchen?"

"If you want to," I smiled shyly.

"We can *all* help," Mason said, eyeballing my other mates. "After all, it wasn't Posy's turn to cook, but she did anyway, *and* after the trauma of what happened at the diner."

"I like to cook." I shrugged a little. "I find it relaxing. And it's nothing fancy."

"It will be delicious, I'm sure," King Julian said graciously as he pulled out a chair for Lilah. "Thank you for preparing it."

Blushing, I ducked into the kitchen with my mates following me. While Lilah slept this afternoon, I'd been restless and thought making dinner would be helpful as well as give me something to settle my nerves. I had to shove Cole out of the house, though, when he fussed over me doing anything. It took a while to convince him, but he'd finally given in and went to see what was taking Ash so long, leaving me in blessed peace.

Now, I handed out oven mitts to Mason, Jayden, and Cole so they could pull the three big pans of lasagna out of the oven.

"Wyatt, please take the trivets and put them on the table so they can set the hot pans on them."

"Sure. Um, what's a trivet?"

I giggled, then pointed to the stack of them I'd found in a drawer earlier. He winked at me before picking them up and doing as I'd asked. The rest of the boys followed him, and I went to the fridge and pulled out the two large bowls of salad I'd put together. Pursing my lips as I debated, I finally decided to grab all five bottles of dressing, since I didn't know what anyone would like.

And since there are five, each of my mates probably likes a different one.

Wyatt came back to the kitchen to see if I needed anything else.

"Could you put one salad bowl at either end of the table? And what about drinks? Should I pour them out here and bring them in?"

"Uh, yeah, I guess. We usually just drink straight from the bottles, but we can be classy tonight." He grinned, then pecked my cheek before leaving with the salads and dressing bottles.

I followed him back into the dining room.

"What does everyone want to drink?" I asked, twisting my fingers as all eyes landed on me.

Almost everyone wanted water, except Ash and Ranger requested sweet tea and Luke wanted to know if we had any apple juice.

That one made me raise my eyebrows. Who drank apple juice with lasagna? Or for dinner?

"He loves apple juice," Lilah said with a laugh.

154

"I'll bear that in mind." Gisela looked up at her mate, then over at me. "I'll come help you, Posy."

"No, you stay here so you can get to know my sister." Luke put a hand on her shoulder, holding her in her chair. "*I'll* help."

So it was Luke who went with me back to the kitchen and fixed the drinks. Good thing, too. The tray was pretty heavy once we had eleven full glasses on it.

"I've got it, luna," he said and picked it up like it weighed nothing.

Finally, we were all seated around the table and digging in. Jayden sat on my one side and Mason on the other, and I watched to see if everyone liked what I'd made before I took a bite.

"This is amazing, Posy!" Jayden held up a big forkful. "I haven't had lasagna this good in a long time."

"Yeah, I'm not a huge fan of Italian, but this is great." Cole smiled at me from across the table.

"That's because you think Italian means *only* spaghetti and lasagna," Jayden retorted.

That made the others laugh before they also offered their compliments, which made my cheeks turn pink. I noticed only Mason, Jayden, Lilah, and I took any of the salad - and Mason and Jayden took such a small amount, it looked like garnish next to their slabs of lasagna.

Carnivores, Lark giggled.

"You're not going to eat any veggies?" I gave Wyatt, Ash, and Cole innocent looks.

"No!" Wyatt scowled. "I don't like them, and you can't make me eat them."

"Oh, really?" I raised an eyebrow and kept my face straight.

"Really."

"I brought out all the dressings because I figured you each had your own favorites." I tilted my head and widened my eyes. "Why else do you have so many different ones and the veggies if you don't eat salads?"

"Mom and Mama stock the fridge every week," Ash explained. "That's why we have it. We usually end up throwing *that* stuff away or giving it to someone."

"We don't eat *salads*." Cole actually shuddered a little at the thought.

Suddenly, that little imp of mischief inside me stirred again.

"But it's healthy for you. Don't you want to be healthy?" I pooched out my bottom lip. "And I went to the trouble to make it for you and everything."

155

I looked at Cole with big eyes, then did the same to Wyatt and Ash.

"Pass us the freaking salad," Ash groaned and banged his head on the table.

Everyone else burst out laughing.

"I'm kidding, Ash." I giggled. "Eat whatever you like."

His face was blank for a second, then he smirked.

"Oh, you're asking for it, cupcake."

"Lilah, I'm glad we'll be able to continue *our* prank war," Luke spoke up suddenly. "Since we'll be going to the same pack and all. I was so worried that we'd be separated after we found our mates."

Lilah's eyes were filled with love as she looked at her older brother, who had one arm draped over the back of Gisela's chair.

"Did you have a role in mind for Luke, King Julian?" Cole asked.

"Well," the king laid his fork down and wiped his mouth with his napkin, "I figure Gisela will act as the kingdom's beta and Luke will act as the pack's beta. A beautiful arrangement, if you ask me."

"Isn't the pack and the kingdom basically the same thing?" Lilah asked.

"For kingdom events, Gisela will act as your guard. For pack events, Luke will."

"That's fine with me. I'm always happy to guard my baby sister." Luke smiled at her, then turned to meet Gisela's gaze. "Especially since it means I'll be on duty with my Ela."

Lilah continued to look confused, and Wyatt took it upon himself to explain what I myself had just realized.

"You'll basically have two beta guards at all times."

"My queen deserves the best, and that's what she will get."

King Julian picked up her hand and kissed the back of it, and Lilah's delicate skin flushed red.

"So, Julian," Ranger interrupted their starstruck staring, "what did you break in the living room? I heard a crash."

"A clock." The king shrugged. "Sorry. I'll replace it or repay the cost."

"I owe them money, too," Lilah said to him, then turned to me, "for all the clothes and things you bought me today. I thought I was using pack funds for emergencies or something. I didn't realize it was the alphas' personal money."

"I can pay for that," Luke offered right as King Julian said, "Start a tab for us and I'll pay it before we leave."

"No." I held up one hand. "It's a gift, Lilah. A small token for our new queen. Please accept this from us."

She hesitated for a second, then nodded.

We chatted for a little longer, lingering over our drinks, and I sighed as I stared at all the dishes piled on the table. I was tired, despite my two-hour "nap" after hitting my head. The last few days had worn me out, and now I had a mountain of dishes to tackle.

"What is it, honey?" Cole's eyebrows drew together. "You seemed sad for a second."

"Just dreading doing the dishes." I summoned a smile. "But the sooner I start, the sooner I'll get done."

"Huh-uh." Mason wrapped an arm around my waist and held me in place when I went to stand up. "You cooked. You don't do the dishes. We'll handle that."

"Yeah, Posy. We have a kitchen routine," Ash explained. "We have a rota of who cooks when and who's on dish duty. Mom and Mama do the grocery shopping from lists we give them, even though they always add other stuff."

"Well, that's going to change," I said and smothered a yawn.

"Oh, really?" Ash threw my words back at me.

I blamed my tiredness for the mini rant I went on next.

"*Really*. I like to cook and I want to do it, although I would still like and appreciate your help sometimes. Also, I'd like to do my own grocery shopping. If one of you doesn't want to come with me, I can take one of the betas. The only thing I do not want any part of is washing the dishes. I mean, like ever. I hate doing the dishes!"

Cole shot to his feet and came around the table toward me with a strange light in his fern-green eyes. A little scared because I didn't know what he intended, I huddled against Mason's side and felt his arm tighten around me.

"He's not going to hurt you," he whispered into my ear and dropped a kiss on my head. "You've made him happy and he wants to hug you."

Relief made me almost boneless as I slumped against him. Then Cole was there. He picked me up and held me like a baby.

"You opened up to us. You were comfortable enough to *complain*."

He shoved his face in my throat, and I felt something wet on my skin.

Oh, my heart.

Lots of other arms suddenly wrapped around both of us as my mates squashed us in a group hug. Their delicious scents surrounded me and sparks danced all over my skin.

"I love you all," I murmured.

"We love you, too, Posy." Cole raised his head and kissed my nose. "So, so much."

Each of my mates kissed me either on the forehead or cheek and told me how much they loved me. My pulse picked up as I felt their hands rub my arms and legs and back.

We their life now, Posy. Lark preened under their attention.

I know, wolfie, and they are ours.

#

Lilah

Julian and I caught each other's eyes as the alphas squished Posy in a group hug, and I knew we were both thinking the same thing.

"Let's go into the living room," I murmured, and Julian pulled out my chair for me.

We made ourselves comfortable on the plush couches, me on Julian's lap and Gisela on Luke's. Ranger sprawled in solitary splendor on the chaise lounge, turned on the television, and found a baseball game. I snuggled in Julian's chest, inhaling his delicious scent, and he tightened his arms around me.

"Happy, sweetheart?" His warm breath in my ear made me all quivery inside.

"Yes. Are you?"

"More than you can imagine."

—lo? Hello? Hello?

"Oh." I sat up straight with a little jolt.

"Lilah? What is it, darling?"

I held up one index finger.

Kestrel?

Tired, Li. So tired.

It's okay. Our mate found us. His wolf, Onyx, is dying to meet you, but they both understand. You can rest, all right? For as long as you need to. They'll take care of us.

Praise the Goddess, she whispered.

KESTREL!

Onyx had heard her.

Mate? she breathed.

Kestrel, he crooned in his deep, dark voice. *Still sleepy, little wolf?*

Uh-huh.

Then sleep. Nyx will keep little wolf safe. Nyx's little wolf. Nyx's pretty little wolf.

Kestrel took him at his word and passed out again, and Onyx continued to chant endearments.

"She's not that little." I rolled my eyes. "She's actually one of the biggest she-wolves I've ever heard of."

"Because she was always meant to be queen. Plus, next to Nyx, she is little. You'll see." He shuffled me a little on his lap. "Sorry he's not more articulate. He's a very primitive wolf."

"He's adorable. I love him already."

"I love *you* already."

He kissed my forehead, the tip of my nose, and finally my lips. Sparks exploded and fizzed through my whole body, and I wrapped my arms around his neck with a soft moan.

He lifted his head, and his surprised expression morphed into one of smug satisfaction.

"Ready to say goodnight to everyone, darling?" he murmured.

I nodded, hypnotized by everything about him. I heard a quiet giggle and a muffled chuckle, but tuned out everything when he leaned down to whisper in my ear.

"If you go with me, I am going to mate you." His deep voice was as seductive as his words, and goosebumps raised all over my skin. "Are you ready for that, Lilah? It's okay if you're not. It just means you'll need to stay here tonight."

Staring into his blue, blue eyes, I saw the stark and undeniable truth: This gorgeous, glorious man wanted *me*. Even better, he was going to *keep* me.

Happiness and love flooded my whole being, and I made my decision. With a tiny smirk, I stretched up and put my lips next to his ear.

"Who am I to deny the king what he desires?"

Four and a half seconds later, we were in a vehicle and speeding into the night. I didn't know where we were going, but I trusted him so much, I didn't really care. As long as we were together, I would travel down any road with him.

24: Leaving Her Mark

Posy

That night, as the boys stripped down to their boxers and t-shirts, I did my routine in the bathroom, changed into my pajamas, and went back to the bedroom.

I found three of my five boys situated as they'd talked about this morning: Ash in the center with Jayden and Mason on either side - and they had asked me to sleep on top of Ash.

I swallowed, not sure I could, but I wanted to try. For them.

"So where do *I* sleep?" Wyatt asked in a pout that made me giggle.

"Jay's had a rough day. I don't think he's up for being your little spoon tonight." Mason patted the space next to him. "Come on over here."

"I don't *spoon* anyone," Wyatt sneered.

"Yes, you do," said the rest of my mates in unison.

"Whatever," he grumbled as he fell into bed with his back against Mason's.

"What's a little spoon?" I asked.

"I'll show you." Cole climbed in, laid on his side, and nestled against Jayden. "See I'm the big spoon and Jay's the little spoon."

"Okay, demonstration over," Jayden grouched. "Off."

Chuckling, Cole released him and plopped on his back, then folded his arms behind his head. The move made his t-shirt ride up, which gave me a glorious view of hard muscles and a line of dark fuzz that trailed into his shorts—

Red flooded my face.

It okay to look at mate's sexy body, Lark laughed.

Stop! I hissed.

"Cole, you know you won't last long like that," Ash told him with a chuckle. "You'll be draped all over Jay before morning."

"I'm sure I'll wake up with Wyatt draped all over me, too," Mason said with a tiny smile, "even though he's pouting right now."

"Will not!" Wyatt barked and elbowed Mason in the ribs. "And I'm not pouting!"

"Will, too," Mason retorted over his shoulder. "You do it every night."

"Hey, it's okay, Wyatt," I intervened, walking over to his side of the bed. "I enjoyed waking up that way."

"You did?" His silver-shot blue eyes blinked up at me.

"Yes." I smiled, flashing my dimples. "I liked being wrapped up in your warmth and strength. It made me feel safe."

"Good! I'm glad because you're probably going to be the little spoon *a lot* from now on."

"Give us each a kiss good night, baby, then come here." Ash yawned and his eyelids drooped. "I want to cuddle you for at least a few minutes before I fall asleep."

Nodding, I leaned down and kissed Wyatt's jaw. He reached up and cupped my cheek with one hand, and I nuzzled into it.

"Good night, cutie," he murmured.

"Good night."

Next, I went around to the other side of the bed and dropped a kiss on Cole's scratchy cheek. He gave me a sultry smile with his pretty eyes half-lidded, and my insides coiled tightly.

"Uh, good night, Cole." Flustered, I patted his shoulder, and he chuckled.

"Good night, honey."

Now for the difficult part.

I bit my bottom lip as I considered my options, then decided to crawl over Cole's legs. Getting on the high bed was hard enough for my short self without the added challenge of scaling his wide body. I almost didn't make it, but one of his hands cupped my bum and boosted me up. I didn't think he meant to launch me so hard, but I flew across his legs and landed on Jayden's in an untidy heap.

Really flustered now, I scrambled over to Ash and sat up with his knees between mine. I blew a wisp of hair out of my face, then noticed that all of my mates were staring at me with wide eyes and pink stains on their cheekbones.

Frowning, I opened my mouth to ask what was wrong, but Mason's big body suddenly crouched in front of me and blocked my view. His serious gray eyes met and held mine as his hands reached up and adjusted my shirt, and it was only then I realized that my girls had been on display.

Squeaking, I covered my face with both hands and struggled not to panic. Curse Peri for convincing me to buy a cropped pajama top! I knew I should have worn a bra with it, but what woman in her right mind would willingly sleep in one? Now they'd think I was the whore and slut my father had always called me.

My breathing grew sharper and shorter, and a little sob tore from my throat.

Mason gathered me against his chest, his thick arms winding around my shoulders and tucking my head under his chin.

"Hey, it's all right. Don't be embarrassed. It's just us. Just your mates."

Another hand ran up and down my back, and I peeked out from my fingers to see Jayden's worried eyes.

"It was an accident, I swear!" I choked out. "I wasn't teasing. I *wasn't*!"

"I know that." He blinked twice. "We all know that. Why would you think we'd accuse you of teasing?"

My mind was getting the present tangled up with past nightmares.

"Father. Father said. Father said I was. Always flaunting what he couldn't have. Father said. Slut. Whore. Bad girl. Father said. Bad girls get punished."

I dropped my hands and gripped onto Mason's shirt although my frantic eyes never left Jayden's. I shook my head quickly, my hair flying everywhere.

"Don't punish me, alpha," I begged. "I didn't mean to! I swear!"

"Shh. You're okay." Mason cradled me closer and stroked my hair. "No one will ever punish you again. You're safe here."

"You are none of the things your father said," Jayden told me with tears in his beautiful eyes. "He was sick in the head, sweetness. You're our innocent girl. Our sweet and pure Posy."

"But I *looked*! I *looked* at Cole's body and ... and then ... and then my shirt ..." I couldn't suck enough air in to talk.

"Baby, you need to calm down and breathe," Mason shushed me and rocked me from side to side. "Can you do that for me? Just breathe. In and out. There. Good job, baby."

Cole got to his knees and crawled over to sit beside me. He laid one calloused hand on my thigh and rubbed soothing circles on my skin.

"You can look at me all you want, honey. You can look at any of us all you want at any time you want. It doesn't make you bad or a tease or a slut or a whore. We're your mates."

"That's right, princess." Ash sat up and peered at me around Mason's shoulder. "We're all yours. Forever and only yours. It's your right to look at and touch us whenever you please."

It took several minutes for me to calm down enough to remember where I was and who I was with. Once I did, shame welled up inside me.

"Hey, now, don't do that." Ash tugged me out of Mason's arms and into his, earning a growl that he ignored. "We love you. We're here to help you and support you and take care of you. There is nothing you can do or say to change how we feel about you."

He dropped feather-soft kisses all over my face, then blew a raspberry in my neck, and I giggled.

"Here, Posy."

Wyatt leaned around Mason to hand me a wad of fabric. Taking it, I found it was a t-shirt rich with the smell of vanilla.

"Thank you," I whispered.

"You're welcome."

Ash took it from me and put it over my head, then pulled it down past my hips. Covered by Wyatt's shirt, I wiggled out of my pajama top and flung it to the floor, then slipped my arms through the t-shirt sleeves.

"Mmm." I pulled the collar up to my nose and inhaled deeply. "Now I'll smell you all night, Wyatt."

"Good."

He laid back down, and his silence was starting to alarm me. My chatty boy was never this quiet. Had I offended him? Disgusted him? Made him mad at me?

I looked at my other mates to see what they made of his behavior. Cole was returning to his spot and Ash was fussing with the hem of my shirt, but Jayden and Mason were staring at Wyatt, who had one arm folded across his chest and the other over his eyes. Jayden and Mason looked at each other for a second, then turned to me.

"Don't worry, little flower. He's okay. I promise," Mason whispered in my ear and kissed my neck, raising goosebumps everywhere. "Good night, Posy."

"Good night, Mason."

I wasn't happy that Wyatt seemed off, but I trusted Mason. He knew him better than I did.

"All right, cupcake. I can't keep my eyes open any longer."

Ash laid down and pulled me with him, then bundled me up on his chest. Surprisingly, it was fairly comfortable once I got used to it.

"Good night," I whispered and kissed his collar bone.

"G'night," he slurred and fell asleep almost as soon as his head hit the pillow.

Like a toy that's been switched off, I thought with a smile.

"Good night, sweetness."

Jayden leaned up and kissed my cheek, then laid his head on Ash's shoulder and stared at me.

"Good night," I murmured.

I wanted to stay awake so I could watch him watch me, but it had been a long day, and it caught up to me all at once. Ash's maple syrup and Wyatt's luscious vanilla scents combined to relax and comfort me, and I drifted off listening to the steady heartbeat under my ear.

#

Wyatt

163

I waited until I was sure our girl was asleep, then slipped out of bed. I needed to leave before I exploded. I silently made my way down the stairs and headed for the one place I knew I could find *some* relief from the absolute rage swirling in my chest.

I could have talked with Mase and Jay about it, but Jay was exhausted after reining Quartz in twice today, and I couldn't keep depending on Mase to fix everything all the time. Not after Posy made me and Ash realize how much we took him for granted.

Call Papa or Dad, Granite encouraged me, but I shook my head.

They're busy with the heathens.

Stomping along, I threw open the door to the training room with a grunt. Not stopping to wrap my hands, I went straight to the heavy bag and let everything out. With each punch, I imagined I was killing Alpha Kendall Briggs again and again.

An hour later, my knuckles were busted and bloody. Sweat streaked down my face and body in rivers, and every muscle burned. Exhausted, I dropped my forehead against the bag.

"Done?" Mase asked from somewhere behind me.

I nodded, but didn't turn around.

"What's it about, Wy?"

"Dude. She had a panic attack because she accidentally flashed her tits *to her mates*."

"She's okay now. It will get easier as she grows more comfortable with us and there's some time and distance between the present and her past."

"Yeah, but we can't even touch her!" I banged my head on the bag. "She had a panic attack when I tried to hug her, remember? It's not even about mating, although I want to do that so bad, I hurt. But I want— I want to be able to hold her, just hold her, and it's killing me that I can't."

"Listen, I know it's hard, but all we can do is be there for her. We can't rush her. It'll take a lot of patience on our part, but she's worth it. Or don't you think so?"

"Of course I do!" I snarled. "I don't begrudge her the patience and time it'll take."

"Then are you— Are you disappointed with our mate?"

"Goddess, no, Mase! I love her! I love her down to my bones. I'll give her all the support I can. I'll do anything for Posy."

"Well, what are you struggling with? You haven't lost your temper like this in a long time."

"I. Hate. Him." I clenched my jaw so hard, I was surprised my teeth didn't crack. "I hate him so much for what he did to our girl."

164

An arm suddenly laid across my collar bones and another one wrapped around my head. Mase pulled me away from the heavy bag and back against his chest - and I couldn't hold it together any longer.

Standing in my big brother's arms, I sobbed like a kid who'd lost his stuffy. My rage melted into sorrow for all the things that Posy had lost or been denied by the man who should have loved her.

Mase didn't say a word. He just hugged me and petted my sweat-soaked hair and let me cry.

Finally, my eyes ran dry, and I wiped my snotty nose on his t-shirt.

"Better?" he asked.

"Better." My voice crackled harshly. "Thanks, Mase."

"Anytime, pup."

He gave me a noogie, and I shoved him away with a scowl.

"Now how about a shower?" he asked. "I'll go grab some fresh clothes for you and a new shirt for me and be back in a minute."

"Okay. Kiss Posy's cheek for me." An image filled my mind and I smiled. "They're perfect, though, aren't they?"

"What are?"

"Posy's pretty nipples."

"You douche!" He scowled at me. "I didn't need a second boner tonight."

Glancing at the growing tent in his boxers, I burst out laughing.

"Looks like you're taking a shower, too, bro." I smirked at him. "A cold one."

#

Posy

I woke up the next morning with something hard poking my thigh, and I pushed myself up on my elbow to investigate. I slid my hand down Ash's abdomen and under the sheet to see what had ended up in bed with us, but Ash caught my wrist and drew my hand up to his chest.

"Sorry, princess," Ash muttered.

"What is that?" I whispered, aware the others were still sleeping.

"Um, so my brothers will probably want to be part of this discussion, so let's postpone it for now."

I was confused.

"Did I— Did I do something wrong?"

"No, baby." He grinned at me. "You're too perfect, that's all. Listen, don't worry about it. Like I said, we'll talk about it later. Trust me, all right?"

165

"Okay." My brain woke up and had questions. "Are you always the first one awake?"

"Almost always, just like Wyatt is usually the last one. You're an early riser, too?"

"It became a habit over the years," I murmured.

I didn't want to go into details about how Father forcibly woke me up before dawn most days. Ash was perceptive, though.

"He made you, didn't he? And I bet he didn't do it in a nice, fatherly way, either." A frown darkened his face. "What did he do to you?"

"Let's not talk about it. It's in the past. I just want to forget it."

"Remember we talked about triggers? I don't want to do anything to trigger you, and I know my brothers feel the same way. It hurts us when we see you panic like last night."

"I'm sorry! I didn't—"

"No, Posy, no one is mad. No one is upset with you. You're not in trouble. We just want to help. If you're not comfortable telling us, that's okay, too."

"I don't think any of you would ever do the things he did," I hedged.

"At least give us some idea of how *not* to wake you up," Jayden said, startling me.

I hadn't realized he was awake.

"I'm sorry. Did we wake you?"

"No, I've been up for a bit." He reached over and stroked his index finger down my cheek. "Good morning. Now, tell us. How should we not wake you up?"

"Don't throw ice-cold water on me." I hid my face in Ash's neck. "Or boiling hot water."

Ash's whole body stiffened, and Jayden muttered something under his breath that I couldn't quite hear.

"You're right." Ash sounded like he was talking through gritted teeth. "We would never do either of those even by accident, so I think we're safe there."

Needing a change of topic, I sat up on Ash's stomach and looked at each of my mates. Cole had rolled on his side at some point in the night and now has his arm wrapped around Jayden's waist. Ash and Jayden's messy bed-heads were clunked together. Mason lay flat on his back with one elbow laying on Ash's abdomen and his other arm wrapped around Wyatt's head where it rested on his shoulder.

They look so cute, like a pile of puppies!

I giggled.

"What is it, pretty girl?" Ash smiled at me.

I shook my head, wanting to keep the precious image to myself.

"So I thought about marking you," I said instead, "and decided I would like to do that. I'm anxious, though, because I don't know what I'm doing. What if I hurt you? Or do it wrong?"

"You won't do either," Jayden said. "All you do is give Lark the reins and she'll take it from there."

"So your wolves will do the same when it's my turn to be marked?"

"Yep."

"Does it hurt?"

"Mom and Mama said it does a little at first," Ash said, "but then it turns to pleasure."

"Okay." I nodded. "Let's wake the others and do this."

"What? Right now?" Ash squeaked as Jayden's jaw dropped.

"Why not?" I shrugged.

Ash and Jayden looked at each other, then turned back to me with matching grins. Taking that as a sign of approval, I reached over and shook Mason's shoulder, which woke Wyatt, who grumbled a bit and tried to roll over and go back to sleep. As soon as I explained what I wanted to do, though, he woke up quickly. I turned to Cole and saw Jayden had woken him up.

Lark, are you ready to do this?

Yes! Who I start with?

Thinking for a second, I decided to go with who was closest.

"Ash, do you mind sitting up?" I asked with a shy smile.

"Not at all."

He scooched me down to sit on his thighs, then sat up with his hands on my waist. Giving me a grin, he bared his neck to me.

"Ready when you are, cupcake."

Swallowing hard, I braced my hands on his shoulders and let Lark take the lead. She lowered my lips to his throat, and his sweet scent engulfed me, so rich that it made me a little dizzy. Lark kissed around a bit until she found a spot that made his body shudder under us.

There! she crowed and dropped my canines.

Ash grunted when they sank into his skin, then his whole body relaxed and a little moan vibrated through his chest. Lark hummed happily as she pulled back and licked up the tiny trickle of blood.

A little jolt of energy hit my stomach, startling me, until Lark explained it was a normal effect of marking our mates.

"Wow." Ash's dark brown eyes glittered, his pupils blown wide, and his hands tightened on my waist. "If other males knew what that felt like, they'd beg their mates to mark them. Thank you, Posy. I'm honored by this."

I giggled, then leaned back and examined the mark. To a human, it would look like a tattoo of a full moon with a star off to the side. Only another shifter would see it as a mate mark.

"Why is there a star?" I asked as I turned to Mason.

"I have an idea that four more stars will appear, one when you mark each of us."

I nodded. That made sense.

Now that I had confidence, I reached over and grabbed his shoulders.

"I'm next?" His eyebrows flew up.

Giggling, I buried my face in his throat and let Lark do her thing. He had a similar reaction to Ash, which made me smile, and more energy flooded my belly. After Lark cleaned up the blood, I looked at his mark and saw two stars.

"Thank you, little flower." Mason framed my face in his palms and kissed the tip of my nose. "This means the world to me."

I kissed his nose, too, then turned to Ash.

"Is there another star?"

"I don't know. Look at it and see."

Yep! There were now two stars around the moon. Bouncing excitedly, I clapped my hands. Ash groaned deep in his throat and shifted me off his lap and into Jayden's.

"Ash?"

"Jay's turn, right?" He smiled, but it looked a little strained.

Before I could ask if I'd done something wrong, Jayden put a finger under my chin and turned me to face him. His dragon eyes glimmered.

"He's fine, Posy. Will you please mark me now?"

With pink cheeks, I nodded and repeated the process with him. Energy licked up and down my breastbone, flickering like a flame and tickling a little. He slid a hand into my hair and held my head in place for a second after Lark finished, then let me up to see the finished mark of three stars.

I double-checked Ash and Mason's marks and found stars had been added to theirs as well.

Looks like Mason was right!

"Sweetness, thank you for marking me. I will cherish this moment forever."

Oh, my heart.

To hide my red face, I lunged at Cole and landed on his chest. He caught me in his arms and chuckled.

"Hey, honey."

In my excitement, I grabbed his jaw and twisted his head to the side. His continuous chuckles bounced me up and down, but I didn't

168

care. Lark bit down, and Cole's chuckles turned into a rumbly groan. Even more energy shot through my arms, down my hands, and into my fingers. I checked his mark when Lark finished and, sure enough, four stars sparkled around the moon.

"Thank you, honey. To echo my brothers, this is an honor that I'll treasure."

Then he ruined his sincerity by tickling my ribs. With a squeal, I rolled over him, giggling when he groaned again. I hopped down from the bed, raced around to the other side, and jumped onto a sleepy-eyed Wyatt.

Well, *tried* to jump. He had to grab me before I could slide back off the edge.

Once he had an arm looped around my waist, he drew me into the curve of his body. Lying on our sides, we faced each other and his lazy grin made my heart flutter.

"Saved the best for last, huh?" he teased.

"Yep! My fifth star." I looked at him more closely and frowned. "You look tired, Wyatt. Did you have a bad night?"

"It's all good, cutie. Might go back to sleep for a bit, though. You okay with that?"

"Of course." I leaned in and kissed his chin. "Sorry for waking you so early."

"Don't apologize. I'd miss any amount of sleep if it means you'll mark me."

"You're so sweet." I giggled. "Ready?"

"Yep. Do me, baby."

Ash made a strangling sound, Cole threatened to smack him upside the head if he didn't stop, and Mason elbowed him hard in the ribs.

"Behave!" he commanded.

Wyatt rolled his eyes, but didn't respond to any of them, which was mature for him. I didn't know what I'd missed, but shrugged and let it go.

Granite say it a dirty thought. Lark giggled. *Wyatt naughty!*

Then she took charge. She nestled my face in the crook of Wyatt's neck and almost immediately found the spot that made him quiver. My canines dug deep for the final time, Lark lapped up the blood, and a last burst of energy zipped down my legs all the way to my toes.

Just to be sure, I checked his mark and saw five stars.

"I did it!" I beamed as I met his eyes.

"Yeah, baby, you did." He trailed his fingers up and down my spine, making me tremble. "Thank you so much for marking me. I'm yours forever, and that makes me so happy."

"I'm glad you're happy." I grinned at him. "I am, too."

"How do you feel?"

"Amazing! I'm so full of energy, I could burst! Let's do something fun and exciting today!"

"I got you, Posy." Ash piled on top of Mason and Wyatt to stare down at me. Ignoring their irritated protests, he said, "I have the perfect plan. Go grab your shower. You're going to love this!"

"Okay!" I stretched up and kissed his chin. "Thank you!"

Giving Wyatt a quick hug, I scooted off the bed and grabbed a handful of clothes from my dresser. Halfway to the bathroom, I had to stop and do a little shimmy. All the excitement bubbling up inside me had made me hyper.

Pausing at the door, I glanced back at my mates to see five pairs of eyes fixed on me. For some reason, they all had moved their pillows to their laps, and I tilted my head in confusion.

"Go ahead, sweetness," Jayden encouraged me.

Boys, I thought with a roll of my eyes and closed the door behind me.

25: Ticklish Matters

Posy

"So what are we doing today, Ash?"

I looked up at him as Jayden cleared our breakfast dishes from the table. I was slopping over with energy and excitement and hoped he had a good plan to wear some of it off or I was going to go stir-crazy.

"Lark said you haven't shifted in a long time, so I thought we could all go for a run."

"In the woods?" My eyes widened with delight.

"Yep!"

With a happy squeal, I clapped my hands and wiggled in my chair.

"How long has it been since you let Lark out?" Wyatt asked.

"I don't know. Maybe ten months? Either she or I were always too weak."

"Almost a year?!"

"Even then, it was only in my room. She hasn't run in the woods since shortly after my mother died and my brothers snuck me out while Father was at a meeting in another pack."

Cole slammed a hand on the table, which made me jump and clamp a hand onto Wyatt's thigh.

"If your idiot brothers had done something sooner, you wouldn't have had to suffer for so long!" he barked, his eyes hard and sharp.

Taken aback by his outburst, I huddled into Wyatt's side, and he put an arm around my shoulders.

"Not so loud, Cole," Wyatt scolded him, but Cole ignored him.

"Those morons should have asked the king for help sooner, but no, they wanted to be hot shots and fix it themselves. Their ego and ambition blinded them and you suffered because of it."

"They— Father— A wolf must obey the alpha." I managed to string together a sentence, although it came out as a whisper.

"They had options," he spat out. "They chose force. It didn't work the first time they tried it, so what did they do? Tried it again!"

As Cole's anger grew, so did his volume. Trembling, I pressed harder against Wyatt and fought back the fear.

"Calm down, dude." Ash's dark eyes flicked from Cole to me and back.

"And what did those bright boys do next? They waited!" Cole was not calming down. "They knew what your father was doing and they chose to leave you there with him until your birthday, after which

171

they were going to try to use force again! All they had to do was ask for help, which they ended up doing anyway!"

A fierce growl echoed around the dining room, and I clung to Wyatt as I shook.

"Cole." Mason loaded his voice with alpha power. "You're scaring our girl."

Cole came out of the haze his anger had created and looked at me with wide eyes.

"Oh, baby, I'm sorry. I shouldn't have taken that tone or raised my voice." He came around the table and hunkered down next to me. "I'm not mad at you, honey. I'm so sorry I lost my temper and scared you."

Swallowing hard, I looked up at Wyatt. He gave me a half-smile, then nudged my nose with his. Feeling his strong arm around me, I knew I was safe with him beside me. He'd never let anything happen to me. And I knew Cole wasn't a threat. He wouldn't hurt me, not ever. I was reacting the way my father had trained me to react to loud voices and anger.

Gisela had told me I could work on changing that, and I figured now was as good a time as any to try. I wasn't so scared that I froze or felt the need to run or hide. I was surrounded by my mates in our house, their special scents calming me more than any words could do, and I knew there was no threat of physical harm or violence.

Getting my breathing under control, I loosened my hold on Wyatt and turned to Cole. His eyes shone with regret, and I slowly reached up and laid my palms on his cheeks. I was proud to see my hands had stopped shaking.

"It's okay, Cole. You have a right to your emotions and opinions."

"But not the right to scare you," he muttered as he covered my hands with his.

"I'm not scared anymore." I smiled. "Don't feel bad."

His eyes closed for a second, then popped open.

"I worry that your kindness and naivety and soft heart will get you into trouble someday. You forgive too easily."

"I don't think anyone can be too kind," I disagreed. Hesitating for a second, I gathered my courage and asked, "Did you really mean what you said? You think my brothers could have done something differently?"

"I do. There is always something you can do, even under an alpha's command."

That may be true, but Cole is very powerful. I can't imagine he was ever made to submit like James and Aiden were, I thought with a frown.

172

They should have called the king as soon as James turned eighteen and Father stayed alpha, Lark retorted.

"It's okay if she has a soft heart, Cole," Wyatt said. "She can forgive as she likes, and we'll always be there to help her if something bad comes out of that."

"And," Ash chimed in, "her brothers were young and dumb and scared."

"They're older than you," Cole retorted, "although I agree with dumb and scared."

"Yeah, but I had Jay's parents and, later, yours to guide me. All of us did. Who did James and Aiden Briggs have? An old beta who was as broken and controlled as the rest of the pack?"

"Stop making excuses for them!" Cole barked.

"I'm not making excuses or justifying anything they did. I'm only reminding you of their predicament. You can't know how you would react in a situation until you're experiencing it."

As they went back and forth, I thought about everything - what my brothers had told me, what my mates said now, and what I knew from my own experience. I took my time and tried to look at it from different angles.

Could James and Aiden have done more or asked for help sooner? Maybe. Were they wrong for wanting to solve the issue on their own? Probably. Did I suffer due to their inaction? Definitely.

The longer I thought, the more questions came to my mind, and I didn't have answers for all of them.

Would I ever trust them with my life again? Could I rebuild a relationship with them? Did I want to? And if I did, what would I do if they turned their backs on me a second time?

In the end, I decided that I didn't want to think of my brothers as the cruel bullies my father had forced them to be. I wanted to think of them as my best friends, like they were in the photo they'd given me, the one Wyatt had hung up in my special room.

I could never forget everything that they had said and done under my father's rule. I would most likely always have a little fear of them as well as worry that they'd abandon me again. Even so, I had no room for hate in my heart.

And if that makes me naive or too kind, so be it. I lost years with my brothers. I don't want to lose any more.

Mason's voice brought me out of my thoughts.

"Regardless, they're aware of their mistakes now. They won't make them again."

Something about the way he said that made me suspicious.

"Did you do something?" I asked him. "Before we left Green River, did you do something to my brothers?"

"We had a talk with them. That's all."

I held his gray gaze, but he didn't even blink.

He would never lie to you, sweetheart. It really was just a talk.

Garnet's voice was crystal clear in my head. I'd been able to hear my mates' wolves before I'd marked them this morning, but it was in an underwater sort of way. This was so much better.

Thank you, Garnet.

"All right. I trust you, even without Garnet vouching for you." I gave him a sweet smile that showed my dimples.

"Now that we got that out of the way, let's run!"

Ash leapt to his feet, reached between Wyatt and Cole, and picked me up under my arms like a little kid. Ignoring their protests, he lifted me straight up until we were face to face. Startled by the suddenness as well as how high I was off the ground, I wrapped my arms and legs around him and clung tightly.

"Don't drop me!" I squeaked.

"Of course I won't, princess."

"Aren't I heavy? Father said the reason he didn't feed me was because I was too fat."

His whole body tensed up, and I snuck a peek at his face. Sid flashed in his eyes for a split second before Ash reined him back in.

Why did that make him angry? I wondered.

Because you no supposed to see every rib and bump of you spine! Lark growled. *Father starve you just to torture you!*

"You aren't heavy or fat." Ash's voice turned gruff. "You're actually too light. We'll help you get to a healthy weight, okay?"

"Okay," I whispered to both him and my wolf.

"Besides, even if you were as plump as a little piggy, I'd still want to carry you."

Laughing, I kissed his jaw and laid my head on his shoulder.

With my other mates following, he carried me about two hundred feet off the back porch to the edge of the woods.

"You can undress behind one of these." Ash swiveled to show me three giant trees that stood sentinel by a well-worn path. "The betas will have packs for us to put our clothes in, just in case we need to shift during the run."

"The betas are coming?"

"Yes. They are your guards, after all, and you need to get used to each other."

I twisted my fingers nervously into the back of Ash's shirt, and Jayden looked up at me with concern painted on his face.

"Did one of them do something to make you uncomfortable?" he asked.

"They better not have!" Cole growled. "Did they, Posy?"

"Um, no."

He pulled me off Ash, set me on my feet, and bent almost in half to go eye to eye with me.

"*Did they?*"

"No, Cole. I swear they didn't do anything to me. They took very good care of me." I looked at the ground, then back at him. "But I didn't like how Matthew treated Tyler."

"I gave him a warning." Mason came over and patted me on top of my head. "If he bothers Tyler again, I'll discipline him."

"Good. It made me mad and upset to see. Tyler's so sweet and nice."

"Hey! He's not your mate. *We* are!" Ash plucked me away from Cole, slung a heavy arm around my shoulder, and pulled me tight against him. "Never mind. You don't need to spend any time with them."

Feeling mischievous, I grabbed the hem of his shirt, yanked it up, and blew a raspberry on his belly button. He jerked like I'd tasered him, and I used his distraction to dance out of his long arms. The look on his face cracked me up.

"Ha! That gets you back from last night!" I teased him.

"Oh, cupcake, you asked for it now."

He grinned and looked like he was going to pounce on me, but Wyatt came up behind me, wrapped an arm around my waist, and swung me around in circles.

"Me, too, cutie!" he demanded. "Zerbert me, too!"

"Stop spinning me! If I get dizzy, I'll vomit!"

Abruptly, he set me down, and I turned and jumped on him. Using his surprise to my advantage, I tugged up his shirt and blew a raspberry in the center of his chest. I went to run away, but he grabbed me with one hand and yanked his shirt down over me with the other, trapping me against his hard torso. It was a super tight fit, and I could hear the seams tearing.

"Let me go. We're going to rip your shirt!"

"I got plenty of others, cutie."

Giggling, I put my hands on his chest and tried to push away, but now both of his muscular arms were around me and it became a lost cause. I wasn't getting away until he let me go or unless one of my mates saved me.

Then a different solution popped into my mind.

Granite, can I ask you something without Wyatt knowing?

Of course.

Is he ticklish?

Oh, yes. Very. From his armpits to his waist.

175

A wicked grin spread across my face. I skimmed my hands up either side of his torso, and his skin quivered in their wake.

"You're playing with fire, baby," he whispered in my ear, his voice thick and husky.

"Maybe, but you're the one who's about to get burned," I whispered back.

Then I stuck my fingers into his armpits and wiggled them. He jerked back and tried to catch my hands with his, but he was giggling too hard to be effective. Changing tactics, he pressed his arms against his sides, trapping my wrists.

"Caught you," he laughed.

"Oh, yeah?"

I angled my fingers to attack his ribs, and he doubled over with deep belly laughs. Unfortunately, I was still stuck inside his shirt and the whole left side tore out, dumping me onto the ground.

Giggling, I started to get up when I was gently tackled back to the soft grass. Four pairs of hands joined our tickle fight, and none were on my side. Now fifty fingers wiggled behind my knees, under my arms, on the sides of my neck, and over my ribs.

I laughed so hard, fat tears rolled down my cheeks. Then one of my mates had the terrific idea to zerbert my belly button. Flailing wildly, I screamed and wheezed and laughed harder.

"Looks like we found her panic button," Ash laughed.

"No" giggle "stop" giggle "I'm going" giggle "to pee!" giggle.

Laughing, the boys stopped and dropped down on the grass next to me. As I calmed down, I wiped my face and nose on Wyatt's ripped t-shirt.

"Eew. Boogies!"

"Oh, hush." I swatted his arm. "It was ruined anyway."

"Luna? Are you in need of saving?"

I raised my head to see the five betas in a circle around us with black saddlebags at their feet. Tristan and Tyler grinned down at us, and Emerson stuck out a hand in front of me.

"Let me help you up, little luna bunny," he offered.

I took his hand, and he pulled me to my feet, but he used too much force, and I flew into his stomach. My mates growled, and he swallowed nervously as he made sure I was steady on my feet.

"I apologize, luna bunny. You're so tiny and light. I didn't hurt you, did I?"

"Of course not, Em." I smiled.

"All right, betas. You shift first," Mason told them.

They nodded and disappeared behind the giant trees, and it only took a few minutes before five wolves appeared. Their coats were similar with shades of gray and cream, and they stood at least a foot

176

taller and a hundred pounds heavier than Lark, which made her nervous.

The alphas buckled saddlebags onto each beta's wolf, then looked at me.

"Ready to shift, sweetness?" Jayden grinned and squeezed my hand.

"Um. Well, Lark's a little worried." I shuffled my feet. "She's a runt, you know. She's afraid you won't like her anymore because of how small she is."

"Of course we will," Wyatt and Cole said together.

"Don't even worry about that, Lark," Jayden told her, and Mason smiled gently.

"We love Posy, and look how small *she* is." Ash smirked at me, and I stuck my tongue out at him. "Do that again, princess, and I'll bite it."

For some reason, his promise made me blush and feel quivery inside, so I spun away and went behind one of the massive tree trunks to strip down. Despite her nerves, Lark was so eager to run that she shifted faster than she ever had before.

Wow! I laughed at her.

Run! Run with mates, Posy. In the woods!

I know. Have fun, wolfie.

She stretched her front paws out, then did a full-body shake that started with her nose and ended at the tip of her tail. Then she pranced out to our mates, who stared at her with soft eyes and open mouths.

"You're so cute and small, like a pup!" Ash bounced on his toes. "Now I'm even more in love with you! You're like a stuffed animal. Our little wolf doll!"

Lark ducked her head shyly.

"Okay, we'll shift next." Mason looked at the beta wolves. "You're on guard."

Arroyo, Matthew's wolf, dipped his head, and they surrounded me in a wide circle, not close enough to make me feel threatened, but not too far that I felt exposed.

It only took a minute before my mates returned. When they did, Lark froze. Alphas were always the biggest wolves in a pack, since size went along with power, and my boys were some powerful alphas. The betas looked like pups next to them.

Unfortunately. Lark panicked. She submitted and bared her neck, then tried to make herself as small as possible. Flattening her ears down, she arched her back, tucked her tail between her legs, and whimpered.

At the sound, all the wolves in the clearing dropped to their bellies and whined.

Topaz crawled over, still on his belly, and rubbed his face against hers. That made Lark comfortable enough to relax her defensive crouch. Quartz came over next and did the same, and she lifted her tail and wagged it slowly.

Her other three mates joined in then. I hadn't seen their wolves before, so I was curious to learn which was which. Garnet had pitch black fur, Sid was charcoal gray with light gray cheeks, and Granite's coat was a blend of blond, cream, and tan.

After they'd all rubbed Lark's face with theirs, she bounced around happily and started yipping like a pup. Her mates finally stood up and began to yip and wag their tails, too.

I only hoped they weren't laughing at us.

They not, Lark insisted. *They happy we happy.*

I studied the alphas as they frolicked with her. Something was bothering me, and it took me a few minutes to realize what was wrong: Jayden, not Quartz, was in charge of their wolf form. I knew that, if Jayden had him controlled, it was for a reason. Still, his absence didn't feel right.

Quartz, I called him, *are you going to come out for the run?*

Jayden says no, he grumbled.

Well, you tell him that I said yes!

He says good try, but still no. Now he sounded like he was pouting. *He doesn't trust me while you are surrounded by other males, even if they are your beta guards.*

And what do you *think?* I asked him.

He was silent for a moment, then sighed heavily.

I don't trust me, either.

I held back a chuckle.

Well, we'll just have to cuddle together later.

Really? He perked up.

Yep. Just you and me, okay?

And you'll rub my ears again?

Of course.

Promise?

I promise.

26: Running with Wolves

Jayden

As Lark ran her darling little heart out, the rest of us ambled along and Mase took the opportunity to catch us all up on what they'd discovered while interrogating the Tall Pines prisoners.

Most were hardly more than pups. They'd submitted to Ranger at the diner instantly and hadn't put up any resistance when taken to the cells. After the king broke their alpha's command, they'd told him everything he wanted to know.

Conditions at Tall Pines were every bit as bad as Luke MacGregor had described to me. Alpha Halder controlled most of the pack with threats of harm to individual wolves or their families, and he and his bully boys made a spectacle of killing any who voiced opposition to them. The smart ones fled.

Like Luke and Lilah MacGregor, Wyatt said.

You mean Queen *Lilah now that the king has claimed her*, Ash laughed.

We all snickered, knowing *exactly* what King Julian had been doing last night.

And this morning, Quartz complained with a scowl. *Nyx won't shut up about it. I'm going to beat the crap out of him if he doesn't stop his obnoxious gloating.*

Soon, I soothed him. *We'll mark and mate Posy soon.*

But behind the privacy of my mind shield, I wasn't so confident.

I was keeping a secret from my brothers, one that made me sick with worry, but I couldn't tell them because I knew how they'd react.

We'd been down this road before.

When I was twelve, Quartz took control and killed a wolf who was beating his pup. Afterwards, my brothers and I sat down with our dads and had a hard conversation about what we'd do if I couldn't keep him contained. We'd considered several ideas, including using wolfsbane to drug him and maybe even put him down.

It might sound cruel, but a shifter had to be in control of his or her animal half. Otherwise, they became a danger to themselves and everyone around them, turning into monsters that were all needs and now and no restraint.

After that, I put Quartz on a leash and kept him there with a combination of brute force, mental toughness, sacrifice, and my burgeoning alpha power. Sometimes, I could reason with him, but I never dared to relax. It drained me down to nothing most of the time, but I'd managed to keep the beast in his cage for the last few years.

Then we found Posy.

At that store, when she and Lark had become so upset? Yeah, that wasn't me letting Quartz out. That was him letting *himself* out.

The same thing happened when we heard Lilah call for help through the Moonset link, and then again when the king had moved too fast toward our mate with a face full of fury.

That last incident scared me the most. Quartz had been prepared - no, *willing* - to kill Onyx, a wolf he considered his brother, and he'd broken through my hold as if it were tissue paper.

I wasn't as in control of Quartz as everyone thought I was. I wasn't sure how much longer I could pretend to be, either. Mase especially was going to start noticing things soon.

I knew what was going on. Giving a wolf like Quartz someone to love was dangerous. All his instincts, all his thoughts, turned to one mandate: Protect mate. Above all else and above all others, protect mate.

I understood where he was coming from. I loved Posy with every particle of my soul and would protect her just as fiercely.

Even if it is from my own wolf.

Sighing, I went over my options again.

One, I could continue to pretend all was well and hope he didn't kill anyone he shouldn't.

Two, I could drug him with wolfsbane, although the others would notice immediately.

Three, I could inform my brothers and hope they didn't see him as too much of a threat. I frowned, knowing that wasn't likely.

King Julian's arrival had only added to my worries. He was going to be around for a couple of weeks, and he wasn't easy to fool, even with Lilah to distract him. If he figured it out, he'd execute Quartz, me, or both of us. It didn't matter that we were friends or our wolves soul brothers: Quartz was too dangerous, too brutal, to live if he couldn't be controlled.

And I'd want the king to do it. I'd want someone to put us down before a tragedy occurred.

And better him than my brothers. I couldn't bear to lay that burden on them.

I sighed as my mind circled and whirled.

Why are you so stressed, Jayden? Quartz tore his attention away from Lark to ask. *Is it because I took charge yesterday? You know those Tall Pines wolves deserved to die.*

Not all of them, I reminded him. *Some submitted, and others were barely more than pups forced to attack by their psycho alpha.*

They would have killed our mate if they could. Any who threaten her will meet the same end.

This is why I can't trust you, I grumbled in frustration. *How many times have I told you? Anger clouds the mind. It keeps you from seeing the whole picture. Just look at what happened with King Julian and Onyx.*

He fell silent, and I decided to relax for a bit and simply run with the others.

We hopped over downed trees and ducked under limbs as we loped along at Lark's baby pace. Looking at her, I couldn't help but smile. Her small, pink tongue was hanging out, and I knew she probably wouldn't be able to run half as far as we normally did.

Sid asked if we should go back, but Garnet told him that Lark was too happy and we couldn't take this away from her. We all - wolves and men - agreed.

If the little wolf wants to run, then she will run, Topaz decreed, *even if I have to carry her once she poops out.*

Ash and Sid and Wyatt and Granite giggled at the word poop, and I rolled my eyes at their immaturity.

After I first shifted, I'd been jealous of how the others interacted with their wolves. Mase was so dominant that he easily controlled Garnet from day one. Sid was such an easygoing wolf that he gave Ash no problems. Wyatt and Granite worked as partners, and Cole and Topaz were so alike that they rarely disagreed.

Why *I* had to be the one cursed with a brutal monster was a question I asked a lot as a kid. Then, shortly before he died, my real dad told me something that changed my way of thinking about Quartz.

"You were given this wolf for a reason, son," he'd said. "Mase would have broken him, and Ash and Wyatt would have been broken *by* him. Cole would have given up, put him down, and lived wolfless. The Moon Goddess blessed *you* with Quartz because she saw you were patient and perceptive enough to be trusted with him."

If he were still alive, he'd be so disappointed in me right now.

All right then. Time to think, actually think*, and stop reacting in panic.*

Like Cole had ranted about Posy's brothers earlier, I couldn't keep trying the same approach over and over and expecting a different result.

So, what other approach could I try? He was so hard-headed. If only I could get him to cooperate with me—

Hmm. Cooperate. That would require leverage. A carrot - well, a steak - to dangle as a bribe or reward.

And in an instant, I knew. There was only one thing he wanted, the same thing that had gotten us into this fix to begin with.

As if on cue, Lark tipped her head back and sang out an adorable *a-roo!* that made all of us chuckle, even Matthew. Quartz's heart swelled with affection and admiration for his little wolf - and I knew this was the moment to strike.

Do you want to lose this? I asked him. *Because that's what it will come to. You'll kill someone you shouldn't, then Mase and Cole, our brothers, will be forced to put one or both of us down—*

They can try, he interrupted.

—and be stuck with that grief for the rest of their lives, I continued, ignoring him and his arrogance. *Not to mention what Posy and Lark would feel. Losing either of us would devastate them. Do you want to hurt them that way? Because I don't.*

Crippling pain rippled through both of us at the thought of hurting our mate.

No! he growled. *I will not hurt either of them in any way. Not ever.*

Then I need you to be good, I told him. *That means asking permission to take control and obeying if I say no. I promise that there's always a solid reason why I need to be in charge.*

You will no longer force me into a cage.

He said it like a declaration, although I heard the question in his tone.

No, I won't. We'll work as a team, like Cole and Wyatt do with Topaz and Granite.

Those two pussies could rule their humans if they weren't so childish and silly, he snorted. *Sid, too, but he's too lazy.*

I held back a grin at his tone of superiority.

That may be true, I told him, *but I'm offering you the opportunity to work with me. You will not rule me, nor will I rule you.*

And this will keep our mate safe?

I swear that there is nothing we could do to make her safer.

I didn't try to explain that we needed to still be alive in the future to keep her safe.

He ran next to Lark in silence, checking on her out of the corner of his eye every few minutes. I waited, knowing patience was the best - and only - card I had to play in this hand.

Then I will be good, he said at last. *For our mate, to keep her safe, I will be good for the rest of my life.*

I hid my smirk from him. Blackmail, bribery, and reasoning. That's all it had taken. Of course, only time would tell if I could trust him to keep his word.

Thank you, Quartz.

I'd been so busy in my head, I didn't realize everyone but Lark was looking around with raised ears and alert eyes. It was only when I opened the link to ask if we could swing by the river for a drink that I was bombarded by the boys talking about something feeling off, but not knowing what.

I smell a witch, Tyler called out suddenly.

Shut up, kid, Matthew sneered. *Stop trying to show off. You don't smell anything.*

Matthew's in for it now, Quartz smirked, and I nodded.

Strike one: Matthew knew we required the betas to be a tight team that we could count on.

Strike two: When Mase gave an order or warning, he expected it to be followed or obeyed the first time. A second 'conversation' on the same topic would carry a heavy penalty.

Strike three: Tyler didn't deserve it. He was a good kid who'd had a rough life and been forced to grow up far too fast. Becoming Ash's beta so young hadn't helped, but what could we do? We needed a beta, and Tyler needed a good position in the pack to support himself. He was one of very few wolves in our pack who had no family at all to help him, so we'd decided to.

Emerson played peacemaker before Mase could jump down Matthew's throat.

Smell or not, there's definitely the sound of something approaching from the north. How far are we from the border?

Few hundred feet, Cole told him. *Betas, stay close to Lark. Do not leave her side.*

None of us were happy with the situation, but we had to check what was going on. No patrols were in this area because Ash had cleared everyone out. He'd wanted our mate to feel free and comfortable on her run.

The betas formed a circle around her, then my brothers and I formed a circle around them before we veered toward the border.

When we got there, we scanned the area and found nothing.

I'm going to shift, Cole said.

It was a good idea. We might need someone who could communicate outside the mind link, and, of all of us, he was the best at fighting wolves in human form.

He shifted quickly, then went to Cove, Emerson's wolf, and pulled a pair of shorts out of the saddlebag. He'd just tugged them on when a line of twenty or so male shifters bled out of the trees.

One stalked ahead of the rest, their obvious leader. He held the elbow of a brown-haired girl wearing torn and bloody clothes. Her left cheek bore a red handprint and her right eye was bruised and swollen. As the shifter pulled her along, she tripped and fell to her knees, and he dragged her along behind him until she could scramble to her feet.

It made me angry to see, and Quartz let out a sub-vocal growl. As his anger rose, I knew this would be the first test of our new pact.

I glanced over my shoulder to check on my mate and saw Bay, Crew's wolf, nudging Lark under River, Tyler's wolf. She was so small, she could stand up beneath him, and River used that to hide her as well as prevent her from seeing what was happening.

I nodded at them both, then turned my attention back to the intruders.

A few seconds later, the lead shifter saw us ranged in a line along the border. His eyes widened. Growling, he wrapped his fingers of his free hand around the girl's throat. She choked and clawed at his hand, but he only tightened his hold.

"You had one job in exchange for your life, witch." He shook her like a rag doll. "Alpha told you to hide our scent and take us to *her*, not to the alphas of Five Fangs!"

He threw her limp body to the ground and stomped on her twice. As she fell unconscious, something twinged in the air, releasing the smell of Tall Pines wolves and the distinct tang of magic.

Mate! howled Creek, Tristan's wolf.

He stayed true to his charge of sticking by Posy, but his eyes were locked on the brunette. He whimpered as she lay quiet and still on the grass.

Jayden? Quartz's whole body quivered with rage. *Permission?*

Pride filled me.

Not yet. They haven't crossed into our territory.

Four men walked out of the trees, each pair carrying a giant duffel bag that sagged in the middle. They swung the bags back and forth twice, building momentum, then heaved them toward us. They landed at our paws, and Cole swiftly reached down to unzip the closest one.

Staring up at us was a guy's battered and bloody face. He looked about my age, maybe a little older, and I could smell his beta blood. Cole crouched down and laid his fingers on the dude's neck.

Still alive, at least at the moment, he told us.

He went to the other duffel, too, and found a second guy in the same beaten condition, and we were surprised to see he was identical to the first one.

Twin betas. Hmm. Maybe they had tried to claim Luke's abandoned position and Alpha Halder hadn't liked it? Or maybe they were relatives of someone Alpha Halder wanted to punish?

Not important at this time, Quartz rumbled, then nodded at the duffel bags. *Now there are Tall Pines wolves on our territory. Permission?*

My clever wolf had a point, even if it seemed wrong to use them to legitimize a fight. Regardless, I got the feeling we needed to hear what they had to say.

Not yet. Let's find out what they want.

"We bring a warning from Alpha Halder," shouted the leader. "Turn Lilah MacGregor over to us, or more of her friends and family will suffer the same fate or worse."

Permission? Quartz whined.

For their own safety, I alerted my boys that I was about to let my wolf come out to play.

We need at least one alive for questioning, Mase reminded everyone.

And don't kill them if they submit, Cole added. *Most of them look barely older than pups.*

Quartz? I grinned.

Yes, Jayden?

Permission granted.

And that was all he needed to hear before leaping forward and doing what he did best.

27: Morning Mating

Luke MacGregor

Gisela had just slid her tight, wet sheath down onto my morning wood when Alpha Jayden nudged the mind link.

I opened it with caution. I didn't care if he knew what we were doing, but no way was he going to accidentally see or hear my mate like this.

We need you at our house with Ranger and the king.

Is it an emergency, or can it wait fifteen— my balls tightened as Ela rode me hard and fast. *Uh, ten more minutes?*

I can tell your wolf if you're busy, he smirked.

I handed the conversation over to Rain as Ela leaned forward to grab the headboard, her perfect breasts jiggling in my face. Bending my knees, I tilted her even further forward, slid my hands up and down her rib cage, and sucked one nipple deep into my mouth.

From Alpha Jayden's tone, something bad had happened, and I wanted to give Ela every drop of pleasure I could before we had to go to work. Fortunately, after exploring each other's bodies most of the night, I knew *exactly* how to make her come.

Sliding one hand between her firm cheeks, I eased a finger into her tight back hole. At the same time, my other hand slipped into her dripping pussy. My thumb and forefinger pinched the pearl hidden inside, and she clamped down tight on my dick in front and my finger in back.

"Luke!" she screamed as her taut body arced above me, and I grinned.

Withdrawing my hands, I rolled us over, and it was my turn to grab the headboard as I pounded into her. When she came a second time, it surprised us both, and I laughed as I spilled inside her.

While we caught our breath, Rain told us about the Tall Pines incursion. The five alphas wanted us, Ranger, and the king to come over so we could determine who was going to interview which group as well as plan how we were going to take down Alpha Halder.

I wondered who the two wounded wolves were and hoped they weren't who I thought they might be.

"Why don't you link the king and let him know?" I asked Ela. "Ask him to not tell Lilah about the injured guys until I find out who they are."

"Do you know the witch?"

I shook my head.

"Alpha Halder never dealt with witches before, or at least not to my knowledge."

With a shrug, her sultry dark eyes glossed over and her plump lips parted, and I started to grow hard again.

Not the time, I told myself sternly. *We still need to shower, and the alphas are waiting.*

While she linked the king, I scooped her up in my arms and rolled us out of bed.

"He's not acknowledging me," she said, then giggled. "He *is* broadcasting quite loudly through the royal pack link, though."

"What's he broadcasting?" I asked as I carried her into the bathroom.

"Hmm. Let's just say he wants everyone to know how ... happy ... he and his new queen are this morning."

"Oh, my Goddess." I closed my eyes, fervently glad I wasn't part of the royal pack yet. "That's more about my baby sister's private life than I ever wanted to know."

She laughed as I sat her on the counter while I got the shower going. Once the water had heated up, I gathered her back into my arms and carried her under the hot spray.

"I don't want to be the one to tell him that Alpha Halder is still targeting Lilah." I dropped my forehead against my mate's and sighed. "I don't want to tell Lilah, either. I hate seeing her scared."

And if those two wolves in the clinic happen to be my little cousins, which I'm almost positive they are, I'm going to hate telling her that, too. She loves those boys like brothers.

Frowning, Rain muttered, *Those hotheads better not have endangered Junie with whatever trouble they got into.*

They'll have to answer to Lilah if they did, I told him with a smirk, making him chuckle darkly.

"Why don't we send Ranger to tell them?" Ela scratched her fingers through the long stubble on my cheeks and chin. "He can face the king and queen's displeasure at the news and at having their morning mating interrupted."

"Better him than us," I murmured, "and we won't have *our* morning mating interrupted."

Her grin was wicked as she wrapped her legs around my waist, then slid down to where something hard and throbbing awaited her.

#

Lilah

I woke up to a large hand trailing sparks over my bare hip and down my thigh, and a smile bloomed on my lips.

"Good morning, darling."

187

Julian's morning voice was rough and rumbly and brought goosebumps up all over my skin. That made him chuckle, and my eyes popped open to see him lying next to me with his head pillowed on his curled arm. His blue, blue gaze caressed me as gently as his hand was.

My face burning, I murmured, "Good morning."

"I like waking up with you like this, my beautiful queen." He brushed his lips with mine, then pulled back to meet my eyes. "Are you all right?"

I nodded, my blush spreading down my neck to my chest, and his hand squeezed the back of my thigh as he leaned closer.

"I'm sorry it hurt you so much," he whispered in my ear.

The heat from his body and his luscious coffee aroma made me melt against him, but the guilt and worry in his voice broke my heart.

"It's not your fault. It's how nature works. And afterwards, you—" Not having the words, I kissed his cheek above his beard. "You were amazing. I never dreamed I could feel like that."

"You're the one who was amazing."

He kissed me again and, this time, I parted my lips. With a low groan, he accepted the invitation and made love to my mouth with his.

"Julian," I gasped when he finally let us up for air.

He laid open-mouth kisses down my throat to my breasts, and his hand glided to my knee and tugged my leg over his hip. I felt his hardness against my thigh and moaned as my body throbbed with need.

"I want to be inside you again, baby. May I?"

His lips brushed my skin with each word, stoking the fire building inside my belly, but I hesitated.

"It won't hurt this time, right?" I whispered.

"No, darling. From now on, it'll be nothing but pleasure."

The promise in his eyes eased the last of my uncertainty, and I gave myself wholeheartedly to my mate, my love, my king.

#

King Julian

Our first time was not the perfect memory I wanted to make with my queen.

My dad and uncles had given me 'The Talk' when I'd turned sixteen, although I'd never needed the knowledge until last night, when I'd been more than grateful for it. However, even though I'd done everything they'd advised, I still had a devil of a time getting inside her.

She had cried, and all I could do was kiss her tears away while I stayed still, buried inside her and throbbing with the need to move. I felt so selfish, and guilt sank its sharp claws into me. Finally, she wiggled her hips with a moan and asked if it was okay if *she* moved.

Thank the Goddess, I at least managed to make her come before I did.

Afterward, when I saw all the blood, I freaked out. In a panic, I commanded Kestrel to heal her, and she assured me that it was natural and there was nothing to heal. Onyx screamed at me to take care of our mate, so I pulled on my boxers, then ran her a hot bath with a ton of bubbles. She sank into them with a giggle, which made me smile, and I sat on the edge of the tub when she asked me to.

She chatted away about anything and everything, telling me about growing up with Luke as a father figure after their parents passed in the sickness, and I told her about growing up in a male-dominated household after Grandma and Mom died the same way. Then, while she was getting out and drying off, I stripped the bed, remade it, and threw away the blood-stained sheets.

Add another expense to my tab.

When I returned to the bathroom, I found her staring at her towel-wrapped figure in the mirror over the sink. She had her head tilted and her mismatched eyes fixed on her neck, specifically the mate mark I'd put there.

Leaning one shoulder against the wall, I folded my arms and watched her. She touched it gingerly with her fingertips, then her eyes flicked to mine in the mirror.

"I didn't expect it to be so beautiful."

I pushed away from the wall and went over to her, glancing at the tattoo of Nyx's portrait with my crown on his head. If she graced me with her mark, I wondered if it'd be Kestrel wearing the royal tiara.

"Of course it's beautiful, darling. It's on you."

Taking her hips in my hands, I stood against her back and lowered my head to nuzzle her neck with my nose. Watching her in the mirror, I smirked to see her eyes roll back in pleasure. I brushed my beard over her mark, and she shuddered as her nipples hardened under the towel.

"Do we need this?" I tugged at the knot between her breasts.

"I suppose not."

I pulled the towel away and nearly came in my boxers just from looking at her lovely body, so petite and delicate against my larger, heavier frame.

"Julian."

Her heavy-lidded eyes met mine in the mirror, and I grew even harder.

With a soft growl, I carried her back to the bed, opened her legs, and devoured her until she came, then did it again. Once she was sated and limp, she fell asleep with my name on her lips, and I headed for the shower to clean up - and take care of my problem down south.

In the morning, I woke up surrounded by the fragrance of almonds. My queen lay beside me, her lovely red hair spilled across her pillow and her freckled skin glimmering in the bright morning sun. Deep satisfaction filled me.

Mine. All mine. I skimmed my fingers down her waist to her hip. *Mine forever.*

Her gorgeous eyes fluttered open, and a blush spread from her cheeks to cover her whole face. As my hand slid to her thigh, the color flooded down her neck to her upper chest, and I couldn't keep my hands off of her. Her mouth opened under mine and I dove in, loving the soft, shy noises she made. I trailed kisses down her throat to her chest, then enjoyed her breasts with my teeth and tongue and lips.

Her moans turned me into solid steel, and I tugged her leg over my hip.

"I want to be inside you again, baby. May I?"

Her response was hesitant at first, but she agreed after I told her it wouldn't hurt again.

"You're sure, sweetheart?" I stopped suckling her nipple to ask. "We don't have to. I can survive with blue balls until you're ready."

"No, I want you." She squirmed against me and whimpered with need. "Please, Julian. Please!"

Her begging dissolved the last of my guilt and concern. My hand left her leg to cup her mound and rub it slowly, and her breath caught as I bit down on her mate mark. When my fingers delved into her soft folds, they found her wet and ready. My thumb rubbed her rigid jewel, and she tipped her head back with a gasp.

"I want you, Julian. I want you now! Bury yourself deep inside me and make me see stars again."

"Yes, ma'am." I grinned as I rolled on top of her. "Who am I to deny the queen what she desires?"

#

Twenty minutes later, as we lay panting and sweaty in a tangle of limbs, Ranger tapped on the mind link.

With a quiet curse, I cracked it open.

Not now, Ranger, I warned him, then snapped it closed.

So what did my irritating little brother do? Prodded it again.

What. Do. You. Want? I snarled.

Good morning to you, too, sunshine. Alpha Halder made a move. Threatened the queen and sent a message.

Raw fury brought both Nyx and me to complete attention.

He threatened my queen?

Yeah, dude, he did.

NYX WILL DESTROY HIM!

190

What's the message? I asked Ranger, trying to hear over Nyx's roaring.

His wolves left two of her relatives half-dead on the doorstep, so to speak. Ranger paused and took a deep breath. *They said to hand her over or more of her friends and family will follow.*

Who found them? Did they speak to Halder's wolves or did they leave a note? I demanded.

The alphas were taking Lark on a run when they ran into Halder's little band up on the northern border. The alphas dealt with the threat and brought the injured back to the clinic.

Are there prisoners to interrogate?

Eleven of the twenty submitted and are now in the pack cells. Quartz killed the rest.

The first part surprised me. The second did not.

Tell me about the injured. You said they're Lilah's relatives?

Luke asked that you wait to tell the queen until he's certain about their identities. There was also a witch Halder beat up and coerced into hiding his wolves' scent. Luke didn't know her. She's at the clinic, too. Beta Tristan discovered she's his mate.

Where are you now? I asked as I analyzed everything he'd told me, wishing I had more information.

About two minutes from your place.

When you get here, wait in the car until we're ready.

What?! he whined. *It's ninety degrees out here and it's only nine in the morning. I'll wait in the kitchen.*

You'll wait in the car. It has A/C. Turn it on.

I'm hungry, Julian! I'll just grab a snack. I won't look or listen or comment on anything I smell.

Ranger, if you come into this house, I will skin you alive. My queen needs a shower, then we'll meet you outside.

Fine. Now he sounded sullen. *At least bring a snack out for me.*

Why didn't you have breakfast? I rolled my eyes. *I thought you stayed over at the alphas, and I know they always eat a big meal.*

I ended up at Tristan's. Just two unmated males commiserating as everyone around them finds their mates. Of course, now he has a mate, too. I'm everyone's third wheel.

I ignored his attempt to gain pity. He was twenty-two. If he went two more years without finding his mate, then I'd feel sorry for him. He wasn't getting any pity until he had to wait as long as I did.

Ash's new beta doesn't, I reminded him. *You can hang out with him.*

He's seventeen, Julian. He's not even old enough to find *his mate yet.*

I tuned out the rest of his whining as I looked down at my queen's sleepy, flushed face. She would need something to eat, and I was pretty hungry, too. Making up my mind, I gave Ranger new orders.

Go to Roger's Diner and get breakfast for the three of us. I don't care what you pick, but get a variety so there's something Lilah will like. We can eat here before we leave.

Great! Roger's food is the best in the territory, he said happily. *Be right back, bro.*

Closing the link with a solid slam, I stroked the back of my fingers down my lady's cheek. Her face followed my touch like a flower following the sun.

"Darling, we need to clean up. Ranger's bringing us breakfast, then we need to go over to the five alphas."

I thought my wording was generic enough, but something in my tone must have alerted her.

"What happened?" She narrowed her eyes at me.

"I'll tell you after we get showered. Ranger will need to give me more details while we eat, anyway."

She nodded and petted my beard with both hands before holding my face and kissing me. When she pulled back, her eyes sparkled with tears.

"Lilah?"

"I always thought I wouldn't have a mate or, if I did, he wouldn't want me because of how I look. I was resigned to being alone and lonely. Then you came. You called me your lovely and precious mate and you want to keep me." Her cheeks glowed pink and her smile was huge. "I'm happier than I've ever been in my life. I love you, Julian Hemming."

"And I love you, my beautiful darling. Heart and soul, for the rest of my life, I'm yours and yours alone."

28: Learning Curve

Ash

It took nearly an hour to clear the situation on the northern border.

Quartz, his muzzle dripping with blood and gore, demanded we take Lark home the second the fighting was over. Cole suggested that he go wash up in the nearby river, saying our mate shouldn't see him like that. He didn't snap or even argue, which shocked us all.

Like the rest of us, he was completely wrapped around our girl's little finger.

While he was gone, Mase contacted a patrol to bring a clean-up crew, Wyatt linked the clinic to send a rescue team, and Cole and Arroyo stood guard over the wolves who'd surrendered. Tristan shifted and tended to his mate as best he could with what few medical supplies were in the saddlebags.

I shifted, too, pulled on some shorts, and crouched next to Lark where she still hid under River.

"Hey, baby. Everything's okay. You're safe, all right? We're going to be here a little longer, though. Do you want to play with River for a bit while we wait?"

She yipped at me and wagged her tail, and I took that as a yes.

Not wanting her to see all the dead bodies, I told River to take her over to the small clearing that was within view, then sent Bay and Cove, Emerson's wolf, with them. I watched as they distracted her by chasing butterflies, and she happily pounced and raced around the field. I grinned and shared the sight with my brothers through the mind link.

Even Quartz smiled when I showed him, which shocked me again, but also made me happy. She was helping Jay with him already, and the Goddess knew Jay needed that.

Eventually, we got the prisoners transported to the cells, the injured to the clinic with Tristan accompanying his mate, and the rest of us back to our house. Quartz relinquished control to Jay as soon as our mate was safe in our room, another good sign. We left her alone to shift as we gathered with the remaining betas in the living room.

"Go support Tristan," Mase told them. "Link us when you get word on her condition and let us know as soon as those twins wake up enough to talk."

They nodded their heads and trooped out, and I looked at Mase.

"We all know the beta dudes are Luke and the queen's relatives."

"I ain't looking forward to telling them." Wyatt grimaced and scrubbed a hand through his hair. "The queen is already going to be upset to know that Alpha Halder is still after her, never mind that her family has been hurt."

"The *queen* is going to be *upset*?" Cole scoffed. "The king is going to freaking explode!"

"Yeah, but that's only blood and damage if he loses his temper. Queen Lilah might *cry*, and that's a thousand times harder to take."

I smirked at his scowling face. Wyatt never could stand to see a girl cry. It was Peri's main ammunition against him growing up.

"I'll contact Luke through the Moonset link," Jay offered with a smirk. "He can tell the king, who can tell the queen. Let him deal with his mate's tears."

"And tell Luke to bring them and his mate over here. Ranger, too," Cole instructed.

I tuned them out when I heard footsteps coming down the stairs. Seconds later, Posy appeared in the living room doorway and hovered there with uncertainty on her face.

"Come here, cupcake." I patted the space next to me.

With a grin, she ran over and jumped on the couch. Her little arms snaked around my waist and squeezed me tightly.

"Hey, princess," I murmured and stroked her long hair. "Did you enjoy your run before the interruption?"

"Loved it. Lark, too. She was so, so happy."

"Good! Watching her chase butterflies with the betas was adorable."

"She used to like to chase fireflies at night." She smooshed her face into my side and snuggled closer.

"Well, we can do that one evening. Once everything calms down."

"What happened, Ash?" she asked quietly. "River wouldn't let us see anything, but we heard fighting."

"Wait until the others get here. We'll have to tell them the story, too."

She nodded and relaxed against me, and we cuddled until the doorbell rang.

We all got to our feet, and I volunteered to open the door because I wasn't one to be still for too long.

"Where's the wolf who threatened my queen?" King Julian demanded as soon as I had the door open.

"Dead. You can thank Quartz later. Come to the living room and we'll tell you everything."

I greeted Lilah, Luke, Gisela, and Ranger as they followed in his wake. We were sorting out seats and Jay was asking if they wanted drinks or snacks when Sid got my attention.

Something wrong with mate!

Swiveling toward her, I saw one of her hands clutching her throat and the other rubbing her chest. She was trembling, and I realized she was having a panic attack.

In that moment, everyone else became insignificant. Royalty in the room or not, only she mattered. I bolted over, wrapped my hands around her upper arms, and bent almost in half to look in her eyes.

The fear in them devastated me.

"Posy?"

No response.

Something triggered our girl, I linked my brothers.

In a heartbeat, they surrounded us, blocking her from worried and curious eyes.

"Breathe, sweetness. In and out."

"You're safe, honey. No one will hurt you."

"What happened, Ash?" Wyatt demanded.

"I don't know."

She wasn't responding to any of us, and I wondered if we were overwhelming her. Worried at how rigid her shaking body had become, I scooped her up in my arms.

Where should I—

Her room, Jay said immediately. *The balcony garden. It should soothe her when she comes out of it.*

Nodding curtly, I listened to my brother and hoped he was right.

#

Posy

The first thing I noticed when the others walked into the living room was the mate mark on Lilah's neck. Turning to Gisela, I saw she had one as well. Both of them looked radiant and happy, and it was clear as day that they'd finished the mating process last night.

King Julian and Luke looked happy, too, in that smug guy way, and couldn't keep their hands off their ladies.

They'd known each other less than twenty-four hours. I met the boys nearly a week ago.

No compare with others, Lark tried to tell me. *Gisela say go at own pace. Let things happen by nature.*

My mates deserve to be that happy, but I'm a coward. A baby. They're going to get sick of waiting.

I began to shake. Was I hurting my mates? Was I disappointing them?

What if they resent me? What if they don't think I'm worth the trouble and send me back to my brothers?

Just the thought of being separated from them sent my lungs and heart into overdrive.

"Posy?"

I heard the voice dimly, but was too deep in my mind to respond.

What if they find someone else? A girl who isn't scared to give herself to them? What if they already have? What if they're seeing someone on the side? Is that why they aren't pressuring me to mate? They already have that need taken care of?

I heard my mates' voices all around me, but I couldn't get any air in at all now and was getting dizzy. The thought of my mates with another female destroyed me.

Arms lifted me and I didn't bother to struggle. Whatever they wanted to do to me, it couldn't hurt more than what was happening in my heart.

I don't know how much time passed before I came back to senses, but I eventually found myself cradled in Ash's lap. He rocked us gently on the wicker chair out on my garden balcony as my other mates stood or crouched around us, anxiety etched on all of their faces.

"I'm sorry! I'm sorry! Don't send me away," I begged like the pathetic creature I was.

"You are never leaving us," Cole assured me, his green eyes fixed on my face. "This is for forever, Posy. *We* are for forever."

"But we should have completed the mating process by now!" I wailed. "You'll get tired of waiting and replace me with another girl!"

"No, we won't." Wyatt shook his head fiercely. "We were yours and yours alone from the second we found you, and you bound us to you forever with your mark. We wouldn't have it any other way."

"Whether you're ever able to complete the mating process or not, I will never leave your side," Jay vowed.

"Nor will I."

"Nor I."

"Nor I."

"Nor I."

Mason leaned down and wiped my tears away with his thumbs.

"Is that all, little flower," he whispered, "or is there something more bothering you?"

My bottom lip trembled as I met his gray eyes.

"I'm scared," I whispered. "I don't know anything about mating. You'll think I'm dumb."

"Baby, you were locked away when you were *twelve*. Unless your brothers slipped you books on anatomy and sex, how could you know?"

"They didn't, did they?" Ash growled.

I shook my head.

"And your mom never discussed mates or mating with you?"

"She was sick for a long time before she died," I explained. "Nearly a year. By the time I got home from school, she was usually asleep or in too much pain for any serious conversation."

"Either way, you were a little young for 'The Talk,' anyway," he sighed.

I watched as they exchanged looks, then turned as one to Cole.

"Um, so, our parents gave *us* 'The Talk' when we individually turned fourteen. We can share what they told us." When I nodded, he continued. "As you know, the mating process has three steps. Finding each other, marking, and mating."

He swallowed and rubbed the back of his neck, and the other boys shifted or shuffled their feet.

Are they scared of that part, too? I wondered.

"After that, the bond will be completed. Rather than have a human period, from now on you'll go through heat once a year. That's the only time you can get pregnant."

"Pregnant," I repeated in a flat tone.

"Conceive. You know." His cheeks flared red. "Have a pup."

"Yes, I know what the word means. I just wasn't expecting to hear it." I grabbed a strand of my hair and played with it. Their nervousness was rubbing off on me. "So, um, what is mating?"

"All right, here's the short and sweet version," Wyatt said before Cole could answer.

"Oh, no. Anyone but you," Jayden cut him off. "You'll either scare her or traumatize her."

"What? Of course I won't!"

"Your filthy mouth is too crude and graphic."

"Hey! Just give me a chance!"

"One chance," Mason warned him. "Don't screw it up."

Wyatt rolled his eyes, then turned to me and took my hands in his. His eyes held mine.

"Okay, Posy, so you know boys and girls have different parts in their pants, right? The boy's part, which is called a penis, fits into the girl's part, which is called a vagina."

I nodded. I may have never seen a boy's part, but I knew what both were called.

"The penis mostly hangs around until it wants to be inside the vagina. When it does, it gets big and hard so it can fill it up. With me so far?"

"Wait. You mean you would put— Um, *down there?!*" I squeaked, squeezing my legs together tightly.

Ash's chest rumbled against my back and I knew he was laughing quietly. With a frown, I turned and slapped his bicep.

"Stop that," I hissed.

"Okay, princess." He bit his lips, but the humor stayed in his eyes.

With a huff, I spun around and faced Wyatt.

"Yeah, but don't worry. Your vagina gets nice and wet so Mr. Penis can slide right in." Wyatt ignored Jayden, who choked at the 'Mr. Penis' part. "Easy peasy, right? And that's the start of mating. Making love. Having sex. Doing it."

I was silent for a second, trying to process everything, then I remembered something.

"Is that why I occasionally feel something hard in your pants when you're holding me?" I whirled toward Ash again. "Like this morning when I woke up?"

"Yeah, princess. You feel so good that we get excited."

"And those times when you shift me off your lap quickly? That's what's happening?" I raised my eyebrows.

"Yep," Wyatt said. "We don't want to embarrass you or lose control and shoot the juice into our shorts."

"Wait. Juice? What juice?"

I turned back to Wyatt and saw pink on his cheeks. Had something about this finally embarrassed him?

Good, because this whole thing is embarrassing to me.

"The penis shoots, um, juice into you during mating," he explained. "When you're in heat, the juice will make a pup grow in your belly."

"So you only mate when you want pups?" I tilted my head with a confused frown.

Cole scrubbed one hand over his face, Jayden looked like he had swallowed a bug, and Mason closed his eyes and shook his head slowly.

"Well, no. It's another way we bond with each other. And it's fun, feels good, and becomes addicting," Wyatt said. "At least, that's what Papa and Dad say. I guess we'll have to try it and see."

"You've never done it before?" I squeaked in shock.

"Of course not. None of us have. We've been waiting for you since we turned eighteen. Lucky for us, Ash and I have only had to wait a few months. Poor Mason has had to wait three, almost four years now."

And right on cue, all my doubts came rolling in again.

"What if you don't like mating with me? What if I'm not any good at it? What if I'm not enough for all of you?" My breathing grew sharp and short. "Are you going to go to other girls to have fun and feel good? What if—"

"Stop that, sweetness." Jayden came over and picked me up, ignoring Ash's complaints. "None of us have done it before, so we can all learn together. We'll figure out what each of us needs and wants as we go. As for the rest of your worries, we will *never* seek out any other females. You are the only one we want."

"That's right, cutie. None of us gets hard looking at other girls. Only with you," Wyatt assured me. "And you like when we touch and kiss you, right? You don't want any other male to do that, do you?"

"No. It makes me sick to even think that way about other males."

"Good," growled Cole, Mason, and Ash in unison.

"There's a lot of touching and kissing during mating," Wyatt continued, "which we enjoy as much as you do, so no more worrying about that, okay?"

Heat built in my cheeks and scorched my whole face before spreading to my neck, and I dug my head into Jayden's chest. He rearranged me so he was holding me on his hip like a little kid, and I twined my arms around his neck.

"Let's go back to the subject of pups for a minute," Cole said. "We've been talking and we wanted to know how you felt about waiting for a while. You've been through a lot the last few years, and we're still finding our feet as co-alphas of five packs. We think it would be a good idea to wait, at least until we're all comfortable with our roles."

"It would be nice to get to know each other better before pups come along. We have lots of time to become parents," Ash added.

"Parents." Wyatt gulped. "Dude. Am I the only one who freaks out thinking of myself as a parent?"

"No, you're not. It freaks all of us out to think of *you* as a parent," Cole retorted.

Mason caught Wyatt's shoulders before he could launch himself at Cole, and I giggled.

"Seriously, though, it is a huge responsibility," Ash argued. "One we all need to be ready for when it happens, so we should wait until we are."

"We could travel a bit, too, before pups." Jayden sounded wistful as he kissed my temple. "I'd like to visit the ocean."

My eyes widened with interest, and I felt Lark's ears perk up. We'd always dreamed of seeing the ocean one day.

"But it's entirely up to you, Posy," Cole said. "We'll do anything you say concerning pups. You're the one who has to carry and birth them, after all, although we'll be with you every step of the way."

I laid my head on Jayden's shoulder as I thought about it.

Alphas usually wanted pups right away to ensure security for the pack. The fact that my mates wanted to wait - and for all the right reasons - warmed my heart.

And I am not ready for pups.

"Could we wait?" I asked with a shy blush. "At least for a bit?"

"Of course!" Ash said, and all of the boys exhaled a breath of relief. "Don't get us wrong. We want pups, but we're nervous about becoming parents while we're so young. I mean, four of us are still teenagers, and Cole *just* turned twenty."

"While I can't wait to see your belly big and round with a pup," Jayden said with a grin, "we're selfish enough to want you all to ourselves for a while."

"So we wouldn't mate when I'm in heat?" I asked. "How long does it last?"

"Three days," Cole answered, "during which you'll be *driven* to mate. You'll emit a fragrance that we won't be able to resist, and your body will hurt if you're denied. But don't worry. It's only once a year, and we can wear protection on those days until we're ready for pups."

"Protection?"

"It's called a condom," Wyatt said. "It's a rubber sleeve that collects the pup-making juice so it doesn't get inside you."

Mason, who'd been quiet for a while now, started to speak.

"As for when we mark and mate you, that will be your decision entirely. We're not going to rush you into either. When you're ready, when you're comfortable with us, we'll do those things and not before."

"Don't think we aren't eager for both, though, because we are," Ash assured me. "We'll wait as long as you need us to, but we want you badly."

"Really?" My eyebrows flew up. "*Me?*"

"Uh-huh, and that makes it hard."

"Yeah. You have no idea *how* hard, cutie, but you will."

"Wyatt!" growled Cole and Mason.

It took me a second, but I got what he meant, and my face burned red.

"As much as I want to stay here with you, the king is waiting for us." Jayden gave my waist a little squeeze. "He's usually a patient guy, but I doubt that will be true as long as a threat exists against his queen."

I took a deep breath.

I have to face down the embarrassment sometime. Better to get it over with quickly.

"All right. Put me down so we can go back."

"I can carry you," he offered.

I shook my head.

"I will walk on my own power to welcome the king and queen into our home."

He grinned at me and set me on my feet, then picked up my hand and bowed over it. Kissing my knuckles, he looked up at me through his eyelashes, and something in my lower belly twisted.

"As you wish, my lady." His voice dipped low, which gave me tingly shivers. "We're yours to command."

Blushing, I tugged my hand out of his and ran away from his flirty self. Behind me, I heard my boys chuckling as they followed me.

29: Slaughter All

Beta Gisela MacGregor

Watching a friend have a panic attack is both saddening and sobering.

I didn't know what had scared Posy so badly, but it probably wasn't helping her to have all of us stand there gawking. Before I could suggest we move to a different room, however, Alpha Ash swung her up in his arms and carried her away, the other four alphas hot on his heels.

"Oh, my Goddess," Queen Lilah whispered in the ensuing silence.

She put one hand over her mouth as tears sprang to her eyes. A second later, King Julian gathered her up in his arms and pulled her tight against his chest.

"She's with her mates," he murmured with his lips against her forehead. "It's the best place she could be right now."

"I hope we didn't do anything to trigger her." I looked up at my own mate.

"Yeah. Poor little kid."

With a sad half-smile, he opened his arms. I went into them with a sigh and laid my cheek over his heart, inhaling his scent of fresh-cut grass.

"What happened?" Ranger asked in clear confusion. "Why did they leave like that?"

"The little luna was having a panic attack," Luke told him.

"What? Why?" Ranger scanned the room as if looking for threats. "What's to panic about in here?"

"You are so dumb sometimes that I wonder how you graduated high school, let alone college." The king shook his head while glaring at his little brother.

"I am not dumb, your royal douche-ness," Ranger barked back. "I didn't understand something and I asked about it. How is that dumb?"

The queen intervened before they could get any more heated. She stretched up and kissed King Julian's mate mark, and his eyes rolled back.

"Panic and panic attacks are two different things," she told Ranger, then went on to provide more details about panic attacks.

I tuned her out when Luke linked me.

Do these two bicker all the time? he asked.

Yep. Like a pair of hens. It gets pretty funny, to be honest.

Does it ever come to fists flying?

Nah, not that I've seen. Ranger just knows how to get under the king's skin. Every younger brother's talent, I guess.

Hmm. All right. So long as it's safe for Lilah.

I'm sure it is. And besides, Ranger isn't going to be around after this week. The king's going to install him as the new alpha at Tall Pines.

I don't envy him the task of straightening out that mess. Luke slid his big hands around my throat and his thumbs tilted my head up so our eyes could meet. *Do you think Ranger is up to it?*

The king does. I shrugged. *To be honest, I think he's hoping it will help Ranger find a purpose. I've seen for myself how he's steadily growing more and more frustrated with his life.*

A mate would be best for that, Luke mused, *although I know no one, not even a king, can make that happen before the Goddess is ready.*

Ranger said Coal was as excited as Hawk and Onyx when we crossed into this territory. He was either imagining it or else he really is close to finding his mate.

Hopefully the latter. Luke kissed the tip of my nose.

"For the love of the moon! Can the four of you tone down the PDA, please?" Ranger whined. "Single male wolf here, dying for lack of love and attention in his life. I'd appreciate it if you all stopped rubbing your happiness in my face for five minutes."

I glanced over to see the king and queen staring deeply into each other's eyes. With a smirk, I reached up, grabbed Luke by his ears, and pulled him down into a kiss.

"Seriously, Gisela?" He let out an exasperated sigh. "Fine. I see how it is. Okay, then. I guess third wheel Ranger is going to find a ball game to watch and ignore all you lovebirds until you're ready to take recent events seriously."

Darkness gathered in the corners of the room as power - royal, moon, and alpha - rolled off the king in immense, thunderous waves. Ranger, Luke, and I were forced to our knees under the weight of it, and fear like I never felt before had me shaking like a child caught in a nightmare.

"I can assure you that I am taking it seriously, brother. ***Very. Seriously.***"

Another wave of power crashed around the room, and I bowed under the intense pressure, dropping my forehead to the carpet and clenching my fists tightly on my thighs. My heart rose into my throat and thudded painfully hard and fast.

Fingers brushed my left hand, and I knew from the sparks that it was Luke. How he found the strength to do that was beyond me; I couldn't open my eyes much less move any part of my body. However he managed it, I was grateful for his grounding touch.

I wasn't a timid or clingy woman by any means, but fear had hijacked the part of my brain that said I wasn't in real danger. The adrenaline-jacked part was now in charge, and it screamed at me to attack or prepare to defend myself. I couldn't move to do either, though, and Luke's fingers against my knuckles was all that kept me from screaming.

"Julian!"

The queen's voice broke the oppressive silence, and just like that, we could move again.

Luke helped me to my feet, then pulled me up against him and held me as tightly as his big arms could without breaking or suffocating me. I was ashamed of how badly I was shaking, but I couldn't help it. Feeling the fine tremors racking through him, I realized he was struggling, too, and holding me was probably helping him as much as me.

A memory flashed in my mind of the time I went to a drag race, and a jet car came into the line up. When they fired that sucker up, my heart climbed into my throat and I thought it was going to leave my body through my mouth. The immensity of the power generated by the engine, the sheer energy and volume and pressure, was deafening and awesome and terrifying and exciting and unnerving all at once.

Wanting to share with Luke, I sent him the memory.

The king losing his temper feels just like that, I linked him, *only without the exciting and awesome parts.*

Yeah. Let's not do that again anytime soon.

Tell Ranger, not me.

Oh, don't worry. I think he got the message, but if he didn't, I'll remind him later with a fist in his gut.

I grinned, feeling much more stable with my mate's scent in my nose and my face in his chest.

There goes our tough-girl card, Gis, Hawk bemoaned. *Our mates are going to think we're weak pussies now.*

Sorry to drop the knowledge on you, honey, but they already know we have pussies.

After the pounding yours took all night, I'm surprised it's still functioning.

You're such a bitch, Hawk.

Hey, blame Mother Nature for your gender, Gis, not me.

I let a laugh slip out at her last barb, and Luke lifted his head to look down at me. I didn't want to move out of my little nest between his solid pecs, though, and just nuzzled my face in deeper.

"What's funny?" he asked as he nudged the top of my head with his chin.

His beard caught a few hairs and moved them around, making them tickle as they brushed over my neck. Shivering at the sensation, I tilted my head up and met his light brown eyes.

"My wolf and I are engaged in a long-running war of the words. Tell me, mate: Do you think we're weak from how we responded to what just happened?"

"What? Why would I when Rain and I had the same response?"

See? I taunted my wolf.

I'm talking to my mate right now, weak pussy. Leave me alone. Fine by me, petty bitch. I don't want to talk to you anyway.

With a grin, I looked around to check on Ranger. I couldn't see him and wondered if he'd left the room. The king, on the other hand, sat on the couch with the queen on his lap, his face stuffed in her neck and her hands undoing his man-bun so she could play with his long hair.

"That's one way to calm him down," Luke snickered.

"Better than the horse tranquilizers we were using," I chuckled.

"Um, hello again," came a little voice from the doorway. "Would anyone care for a drink or snack?"

#

Lilah

I escaped Julian's arms, ran over to Posy, and wrapped her little bitty self up in a tight hug. The poor girl's pink nose was all the evidence anyone needed to know that she'd been crying, and the tight skin around her eyes showed how much the panic attack had drained her.

"Are you okay?" I whispered in her ear as I squeezed her.

"I'm sorry. It won't happen again."

"Don't be sorry." I leaned back and briskly ran my hands up and down her arms. "And it's okay if it happens again. No one's angry, okay?"

"Okay."

Her red face and lowered eyes spoke volumes on how embarrassed and ashamed she was.

"Don't feel bad, Posy. We all care about you, and we're here for you."

She nodded with a sniff, then her mates came in the room and carefully edged me away so they could drop little kisses on her head and temple and cheek. My heart melted at their gentleness with her.

205

"Posy, if you are agreeable, I'd like to hear the whole story of what happened this morning."

Julian came up to stand against my back, then slid his arms around my waist. Kestrel and I both purred quietly at the pleasure of his big body surrounding us, then she went back to Onyx. He'd been ... upset ... since Ranger linked Julian before breakfast, and Kestrel had been talking and singing to him to help Julian keep him from rampaging.

Or at least under control enough that he didn't kill anyone.

"Of course, your majesty," Posy said, "and I apologize for delaying everything."

"No apology needed, luna. Are you sure you're okay?"

"I am." She gave him a small nod and a smaller smile.

So we all sat down, and Julian called Ranger back in the room. I didn't know where he'd disappeared to or why, and Julian wasn't telling me, even though I'd asked him twice through our link.

Wait. You didn't punish him, did you?

No, darling. Making him bow to me was punishment enough. He doesn't want me to tell you where he went.

Oh. I didn't know what to say to that, so I left it alone.

Ranger came in and flopped on the chaise lounge, which was as far from Julian as he could get and still be in the same room. I tried to read what he was feeling, but his face was carefully blank. Shrugging it off for now, I turned to the five alphas as Julian asked them to explain what happened this morning.

I bit back a chuckle when I saw how they'd arranged themselves.

Posy sat on the couch in Alpha Ash's lap with his hands on her hips. Alpha Wyatt held her hand on one side and Alpha Jayden linked his arm through her elbow on the other side. Alpha Mason and Alpha Cole stood behind the couch, each laying a hand on one of her shoulders.

At first, I had my doubts when I heard she had five mates, but now I was satisfied that my friend was fine. The alphas were closer than brothers, and Posy had them all wrapped around her delicate little fingers. Anyone with eyes could see that those boys were going to cherish her for the rest of their lives.

After the alphas recounted the story, Julian began asking questions.

"Posy, did you or Lark see anything that your mates didn't?"

He made his voice very soft as he talked to her, and I sent him my love and thanks for that through our bond. She was still so fragile, both physically and emotionally, and I appreciated his care for my friend.

He sent me back a wave of love, and my heart fluttered with happiness.

"No, your majesty. They made us hide under River."

She played with Alpha Wyatt's rings, spinning the one on his thumb, and that reminded me I still needed to tell her my idea for the mate rings they'd asked her to design.

"River? Beta Tyler's wolf?"

"Yes, your majesty. Then, he, Cove, and Bay took us over to a field and we chased butterflies. I figured it was to distract Lark, and I wasn't too keen on seeing the aftermath of the fighting, so I sank back into my mind and let her have fun."

"You should have seen Lark trying to pounce on them. She was super-super cute!" Alpha Ash squealed.

He jogged his legs rapidly, making Posy bounce around on his knees. She must not have liked that because she stood quickly, dislodging all her other mates. Alphas Jayden and Wyatt leaped up next to her.

"You tool! What's wrong with you?"

"You scared Posy!"

"Think before you act."

And Alpha Cole whacked the poor guy on the back of his head.

"Owie!"

"Guys, I'm fine." Posy held up both hands. "It just startled me."

Four of them had irritated expressions, but Ash made such adorable puppy dog eyes that no one with a heart could have resisted.

And Posy has a heart that could hold the whole world, I thought with a hidden smile.

"Posy, I'm sorry that I startled you," he said, and that was all it took for her to flung herself back in his arms.

"Alpha Jayden, would you please share a picture of Lark chasing butterflies?" I gave him a sweet smile with my request.

"Of course, my queen."

It came to my mind almost instantly, and I nearly died from cuteness overload at the image of a small brown wolf determinedly trying to catch an orange butterfly.

"Oh, Julian, look!" I cooed and shared it with him.

"Let me see, too, Li," Luke asked.

"Me, too," Gisela said.

I sent it to Luke, knowing he'd send it to his mate.

"Ash, you're right," Julian chuckled. "Lark is very cute."

Posy hid her cherry-red face in the crook of Ash's neck, earning a round of *awws*. This time, Gisela stepped in to spare her.

"Well, sire, how do you wish to proceed?"

"I want to talk to the injured wolves first," Julian said.

"I'm coming, too. I want to know who was hurt because of me." I gave him a stern look when he opened his mouth. "Don't think I'll stay here and wait, Julian. If you say no, I'll just follow you— "

"Darling, I didn't say no. I wasn't *going* to say no." He smirked a little, and I rolled my eyes, which turned his smirk into a grin. "Of course you'll come with me. You have a right to visit your relatives in the clinic. And anyway, you are not leaving my side until both Nyx and I have calmed down a lot more."

"Lilah, let me find out who it is first." Luke frowned at me.

"Thank you, but I can handle it."

"Even if it's Zayne and Zayden?" He raised an eyebrow.

I wanted to be angry that he thought I was so fragile, but I knew he was only concerned for me.

"Yes," I told him. "I need to know what happened, and if it is them—"

"I'm ninety-nine percent sure it is," he interrupted me.

"Then I want to see them."

"Li, I know you're strong enough to do this, but you shouldn't *have* to. I'd spare you from it if you'd let me."

"I appreciate it, but no. I need to know they're okay and find out where Junie is."

"Very well, sister."

He nodded, then his eyes fogged over as he linked with someone. Hoping he wasn't arranging something behind my back, which he'd done before with the excuse that it was to keep me safe, I spun in Julian's arms to face him.

"What else, Julian?"

"While we're at the clinic, I want to interview the witch as well."

"I'll link Tristan and see if her condition is stable enough for that," Alpha Wyatt said. "She isn't a wolf, but we don't know if she's another kind of shifter or a human. Just saying, her rate of healing may be different from ours."

"Noted." Julian dipped his head. "After the clinic, I'll bring Lilah back here. The betas, including mine, will guard her and Posy while the rest of us interview the new prisoners. Unless," he looked down to me, "you have an interest in interrogation, darling?"

"No, thanks," I said in a wry tone. "I will gladly leave that to you, my love."

"All right." He looked around at the others. "Finally, we'll reconvene here to review everything we've learned and use it to plan the end of the Tall Pines pack."

"Wait. We're taking down the whole pack?" Gisela asked with a furrowed brow. "I thought we only needed to take down Alpha L—"

"Don't say it!" Ranger and I shouted at the same time, but it was too late.

"—eo Halder."

SLAUGHTER THEM! Onyx's sonorous roar shook the whole room. *SLAUGHTER EVERY LIVING ONE! STRING UP BY GUTS AND LEAVE FOR THE CROWS! RIP OUT THROATS AND LET ROT IN SUN—*

30: Getting Schooled

Mason

It took nearly an hour for King Julian and his queen to calm Nyx down.

Nyx was a caveman of a wolf, which was probably why he and Quartz got along so well, but I'd never known him to lose it like that before over something as trivial as hearing his enemy's name.

My brothers and I had a brief talk and decided Ash would get Ranger to play basketball with him in the gym. We didn't want to pry, but we needed to know if there was something more going on. Ash was the best choice because everyone knew he couldn't stay still, and Ranger looked like he needed to blow off some steam, anyway.

After they left, we busied ourselves with little jobs that needed done. I gave Luke some paper and a pencil and asked him to draw the Tall Pines layout. Cole began a to-do list in case the king wanted us with him, which was likely. Posy and Jay started on lunch while Gisela and Wyatt set the table.

Ash began to relay what he was learning as they shot hoops, and we found out that Queen Lilah hadn't handled the news well this morning. Nyx had handled it worse. He'd gone on a rampage and destroyed the dining room in a blind rage, furious at both her panic and the audacity of a threat to his mate.

We all rolled our eyes, and Cole linked our maintenance manager to send a repair crew over to the guest house.

"Nyx is on a whole different level of aggression right now," Ranger said as he shot a three-pointer. "Julian, too. He lost his temper right before you all came back into the room. Made Luke, Gisela, and me bow to him because I made a dumb comment. The other two didn't even do anything and he punished them. That's not like my brother at all."

Wow. I haven't seen that kind of reaction out of the king in a couple of years now, Cole linked us. *Right, Mase?*

Yeah, and that time was understandable, I replied.

What time are you all talking about? Wyatt wanted to know. *Was it when the kush-taka wiped out that pack in Alaska?*

Yeah, Cole said, and I was content to let him do the talking. *I'd just stepped up as alpha, and you younger three were still in high school. The beta and the gamma betrayed their alpha, and were then betrayed themselves by the devils they made a deal with.*

I remember you telling us about it when you got back, Jay said. *The alpha was the king's uncle, correct?*

Yes. When he discovered the truth, the king lost his temper and radiated so much power, we all went to our knees under it. Me, Mase, Ranger, the royal guard, even his father.

Dang! That is *some heavy power,* Wyatt said.

Wait until you're *the one kneeling under it,* I told him dryly. *Then you'll learn what heavy is.*

A few minutes later, Queen Lilah and our much calmer king joined us where we'd set up in the home office. We linked Ash to come back, and he and Ranger hit the showers before they returned to the house.

"Lunch is ready!" Jay shouted from the dining room. "Come eat!"

As we devoured sloppy joes, green beans, and French fries, we ended up talking about school, of all things.

"So Ranger, what did you get your degree in?" asked the queen.

"Finance with a minor in communications. Julian has his MBA, but I couldn't stand to do another two years of college. Four almost killed me."

Queen Lilah whirled on the king with wide eyes.

"My mate is so educated!" she crowed.

A line of pink scorched across his cheekbones, and we all laughed.

"An ignorant king wouldn't last long, would he?" he muttered, then more brightly, "Would you like to get your degree, darling?"

"Oh. Um. Not sure. I'll think about it. I don't even know what I'd want to study."

I felt a little tug on my shirt sleeve and looked down at Posy, who was seated on my left side.

"Did you go to college?" she asked quietly.

I hadn't even finished high school before I was installed as alpha. Dad, Mom, and Mama had tried to tell my father that the four of them could hold the pack together until all of us had turned eighteen, but Royal Price wasn't having it. I ended up finishing the last month of school online while taking over the management of a massive pack, and any thoughts of college evaporated as the workload grew more and more overwhelming.

She doesn't need to know all that drama. Garnet paced anxiously in the back of my mind.

I knew what was upsetting him; it upset me, too. She hadn't met any of the family yet, including my father, and I *dreaded* her seeing how he treated me.

"No. Haven't had the time. Maybe someday. What about you? Were you able to get your high school diploma?"

I doubted she had, but wanted to get the conversation off of me. She shook her head and I told her that she could go back to school in the fall if she wanted to. She didn't respond as I expected, though.

"Oh! That reminds me!" Her eyes lit up as she shimmied in her seat. She raised her voice a little to get my brothers' attention. "I've been meaning to talk to you guys about that. Why don't we have secondary schools here instead of going to the human one?"

"It costs too much," Cole said. "We looked into it, honey, and it would take millions."

"The nursery and elementary schools were already established when we combined packs," Jay explained, "but there was only one middle and one high school, and they're located in Ash's former pack's territory. Dark Woods is too far away, and most of the buildings there have been abandoned for what, Ash? Fifteen, sixteen years?"

"Yeah." Ash nodded. "See, Posy, hunters invaded my pack when I was two and killed nearly everyone. A lot of people avoid the area now, believing it's cursed or some crap like that. Anyway, I highly doubt those buildings are usable anymore. Last time I was there, I noticed the roof had collapsed on the middle school."

"We originally thought about rehabbing them for boarding schools, but shifter families are too tightly knit," Cole added. "Parents didn't want to send their pups away for weeks or months at a time, so we passed on that idea."

Posy was silent for a bit, then her eyes gleamed with determination.

"I disagree with some of your points," she said. "I don't think it has to cost millions to create a school."

"That's just the cost to construct the buildings. Then comes staffing issues, supplies, equipment," Cole began to list, but she cut him off ruthlessly.

"You don't need a new building, just one that's unused right now and can be converted. It's not like we need state-of-the-art here. When you combined packs, you relocated the alpha house and primary pack house here, right? Well, did you leave behind even one empty building that's in good shape?"

Hmm. There's the old alpha house and offices in my territory, and the same in Wyatt's.

"And," she continued, "staff would come from the pack. It's huge, isn't it? Surely there are enough shifters who want or need something to do and could cover the basics required for graduation. Survey the pack members to find out who could teach what."

We did have a small number of shifters looking for work, and a couple of widows and widowers who needed something to occupy their time before their wolves went mad from grief.

It may be feasible, I admitted to myself. *It's only two or three hundred kids.*

I was drawn out of my thoughts when I heard our girl arguing with Cole.

"So you're saying, if I do decide to go back and get my diploma, you want me to attend a human high school. Off pack territory. With only Peri, Callie, and Keeley to help me if something happens."

Uh-oh. She's pulling out the big guns now. She knows we'll never agree to anything that could potentially endanger her.

"Tyler will be a senior this year and would guard you, and there are lots of other—"

"And what if some human male decides I'm fair game, hmm? Humans obviously have boundary issues; we saw that during our first shopping trip, didn't we? What if a guy starts to flirt with me and won't take no for an answer and Tyler's on the other side of the school?"

We all growled deep in our throats.

No boy had better even look *at what's ours,* Garnet snarled, *let alone touch her.*

"You're going to be wearing our ring," Jay reminded her. "Humans invented wedding rings, so even little high school boys should recognize that you're taken. That should give you a layer of protection."

"And I promised I'd teach you how to throw a punch," Wyatt said. "I can show you some other self-defense moves. But, Posy, that stuff doesn't happen very often. Ash and I graduated from there in June and—"

"It happens often enough, Wyatt." Ash scrubbed a hand through his hair. "How many times did you or I step between a handsy prick and a female, regardless of species?"

"And I haven't even mentioned all the trouble human girls cause," Posy added.

"What?" we all said at once.

"Ha! Peri and the twins were right." Posy wore a smug look. "None of you knows what goes on when it comes to the girls' side of things."

"Wait. Back it up. What goes on?" Cole demanded.

"I'll let Peri and the twins tell you that, since I've never seen or experienced it myself. I'll just say that you're very lucky none of the pack girls has wolfed out at school yet."

She paused to take a drink, but still held our complete attention. Even Wyatt, who usually filled the air and our link with constant chatter, was quiet and listening.

213

"I know I made you focus on *me* attending the human school right now, but please think about the future of the pack. It would make shifters safer, provide employment to anyone who wants or needs it, and can be tailored to meet the needs of the pack."

We all sat in stunned silence until the king and queen began clapping. Luke, Gisela, and Ranger joined in, and Posy's cherry red flush spread from her cheeks to her whole face and down her throat to disappear into the neckline of her shirt. I could tell she wanted to hide, but she sat in her chair and kept her head up, even though she fidgeted a bit.

"We'll discuss this at length later and see what we can work out." I leaned over and kissed her forehead, then whispered, "I'm so proud of you, little flower."

Now she hid. She ducked around my arm and buried her face in my back. I chuckled and dropped my hand to her thigh, squeezing it lightly.

"You made several excellent points, luna," declared King Julian. "The kingdom has always promoted furthering the education of our young minds. Draw up a proposal and I'll have a look at it. We can work out a funding solution to get what you need. It might not happen in time for this school year, but I don't see why it couldn't for the next."

"Thank you, your majesty." Posy's voice came out muffled as her face dug deeper into me, and I chuckled again.

"All right, now that lunch is over, let's get this show on the road," Ranger said.

He picked up his dishes and cutlery and walked toward the kitchen. The others had begun to clear up, too, when Wyatt stopped in his tracks and looked at Posy with sudden realization.

"We can't leave Posy here alone. I'd better stay with her."

Of course, that set off an intense debate, which ended in an even more intense game of Rock-Paper-Scissors. When I won, Wyatt and Ash pouted like pups, and Cole glared at me. Only Jay looked unperturbed, but that was because he knew she owed Quartz a snuggle session.

Lucky dog.

"I'll miss you," Posy assured the others, "and I'll be waiting here when you get back."

That appeased them enough to get them moving, although they went through two rounds of hugging her and dropping kisses on her upturned face before they got out the door.

Finally, they were gone, and it was just me and our girl. A rare grin stretched across my face.

Guess I'm a lucky dog, too.

31: First Kiss

Posy

Mason asked me to watch TV with him, so we went into the living room and he took a seat on the couch before pulling me down on his lap.

He picked up the remote and searched for something to watch, but I was completely distracted by his delicious smell.

Do I distract him at all? I wondered.

Nerves bit me to be this close to my handsome mate. Shivering, I rubbed my hands up and down my thighs.

"Hey, Posy," he said softly, "if you don't want to sit on my lap, you can tell me. I won't be mad, and it won't hurt my feelings."

"Oh. No, I like it. I'm just—" I ducked my head, then gathered my courage and looked him in the eyes. "I'm nervous, but in a good way, if that makes sense. Like, an excited nervous."

"Excited nervous?" He chuckled. Dropping the remote, he framed my face in his palms. "Me, too, gorgeous."

"*You're* nervous?" I marveled, tilting my head to the side as I studied his face. "But you're Mason Price, the intimidating iceman around whom even his own brothers step carefully."

"I *am*?" He raised his eyebrows, his face not giving anything away, but I saw the merriment dancing in his eyes.

"You are, and you know you are." I grinned and, unable to help myself, kissed his cheek, then his chin.

"Well, one whiff of your chocolate chip cookie scent and I'm a melted puddle for you, little flower."

I giggled and dropped my eyes to the arms he had around my waist.

Oh! This is the perfect time to ask him!

"I love your tattoos. I could study them for hours. Did you draw them yourself?"

"Ha. No. Can't draw for anything." He stretched out his left arm so I could better see the gears and machinery and armor plating of his mechanical arm tattoo. "Wyatt's excellent at it, though, so I told him what I wanted, and he sketched it out."

"Did you have a reason for this particular design?" I asked and never expected my simple question to lance a huge, pus-filled boil.

"Well," he sighed, "I was eighteen and had just been made alpha. My father was on my back about something and made a comment about me being too much of an emotionless robot to be a good leader."

He snorted and shook his head.

215

"*He* made me that way, the hypocrite. Anyway, long story short, it pissed me off and I wanted to do something to piss him off, too. He hates tattoos, so of course it had to be a full-sleeve one, and I wanted something that would stick in his craw, you know? If he thought I was an emotionless robot, I'd show him just how much of one I was inside."

His chuckle was dark and angry, and I held still in his arms.

This was the most I'd ever heard him say at one time, and it was all about himself. He *never* opened up, so I froze, afraid if I moved that he'd stop talking, and I wanted him to drain out as much poison from this wound as possible.

"Eighteen-year-old boys don't handle their anger so well, Posy."

My heart pinched at the pleading look in his eyes. Was he begging for understanding or acceptance?

Both, Lark whispered.

Swift tears flowed down my face and dripped off my chin.

"Aw, Posy. Don't do that. It was me being young and dumb." He pulled his t-shirt up and wiped my face with it. "Listen, I don't want to talk about my father right now. I don't want to waste a second of my time with you discussing that train wreck."

"You can't bottle things up, Mason. It's not healthy, and you deserve the time to tell someone your worries and have them listen to you."

"We can talk about it later, but not today, okay, baby?"

"Okay." Knowing he needed a topic change, I ran my fingers over his right arm. "What about the dragon tattoo? Is there a story behind it, too?"

"No, I saw it in a book of designs at the tattoo shop when I got the first sleeve done and fell in love with it."

I nodded, then lifted my hand and touched the tattoo behind his left ear.

"What about this one? Is Willow—"

He grabbed my wrist and pulled my fingers away from his skin, and my eyes flew to his face. What I saw there told me I'd screwed up really, *really* badly.

I lowered my eyes to the floor and hunched my shoulders to be small, wanting to be anywhere but there.

"I'm sorry, alpha," I whispered. "I'll be quiet now."

He didn't respond, not a word or movement, and my breath became short and sharp. He still held my wrist, his grip tightening a little, but not painfully so. Not yet, anyway.

Oh, no! He's mad. I'm going to get punished. My heart raced. *Is he going to break my wrist?*

"I forgot." He said it so quietly, I almost couldn't hear it over the blood rushing in my ears.

A tiny whimper slipped from my lips before I could hold it back, and it was like a spell had broken. He dropped my wrist and, ignoring my flinches, pulled me into his chest. I whimpered again, afraid of what he intended, but he only wrapped his arms around my head and shoulders and held me. My face was in his throat and my hands trapped between us, and I didn't dare move an inch.

"Shh. I'm so sorry, little flower. I didn't mean to upset or frighten you." He lowered his lips to my ear and kissed the top of it. "You never have to be quiet. I love hearing your voice and answering your questions. I was caught off guard, that's all. I forgot I had that tattoo, haven't thought about it since I found you, and I was struggling with how I felt about that."

I stayed still and silent, my go-to when stressed or scared. He swallowed hard, and I wished I had the courage to see what was in his eyes, but every muscle was frozen.

"Willow was my sister," he murmured in my ear. "My twin. She died during the sickness. We were fifteen."

I sucked in a sharp breath, and my fingers clenched into his shirt.

"My brothers tried to help with the grief, but they had their own losses to deal with. Your mom died in the sickness, too, right? I remember your brothers telling us that."

I nodded.

"Posy, please talk to me," he begged.

I bit my lip and shook my head. I didn't know what to say.

After a long sigh, he laid his cheek on top of my head.

"Willow always hung out with the five of us. After she was gone, I was adrift, like I didn't fit with my brothers anymore. I know some of that was my fault for shutting them out, but I—"

He hesitated, then everything poured out of him.

"I was the first of us to turn eighteen, to step up as alpha. For more than a year, I had to handle everything for five packs. I was *so busy* all the time. The work never ended. The parents helped out a lot, but my brothers were still in school. That isolated me from them even more. Now that Ash and Wyatt are full alphas, I'm still figuring out the new dynamic. I overstep a lot and catch myself treating them the way my father treats me, and I hate that. I'm surprised they don't hate me, too."

"Of course they don't hate you!" I wiggled my arms out from between us and hugged his waist as tight as I could. "They love you, Mason. *I* love you. You're the glue that holds them all together. Without you, they'd fall apart. If you feel alone, *talk* to one of them. Play pool

217

with Cole. Go for a walk with Jayden. Shoot some hoops with Ash. Work out with Wyatt. They're just waiting for you to open up to them, I promise you!"

His chest shuddered under my cheek, and a couple of wet drops hit the top of my head.

Oh, my heart.

"Mason, I'm sorry about your sister. I'm sorry you had to go through such a devastating loss."

"Thank you, sweetheart. Hey, Posy?"

"Yeah?"

"Don't call me alpha. You're our mate. Our luna. I love you. Besides, you're the most dangerous wolf in the pack. *You* don't kneel to any of us."

"Dangerous? *Me?*" I scoffed. I knew a scared little runt like me wouldn't stand a chance against anyone.

"No, really. It's true. You know why? Because you have five alphas behind you, ready to support you in all things. This school project? You know it's going to happen. We have to argue about it a bit first because that's how we are, but there will be secondary schools on pack territory simply because you want it to happen. You see what I mean? The power you hold over us is what makes you dangerous."

I lifted my head and stared into his gray eyes, and a sudden desire sprung up inside me.

"Mason?"

"Hmm?"

"Can I kiss you?"

His whole body tensed against mine for a second, then he relaxed with a sexy smirk on his lips.

"Only if I can kiss you back."

"Of course!" I smiled brightly.

He slid his hands up and down my back and I leaned in so close, I could count every one of his eyelashes.

"Can you feel my heart beating?" he murmured as his gaze dipped to my lips.

"Yes," I whispered. "It's beating as hard as mine."

"I know. I can hear it."

"This is my first kiss," I confessed.

"Mine, too, baby."

Then his big, soft lips were on mine and a zoo of butterflies fluttered around in my stomach. Neither of us really knew what we were doing, but it didn't matter. We figured it out together with little soft kisses that grew into longer, more heated ones.

Without lifting his lips from mine, Mason rearranged us so that my legs straddled his and my bum hung between his spread knees.

218

His hands fitted to my waist, but the longer we explored each other's mouths, the lower his hands slid until he was fully cupping my bum cheeks.

A hot wire of need twisted in my belly as his long fingers squeezed dangerously close to where I'd started to tingle and ache. I wanted to do *things* to him, wanted him to do *things* to me, and I had no idea what those *things* were.

When his tongue licked along the seam between my lips, I got the impression he wanted me to open up, so I did. His tongue slipped into my mouth and explored every corner. I could taste him, *him*, Mason Price, and goosebumps popped up everywhere.

Shivering, I squirmed a little to get closer to him. His sharp inhale and tightening grip on my bum drew my attention to something hard poking my inner thigh. When I realized what it was, my eyes widened and I pulled back a bit to look at him.

"Is that—"

"Yeah. He wants to be inside you." He peppered my throat and chin with little kisses.

"I'm sorry! I didn't mean to—"

"Hush, baby. Just because he stands up doesn't mean you have to do anything about it. Ignore him. I do it *all* the time."

"But now you're stuck like that for ... for how long?"

"He'll calm down on his own eventually," he chuckled, "and if he doesn't, I'll take a cold shower to *make* him calm down."

He didn't seem angry about it, so I decided I shouldn't feel guilty. I *was* curious, though.

"Mason?"

"Hmm?" he hummed as he kissed the notch between my collar bones.

"Can I, um, touch it? Him?"

"What?" He lifted his head and met my eyes.

"Mr. Penis. Can I touch him? I'll be super careful with him, I promise."

A deep groan reverberated through his chest as he closed his eyes, and I scolded myself for asking. I opened my mouth to apologize, but he just moved to lay on his back and pulled me beside him. Then his big hand grabbed mine and laid it on top of his soft sweat shorts.

My fingers found a hard rod that twitched underneath the fabric, and I gulped at the size of it.

And he thinks he's putting that where *when it's time to mate?*

"You still want to do this?" His voice came out as a husky rasp.

"Yes." I met his eyes without blinking, and that seemed to be all the answer he needed.

His hand held mine in place for a moment longer, then showed me how to rub over the long, steely length. He did that a couple of times, then released my hand so he could slide his fingers into my hair and angle my face up for more kisses.

Excited, I stroked him harder and faster, and he broke the kiss to tilt his head back on a heavy groan, his Adam's apple bobbing and the mark I'd given him was on full display. Feeling bold, I laid an open-mouth kiss on it and sucked the skin gently.

"Bite it," he hissed.

"What?"

I was so shocked, my hand clamped around what it had been stroking, and another groan left his lips.

"Bite. My. Mate. Mark," he demanded through gritted teeth.

I didn't want to hurt him, but he asked me to do it. Gently, I nipped at it, and a tremendous shudder ripped through his big body. One of his hands dropped to mine again and guided it faster and harder than what I'd been doing.

And I was worried that I was being too rough, I laughed at myself.

Suddenly, he stuffed his face in my neck and tightened his hand around mine so that I was squeezing him hard.

"*Posy!*"

A patch of warm wetness grew under my hand until the front of his shorts was soaked.

"Mason, did you pee on me? I mean, I understand that accidents happen, but did you seriously *pee* on me?"

He laughed so hard, he almost shook me off the couch.

"No, baby," he said between chuckles. "It's not pee. Does it embarrass you?"

"I'm not embarrassed." I frowned and tried to get him to look at me, but he wouldn't come out from his hiding spot in my neck. "If it's not pee, what is it?"

He finally raised his head, and his gray eyes were full of amusement.

"Pup-making juice."

"Ah." I nodded, remembering Wyatt's explanation. "Okay. So long as it wasn't pee."

He laughed again and shook his head with a silly grin.

Oh, good. He's not upset or angry! In fact, this is the happiest and most relaxed I've ever seen him.

"Uh, Posy, can I make one request?"

"Yes?" I narrowed my eyes in suspicion of what he might ask for.

"Please don't say Mr. Penis again. *Please.* I see Wyatt's stupid face when you do and that is not an image I want in my mind when you're giving me a hand— When you're touching me like that, okay?"

"Okay, Mason," I giggled.

"Oh, and little flower?"

"Hmm?"

"One day real soon, I want to return the favor."

#

Wyatt

"Hey, cutie!" I called as I walked in the kitchen.

The others trailed behind me, all of us on the hunt for snacks after our visit to the clinic. I went straight to our girl and wrapped my arms around her waist from behind.

"Hi, Wyatt. You're back sooner than I expected. Not that I'm complaining!" She gave me a big sunshine smile over her shoulder.

"We brought Lilah back," I explained, stuffing my face in her neck and inhaling her cookie goodness. "The king wants her to rest for a bit, so he's putting her to bed in the upstairs guest room. Then we're heading over to the cells as soon as the betas get here to guard you two."

"Where's Mase?" Cole asked. "He hasn't been answering the mind link for the past hour."

"He's cleaning up and changing his shorts." Posy giggled. "He got juice all over them."

"Not my apple juice, I hope," Luke teased.

From the way fire burned up her cheeks, I had a hunch that she wasn't talking about any kind of fruit juice.

"No," she giggled again. "Not *that* kind of juice. Pup-m—"

I got my hand over her mouth in time, and she looked up at me with wide eyes.

Our naughty girl, Granite giggled.

She doesn't know any better, I told him.

Does it matter?

With a sigh, I tossed her over my shoulder and carried her away from everyone.

"Wyatt? Did I do something? Are you mad?"

"Everything's okay, cutie. I just need to talk to you about something real quick."

When I was sure we were alone, I set her on her feet and took her face in my hands.

"That's not the kind of thing to say in front of others," I told her in a gentle tone, then kissed her forehead. "That's only to talk about in private with your mates. Bedroom talk, okay?"

"Oh! Should I apologize to Luke? Did I embarrass him?"

"No, cutie." I chuckled. "He's good, but I didn't want *you* to be embarrassed once you realized you said something in front of him that you shouldn't have."

"All right, Wyatt. Thank you for watching out for me."

I melted at her sweet, earnest face. This girl had my whole heart.

Hiding my smile, I hardened my expression and gave her a stern look.

"Now, Posy, I want an honest answer to this question."

"Of course. I'd never lie to you, Wyatt, or any of my mates."

"Tell me exactly what you and Mase were doing while we were gone." I grinned as red flooded her cheeks again. "And don't you *dare* leave out a single detail."

32: Get Well Soon

King Julian

Even with their bruised and swollen faces, the twin betas would have been impossible to tell apart if not for the blond highlights one had added to his dark hair.

"Julian? Let me in, please."

My beloved queen put her hands on my back and shoved, and a grin pulled my lips up.

Goddess, I love this woman.

Nyx perked up a little as Lilah's aggression caught his interest.

Pushy mate. Pushy mate is sexy. Jul, tell mate to be pushy in bed tonight.

I snapped the link closed as he projected a steamy image of us dominating our 'pushy' mate. While I was all for it, now was not the time - and I didn't need a tent in my pants while I talked to her family.

With a quick glance, I knew there was no threat in the room. The two guys were in such bad shape, I doubted they could blink without pain, much less hurt my queen. Turning to the side, I reached behind me and slid my hand to the small of Lilah's back, then drew her in front of me.

Her eyes went right to the two hospital beds that were positioned side-by-side, and she slumped against me with a whimper. I quickly wrapped my arm around her waist and held her close to my side.

"Oh, no!" Her voice wobbled and cracked.

"Who are they?" I asked.

"Zayne has the highlights," she sniffed as tears rolled down her cheeks. "His wolf is Delta. Zayden's wolf is Lake. They're twenty-one. Their sister Junie is my best friend."

Not what I was asking, but good information nonetheless. I'd been calling them Highlights and No Highlights in my head, but I didn't think she would appreciate hearing that right now.

"I meant, how are you related to them?" I clarified.

"They're my cousins. My mom and their dad were siblings. Oh, my Goddess, my aunt must be so worried. I hope she and Junie are okay."

"Killed her," came a quiet croak from Zayden's bed, and Lilah immediately ran over to his side.

"Zayden?" She picked his hand up and rubbed her thumb over his bruised knuckles. "Zayden, what happened?"

"Killed Mom." His voice gained a little strength as his swollen eyes slit open a bit. "Alpha killed Mom."

"No!" She covered her mouth with one hand. "No, no, no! Not Aunt Susie!"

"Took our Junie. Alpha took our Junie."

"Zayden, what are you saying?" she whispered.

"We fought him. Him and half the pack. Couldn't stop them." His voice broke and a tear streaked from the corner of his left eye. "Killed Mom. Took our Junie. Our Junie."

Closing his eyes, he passed out with his sister's name on his lips.

Poor guy, I thought at the same time Nyx said, *Half the pack?*

I frowned, wishing we could get more information from these two, but it obviously wasn't happening any time soon. I needed to talk to the doctor and find out—

Lilah's knees gave out, and I grabbed her before she hit the floor. Swinging her up in my arms, I cradled her against my chest. She clutched my shoulders and buried her face in my neck, her hot tears trickling down to soak my shirt.

"I can't. Julian, I can't!" she gasped. "Not Junie. Please, *please*, not Junie!"

"Look at me, Lilah."

She only sobbed harder, breaking my heart.

"Darling, look at me."

"This is all my fault!" she wailed.

"Lilah. Look. At. Me." I waited until she lifted her face. Her eyes were wild and her skin flour-white, making all her freckles stand out like tiny bruises. "None of this is your fault."

"But Junie—"

"I'll go get her, shall I? I'll bring her back here to you."

"Promise?"

"I promise, darling. I'll take care of this. You don't have to cry anymore. I'll fix it, baby."

"Your majesty? A word?"

Luke's voice surprised me. Concerned for my queen, I'd forgotten I wasn't alone.

I'd split us all up once we arrived at the clinic. I sent the four alphas to talk with their betas and interview the witch, but kept Ranger, Gisela, and Luke with me.

I turned with Lilah in my arms and raised an eyebrow in question as I looked at their three concerned faces.

"Sire, how about I find a chair for her?" Gisela asked. "My queen, would you like to sit down?"

"I don't want to be separated from her," I growled.

"Of course not. I'll bring one in here," she offered. "I'm sure she'll want to sit by their bedsides for a bit."

224

I hesitated, not wanting her out of my arms, but Gisela pointed out she'd be more comfortable, and Lilah said she'd like that, so I nodded. My beta slipped out of the room, and I looked at the other two.

"Want me to fetch the doctor?" Ranger scratched his scruffy chin.

"Yes, please, Ranger. And thank you."

His eyebrows flew up for a second, then he grinned before also darting out of the room.

Glad he understands that that *is as close to an apology as he's going to get.*

"Your majesty," Luke began, "the twins are still part of the Tall Pines pack. Like he did with us, I'm sure the alpha will torment them through the pack mind link. Is there anything you can do to help with that?"

There were several things I could do, and I took the time to debate each one. Finally, I nodded.

"I'll take care of it once they're conscious again."

"Thank you." Luke dipped his head.

Gisela came back in with two male orderlies, each pushing a trolley that carried an armchair, and Lilah started to wiggle around in my arms.

Put me down, please, my love.

I lowered her to her feet and kept my hands on her waist until I was sure she was steady. She and Gisela directed the orderlies to set the chairs on either side of the twins' beds, then thanked them.

"Of course, your majesty," one replied with a polite little bow.

The other one looked petrified to be in my presence. He kept glancing at me out of the corner of his eye, and Nyx took far too much pleasure in the fear pouring off of him.

Psychopath, I grumbled.

After the orderlies left, Lilah got comfortable in the chair next to Zayden, her eyes jumping from his face to Zayne's every few seconds.

On one hand, I knew she needed to be near them, but there was too much to do for me to wait around here. On the other hand, I wasn't sure we could be apart from her right now. Nyx was calm, but only in the way the eye of a hurricane is calm.

Set guards and go, he grunted. *Nyx will be good.*

You sure?

Nyx sure. Set guards.

"Luke, Gisela," I said, "stay here with Lilah. Contact me if either of them wake up and are coherent enough to talk. I'm going to find Ranger and talk to their doctor. I'll let you know what he says."

"Yes, sire."

"Certainly, your majesty."

I leaned down and gave Lilah a gentle kiss. She gave me a questioning look when I stood up.

"I'll be back. You sit with your cousins, darling."

"Thank you, Julian," she said with a smile.

I left the room and followed Ranger's scent until I met him coming back with a doctor.

"Your majesty." The doctor, an older shifter with graying hair, bowed at the waist. "Would you care to talk in my office?"

"Lead the way." I held out one hand in a gesture to proceed, which he did.

Ranger fell into step beside me.

"You shouldn't have promised her that," he muttered.

"What?"

"That you'd go get this Junie chick and bring her back."

"Why not?" I scowled.

"For all you know, she's already dead."

"Don't say that!" I barked. "Don't tempt fate. It would kill Lilah."

"Just being a realist." He threw up his hands. "What if there's no happy ending here, Julian?"

Plowing one hand through my hair, I let out a gusty breath. He was right. There were some things not even a king could do.

"I don't know, Ranger, but I'm going to do everything in my power to make one happen."

#

Ash

Tristan's mate looked to be on death's door.

Tubes stuck in her everywhere and an oxygen mask covered most of her face. She'd been changed into a hospital gown at some point, and her skin looked milk white against the blue fabric. She was still as a stone; not even her eyes moved under her purple-veined eyelids.

Tristan sat rocking in a hard, plastic chair, his hands clasped between his knees and his eyes fixed on her battered face. Our other betas were scattered around the room, their faces grim as they waited with him in quiet solidarity.

"How bad are her injuries?" Cole broke the silence.

"Severe concussion." Tristan listed them in a flat monotone. "Broken right wrist and left ankle. Four fractured ribs, one of which punctured her lung and caused it to collapse. Some damage to her kidneys."

"What are her odds?"

"Doc says fifty-fifty. Says she'll either wake up or she won't and—" The monotone faltered for a second, and he swallowed hard. "And I don't even know her name."

"Is Luke MacGregor somewhere nearby?" Crew asked quietly. "Maybe he could see if he knows her."

All their eyes fixed on us.

"He's here at the clinic, but he said he'd never known Alpha Halder to use witches before." I shoved my hands in my pockets. "We'll get him to come by, though. Won't hurt to ask him."

"Did you find anything on her or in her clothing?" Cole asked. "ID of any kind?"

Tristan frowned and shook his head.

"I haven't looked. The nurse put her stuff in that bag." He pointed to a green plastic drawstring bag in the corner. "There was no purse or anything, so I didn't think it was worth going through."

"Do you mind if we look?" Jay asked. "Just to make sure?"

When he shook his head again, Wyatt went over and picked it up.

"We'll be right back," he said.

Tristan nodded, already dismissing us as he went back to his silent vigil.

My brothers and I followed Wyatt down a couple of doors until we found an empty room. He dumped the bag on the bed and spread the items around. With more class than I thought him capable of, he quickly bundled up the bra and panties and stuffed them back in the bag without a single dirty comment.

There wasn't much to go through. A torn blouse. A pair of jean shorts that Jay grabbed to search the pockets. Socks. Canvas sneakers. A black drawstring pouch that held a deck of tarot cards, as I discovered when I looked.

Since there was nothing else, I examined the cards closer. The bag was nothing special, just soft velvet, but the cards were beautifully illustrated.

"She won't like that you touched those," Cole chided me.

"She can re-consecrate them later," I said with a shrug and continued to look through the deck.

The cards were in various stages of being finished. The illustrations were sketched in on some, but not colored. Others didn't have gilded edges. A few were completely blank. It looked as if the artist hadn't finished the deck before selling it.

Why would a witch want an unfinished deck of tarot cards? I asked myself.

Because she making them, Sid answered in a *duh* tone.

What?

She making own cards and not finished yet.
Dang, buddy. You're a smart cookie!
I get cookies? Sid bounced around happily.
Sure, buddy.

"What did you find?" Cole hovered at my elbow and looked at the cards.

"Just that she's in the process of making a set of tarot cards, and she's a great artist."

"See if she signed them," said Wyatt, who was a great artist in his own right.

On the hunt now, I shuffled through the deck slower this time. The backs were solid navy blue, so I didn't bother to look there. I focused on finding cards that were definitely finished and found three I thought were: The Tower, the Ace of Cups, and the Moon. I knew a little about witches, but I didn't know jack about reading tarot cards. I picked the Moon card simply because it had a wolf on it.

"Her pockets are empty," Jay said. "Did you find a signature, Ash?"

"Maybe." I held the card closer to my face, angled it to catch the light, and spotted a tiny line of text in the bottom right corner. "Oh, yeah! I'm the GOAT!"

The boys crowded around me. Wyatt reached for the card I was holding, and Cole slapped his hand down. Before Wyatt could retaliate, Cole explained that the witch would already need to re-consecrate the cards from my touch. She didn't need to do it twice simply because he was curious. Wyatt huffed, but nodded.

"Let me check one of the other ones," I said, "to make sure they match."

They nodded and stepped back, and I grabbed the Ace of Cups. My eyes went to the bottom right corner and saw the same lettering.

"Man, she must have used a brush that had one little strand of camel hair to write this small." I shook my head in amazement, then gathered up all the cards and put them back into the black pouch.

"What are you doing?" Jay asked.

"Going to tell Tristan his mate's name."

"How do you know she's the one creating the cards?" Wyatt demanded.

"Why else would she have them?" I shrugged. "Besides, it feels right."

"Well, just tell Tristan what you found. You don't need to claim that it's her name. See if *he* thinks it 'feels right'," Cole suggested.

We put the rest of her stuff back in the plastic bag and returned to our betas. I did what Cole said and explained what I found.

"What's the name?" Tristan asked with hope in his eyes.

"Ariel Del Vecchio."

A sharp inhale came from the girl lying on the bed, audible even through the oxygen mask and over the beeping machines she was hooked up to. She hadn't moved, didn't even look to be breathing, and her eyes were still closed.

Tristan raced over, picked up her hand without an IV in it, and leaned over her.

"Ariel?" he whispered. "Is your name Ariel?"

Her eyelids flew up, revealing big hazel irises that locked onto his face.

"Mate?" she rasped.

"Mate," Tristan confirmed with tears sparkling in his eyes.

His grin threatened to split his face in half, and her answering smile was just as big.

"Go get a doctor," Cole told Matthew, who ran out of the room.

Tristan and Ariel were staring into each other's eyes, and we gestured for the betas to step out into the hallway with us.

Once there, we all heaved a sigh of relief. The tension in that room had been incredible.

"So, we need you up at the house," I told them. "The king wants to interview the prisoners and won't leave the queen unguarded. Plus, Posy will be there, too."

"Is she there alone right now?" Emerson asked, suddenly alert. "Is our luna unguarded?"

"Mase is with her," Jay assured him.

"Tristan will stay with his mate, of course," Wyatt said. "If you guys need anything, go get it now and rendezvous at our place. I don't know how long we'll need you on guard duty."

"Sure thing, alpha," Crew said. "Be there in twenty."

He took off down the hall, and Emerson soon followed.

"Ty, we're going to wait until Matthew brings the doc around," I explained, "then we have to go check in with the king. You need to swing by the O and grab anything?"

"No, I'm good. Thanks, though."

"Need a ride up to the house?"

"If you're going that way." He shrugged. "If not, I can shift and let River run."

"Well, it's your lucky day. You get to ride with us!" I grinned at him. "Who's a special puppy?"

"I am not a *puppy*, alpha," he growled and scowled up at me.

Laughing, I slung my arm out and caught him in a headlock.

"Hey! Stop that, alpha! Abuse of power! Abuse of power!"

I gently scrubbed his head with my knuckles, then released him.

I loved this kid and wanted him to loosen up a bit. His life had been garbage for so long, he needed something great to happen to him.

He will find mate on birthday, Sid yipped and pranced around.

Maybe, I agreed. *That would be something great, although unlikely.*

No, he will, Sid insisted.

I didn't like arguing with my wolf, so I let it go. Time would tell which of us was right.

33: Ice Pops and Party Planning

Posy

"Let's torture Tyler," Queen Lilah whispered in my ear.

Swinging my head around, I saw her wicked grin. She winked at me, and I instantly understood.

We had taken over the pool-side cabana in the backyard, relaxing on the cushioned loungers and sucking on ice pops that the betas took turns fetching for us. We'd gotten a text from Peri, asking if she could come over and hang out, and we were plotting how to get her here.

I couldn't drive, and the king had asked the queen to stay on our property with the betas until he returned. Since he'd *asked* her instead of *ordered* her to, she wanted to reward him by complying.

"Tyler?" I called, and he came right over.

"Yeah, luna? Want another ice pop?" he asked with a big grin.

"No, thank you. Do you know how to drive?"

"Yeah, but I don't have a car or anything." Now his eyes were puzzled, as if he couldn't work out where I was going with the question.

"Could you please go pick Peri up for us? She can't drive and we want to hang out with her."

"Luna, my orders are to stay here and guard you." Tyler straightened to his full height and pulled his shoulders back.

"Out of curiosity, can a luna's orders override an alpha's?" I asked Queen Lilah.

"Asking for a friend, are you? Well, I'm not sure, but I know a queen's can."

She gave Tyler a sweet smile, and his cheeks and the tops of his ears flushed red.

"Your majesty, I'd be failing in my duty if I left my post to run an errand."

He swallowed hard, his Adam's apple bobbing, and the conflict was clear on his face. I opened my mouth to put him out of his misery, but Luke stepped in before I could say anything.

"Ty, we're on pack territory and there are five other betas here, one of whom is the king's. Your luna will be safe and protected." His stern expression relaxed into a kind smile. "Take a word of advice, son. Piss off your alpha a dozen times before you piss off your luna once."

Tyler jerked his head in a quick nod of acknowledgement, then looked at me.

"All right, luna. Which car should I use?"

"Take your pick." I shrugged, not really caring.

"Um, actually, luna, the alphas are fussy about their vehicles," Matthew was brave enough to say despite my glare. "For example, Alpha Mason does not let anyone drive his truck."

He and the rest of the betas joined us and claimed their own loungers.

"Hmm. Well, they took Cole's and the king's vehicles, which leaves Wyatt, Ash and Jayden." I tilted my head and raised an eyebrow at him. "Of those three, which of my mates would mind the least?"

"Don't touch Alpha Wyatt's car if you want to keep breathing," Emerson muttered, and Matthew and Crew burst out laughing.

"Alpha Jay won't care, Ty, so take his," Crew said, still grinning. "He only sees vehicles as a tool to get from point A to point B and doesn't understand his brothers' obsession."

"What about Ash?" I asked, curious now.

"Normally, I'd say he wouldn't care either, but he just got it like a month ago. I think he's still a little possessive of it."

"A boy with a new toy," the queen chuckled.

I grinned and told Tyler where to find the keys. Once he was gone, Luke plopped on the lounger next to Lilah and pulled his mate down to lay on top of him.

"Sister, why are you being so cruel to that boy?" he asked.

"What are you talking about?" she demanded. "He likes her! She likes him! What does it hurt to arrange some one-on-one time for them to get to know each other better?"

"Even though they're clearly attracted to each other and their chemistry is obvious to everyone, you can't *know* that they'll be mates."

"I think that sentence contributed more evidence to my argument than yours, dear brother."

"We aren't doing anything wrong, are we?" My wide eyes bounced between the two. "It won't hurt anything for them to become friends, regardless of whether or not they're destined to be mates. Your mate should be your friend, too, right?"

"Yes, luna," Luke said, his voice gentler than usual and calming my worry. "Your mate should be your friend, too."

"When's Peri's birthday?" the queen asked.

I knew she was really asking when we would know if they *were* mates.

"Cole said it's next week. Hey, Emerson?"

He broke away from his conversation with Matthew to grin at me.

"Yes, little luna bunny? More ice pops?"

"Sure. That would be great. Would you please bring some for everyone? And do you know Peri's birthday?"

"June thirtieth. Next Wednesday," he said as he jogged over to the freezer in the outdoor kitchen.

"Do you know when Tyler's is?"

"July eighth."

"We should throw big parties for both of them!" I clasped my hands together under my chin, my eyes already sparkling as ideas came to me.

"Peri's parents already have that in the works," Crew told me. "They always have big celebrations for all their kids' birthdays, your mates included. I think it's a pool party for her this year."

"And what about Tyler?" I asked him. "Do his parents plan a big party?"

All three betas froze, Emerson in the act of handing the queen her ice pop. My eyes darted from one of them to the other, wondering what I'd said.

"He doesn't have any family." Crew gave me a small smile. "He lives at the O."

"The O?" My brow furrowed.

"The orphanage," Matthew muttered.

Two words and my heart broke.

"For— For how long?" My voice wavered, my eyes stung, and my ice pop fell to the concrete floor.

"Since he was twelve or so." Crew began to look a little panicky. "Are you okay, luna?"

"What happened to his parents?" I whispered.

"Well, you see, Alpha Jay—"

"That part is not our story to tell," Emerson cut Crew off. "They died, luna. Violently and in front of him. That's common information in the pack, and if Ty wants you to know more than that, he'll tell you himself."

Holding back the tears was a lost cause now. I cupped my hands over my nose and mouth and let them flow. Handing her ice pop to Luke, Lilah got out of her lounger, sat on the side of mine, and hugged me.

"Why did you tell her that?" Matthew hissed. "The alphas are going to kill us for upsetting her!"

"You're the only one who needs to worry," Crew snickered. "You pissed Alpha Mason off twice in as many days and over the same issue. You know he's going to tear you a new one as soon as he gets a chance. What's one more offense at this point?"

"Shut it, Crew."

Ignoring them, I hugged Lilah back and cried a little bit. Tyler was as sweet as pie; I'd imagined him surrounded by a happy, loving family.

"Little luna bunny, what's wrong?" Emerson laid a hand on my head.

"Who makes his birthday cake?" I sniffled. "Does he even get presents?"

"Well, alphas Ash, Jayden, and Wyatt took a special interest in him when he was orphaned. I think they make sure he's taken care of. I remember last year hearing them tell the den mother to order him blue cupcakes."

"Who does ... he share ... them with? Who's there .... to celebrate ... with him?" I hiccuped, getting more worked up, not less.

"There are other kids in the O," he assured me. "Although most of them are younger than Ty, he's friends with them. And this year he's a beta. We're planning to do something for him. Do you want to celebrate with us?"

I nodded and got myself under control. He and Peri would be back soon, and I didn't want him to know I'd been crying for him. He might mistake it for pity.

"Luna?"

A big, tanned hand held out a box of tissues, which I took gratefully. After I blew my nose and wiped my face, I raised my eyes to see everyone staring at me with concerned expressions. Except for Gisela, who was fast asleep in her mate's arms.

"I'm fine," I croaked.

"Want another ice pop?" Crew leaped up to get it before I could reply. "It'll feel good on your throat, and you dropped your last one."

"Luke, where's *my* ice pop?" The queen glared at her brother.

"What? It was melting. Just grab another one."

"That is not the point. It was *my* ice pop."

"I got you, Queen Lilah." Crew handed her one.

As she thanked him, he gave me mine and I smiled at him.

"Luna bunny?" Emerson crouched down next to me. "When's the last time *you* had a birthday party? Or cake? Or presents?"

I shrugged, then smiled brightly when I remembered.

"Ash got me a present this year!" I grinned. "A set of hair pins with the prettiest flowers! I didn't even *ask* for them and he got them for me!"

I didn't understand the emotion burning in Emerson's eyes, but an idea popped into my mind and distracted me.

"We are going to give Tyler a big party. Here at the alpha house. And he's going to get a cake and presents. And you're all coming."

"Sounds great." Emerson chuckled. "Tell us how to help and we'll do it."

"Queen Lilah," I swiveled to look at her, "you'll help me plan it, right? I've never planned a birthday party before."

"Of course, I'll help. It'll be loads of fun. Is it going to be a surprise or not?"

I bit my lip. I didn't know Tyler well enough to know if he liked surprises. He might go the whole day thinking everyone had forgotten him, and I didn't want him to feel bad for a single second on his biggest birthday.

"How about I invite him for a birthday meal," I thought out loud, "but have a pool party set up back here? Is that too boring?"

"I think it's a great idea," she chirped and clapped her hands.

"I doubt he'll go swimming."

We both looked at Matthew, who rubbed the back of his neck and looked at his feet. Glancing at the other two betas, I saw an uncomfortable expression on their faces, too.

What do they know that I don't?

"Oh. Well, he doesn't have to swim. Just eat the cake and ice cream and open the presents. Other people can swim if they want to."

I finished my ice pop and added the wrapper to the tidy stack on the floor.

"I'm here, fan club!"

A sudden shout made all our heads turn to see Peri pelting around the side of the house.

"Thank you for waiting! Sorry, no autographs at this time!"

The queen and I laughed as she came to a stop right in front of us and jumped up and down in her excitement.

Tyler ambled along behind her and his eyes flicked to her bum as she bounced around. That made the queen and me dissolve into giggles. Fortunately, Peri thought it was because of her antics.

"Hey, Per. I thought you went to Disney with the Horde?" Matthew asked as he handed her, the queen, and me each an ice pop.

These guys are definitely trying to give me a sugar rush. But they're so good on a hot day!

"I *was* with them, but I flew home the day before I went shopping with you guys. We did the theme parks the first week, which was *ah-maz-ing*, but the boys got to pick the activities for this week. You know what they picked? A monster truck show, a dirt bike rally, and a car show." She screwed her face up, and I giggled. "So, since Mama and Papa are there to help with the little ones, Mom and Dad let me come home rather than be tortured."

She brought out her phone to show us all some photos from the trip. The last picture in her album was of her hugging Callie and Keeley Breckenridge goodbye right before the family boarded the plane.

"Oh, we should have invited the twins over!" I said, feeling bad for forgetting them.

"The alphas gave them a job." Peri waved a hand dismissively. "Asked them to go to the clinic and sit with a pair of visiting wolves who were injured somehow. I didn't get the full story."

"Oh?" I traded a glance with Queen Lilah.

"Yeah, apparently they're the king's family or something." Peri looked at the queen. "Do you know who they are?"

"My cousins." Queen Lilah dropped her eyes to her lap. "I didn't like leaving them, but Julian needs to interview some prisoners and didn't want me to stay without him. I only agreed to come back here when he asked the alphas to find someone to sit with them until they woke up."

"Oh, Goddess! What if they turned out to be mates?" Luke chuckled. "Identical twins with identical twins."

Peri's eyes brightened and she pulled out her phone. Tapping away, she explained she was texting Callie and Keeley to ask that very question.

"Why not just link them?" Crew asked her.

"Can't send emojis through the link. Duh." Her phone tinged and she read the reply, but from the way her shoulders drooped, we all knew the response. "Aw, rats. Not mates."

"Can you ask them how Zayne and Zayden are?" Queen Lilah asked in a hopeful voice.

"Of course, your majesty."

While she texted the twins again, Emerson asked Luke about their injuries.

"The king talked to their doctor," he said as he shuffled his sleeping mate into a more comfortable position. "Lots of broken bones and deep bruising and concussions, but no internal injuries. Lake and Delta, their wolves, will sort them out eventually."

"The twins say the twins are still asleep, but they seem much more comfortable than they did at first," Peri told the queen. "Callie says their faces look more relaxed and some of the bruising has even gone down."

"Oh, that's good news." The queen grinned and squeezed her brother's shoulder, who smiled back.

"What about Tristan's mate?" I looked at the betas. "Any update?"

Ash had told me a little about her condition and that they had found out her name at least.

"Tristan says she's awake, but in a lot of pain," Crew told me. "He hasn't been able to get much information out of her yet."

"As soon as she's more coherent, he's going to ask her if he can mark her. Then Creek can help heal her," Emerson added.

"If she knew they were mates, she has to be some kind of shifter, right? A human witch wouldn't feel a mate bond, would she?" the queen asked.

"Ha ha ha. She *is* a shifter!" Matthew was overcome by laughter, but still managed to get out, "She's a *bird* shifter! Ha ha ha."

"I've never heard of such a thing," I said, shocked. "Are you making a joke? Or is it true? And if it's true, why is it so funny?"

"Yes, she's a bird shifter, which are very rare," Emerson said, "and I don't know why Matthew finds it so hilarious."

"A *bird*! Ha ha ha! She shifts into a *bluebird*! Ha ha ha!" Matthew was reduced to a pile of giggles by this point.

We all ignored him when Tyler, who had been quiet since he'd returned with Peri, started to speak.

"Queen Lilah, I'm not sure if the king is aware that she's a bird shifter. Tristan only linked us that information a few minutes ago. You may want to let him know."

"Of course, but I can see that you know something you aren't saying." The queen tilted her head and narrowed her eyes at him.

"Um, so, the alphas let me check books out of the alpha library. It's a really impressive collection, which isn't surprising considering it's five packs' accumulation over three or four hundred years."

"I'd like to see it!" I bubbled and suddenly remembered that Jayden liked to read.

I bet he camps out there all the time.

"I'll be happy to escort you anytime." Tyler's smile transformed his face from handsome to gorgeous, and I heard a little sigh slip out of Peri. "Anyway, a couple of summers ago, I found a biography on the royal family."

"I bet that was *such* an interesting read. Little nerd," Matthew scoffed.

"He's not a nerd for wanting to educate himself!" I scolded him, and Lark's growl underscored my voice. "You would benefit from the same, only you should start with a book on manners!"

Luke, Emerson and Crew chuckled, and I expected Matthew to turn red with rage, but I was wrong. His face went white and his eyes bugged out.

"Third strike, Beta Matthew." Crew shook his head, still chuckling. "There's no way Garnet missed hearing her little wolf bark at you. You just don't learn, do you?"

"It *was* an interesting read, actually," Tyler spoke before Matthew could reply. "The part I'm thinking of, well, I don't know how to say this, Queen Lilah."

"Just say it, sweetie."

Pink fired over Tyler's whole face at her endearment, and he stammered a bit as he answered her.

"The king's grandfather kept a bird shifter. In a cage. As a pet. For years. Maybe his family knows more about them than we do."

Everyone was silent for a moment, processing the new information.

"Do you think you could find that book again?" the queen asked Tyler. When he nodded, she said, "I would like to see it. I'll also notify the king about Tristan's mate. Thank you."

"Always your servant, your majesty." He nodded.

"You know, if the library is that extensive, there might be something on other species of shifters." Emerson pursed his lips. "Ty, maybe you could look into that, too."

"Of course."

"Okay, let's have some fun after all the serious talk." Peri held up her tote bag with a bright smile. "Who wants to go swimming?"

I bit my lip. Everyone seemed relaxed and okay with the idea, but Tyler looked as distressed as I felt. I wondered if he shared the same reason for not wanting to put his body on display.

I hoped not.

Adult werewolves are very tough, and scarring one is quite hard to do. Some injuries take longer than others, like growing back a limb, and too many at once can overpower a wolf's abilities, like what happened to me, the queen, and her twin cousins. However, after we get our wolves, there isn't much we can't heal, and to leave permanent marks takes either silver or mercury.

Or both, as my father preferred.

So, no, I wasn't going swimming any time soon. Nobody needed to see how he'd ruined my skin beyond repair.

"Anyone who wants to swim is welcome to, but I don't have a suit," I murmured.

Instead of dampening Peri's spirits, the words lit her up.

"You don't have a *swimsuit?* Oh, girl. You know what that means, right? More shopping!" she yelled.

"Oh, no." I hid my face in my hands.

"Quit yelling," Gisela grumbled with a frown without opening her eyes. "Neither the queen nor luna can leave the property. No shopping today."

Now *that* dampened Peri's spirits.

"Can I at least have another ice pop to console myself?" she grumbled.

"Of course!" Tyler smiled at her. "What color would you like?"

"Red, please."

He booked over to the freezer, and the queen and I grinned at each other.

"What?" Peri demanded.

"He never asks us what color *we* want," Queen Lilah purred. "We have to take whatever he brings over."

Peri's face went blank for a second, then bright pink bloomed on her cheeks and her mouth opened and closed, but no words came out.

"Hey, Ty," Emerson called out, "where're you going?"

We all swiveled our heads to see Tyler heading toward the house.

"Just going down to run down to the store and grab some more ice pops."

"Dude, there are like fifty in there."

"Peri asked for red, and they're all gone."

"Oh, that's okay!" Peri jumped up and frantically waved her hands in front of her. "Purple's fine, or blue. You don't have to make a special trip."

Tyler slowly walked over to her, a frown pulling his eyebrows together.

"I can go get some. I don't mind."

"No, really. I'm good with anything. Except green. If there were only green left, then sure because I really don't like the green ones, but anything else is good."

She was pink-faced and rambling by the time he came to a stop right in front of her.

"I need popcorn," Queen Lilah whispered, and I grinned.

I need to vomit. Lark rolled her eyes.

Hush! I hissed. *They're adorable.*

"No green. Got it." One side of Tyler's mouth picked up in a half smile.

"It's that lemon-lime flavor. What kind of flavor is that for an ice pop? I don't even like it as a soda flavor. Lemon-lime is a terrible flavor for an ice pop..." Peri's voice slowly faded into nothing.

She and Tyler stood there staring into each other's eyes, and the queen and I muffled our giggles behind our hands.

Crew meandered over to them and held out a blue ice pop. Neither Tyler nor Peri noticed or moved. I wasn't even sure they were breathing at this point.

Then, for some crazy reason only he knew, Crew took his life in his hands and laid the ice pop against Peri's bare neck.

The screech that came out of that girl could have broken glass. Whirling on Crew, she grabbed it and whacked his chest with it, and he took off. She ran after him, screaming threats.

Tyler blinked and looked like he was waking up from a dream.

"If they don't end up being mates, I'm going to have words with the Moon Goddess herself." Gisela sat up between Luke's legs and scooted to the end of the lounger. "Now, I'd like an ice pop, too, mate, and I don't like the green ones, either."

"Me, too!" the queen chirped.

"Me, three!" I added because why not?

While Luke fetched them, we watched Peri chase Crew.

"Hundred bucks says she pushes him in the pool," Emerson said.

"Hundred bucks says he picks her up and tosses her in the pool," Matthew countered.

"Hundred bucks says she accidentally falls in the pool and pulls him in with her," Gisela smirked.

"Hundred bucks says *he* accidentally falls in the pool and pulls her in with him," Queen Lilah said with a giggle.

"Babe? You getting in on this bet?" Gisela called out to Luke.

"I never bet," he called back.

"Your loss." She shrugged. "Tyler, what about you?"

He shook his head. Living in the orphanage, his wallet was probably as empty as mine.

"What's your wager, little luna bunny?" Emerson sat on the end of my lounger.

"Um, I don't have any money to make a bet with." I shrugged.

Every eye fastened on me.

"Your mates are extremely wealthy," Emerson said slowly, "and it's a measly hundred dollars."

"That's *their* money, not mine." I shook my head. "I don't want to waste what they've earned."

"Luna bunny, if you lose, I'll spot you the cash. You can pay me back by baking me cookies or something."

I perked up and agreed with a nod. Now I needed to make a really good bet so I didn't waste Emerson's money.

No include the pool, Lark advised.

"Hundred bucks says she catches him and shoves the ice pop down his throat."

"Bet," said the others in concert.

Luke brought over a handful of ice pops and we settled in to watch the show.

34: Interrogations

Ash

"So, Mase." I bumped his arm with my elbow. "What did you and Posy find to do while we were at the clinic?"

I knew full well what they'd done. Wyatt hadn't wasted any time in linking Jay, Cole, and me once Posy spilled the beans. None of us were surprised that she did; our cupcake couldn't keep a secret to save her life.

I only asked because I wanted to make Mase writhe in embarrassment, but should have known better. He just looked at me out of the corner of his eye, then grinned a lazy, satisfied grin.

At least you got reaction out of him, Ashy, my wolf pointed out. *That hundred percent better than stone face.*

Good ole Sid. Always looking on the bright side.

"Do you want me to tell you, or play the memory for you?" he smirked. "And are you sure you want to interview prisoners with a hard-on?"

"Aw, Mase!" Wyatt and Cole groaned together while Jay snickered quietly.

"All right, boys," Ranger strode into the cell block. "Let's do this."

"Show us later," I hissed at Mase. "Show us *everything.*"

Because of Onyx, King Julian had decided to wait in the anteroom and watch through the two-way glass. Ranger would start the questioning and we'd jump in. The king would join us if he could or wanted to.

As my brothers and I flanked him, Ranger went to the closest prisoner, who looked defeated and hopeless already.

"On your feet," Ranger barked at the guy, who did as he was told, but kept his head down. "Name?"

"Julio Serrano," he said quietly with a slight Spanish accent.

"You surrendered without a fight. Why?"

"What Alpha Halder is doing is wrong. Someone needs to stop him, and there are not enough of us left in the pack who have the will to fight him. We need help."

"Not enough left? What happened to the others who fought him?"

"Many he killed. A few fled. Our beta, Luke MacGregor, most recently. Everyone who tried was caught and tortured or killed. Luke and his sister are the only ones who haven't been dragged back yet."

Julio finally raised his head and looked in Ranger's eyes.

"We prayed they made it somewhere safe, somewhere they could get help for us, but the alpha told us yesterday that he'd found them. He gathered twenty of us and ordered us to deliver a warning."

"What kind of help were you hoping for?" Mase asked.

"We've tried for the past year to get word to the king that our pack was in trouble." Julio shook his head. "Alpha Halder is going to destroy Tall Pines and everyone in it if he isn't stopped."

"Those boys in the duffel bags, the twins. Who are they?"

Jay's question seemed dumb at first, because we already knew the answer, but I realized it was a good way to confirm if Julio was telling the truth and knew what he was talking about.

"They're the MacGregors' cousins. Zayne and Zayden Maxwell. Poor little Lilah is going to be crushed if they're dead. That is, if she herself is still alive."

Julio's dark eyes grew moist and glittered, and it was clear he cared about the queen, even if he didn't know that she was the queen yet.

Part of me wanted to tell him about Luke and Lilah, but Halder could still link him and he with his alpha. I wanted to believe Julio's honest face, but knew we couldn't risk it. Glancing back at Ranger, I saw the same warning on his face that Mase was sending through *our* link, and we all shared a quick nod of agreement. We were here to get information, not give it out.

"Did Alpha Halder target them because the MacGregors ran away?" Jay asked.

"Yes. He wants Lilah. He's obsessed with hurting and terrifying her. He wanted to show her that he will do anything to get to her."

"So he knows she's here at Five Fangs?" Cole growled.

"He does now. Ever since the witch led us here this morning."

"Who was the shifter leading your group?" I moved a step closer. "The one who hurt the witch?"

"Ryker Schultz," Julio spat. "He was loyal to the alpha, not the pack."

That last statement was very telling. There should be no distinction between the two. I took it to mean this Ryker guy had been Halder's follower because he wanted to be, not because he was forced to be.

"Well, he's dead now," Jay smirked, Quartz glimmering in his eyes for a few seconds. "How many others in the pack willingly serve your alpha?"

"Maybe forty. No more than fifty, for sure, but the rest of the pack will do what he orders. He holds their families hostage in one way or another."

"Yours, too?" I crossed my arms over my chest and stared down at him. "Is that true of the whole group you were with this morning?"

"Most of them. Before we left yesterday, he gathered our mates and pups in the dining hall." Julio pointed to one shifter standing in the corner. He looked to be about my age. "Elijah's mate could go into labor at any moment. It's their first pup."

Julio turned, scanned the group, and pointed to another guy, this one maybe in his late twenties, and I saw nothing by fear in this shifter's eyes.

We scaring him, Ashy? Sid asked.

I don't think it's us, buddy. Let's hear what Julio says.

"Two days ago, he had his men beat Adam's six-year-old pup to make him cooperate. She has a cracked skull, among other injuries. Last night, Alpha Halder himself went to the pack hospital, unhooked her from the machines, and carried her into the dining hall. They have no access to a doctor or pain medications, nothing."

A little she-wolf? Ashy, he do that to a little she-wolf?

Upset, Sid began to pace. He had a special place in his heart for pups.

I know, buddy. I know.

Ashy, a little she-wolf.

Hang on, okay? We need to find out more, then we'll take care of it.

Julio hung his head and turned to face us again.

"And my daughter. He took my daughter to the cells, along with a few other children and teens. I can't— I can't let myself think about what's happening to her. To all of them."

More pups? He hurting more pups? Ashy—

I know, Sid. Calm down. We can't do anything right this second, but I promise we will. We'll end it one way or another.

"Why now?" Mase folded his arms and stuck his hands in his armpits, his eyes cold and his face completely closed off as he stared at Julio. "Why is all of this happening now? You said you've been trying for a year to get word out that something was wrong. What happened a year ago?"

"Lilah MacGregor turned eighteen." Julio shrugged. "By shifter law, he could pursue her as a chosen mate if she didn't have a true one."

"Dude, that doesn't make any sense," Wyatt grumbled. "All this murder, torture, and coercion because he wanted to choose a mate? Why is he destroying his pack when he could just choose another female?"

243

"I told you, he's obsessed with her," Julio said. "My mate Elena thinks something snapped in the alpha when Lilah refused him."

"Well, he isn't going to be alive much longer to hurt anyone else," Ranger muttered, then looked at Julio. "Do you know when he'll make his next move?"

"He already has." Another shifter spoke up.

Our eyes cut to a man crouched on the concrete floor, the thick chains rattling as he stood. He was a tall one, almost as tall as me - and there weren't many wolves in the world just shy of seven feet. He had a heavy build similar to Mase's, but not as heavy as Cole's, and his brown eyes were flat and dead.

"Don't trust that *puta*," Julio cautioned us. "Raph follows the alpha willingly."

"Threats are only one way to get people to do what you want." Raph smirked at Julio.

"What were you promised?" Jay, of course, got there before the rest of us.

"Anything." Raph's smirk turned into a grin. "The beta position, money, houses, cars, as many bitches as I cared to break."

The other prisoners stirred in their chains, their faces alternating between fury and disgust, and both Cole and Wyatt clenched their hands into white-knuckled fists at that last part.

"Then why did you surrender? You could have made a run for it. You could have fought." I raised an eyebrow at the douche.

"And *died*. I know Quartz's reputation." Raph nodded at Jay. "I wasn't sure even surrendering would get me out of there alive, but fighting and running were death sentences, and I ain't ready to die just yet."

"Could still happen." Garnet rattled in Mase's voice, which was unusual enough to make my brothers and I give him space.

He hadn't lost his temper since becoming alpha three years ago. Even before that, it was a rare occurrence, but when he did, he wrecked *everything*.

"Ah. Mason Price, right?" Raph jerked his chin up in acknowledgement. "I've heard about you, too. First alpha of Five Fangs. Mr. Ice. The man who cannot be shaken. If I wasn't chained up, we'd see just how true that is."

He's picking a fight? With Mase? Wyatt asked incredulously. *Contrary to what he said, I think he* does *have a death wish.*

It's a distraction. Don't get worked up by anything he says, Mase said, his tone even as always.

I'd always envied him that calmness, and I never realized it was a mask until Posy had pointed it out the other day.

"Heard you found your mate."

The turn in Raph's goading got our complete and immediate attention. Our wolves' ears all picked up, and a snarl of warning ripped from both Topaz and Quartz. Even Sid, my mellow little buddy, had his teeth bared and his hackles raised.

"How do you know about her?" Wyatt demanded, Granite heavy in his voice.

"Blame the little boy you sent to Tall Pines with the paperwork severing the alliance between our packs. Bubbling over with the news, he was. Bubbling over with blood, too, by the time we were done with him."

Who did we send? I asked in a panic. *He killed one of our wolves and we didn't know it or feel it in the pack bonds? How?*

I sent Gamma Reuben, Wyatt replied. *He's not dead. I can feel him, but he's not answering the mind link. Neither Five Fangs nor River Rapids.*

End him, Mase, or move and let me, Cole growled. *Before he can spread any more poison with his mind games.*

Or before one of our wolves breaks loose, Jay added.

If I was struggling with Sid and Wyatt with Granite, I could only imagine what Jay was going through with Quartz.

He could still be valuable, Mase argued.

He's talking about our MATE! Cole and Topaz howled in unison.

And there goes Cole's temper. This is not going to end well.

"What's it like to share the same pussy every night? Whose name does she scream when she comes?" Raph taunted. "Ha! I bet she's such a whore, she wouldn't care if *I* drilled her. Hmm. Now that's an idea. How about a deal, boys? You let me take a turn or two with your little slut, and I'll tell you Alpha Halder's next move."

We all wolfed out, even Ranger and Mase, and were ready to rip apart this abomination of a shifter. Then a triad of power - alpha, royal, and moon - rumbled around the room like a roll of thunder.

"*DOWN. NOW.*"

Everyone fell to their knees, and our wolves dropped on their bellies.

King Julian stalked toward his prey with slow, even steps, his eyes glowing green with wolf-light. He hunkered down next to Raph and settled his elbows on his knees, letting his hands dangle between them.

For nearly a minute, the king stared at Raph's bowed head. Then he turned, released the rest of us from his hold, and motioned Julio over.

"Look at every Tall Pines shifter in this cell block, Julio. Are there any others among them who served your alpha willingly? Wolves

245

who are in no way coerced or threatened? Take your time and look carefully, then come tell me who."

"Yes, sire." Julio bobbed his head.

As he followed the king's command, Mase linked the cell guards to bring us some clothes, since ours were now fabric confetti spread around us. When they did, all of us except Quartz shifted back and pulled on the shorts they handed us.

I need Posy, Wyatt muttered. *I need to see her. I need our girl. Right the freak now!*

We all do, brother, I replied. *Hang in there. The king will smash this bastard, then we can go to her.*

Quartz, who still hadn't relinquished control to Jay, moved to King Julian's side and stood eye to eye with Raph. His hackles were down, and he wasn't snarling or growling, but his ears were up and his eyes locked on his target.

"Nyx doesn't like this prick's dirty mouth. What about you, Quartz?" the king crooned. "Do *you* like his dirty mouth?"

Quartz moved his head from side to side very slowly.

"Listen, Raph. It is Raph, right?" The king grabbed a fistful of hair and made Raph nod. "Oh, good. So, Raph, you're a dead wolf. You know it, I know it, and everyone in this room knows it. I *was* going to make it quick. You tell me what I want to know, I rip your throat out, business done. But you had to go and open your filthy mouth."

King Julian shook his head and looked over at Quartz, whose gaze hadn't wavered.

"You have to admit the cur has some heavy balls to talk about *your* mate while he's chained up in *your* cells in the heart of *your* territory. But I'll tell you a secret, Q."

The king leaned closer to Quartz's right ear and pretended to whisper.

"He doesn't need his balls to answer my questions, now does he? Maybe you should relieve him of that burden."

With a grin, Quartz lunged.

35: Plan of Attack

Cole

The sound of our mate's giggles floated to our ears from the backyard, and the tension washed right out of us.

No sweeter sound in the world, my dudes! Ash chirped, and we all grinned at each other.

Walking around the side of the house, we saw Posy running after Tyler, her long brown hair flying everywhere.

"Come on, Tyler! It's not fair! You know I have these short dinosaur arms!"

Tyler let out a peal of laughter, and I raised my eyebrows.

I don't think I've ever seen him this happy. Wyatt sounded as amazed as I felt.

Our mate is an angel, Jay said. *She makes miracles everywhere she goes.*

Tyler ran a few more feet, then tucked into a little roll and flopped on the grass, pretending he tripped. Posy jumped on him and squashed him in a hug.

"Ha! Tag! You're it!"

Then she scrambled to her feet and took off, little giggles coming out in pants as she ran.

Ash, of course, *had* to be involved in any physical activity and raced after her. Catching up to her in four strides, he slung one long arm around her waist and grabbed her, then swung her around and around in dizzying circles.

"Aaa-aaa-aaa-aaash!"

He put her back on her feet and giggled as she staggered around like a drunk. Making a cage of his arms, he followed her to make sure she didn't fall, and everyone laughed as she bounced between his forearms like an out-of-control bumper car.

Finally, she was able to stand on her own, and Ash hugged her, still chuckling.

"Not funny, Ash," she muttered, although she hugged him back.

"Thank you, betas. Have a good evening." Mase, the killjoy that he was, dismissed them with a nod.

"Wait. They're leaving? All ready?" Posy asked, her voice pitching high at the end.

"Aw. Is wittle wuna bunny sad her fwends are weaving?" Emerson pooched out his bottom lip, and she swatted his arm.

"Don't worry, luna. You'll see us again tomorrow." Crew patted her on top of her head. "We'll be guarding you while the alphas go with the king to straighten out Tall Pines."

I knew the instant her brain processed his meaning because her face fell and all the light went out of her eyes.

Crew upset our mate, Topaz growled. *Punish him!*

Chill, dude. Jeez!

"What's wrong with you?" I muttered at Crew.

Shouldering the beta out of the way, I wrapped myself around Posy and snuggled her face into my chest. Well, more like the upper half of my stomach. Our girl was *short*.

"What?" Crew protested. "It's true, isn't it?"

"Yeah, but you didn't have to drop it on her like that!"

Comfort our mate!

I am, Paz. Calm down.

I rolled my eyes. Goddess only knew how crazy he'd get if Posy ever had a real emergency.

"Oh! My bad, luna." Crew's eyes widened. "I thought you knew."

"Don't worry about it," Posy mumbled into my shirt.

Emerson offered Ty and Peri a ride home, and the betas left without much more ado. The king linked Gisela to bring Luke and Lilah to the clinic, where he and Ranger were currently checking in on the Maxwell twins and Tristan's mate. Afterwards, the king was going to take them all out to dinner, so we were free to just be with our mate.

Posy started to straighten up the cabana, so I helped her. My brothers, on the other hand, stood on the far side of the pool debating something.

"What's with all the ice pop wrappers?" I asked, holding up a bunch.

She just giggled, took them from me, and tossed them in the trash can. While we were washing our hands in the outdoor kitchen, I linked the boys.

What are you discussing?

We want to order delivery for dinner, Ash told me. *Two votes for Chinese, one for Italian, and one for pizza. Preference?*

Chinese, but let me check with Posy.

"We're ordering something for dinner tonight." I looped an arm around her waist and reeled her in again. "I'm feeling like Chinese. What about you?"

"Never tried it," she said, wrapping her arms around my waist and laying her cheek against me.

Chinese it is, then, I told the boys. *She's never had it, so order a variety to see what she likes.*

248

"I'm sorry we have to leave you tomorrow," I said quietly. "None of us wants to, but Tall Pines—"

"I understand." She turned her face up to give me a brave smile. "I just didn't make the connection that you would *all* be going."

Jay came over and twined a strand of her long hair around his finger.

"Crew said he spilled the beans about us leaving. We wanted to tell you ourselves." Jay frowned. "Fortunately, it's not often that all of us have to go. Unfortunately, this is one of those times."

"It's okay." She snuggled further into me while looking at Jay. "I'll have the betas to keep me busy during the day, and your scents in our bed to comfort me at night."

A bolt of lightning shot through me when she said that last part.

Can't wait to get our scent between her legs, too.

That isn't helping, Paz.

Sorry, boss, he muttered, then grinned. *But it's true.*

Knowing she might feel my hard-on at any moment, I turned her over to Jay, who took our girl in his arms with a grin.

"How long will you be gone?" Posy asked.

"Two days at best," Jay said, "but probably three. Four or five if things go sideways."

Goddess, I hope it doesn't go sideways, I linked him.

You and me both, brother.

"The king and Ranger will be joining us later so we can go over the plan with you and the queen," I told her.

"Let's set up in the dining room," she suggested. "There's plenty of space, and we won't have to move when the food gets here."

"Sounds good."

#

She liked the egg drop soup, sesame chicken, and cheese wontons, but not the spicy dishes. We made sure to note what she made a face at so we didn't order it again.

By the time we finished and cleaned up, the king and his entourage had joined us, and he outlined the bare bones of our plan. We'd all agreed to keep the finer details to ourselves for several reasons.

One: Not used to situations like this, Luke, the queen, or Posy might unwittingly give something away that could get back to the enemy. We knew it was unlikely, but we couldn't afford any risks. Not when so many lives were on the line.

Two: They would worry.

Three: They definitely wouldn't approve of some parts of it.

"Tristan's mate, Ariel, will cover Gisela and Ranger's scent," King Julian began. "They'll scout ahead after dark. I've already gone over their roles with them."

"Is Ariel well enough to do that?" Posy wanted to know.

"Yes. Tristan marked her, and Creek helped her finish healing," the king told her. "While we were visiting with them, she volunteered before I could even ask."

"You can get to know her better while we're gone," Wyatt chimed in.

"I look forward to that," she said with a happy smile. "And how are the twins?"

"Getting better. You can go with Lilah to visit them tomorrow if you'd like." When she smiled and nodded, he continued. "In the morning, the alphas and I will head out. The betas will stay to guard you, and Luke to guard Lilah."

"Luke, you're okay with Gisela going into danger without you?" Posy looked at him with wide eyes.

"She's the king's beta. She didn't get the job simply because she's gorgeous." Luke grinned down at Gisela, who elbowed him in the ribs. "She says she can do it. Who am I to doubt her?"

I could see from Posy's face that she was going to need to process his response, so I motioned for the king to continue.

"We have a place off pack territory where we'll wait for Gisela and Ranger's report," he said. "We'll revise as needed based on their information, then we'll go in and deal with Alpha Halder."

"That sounds too simple," Posy said with a frown.

"Simple works best sometimes," he told her.

"I meant, it sounds like there is a lot more to the plan than you're saying."

I chuckled at her little frown.

"There is," he acknowledged.

Her cheeks reddened, and I wondered if she thought he was snubbing her. I opened my mouth to reassure her, but she had more to say.

"Lilah and I might be able to contribute some ideas if we knew more details."

"We've got everything covered. We're as planned as we can get it until Gisela and Ranger infiltrate the pack and gather more information," said the king.

Posy seemed content with that, but Queen Lilah was far from it.

"Julian, that kind of arrogance may get you hurt or the hostages killed," she chided him. "Why wouldn't you want as much help as you could get? Posy's right; we may have ideas you haven't thought of."

Ding, ding, ding! May day! May day! Topaz yipped.

Yeah. I grinned at him. *But it's the king's plane crashing, not ours.*

My good humor fled when Posy whimpered and huddled against my side. I tucked my arm around her and held her close, confused by the little tremors that racked her body.

"Don't worry, honey." I tried to guess what was upsetting her. "She's only speaking her mind. She's not being mean to him."

"He'll get mad." She shook a little harder. "The king will get mad again."

"The alphas and I have gone over everything twice," the king said patiently. "The plan is as solid as we can make it until we get the intel from Gisela and Ranger."

"What is it you don't want us to know? You're hiding something, aren't you? That's why you don't want us to know all the details!"

"Please," Posy whispered, "please, Queen Lilah."

There was no way the queen heard her hushed voice. I rubbed my hand up and down her back and kissed her forehead.

"It's okay," I told her. "Everything's okay."

"You'll have to trust me, Lilah," the king said. "I have a lot of experience with this kind of thing. I know what I'm doing."

"Can you guarantee that no one dies in this expert plan of yours?"

"You know I can't. There's always a chance for casualties—"

"That is my *family* you're calling a casualty!" The queen stood and gripped the edge of the table so hard, her fingertips turned white. She was trembling as hard as Posy. "He has *hostages*, including my best friend and cousin, Junie, who is the gentlest creature on Earth!"

"Calm down, fire hair," King Julian said, also standing up. "I told you I'd go get her and bring her back to you, and I will keep that promise. I won't fail you, Lilah."

"He's mad. He's mad. He's mad," Posy chanted in short, shallow breaths.

Get her away from here, Topaz muttered. *This isn't a good place for her right now.*

Agreeing with him, I linked the boys to let them know what was happening, then stood and swept her up in my arms. As I moved toward the door, the king reached for his mate, most likely to pull her into a hug, but Posy didn't perceive it that way.

"Don't let him hurt her," she begged. "Cole, don't let him hurt her. Please, Cole. *Please!*"

251

Queen Lilah's muffled sob followed us out of the room.

"Shh, honey." I kissed her forehead as I went up the stairs. "No one would dare hurt the queen, least of all her mate. Plus, *my* brothers are there, *her* brother is there, and the king's beta, who is her personal guard, is there. She couldn't be any safer locked in a vault."

"But he's mad!"

"Breathe, Posy. They're having a disagreement. People can disagree without hurting each other. He didn't even raise his voice to her, let alone his hand, and he never would."

I opened the door to her room and headed straight for the French doors. Once on the balcony, I settled into the wicker rocking chair with her cradled on my lap.

"Shh, baby. Shh. Everything's okay. Shh."

I wasn't good at whispering sweet nothings, and I couldn't sing, so I hummed a mindless little tune while she tucked her face in the crook of my neck and gripped my shirt in tight fistfuls. When her breathing settled down, I figured she was calm enough to ask a few questions.

"Are you okay, honey?"

She nodded.

"Did you think the king was going to hurt the queen because she was disagreeing with him?"

She nodded again.

"It can be scary when people disagree," I said, "especially if they start to raise their voices."

She nodded a third time, and I sighed.

Comfort mate! Topaz growled again.

I am, dude! I growled back, then linked my boys. *Any ideas what I should do?*

Just keep doing what you're doing, Jay said. *Talk to her. Your voice, your scent, your touch, it's all comforting to her.*

I trusted him because he wasn't as much of a Neanderthal as the rest of us. Mase wasn't, either, because he was observant, but Jay was best because he *understood* things.

"Your fairy lights are going to come on soon." I brushed her hair out of face. "Won't that be pretty? It makes me very happy that you like it out here. Ash and I tried so hard to make this a place you would love."

"I *do* love it." Her lips moved against the skin of my neck, making me shiver. "You did a great job."

"My brothers are worried about you," I whispered in her ear. "Can they join us, or do you want to go back? Mase says the queen feels awful and wants to apologize."

252

"I don't want to see the king and queen right now. I feel like a fool. This is the second time I've embarrassed myself in front of them."

"You're not a fool, and there's nothing to be embarrassed about." I kissed her temple. "No one is mad at you. You're not in trouble. In fact, the king is grateful that you wanted to protect his mate."

"I'm sorry I'm so much trouble." Her voice caught in her throat. "Cole, tell me the truth. Am I a burden?"

I closed my suddenly stinging eyes for a second, then moved her so that her knees straddled my thighs and we were eye to eye.

"Oh, Posy. Sweet, sweet girl," I murmured. "Of course not. You are neither trouble nor a burden."

"I *feel* like I am. Sometimes, I feel like I'm making you all as weak as I am."

I am way out of my depth here, I frantically told the boys. *A little help?*

Kiss her, said Ash and Wyatt at the same time.

Tell her what's in your heart, Mase suggested.

What if it's the wrong thing to say?

If it's in your heart, how could it be? Jay asked. *Now say it before she misinterprets your silence.*

Taking a deep breath, I cupped her face in my hands and kissed the tip of her nose.

"No, Posy, you're not making us weak. You *are* making us something, though. You know what that is?"

She shook her head, her pretty blue eyes reflecting the fairy lights as they turned on all around us.

"Better men, honey. You're making us better men."

She stared at me for several long moments, then leaned forward and touched her mouth to mine.

Kissies! Finally! Topaz skipped around and yipped. *Kissy-kissies from our mate!*

I tuned him out as I focused on not screwing up.

Her lips moved against mine, and I followed her lead. The last thing I wanted to do was scare her by being too aggressive. She didn't seem to like that, though, because she ended the kiss and pulled her head back a bit.

"Cole?"

"Hmm?"

"Will you kiss me?"

"Wasn't that what we were just doing?" I teased her and grinned when she pouted.

Unable to resist, I swooped in and sucked on her bottom lip. She squeaked in surprise, then melted into me and ran her little hands up and down my chest. My tongue snuck inside her mouth and learned her flavor, and I couldn't get enough.

Without breaking the kiss, I stood up, and she quickly wrapped her legs around my waist and her arms around my neck. I gripped her bottom in my hands, meaning to carry her inside, but only got as far as the closest wall. Pushing her back against it, I crowded into her, loving the feel of her soft curves.

"Cole!" she gasped when I let us both up for air.

That set me on fire. If I wanted her before, I *craved* her now. My dick strained against the fabric separating us and I ached to be inside her, although I knew it wasn't going to happen anytime soon. I needed a little relief, though, so I rocked my hips against her core.

She gasped again, and I checked that she was okay with what was happening. When she nodded, I did it again and again, each time a little harder and faster. She pulled out my hair tie, knotted her hands up in my hair, and tugged gently. Our lips latched onto each other again and my tongue ran over her teeth and licked the roof of her mouth.

Drowning in her sweet taste and scent, the mate sparks dancing everywhere, I buried my face in her neck, squeezed her bottom, and slammed against her until the predictable happened. Tipping my head back, I clenched my hands around her bum and came in my shorts like a horny pup with his first titty magazine.

At least it was with our mate this time, Topaz reasoned. *She made it feel a million times better than your hand, didn't she?*

Get out of my head, Paz.

How? It's my head, too. Speaking of head, do you think she'll ever put her plump lips around—

Strangling on a groan, I opened my eyes and met Posy's concerned blue gaze.

"Does it hurt when you shoot pup-making juice?" she asked.

"No, honey. Far from it. It feels good."

She blushed and ducked her head and looked up at me through her eyelashes.

"How did you know what to do?" she wanted to know.

"Instincts, maybe?" I shrugged. "My body seemed to be on autopilot. And Topaz had some ... advice."

At least, I guess Hump her! Hump her hard and fast! *counts as advice.*

"Are you okay, honey? I feel guilty that I got something amazing out of that and you got nothing."

"I got plenty," she murmured and kissed me.

I hesitated for a second, then went for it.

"When we come back, would you like one of us to make you feel like that?" I asked.

"It— It feels good? Because you looked like you were in pain. Mason did, too, when we were on the couch."

"I promise you, it feels good. *Real* good." My grin nearly split my face.

"Maybe then. Can I keep my clothes on? At least at first?"

"Baby, you can do whatever you want. Like Jay told you, we're yours to command." I stepped back and put her on her feet, careful not to rub my wet shorts against her dry ones. "I'm going to clean up and change, honey. Do you want to wait for me, or go down on your own?"

"Um, actually, can you ask Jayden to come up? I owe Quartz a cuddle."

She wouldn't want to cuddle him if she knew what he did earlier, my wolf snickered.

Do. Not. Tell. Her. Not ever.

Chill, boss. I know that. Jeez! Give me some credit.

"Don't you want to say goodnight to the queen first?" I narrowed my eyes a little, concerned that she wanted to hide up here. "Baby, your friend is sad. You don't want her to go to bed sad, do you?"

She bit her bottom lip and twisted her fingers, then shook her head.

"Okay, I'll go down," she sighed, "but then I'm cuddling with Quartz!"

Chuckling, I ran my fingertips down the side of her face.

"I'll hurry and be right back, then we can go down," I told her.

"I'll go by myself." She tipped her chin up, and pride swelled my chest.

And she thinks she's weak? Topaz shook his head.

Yeah, but she'll grow more confident as we keep showing her— Just how strong she is, he finished for me.

End of Book One